SHADOW
FIRE

CHRISTINE FEEHAN

JOVE
New York

A JOVE BOOK
Published by Berkley
An imprint of Penguin Random House LLC
penguinrandomhouse.com

Copyright © 2022 by Christine Feehan
Excerpt from *Red on the River* copyright © 2022 by Christine Feehan
Penguin Random House supports copyright. Copyright fuels creativity, encourages
diverse voices, promotes free speech, and creates a vibrant culture. Thank you for buying
an authorized edition of this book and for complying with copyright laws by not
reproducing, scanning, or distributing any part of it in any form without permission.
You are supporting writers and allowing Penguin Random House to continue to
publish books for every reader.

A JOVE BOOK, BERKLEY, and the BERKLEY & B colophon
are registered trademarks of Penguin Random House LLC.

ISBN: 9780593439128

First Edition: April 2022

Printed in the United States of America
1   3   5   7   9   10   8   6   4   2

The Carpathian Novels

DARK TAROT	DARK HUNGER
DARK SONG	DARK POSSESSION
DARK ILLUSION	DARK CELEBRATION
DARK SENTINEL	DARK DEMON
DARK LEGACY	DARK SECRET
DARK CAROUSEL	DARK DESTINY
DARK PROMISES	DARK MELODY
DARK GHOST	DARK SYMPHONY
DARK BLOOD	DARK GUARDIAN
DARK WOLF	DARK LEGEND
DARK LYCAN	DARK FIRE
DARK STORM	DARK CHALLENGE
DARK PREDATOR	DARK MAGIC
DARK PERIL	DARK GOLD
DARK SLAYER	DARK DESIRE
DARK CURSE	DARK PRINCE

Anthologies

EDGE OF DARKNESS
(with Maggie Shayne and Lori Herter)
DARKEST AT DAWN
(includes Dark Hunger *and* Dark Secret*)*
SEA STORM
(includes Magic in the Wind *and* Oceans of Fire*)*
FEVER
(includes The Awakening *and* Wild Rain*)*
FANTASY
(with Emma Holly, Sabrina Jeffries, and Elda Minger)
LOVER BEWARE
(with Fiona Brand, Katherine Sutcliffe, and Eileen Wilks)
HOT BLOODED
(with Maggie Shayne, Emma Holly, and Angela Knight)

Specials

DARK CRIME
THE AWAKENING
DARK HUNGER
MAGIC IN THE WIND

MURDER AT SUNRISE LAKE

Titles by Christine Feehan

The GhostWalker Novels

PHANTOM GAME	RUTHLESS GAME
LIGHTNING GAME	STREET GAME
LETHAL GAME	MURDER GAME
TOXIC GAME	PREDATORY GAME
COVERT GAME	DEADLY GAME
POWER GAME	CONSPIRACY GAME
SPIDER GAME	NIGHT GAME
VIPER GAME	MIND GAME
SAMURAI GAME	SHADOW GAME

The Drake Sisters Novels

HIDDEN CURRENTS	DANGEROUS TIDES
TURBULENT SEA	OCEANS OF FIRE
SAFE HARBOR	

The Leopard Novels

LEOPARD'S RAGE	CAT'S LAIR
LEOPARD'S WRATH	LEOPARD'S PREY
LEOPARD'S RUN	SAVAGE NATURE
LEOPARD'S BLOOD	WILD FIRE
LEOPARD'S FURY	BURNING WILD
WILD CAT	WILD RAIN

The Sea Haven/Sisters of the Heart Novels

BOUND TOGETHER	AIR BOUND
FIRE BOUND	SPIRIT BOUND
EARTH BOUND	WATER BOUND

The Shadow Riders Novels

SHADOW FIRE	SHADOW KEEPER
SHADOW STORM	SHADOW REAPER
SHADOW FLIGHT	SHADOW RIDER
SHADOW WARRIOR	

The Torpedo Ink Novels

SAVAGE ROAD	VENDETTA ROAD
ANNIHILATION ROAD	VENGEANCE ROAD
RECKLESS ROAD	JUDGMENT ROAD
DESOLATION ROAD	

For Diane: it's been a long road
but we're still hanging in there!

FOR MY READERS

Be sure to go to christinefeehan.com/members/ to sign up for my PRIVATE book announcement list and download the FREE ebook of very yummy *Dark Desserts*. Join my community and get firsthand news, enter the book discussions, ask your questions and chat with me. Please feel free to email me at Christine@christine feehan.com. I would love to hear from you.

ACKNOWLEDGMENTS

As in any book, there are so many people to thank. This would never have made it to deadline without the help of Cheryl Wilson, who stayed up long hours editing when we were under the gun to get it in on time. Thank you so much, my dear friend, for going the extra mile. I'm so grateful to have you! Sheila English, dropping everything to get me the things I needed so I could stay in the chair. Denise! You took care of business for me and my dog when he was so sad. And Brian Feehan. What would I do without your constant encouragement? You always make me believe I can hit the deadline no matter what is going on. This was a tough one, and I loved this book and wanted it to make it to my readers, so thank you all!

CHAPTER ONE

Clearly I should have invested in pizzerias instead of strip joints and sex clubs."

Elie Archambault paused in the act of bringing a slice of pizza dripping with cheese, salami and olives to his mouth, staring at the speaker before he burst out laughing. "No one makes pizza the way Tito and his father, Benito, do. There isn't a pizzeria in the world that can top this one, right, Emme?"

Emmanuelle Ferraro Saldi reached over and casually grabbed the slice of pizza from his hand and took a bite, nodding to agree with him.

"Hey. That's the last piece of salami and olive," Elie protested. "Dario," he added, "you shouldn't talk about strip joints and sex clubs in front of Emmanuelle."

Dario Bosco rolled his eyes. "Emme frequents strip joints and sex clubs. She knows more about what goes on in them then I do."

Emmanuelle ignored the statement, making moaning noises deliberately as she ate the slice of pizza, and hastily gathered up the remaining olives that were loose on the platter.

Elie shoved his shoulder into hers. "You're a demon, woman. I don't know how your husband puts up with you."

"He thinks she's an angel," Dario said, feigned disgust in his voice.

Emmanuelle wasn't in the least bit fazed. She continued to eat the slice of pizza as if she was enjoying it immensely—which she was.

"Val never did have good sense that I could see," Elie said.

Emme kicked him under the table.

Elie laughed. "We need our waitress back so we can order more pizza, but there're so many people in here, I don't think we'll ever see her again."

Petrov's Pizzeria was packed, as it always was regardless of the day of the week. Saturday nights just happened to double the traffic. Fortunately, Benito always reserved two large booths, back in the shadows, for the Ferraro family and their bodyguards, just in case they decided to drop in.

Ferraro territory started right on the edge of what some people referred to as "Little Italy." Most of the land, businesses and homes were rented or leased by the Ferraro family. All were protected by them. For years it was whispered that if one went to the Ferraros with a problem, that problem would inexplicably disappear.

Rumors swirled around the mysterious family, six brothers and one sister. They always wore their signature pinstriped suits and were often surrounded by bodyguards, although no one ever thought they needed them. Wealthy, arrogant and formidable, the members of the Ferraro family were known to be lethal if crossed.

Now, after Emmanuelle Ferraro, the youngest and only female, had married a Saldi, uniting the two families, the neighborhood was doubly safe. The Saldi family was a crime family, no two ways about it. No guessing. No rumors. Valentino headed the Saldi family now that his father, Giuseppi, had stepped down after his own brother had tried to assassinate him and take over. The neighborhood might not know why the Ferraros had helped the Saldi family, but Elie knew. He'd

helped when Val had worked to bring down his uncle's human trafficking ring.

"You sure you want to go through with this marriage of yours?" Dario asked Elie. "You haven't even seen this woman."

"Yes." Elie's reply was clipped, indicating he didn't want to continue the discussion.

Dario sighed. "Since I can't talk you out of it, at least come to the club tonight. It's your last night of freedom before you're stuck with some woman who might have a fucking headache every night."

"*Dario.*" Emmanuelle sat up straight, glaring at him in protest.

"Some men have certain needs, Emme," Dario said, shrugging. "I'm not going to pretend I don't, and I won't apologize for who I am. Arranged marriages for business or otherwise rarely work for someone like me because the woman isn't going to like who they get. I'm just being honest."

"You're suggesting that Elie go out to a kink club the night before he marries. Is that very honorable?" Emmanuelle demanded.

"It's a moot point," Elie interrupted the argument.

Emmanuelle was the tie that bound the two men together. Elie regarded her as a sister. He had grown up an only child, moving from one household to another in his native France. Elie and Emme had clicked some years earlier and everyone expected them to marry when he'd come to the United States. Emmanuelle's heart was already taken by Valentino Saldi, Dario's cousin. Elie loved Emme but there had only ever been a sibling relationship between them.

Dario had come to love her through his relationship with Valentino. Who couldn't love Emmanuelle? Dario wasn't an easy man to be around. He had served as Valentino's bodyguard for years. He rarely talked to anyone outside the circle of people he accepted as family. Elie felt lucky to be included. The Ferraros had a way of taking over those they chose to bring into their inner circle and Dario, like Elie, had found his way in when Emmanuelle had married Val.

"A moot point?" Emme repeated, raising an eyebrow suspiciously.

Elie held up his left hand, where a ring circled his finger. "Technically, I'm already married. The lawyers took care of the paperwork and we were married by proxy yesterday. I signed here. She signed in France. So, no kink club, but thank you for the offer, Dario. It was considerate. I don't cheat on my wife."

"What does she look like?" Dario asked.

Elie shrugged. "I have no idea. The lawyers took care of it. I didn't even look at the papers. I signed on the dotted line and walked away. I presume she did the same. She'll be here tomorrow and we'll have a very brief private ceremony just for the sake of photos and formality, but the paperwork is already done."

Emmanuelle brushed her hand down his arm. "Congratulations, Elie. I hope she makes you very happy. I know you believe you can make this work."

Dario's dark brows drew together. "Won't understand you in a million years, Elie. This complete stranger comes into your life. You don't know a thing about her and you expect your marriage to work. Emme is one in a million. Maybe one in a billion. Odds could be even higher than that. Val is so fuckin' lucky, he doesn't even know how lucky he is."

He stated his opinion without looking at Emmanuelle and he spoke in a flat, matter-of-fact tone. "I'm aware a man like me is never going to find a woman who can put up with my . . . proclivities." He shrugged. "But then I don't trust anyone enough to have more than an hour encounter with them and only on my terms, especially now that Valentino forced me to take over this idiotic role in the family. He's only made my suspicious nature worse."

"Your point being?" Elie said.

"You're like me."

Elie couldn't deny it. Maybe he wasn't exactly like Dario. He wasn't nearly as dark. He didn't know too many people who were. Dario had demons. Elie liked his way and he knew

how to get it. He already knew he intended for his bride to learn that lesson about him very quickly. He'd been honest in every answer he'd given to the questions asked of him when filling out the pages and pages of very explicit material needed for his arranged marriage. He had her answers and she had his. She should know that about him and what he expected of her.

He had read her answers dozens of times and knew what she expected of him. He had her sexual answers laminated and put up on the master bedroom wall right over the bed to remind her of what she said so there were no mistakes. His were there beside hers. Supposedly he would be matched with the perfect compatible woman to give them the highest odds of a successful marriage. Divorce for shadow riders was nearly a death sentence. It would mean the end of shadow riding. He wouldn't, for one moment, put up with that.

Shadow riders had a unique ability to utilize portals within shadows to travel from one place undetected to another. They were required to begin training as toddlers in order to acquire the necessary skills to become deadly assassins to mete out justice to the criminals who managed to escape the law.

"I might be a bit like you are, Dario," Elie admitted. "She'll have to learn to accept me. I bought us a house on the lake," he added. "I spent so much time at your home with Val, Emme, that I started looking for a piece of property I wanted for myself. It took quite a long time to find the perfect place and I had to really negotiate with the owners to get it." His eyes lit up when he referred to the negotiations. He'd had fun with that part of it.

"In other words, the property wasn't on the market," Emmanuelle interpreted.

"Exactly. And I wanted the property around it so I could make sure we were protected," he added. "One stubborn old coot was a holdout. In the end he caved, but I paid more for his property than I did for the original one I wanted. The nice part was, he owned more actual land. The house I wanted came with a hundred feet of river frontage with two permanent

docks. The old coot gave me an additional three hundred feet of river frontage with several additional docks. Plus, the property behind his place. His house needs work, but the property itself was worth every penny of the fortune I paid him."

Berta, their waitress, came to their table looking a little harassed. Given that every table seemed to be filled and the long line of waiting customers, they couldn't really blame her. "Anything else I can get you?"

"Place is hopping as usual," Emmanuelle greeted. "Never slows down around here."

Berta shook her head. "We've hired three more waiters. It's that crazy. Still looking for someone else. I heard construction was finished and Masci's Deli was back in business after the fire. Did your family keep the apartments above the deli? Are they looking for renters?"

"The deli's open and running," Emmanuelle said, "but the apartments aren't quite finished. There's only two of them, but we wanted to upgrade them. Signor Pietro needed Masci's finished fast and we concentrated on his business first. The rentals should be finished soon. If you have someone in mind, have them fill out an application and make sure they put your recommendation on it so my cousin will flag it."

"Thanks, Emme," Berta said. "Where's Val? I never see you without him."

"On his way. He'll want his usual ridiculous pizza and Elie hogged all the salami and olive pizza so we need another with double olives."

Dario didn't look up from his phone but pointed toward the empty antipasti plate. Emmanuelle rolled her eyes. "More antipasti as well. You might double up on the salami and olives there, too."

Berta laughed. "All of you are going to turn into olives if you don't watch out."

"Wine," Elie reminded. "Same as before."

"Our family wine," Emme added for clarity, indicating the bottle. "Same year. Same vineyard. It's our favorite."

"Got it." Berta hurried away, shaking her head.

"Dario, how do you order if I'm not with you?" Emme demanded. She clearly was trying to sound exasperated but she sounded more amused than anything else.

He raised an eyebrow. "Val insists I have bodyguards. They're practically useless. I have to give them something to do."

Emmanuelle heaved a sigh. "I don't know how any of you get away with being in this century. Why did you buy the house before your wife arrived, Elie? Did it occur to you she might want to choose her own house with you? It's kind of a big thing, where a person is going to live for the rest of their life."

Dario made a little sound of total disgust. "Emme, seriously? A man needs to lay down the law to a woman from the beginning or she thinks she can get away with everything."

"That is so ridiculous and archaic, Dario. You just say things like that to get a rise out of me. You don't really believe that."

He looked up from his phone, his expression deadpan, one eyebrow lifted. "If I ever find a woman, which I won't, she will do what I say when I say it."

Emmanuelle might think Dario was joking, but Elie knew he wasn't. Dario would rule his world with an iron hand. He was all about control. Elie could tell him—just as Val could—that it didn't always work that way when it came to those you loved, but Dario would have to find that out for himself. Elie didn't know Dario's past. He only knew that something very traumatic had taken place that only Valentino was aware of. Whatever it was had shaped Dario into being extremely protective of those he cared for, and a vicious killing machine when it came to their enemies.

"Dario, I swear, if you even look at a friend of mine, I'm going to put a sack over her head," Emmanuelle threatened.

The briefest of smiles flirted with Dario's hard mouth. Elie couldn't help but laugh. Emme had a way about her. It was impossible not to love her.

He glanced over to the table where her bodyguards covered

their grins behind their hands, pretending they couldn't hear the conversation. Levi and Axel, ex-military, ex-mercenary, trained by Dario and always assigned to be Emme's personal protectors. Elie knew them to be serious, astute and very intelligent men. Dario trusted few men, and if he trusted these with Emmanuelle's protection, they had to be good men. More, the Ferraro family had investigated them thoroughly, not for criminal activity, but for their ability to protect Emme. No one found them wanting. It was easy to see they not only were good at what they did, but had developed a real affection for Emmanuelle.

Elie rubbed the ring on his finger. It had been made by one of the Ferraros' many cousins, Damian Ferraro, a gifted jeweler who knew the exact ring needed before his customer did. In this case, his ring had to be able to travel with him into the shadows. Elie had been surprised to find his bride's engagement ring had been fashioned from gems incapable of traveling into the shadows. He'd even questioned Damian as her papers declared her a rider. That would mean she would have to remove her ring before entering the shadows. Her actual wedding ring could be left on. Elie supposed it didn't matter if she removed her engagement ring. He just found it odd that Damian had given his woman a more traditional gemstone, a blazing flawless emerald surrounded by several diamonds.

"You only say that because you know your friends won't be able to resist me," Dario said, reaching for his wineglass.

"What's to resist? You never talk to anyone. You don't look up from your phone. And you're bossy beyond belief. I'm not even going to talk about your rather scary and unbelievable sexual preferences."

Elie had taken a drink of water and immediately choked on it.

"You don't know the first thing about my sexual preferences." There was no change in Dario's expression, on his face or in his voice.

"You don't know that," Emme challenged.

Those dark eyes that at times reminded Elie of twin pits of hell moved over Emmanuelle's face. "Babe. Be serious."

Emme leaned across the table and lowered her voice to a mere thread of sound. "You wouldn't know if I was around in one of your kink clubs."

"Don't bet on it, Emme. I have a sixth sense when it comes to you. And you would never invade my privacy."

Dario had her there. Elie knew, just as well as Dario did, that Emmanuelle might tease both men, but she would never use her ability to spy on them.

She did accompany her husband when he conducted business meetings in the strip or sex clubs. She was always in the shadows, unseen by his associates, or the many women who worked the clubs and did their best to entice their boss into lap dances or blow jobs. Elie knew it was particularly painful for Emmanuelle in the beginning to see the women fawning all over her husband, especially if Emme had helped them earlier and they'd pretended to be her friends. It also made it difficult to fully have faith that if Val didn't know she was right there watching his every move, he wouldn't take advantage of the many offers thrown at him. She'd confided in Elie that it worried her if she became pregnant and couldn't ride the shadows or accommodate Valentino's rather demanding sex drive, what he might do.

Elie thought a lot about her concerns. His wife would no doubt have similar concerns given the fact that she would know he didn't love her. He had an extremely strong sex drive. Not only that, but he would be inclined to take his wife to a club if he could guarantee privacy and no cameras. He trusted Dario to give that to him so the chances were good that it would happen. She might have those same insecurities. He would have to find a way to make sure his wife didn't feel uncertain of him.

Elie had advised Emmanuelle to talk to Val, to be open with him and he hoped she'd done so. He wanted to establish from the very beginning with his bride that they would be talking over every possible concern she had. He would expect

her to communicate those with him, and if she didn't, the longer she waited, the more the consequences. He hoped she had read every single one of his answers to the questions posed by the computer to make their match. He'd been honest. Very honest, just as he expected her to be. He'd read her answers so many times, he practically had them memorized. If she'd read his, there would be no surprises. She would know what kind of man she was getting.

"Fine, Dario," Emme said. "But you spend far too much time at that silly club of yours."

"That's not possible when I'm always at your house eating," Dario countered, back to looking at his phone.

There was a mild disturbance, hushed whispers moving through the pizzeria. Elie knew without looking that Valentino had made his entrance. He was an impressive figure, tall, with wide shoulders, thick, glossy dark hair and intense green eyes. He came straight to the booth, making it difficult for his bodyguards to keep up with him, although they managed. Both men, Lando Regio and Pace Detti, were experienced, trained by Dario and given the job when Val had insisted Dario take over the territory Val's uncle's death had left open.

Val came up behind his wife and bent over Emmanuelle to tip back her head and take her mouth, kissing her intimately right there in the pizzeria. Emmanuelle laughed softly when he lifted his head. "You'll get us kicked out. I heard Benito has some kind of rule, no PDA or we're thrown out. Taviano told me." Taviano was her brother.

Valentino nudged her over with his hip and sank down onto the seat, up close, thigh to thigh. "Did Taviano and Nicoletta get kicked out? If they didn't, we'll have to see if we can make that happen." Deliberately, he leaned into her and bit down on her neck.

She squealed and pushed rather half-heartedly at him. "You can't get us kicked out until after I eat more pizza. Elie ate nearly all the olives."

Val laughed. "I doubt that. You would have put a fork through his hand."

Even Dario smirked at that while Emme tried to look indignant. Elie nudged her foot under the table.

"What have you three been up to while I've been working?" Val asked. "I see you didn't leave anything for me. Not even wine."

"Ordered you fresh, babe," Emmanuelle said.

"Talked about your wife hanging out in the sex clubs," Dario said. "Told Elie she knew far too much about them."

"Stop saying that," Emme protested, wadding up her napkin and throwing it at Dario.

"Well, you do."

"I *guard* my husband, you cretin. Someone has to. You're too busy looking at your phone. And you aren't fooling anyone, Dario. You're playing games on it. No one has that many emails."

Dario lifted an eyebrow as he crumpled the napkin he'd caught in his hand. "I'm answering letters from women, turning them down as gently as possible, nosy woman."

"You are *not*," Emmanuelle snipped. "There is no way you're on a dating site." There was a small silence. "Are you?" Dario didn't deign to answer. She looked suspiciously up at her husband. "Tell me you didn't sign him up on a dating site, because I know he didn't sign himself up."

Val nuzzled her neck. "He needs a good woman to settle him down, Emme." He sounded innocent—too innocent.

Elie tried not to laugh. There were snorts of derision and various other forms of amusement coming from the large table of bodyguards behind them.

"Don't think anyone believes your bullshit, Val," Dario said. "I should forward you all these crap responses. These women are nuts."

"Then why haven't you deleted your account?" Emmanuelle demanded.

"I can tell you," Elie said. "It's like watching a train wreck. You know you should look away, but you can't."

"Is that speaking from experience, Elie?" Val asked, sliding his arm around the back of the booth.

Tito arrived, grinning as he placed an all-meat pizza in front of Val and the salami and double olive in front of Emmanuelle and Elie. Berta followed with the antipasti, a bottle of wine and another pizza, which she placed in front of Dario with a tentative smile.

"I thought you might still be hungry, Dario. It's on the house."

He barely glanced up, but he did acknowledge her with a nod. She beamed at that small gesture and hurried off.

Emmanuelle sighed. "Don't you dare encourage her."

"Encourage who?" Dario frowned and looked up from his phone.

"Never mind." Valentino reached for a piece of pizza. "You're hopeless, Dario. There's no need to worry, princess. Every woman is safe around him. Now that he's got that dating app to stare at, that's all he wants to do. He'd never see a flesh-and-blood woman flirting with him."

Dario shoved his phone in his pocket. "Elie is really going through with his marriage tomorrow, Val. I couldn't talk him out of it."

"Did he try, Elie?" Val studied Elie's expression.

"He offered to let me come to the kink club free to give me one last night of freedom."

Emmanuelle scooped up olives before Elie could get to them. "Not this again. We've had this conversation. Elie's already married. Tomorrow is just a formality. Stefano will walk his bride down the aisle and I'll be her matron of honor. Pictures will be taken. Cake, that sort of thing. The family will be there for you, Elie." She narrowed her gaze on Dario. "By *family*, that includes you. Wear a suit."

Elie found himself watching Emmanuelle and Valentino as they cuddled close together, his knuckles occasionally brushing her cheek. She looked up at Val and he smiled down at her with far too much open love. Elie wasn't certain it was good for Val to show that much real affection for his wife in public. Valentino was head of the Saldi crime family. Loving his wife the way he did could be a major liability for him.

Still, Elie wondered if maybe he'd acted too hastily in deciding to pursue an arranged marriage. He had done so because the woman he was supposed to marry had rejected him, refusing to see him. She had returned his letters unopened. She wouldn't open her door to him. Eventually, knowing he would have to make a decision, he had made the trip back to France with the intention of confronting her, but she was gone.

She had a sister and a father, but they no longer lived in the same house, and Brielle, the woman he *should* have been marrying, wasn't with either of them. Her sister, Fayette, was considered by her parents to be the beauty of the family. When Brielle had come home and told her father that she wasn't going to marry Elie Archambault, her father, Gaspard, apparently, had been furious.

Gaspard had gone to the head of the Archambault family and offered his daughter Fayette. It was such an honor to marry into the Archambault line. To have Fayette politely turned down had made him even angrier with Brielle and he had disowned her unless she agreed to go to Elie and insist he marry her. She had not done so. At eighteen, she had gone off on her own, refusing to give in to her father's demands, and ignoring Elie's many attempts to contact her.

Now, he was married to a woman he didn't know and didn't love. He would be faithful to her, because he was a man of honor, but he would never have what Emme and Val had. And damn Brielle to hell for not listening to him. He made a mistake. Granted, it was a bad mistake, but he'd been young and his world had been turned upside down. It wasn't an excuse to act the way he had, but she could have just heard him out. Neither one of them would be in the mess she'd landed them in. Not only them, but at least two other riders.

"You find anything out, Val?" Dario lowered his voice as he leaned over the table to snag a piece of pizza.

Elie leaned in on the pretense of catching up the bottle of wine to pour everyone a glass. He counted himself lucky that he was regarded as a sibling in the Ferraro family and therefore whatever Val and Dario allowed them to be privy to, he

was as well. They had broken up a human trafficking ring together. Elie had taken great satisfaction in helping to rid the world of even a small branch of that depraved network.

"Unfortunately, yes. We delivered a blow to the trafficking ring, no doubt about it, a pretty good one. I met with Tibberiu Messina and it appears as if the rumors might be true. Before we ever started trying to ferret out who was behind the ring in our territory, Dario and I discussed the possibility that we would be put on a hit list, but we thought getting rid of the ring was worth the danger to us."

Valentino dropped his free arm around Emmanuelle's shoulders when she turned her face up to his, a look of alarm hastily hidden when she ducked her head.

"Messina said someone else has been investigating this same ring as well, very aggressively, but so far no one seems to be able to uncover their identity. The fact that the scrutiny has been so intense has put enough pressure on them that they've slowed bringing in girls from Europe and have turned their attention to stopping those opposing them."

"Does Messina have any idea who was in bed with Jason Caruso?" Dario asked.

"I thought when you got Jason, he was the head of it all here and that would be the end of it," Emmanuelle said softly. "Wasn't the trafficking ring all his idea?"

Elie heard the unconscious plea in her voice. She didn't want Val or Dario to be in any more danger than they had been in. He could have told her that both men, as heads of the crime families, would always be in danger. He could tell, like him, Dario and Val wanted to comfort her and assure her they would be fine, but they couldn't do that and be truthful.

Elie knew Dario had interrogated Jason before the man had died. Dario wasn't gentle in his interrogations, and in the end, few men held out any secrets. Jason wasn't the kind of man able to even try to hold out. Stefano had been apprised immediately of what Dario and Valentino had suspected when they realized Jason Caruso was the man behind the trafficking ring. It had been virtually impossible for him to have been the one

to have set up such a widespread and successful business. It was clear they hadn't conveyed everything they'd learned to Emmanuelle, and Elie didn't blame them. What good would it do, other than to worry her?

"Princess, even if it was his idea initially, he would have needed someone else to help him get started," Val said. "Someone to back him financially. The entire thing was far too widespread, in too many states, for someone like Jason to have run it on his own."

Emme pressed her lips together and then started to drink from her wineglass. Val took it out of her hand. She didn't drink as a rule. If she did, it was rarely more than one glass of wine. He picked up the glass of water and handed it to her. "Baby, you know you'll have a headache if you keep drinking wine."

"Maybe it will be worth it."

He brushed his lips along her temple very gently. "Don't be stubborn. I know this is upsetting."

"You think? There's a hit out on you *again*, Val. Both you and Dario."

"And Elie," Valentino said. "He's included on the list."

"There's a list? As in my family? Stefano? All of my brothers?" Emmanuelle pushed.

"No, your family isn't included on the list, princess. Your family has a reputation and very few people understand them or want to mess with them. You aren't on the list. Elie is. I am. Dario is. Four of my men are. I find the choices interesting."

"Well, I don't." Emmanuelle looked down at the table. "Damn it, Val. Why is it that there's always someone wanting to kill you?"

"I told you he's a complete bastard," Dario answered in his monotone. "Absolute complete bastard. No one but you likes him, Emme. Even Stefano had him at the head of his list of men to do in until you made your plea to save him. Then that put me at the top of the hit list, which, quite frankly, I didn't appreciate. But to answer your question, he's a bastard."

Elie nodded his head and took another slice of pizza. "I

have to agree with Dario, Emmanuelle. His own men will tell you the same. If you were telling the truth, you just really like him for sex. Remember when we were making those pro and con lists? Even my good looks won out. I'm a better dancer. I'm not as arrogant."

"But I'm better at sex," Val pointed out complacently. "I'll take it."

Dario smirked. "Yeah, you kind of lost out on that one, Elie."

Elie laughed. "I guess I did."

He was gratified to see that even Emmanuelle laughed. It might not be her normal laugh, but she definitely found the exchange funny. Elie had learned, after the disastrous loss of Brielle, that ego wasn't all it was cracked up to be. Sometimes sacrificing for those he loved was worth taking a hit now and then.

"You better not know anything about Elie and his abilities when it comes to sex," Val said suddenly.

Elie laughed again, this time with Emme. Dario's smirk was just a little more noticeable, even though brief. "They don't even equate me with the Ferraro family," Elie said. "Sheesh. I'm an Archambault. In the grand scheme of things, that should trump the Ferraros but no one is in the least bit intimidated by me."

Dario swirled a breadstick in oil and salt. "I don't exactly get that entire Archambault thing. What does that mean?"

Elie had been kidding. He didn't want to explain and make himself sound like he was bragging. He took a bite of pizza and chewed, stalling for time, trying to think how to answer.

"The Archambault family, as you know, come from France," Emmanuelle said. "What you might not know is, without a doubt, they are the fastest riders in the world. They are the only riders who can police other riders. If a rider has committed a crime, the Archambault family investigate and are the ones tasked with dealing with the criminal no matter where he or she is in the world. Elie has always been considered one of, if not the fastest and the most skilled rider and

fighter in the family. We've been lucky to have him train with us."

Elie took another bite of pizza, avoiding looking at the two men. He detested anyone talking about his skills. His abilities were what had gotten him in trouble in the first place. He had been born with lightning-fast reflexes, and yeah, he was grateful for that. At the same time, he'd been taken from his parents at the age of two and sent from trainer to trainer to develop skills. The more promise he showed and the better he became, the more trainers he was sent to, so that he was never in one household very long.

As an athlete and a rider, it was a great way to develop skills, but as a human being and a child, it didn't do so much to help him understand relationships. He didn't really know his parents, even from their occasional and very brief visits. He'd learned to be a brash, arrogant, too-full-of-himself rider, praised for all the wrong reasons. Girls fell for his good looks and his name. He came from a family of a great wealth, so as a young man in Paris, he could easily find women who would want to be seen with him at all the right events.

He had things easy for all the wrong reasons. He'd gotten into the clubs and then the underground clubs with his money. The kinky sex had at first intrigued him and then become a huge part of his life. It was part of a rider's life to be written up in magazines, photographed with women on their arms at every opportunity. They were supposed to be in the blaze of lights, hiding right out in the open, always having an alibi if any criminal was assassinated, but eventually, Elie's lifestyle was too much for those in leadership of the Archambault family. They wanted to rein him in.

"Now you're stuck with me, Emme, and by association, Val and Dario, you are as well," Elie said, striving to look complacent. "And, Dario, I do expect you to come to the wedding wearing a suit."

Dario heaved a sigh. "This family business is such bullshit. Emme, I blame you. Before you seduced Val, all I had to do was beat up a few guys, or kill them. Then you tell me I've got

to make nice with your brothers and attend these family dinners every Sunday. Now you expect me to show up at weddings, too."

"You poor thing," Emmanuelle cooed, making it clear she had zero sympathy for him. "You love Sunday dinners. You can't get enough of Taviano's and Francesca's cooking."

"Or yours," Valentino added. "He practically lives at our home in the evenings just so he can eat."

"That was the deal," Dario reminded, unrepentant. "If I took the bullshit position of head of the family until you found someone else you trusted to do it, I could still eat with you. Which reminds me. How come you haven't found anyone? I've cleaned up the territory—well—mostly cleaned it up. Found new men and brought it all under control. We're making money for you and I've even cleaned up the ports. Isn't it about time you managed to find someone to take my place so I can guard your ass?"

Valentino shared an amused grin with Elie. Elie knew Val had no intention of finding anyone else to take Dario's place. He wanted his cousin to stay exactly where he was.

"It isn't that easy, Dario."

"I'll just bet it isn't. I know you're not even trying."

"It has to be the right man. Someone we both trust implicitly," Val said. "If Elie wasn't French, I'd suggest him, but we can't choose a Frenchman. We'd have a war on our hands." His grin faded and he leaned closer to his cousin. "I don't want to lose that territory, Dario, and all the other families are poised to take it if we can't keep it."

Dario sighed. "I get it. We're not losing the territory. I'm holding it for you."

"For us. This is *our famiglia*. We own everything together." Val threaded his fingers through Emmanuelle's. "We hold it together or we lose it together." He looked around the table, including Elie.

Stefano Ferraro had been the first man ever to make Elie feel as if he had a home and family, as if he truly belonged somewhere. Now he had acceptance from Valentino and Dario

as well, just as if he was part of their family. He knew that was also due to Stefano taking him in and he would be forever grateful.

Elie nodded his head. He didn't even mind the hit put out on him so much at that particular moment.

CHAPTER TWO

Elie stood just one step down from the priest about to formally marry him to his bride. He really should have taken more than a cursory interest in her. Stefano Ferraro was walking her down the aisle because, apparently, she didn't have any family willing to accompany her to the United States. What the hell was that all about? His protective instincts were already kicking in. She might be a complete stranger, but she belonged to him. She was his.

Nobody treated his wife with the kind of utter disdain that would leave her alone in a foreign country as she married a stranger. He couldn't conceive of parents who would do such a thing to their daughter—especially shadow riders. If nothing else, they should be grateful she was marrying to produce children for their community. Hell. He hadn't looked at her age. He was just as guilty as her fucking parents.

Soft music played the wedding march and for some unknown reason his heart accelerated just a little. That made no sense at all. Emmanuelle had agreed to act as a witness and she

came up the aisle first, dressed beautifully in a long burgundy gown. Her brother Vittorio was also a witness and stood beside Elie in his tuxedo. The Ferraros were out in force to support him. Valentino and Dario were there. No one was there for his bride. He detested that. He caught sight of Emmanuelle casting little glances around the chapel with a slight frown on her face. She also didn't like the fact that his bride had no one supporting her.

Elie was many things, including a demanding, arrogant, very dominant bastard, but he was also loyal, protective and faithful. His woman would have a balance in her life, regardless of the demands he put on her. And she would have all the support she needed from his friends and the family he'd surrounded himself with. They might not be his blood, but the Saldis and the Ferraros had made room in their hearts for him. They would for his bride as well. He could give her that.

Emme made it to the altar and they turned to watch his veiled bride start toward him on Stefano's arm. Stefano was a tall man, but even so, Elie's woman looked half his size. He had always dated tall runway models in Paris, his native home. This woman looked as though he could break her in half at the first touch. For a moment his heart clenched hard in his chest and he couldn't help pressing his hand over it.

For years, he'd seen Brielle in the café where she worked. He'd had no right to look at her. She'd been a young teen. Then she'd worked in the restaurant where he'd brought the models he dated. Mainly, he brought them there so he could catch glimpses of Brielle. It was wrong, and he knew it, but it was a compulsion he couldn't stop. He was careful never to date anyone who looked like her. He didn't do substitutes, not even in his mind.

He'd been a fool not to put a height requirement in the paperwork for the arranged marriage. He didn't want to ever cheat the woman he married by thinking of Brielle when he was with his wife. Shit. Here he was, the woman was walking up the aisle toward him, and he was thinking of Brielle. The

way she moved, her diminutive size, even veiled, reminded him of her. It was so wrong. He tried to concentrate on other things. The dress. The veil.

Her dress was from a French designer he recognized. Very elegant, see-through champagne-colored glitter tulle covered a formfitting silk underslip. Long sleeves of the same glitter tulle encased slender arms, coming to elegant, beaded points over his bride's delicate, finely boned hands. Strings of luxurious crystals and pearls ran around the neckline and over the sleeves. There was a slit in the A-line skirt where her leg occasionally peeked out as she walked toward him.

In her wedding dress, his new bride appeared very fragile. A stirring of unease went down his spine. He had stated very plainly that looks didn't matter—he didn't have a preference. He definitely should have thought that through and not just because she reminded him too much of Brielle.

Elie preferred rough sex. This little tiny pixie looked as if he might injure her holding her hand. This could be a disaster. He just kept himself from groaning aloud. The truth was, he deserved what he got. He'd lost his chance at the woman he was meant to be with through his own careless arrogance. He'd said hurtful, ugly things that he couldn't take back.

He had made promises to this woman and he meant to keep them. She had her head bowed, looking down at her feet, as if she wasn't used to walking in heels. He couldn't believe the heels added two or three inches to her already diminutive height. Suddenly, she looked up, her eyes meeting his through the lace of her veil. He felt the impact, although he really couldn't see her. She stopped abruptly right there in the middle of the aisle, forcing Stefano to stop as well.

"No. Absolutely not." Her voice was pitched low, but it carried to him. "Is this some kind of monstrous joke?" She tried to turn away from the altar, but Stefano held her firmly. "I didn't agree to this."

Elie didn't wait to find out why his bride was rebelling, not with his entire family waiting. He strode down the aisle to confront his *wife*. Technically, they were already married. This

ceremony was just a formality. If she didn't want it, that was too damn bad; he wasn't letting her out of the marriage. They had an arrangement. They both signed the papers. There was no getting out of it unless both parties agreed and he damn well didn't agree.

He walked right up to her, caught her veil and shoved it back over her head. His breath caught in his throat. *Brielle Couture.* His Brielle. He would know her anywhere. He dreamt about her nearly every night. She didn't look the same; she'd lost weight until she was almost a thin shadow of herself. Before, when she was eighteen, she had generous breasts and hips. Now the curves were there, but the rest of her was very slight. She was beautiful, just as she had been those years earlier, but she definitely didn't look the way she had before.

Her green eyes flashed like the edges of twin swords. "I'm not marrying you." She hissed it. Decreed it. Acted as if she had a say in the matter when she didn't.

"Too late, you already *did* marry me." He kept his voice pitched very low so only Stefano and Brielle could hear. "We're man and wife and I absolutely refuse to allow you out of our agreement. You're a shadow rider. Your word is everything. Would you really go back on your word?"

She tilted her chin at him. "I'll appeal to the head of the shadow riders." She all but hissed the declaration, keeping her voice pitched just as low. "They have to know what an arrogant, smug . . ."

Elie studied her defiant little face. Her entire body trembled. There was faint color beneath her pale skin. Her breathing had changed. He didn't know the first thing about relationships, but he did know women and their reactions to him. At that moment, their shadows weren't connected. Brielle might protest their marriage, but she was attracted physically to him whether she wanted to admit it or not. That gave him somewhere to start.

"Stefano is head of the shadow riders here." Elie cut her off and gestured to the man who still held her arm.

"Is there a problem?" the priest asked.

"Give us a minute," Stefano said smoothly. "This isn't the

place or time to air your differences," he added, lowering his voice again.

"I'm not marrying him," Brielle insisted. For the first time she looked around the church at their interested audience. She lowered her eyes, color sweeping up her neck into her face.

Elie found it rather adorable that she blushed. He didn't know too many women who blushed and rather liked the idea that his wife did. "You already did marry me legally, Brielle," he reiterated. "Stefano, she was always meant to be mine. I said some unfortunate things in my youth to her which she has never forgiven, although I apologized numerous times. We were matched together when we both put in for an arranged marriage. What are the chances of that? We were married by proxy, and both signed legal documents. I don't wish to terminate the marriage."

"Is this true, Brielle?" Stefano asked.

Brielle sighed. "Yes, but—"

Stefano shook his head. "If what Elie says is the truth, then you must continue with the formality of this wedding. After, we will sit down together and mediate the problems between you. At the moment, there does not appear to be a true reason to terminate the arrangement. If anything, it appears as if the two of you are meant to be together and fate is determined to make certain you are. We will proceed with the formal wedding and the two of you can work this out through mediation after the ceremony."

Brielle shook her head. Her nails dug into Stefano's forearm without apparent awareness. Elie wanted to capture her hand and ease the tension out of her by gently rubbing her fingers. She looked both terrified and furious. She had no one. Not one single person to aid her. Stefano was her only hope.

"I can't marry him. You don't understand."

The little break in her voice shook him. He would have gathered her into his arms to comfort her if she would have let her, but he was the last person she wanted comfort from.

Stefano bent his head to hers. "Brielle, you are already his

wife. I assure you, I am a fair man. I will listen to everything you have to say if you really wish to get out of this arrangement. Shadow riders do not break their words lightly, so I am aware you must have reasons to want to walk away from a contract that you entered into of your own free will."

Brielle searched his face for a long time before she nodded her head. "I have to trust that you're a man of your word. I don't have anyone else to rely on."

"Where is your father?" Stefano asked. "He should have accompanied you."

Her chin went up again, and her eyes, although clouded with pain, met Stefano's defiantly. "He disowned me when he believed I was rejected as not good enough to marry an Archambault. He wanted me to go to Elie and beg forgiveness for my shortcomings and plead with him to reconsider. When I refused, he wouldn't have anything more to do with me."

Stefano's gaze met Elie's and there was a flash of pure anger. Elie knew that same anger was in his eyes. "Let's get this done and we'll talk in private after, Brielle," Elie said. He turned over in his mind the way she'd phrased that to Stefano. *He believed I was rejected as not good enough.* Not that she was rejected as not good enough. He filed at that away to pull out again when they were alone.

He held out his hand and Stefano put Brielle's hand into his. He immediately locked his fingers over hers so she didn't have a chance to pull away. Touching her was like touching a match to a flame. Heat sizzled between them. He felt electricity race up his arm, through his nerve endings and down his spine. She reacted with a little gasp and a quick jerk of her arm. He held her tight to him, refusing to relinquish her hand. They made it to the altar and stood before the priest.

The priest immediately began to give an abbreviated reading and then gave a short homily as the two faced each other. Elie looked down at his bride, not really hearing what the priest had to say. Brielle tried to look anywhere but at him. He had both of her hands in his, refusing to let her escape

what this ceremony meant. It was a commitment and they both knew it. He was one hundred percent in. All the way. He wanted her to see that he meant it.

She kept shaking her head and trying to inch her hands away from his. She was adamant that she wasn't marrying him. He tried to think what had happened to her in the intervening years since he'd last seen her. She was very thin in comparison to when she'd been eighteen. She'd had an hourglass figure then. She wasn't a rider at the time. He'd been told she had washed out of the program, yet now, her résumé claimed she was a shadow rider. She'd been a virgin with no sexual experience and yet her questionnaire had included specific, very exacting questions regarding sexual preferences and she had answered she was familiar with bondage and other kink and she had listed what she was willing or unwilling to do.

Elie wasn't a man who got angry fast. He'd conquered those emotions after he had lost his temper with Jean-Claude Archambault and spewed crap that hurt Brielle and ended their relationship before it ever began. He'd worked hard to overcome a natural tendency to be passionate about everything in his life. He found himself getting angry at the mere thought of Brielle learning about sex, any kind of sex, from other men. He'd lost that opportunity as well through his own carelessness and her stubbornness.

He had taken full responsibility for what happened between them, but as time went on and he'd tried numerous ways to apologize to her, and she'd refused even to open a single letter from him, he had come to realize both of them were to blame. She might be younger than he was, and she felt humiliated, but she still could have listened to his explanation.

The priest ceased speaking and looked at Elie expectantly. Vittorio Ferraro, his best man, nudged him to take the wedding ring Damian had crafted for his bride. Elie took it almost reverently. The circle was bluish black in color and made of a particular element that could enter the shadows with a rider.

Where her band was thin and dainty, it still matched the thicker band Damian had crafted for Elie to wear. Inside each ring, Damian had etched *à toi pour toujours*, meaning *forever yours*.

He took the ring and repeated the vows in a firm voice, promising to love and cherish this woman for all his days. He pushed the band onto her finger and wasn't surprised when it fit perfectly.

Emmanuelle handed Brielle Elie's ring, the one he had reluctantly removed just before the ceremony started. He had wondered at his reluctance. Now he knew why. Subconsciously, he must have known his bride was Brielle. Brielle's voice was low, shaking, as she stumbled over the vows to love and cherish Elie. He knew she wasn't really doing more than parroting the priest when she promised to obey him. He thought she'd stop the entire ceremony. Emme nearly threw her bouquet at him. Maybe Brielle heard and didn't care because she planned on petitioning to get out of the marriage immediately. She did take his hand and push the ring onto his finger.

The priest pronounced them man and wife and said he could kiss his bride. He'd been waiting for that moment. Hot blood roared through his veins, and thundered in his ears, drowning out every civilized sound. The chapel, and everyone in it, receded until there was only Brielle, the woman he'd had so many erotic fantasies about. The woman he'd thought about for years.

Elie swept her into his arms before she could think to protest. Maybe she wasn't going to protest. He didn't know because the moment he gathered her close, her body fitted to his, the familiar electricity ran like a hot live wire between them, connecting them instantly. The air seemed to crackle and lightning shot through his body in jagged streaks. He had never been so aware of another human being in his life.

He tilted her chin with one hand and lowered his mouth to hers. The moment their lips touched, it was as if a match flared into a bright, hot flame, scorching them both. She gasped and he took advantage, sweeping his tongue into the heat of her

mouth. At the first taste of her, every nerve ending in his body came roaring to life, instantly aware of every part of her. Soft skin. The way her breasts rose and fell against his chest. The way her feminine mound pressed tight against his thigh and her firm belly rubbed against his cock where it pushed intimately against her very elegant gown.

Elie was very aware of Brielle's small hands on his chest, shaking. Her body trembling against his, even as her mouth moved like hot magic, sizzling raw fire, so that his blood rushed through his veins and thundered in his heart. He realized his reaction to her was so much more and always had been.

That reaction had started so long ago, when he'd first heard her voice in that café. He'd walked in and she'd asked him what he wanted to drink. Something in his chest, locked up so tight, had suddenly broken free. Tuned to her. Specifically to her. Brielle. He just hadn't known, because no one had bothered to tell him what it meant—that she was his other half. Now she was exactly where she was always meant to be. In his arms. Vows sworn before priest and family to be his and only his. She knew it, too. He tasted it in her kiss. Felt it in her touch. She might not want to admit it, but she would eventually, because he wasn't letting her go.

Vittorio cleared his throat. Brielle's fingernails dug into Elie's upper arms and he reluctantly lifted his head. Very gently he turned his bride toward those watching, keeping one arm around her waist, steadying her as the priest introduced them as Mr. and Mrs. Elie Archambault. Brielle held herself stiffly, but she didn't pull away from him.

He pressed her palm onto his forearm. "There's a small reception. The Ferraros went to a lot of trouble setting it up for you. They had no idea you would object to the wedding."

She gave a little shake of her head as he walked her down the aisle toward the door. "I can't pretend I'm happy in front of all of them, or that I'm going to stay married to you."

"Yes, you can, and you will. This family, as you well know, is huge in the rider community, not to mention they took me

in when I had no one. You will treat them with respect. It isn't too much to ask to keep up the pretense for a couple of hours. Stefano will keep his word and hear you out. I'll be very interested in hearing why you think you have reason to go back on your word when the word of a rider is everything in our world, especially when it comes to an arranged marriage."

Again, color stole up her neck and into her cheeks as he handed her into the limousine that would take them to the luxurious Ferraro Hotel. Brielle scooted all the way across the seat from him.

"You should have stopped the marriage the moment you knew it was me," she said, looking straight ahead.

"I had no idea you were my intended bride, not until I lifted the veil. The lawyers brought papers to me to sign and I signed them. I presume you did the same thing if you weren't aware I was your husband until you saw me when you looked up."

She turned her head to glare at him. "We *aren't* married, and we aren't going to be. To be married, you actually have to consummate the marriage. I did read the rules of the arrangement prior to signing it, didn't you?"

He held her gaze deliberately. "I not only read them, I have your answers on the wall of the bedroom framed, laminated and underlined in red."

This time the blush went from pink to a much deeper shade of red. Her breath hissed out between her teeth. "You always were far too sure of yourself."

"I've always had good reason to be sure of myself, Brielle. I believe the kiss was a mutual exchange, not just one-sided."

His sweet little bride lapsed into French with a string of curse words that cast aspersions on his lineage, clearly designed to make him lose his temper, but only made him want to kiss her again. She really was a beautiful little thing, and fiery as hell.

Elie leaned close, his lips against her ear. "I'll have so much fun restraining all that passion until you're screaming my

name and begging me to let you come for me." That bought him another flair of heat from her jeweled eyes and that unrestrained blush that he wanted to see covering her entire body.

She didn't swear at him this time, only turned her head to stare straight ahead again, the color deepening to a dark rose and her breathing quickening to a ragged one of arousal. Her fingers nervously plucked at the skirt of her wedding dress. Elie wanted to ask her so many questions, but he remained silent. Brielle was clearly struggling, confused and horrified by her body's reaction to him. He didn't want to upset her more, not before the party.

It didn't make sense that she was so opposed to their marriage, not when their chemistry was so off the charts. She had agreed to an arranged marriage because, like Elie, she must have believed they were meant to be together. She had made up her mind they wouldn't be. That was why she was marrying what she thought was a complete stranger.

She had insisted on only marrying someone who was in the United States, just as he insisted his bride had to be willing to live in the United States. Brielle hadn't known he lived there. She hadn't kept up with him and that annoyed him. Seeing him, she had been more adamant than ever that she wasn't going to marry him. Why?

That nervous plucking at her dress was going to drive him insane. He couldn't help himself. Elie placed his much larger hand over hers to still her fingers. He didn't look at her expression, but he did close his fingers around hers to warn her not to fight him. Beside him, Brielle tensed, but she didn't attempt to pull her hand away. She did something amazing to his heart each time he touched her, or even looked at her, let alone breathed her in. Spending so much time with Stefano Ferraro these last few years had been good for him when it came to understanding relationships, but it had also honed him into a man willing to protect his loved ones at any cost. He realized he had an emotional connection to Brielle as well as a physical one. Perhaps it was all the time he spent on thinking

about her, wishing he hadn't screwed up and wondering why she wouldn't give him a second chance.

The limousine pulled up to the entrance of the Ferraro, the luxury hotel owned by the Ferraro family. The door was opened and Elie slid out and held out his hand to Brielle. She hesitated. He waited, knowing she was gathering her courage. She had a great deal of pride and it wasn't as if she wanted to be pried out of the limousine and carried in over his shoulder. She would be terrified he might just do that—which he would.

"I'll get you through this and then you can present your case to Stefano," he assured, speaking low. "He's a fair man and will hear you out." He didn't tell her he had no intention of allowing her out of the marriage and would block every argument she presented.

Elie had dozens of questions he wanted answered in front of Stefano, because Stefano really was fair. He was also head of the riders in Chicago and Brielle fell under his leadership now. She had no choice but to obey him. Riders adhered to a very strict order of rules and there was no way around them, not unless Brielle wanted to be banished from the entire worldwide society of shadow riders in all capacities.

Brielle placed her hand in his and stepped out of the limousine, allowing him to pull her close to him. Elie wasn't too surprised to see Emilio Gallo there, accompanied by Elie's two dedicated bodyguards and two others he didn't recognize. Emilio, as head bodyguard for the Ferraro family, had insisted that not only would Elie be guarded as all riders were, but his bride as well. Emilio had assigned two brothers to him three years earlier and he had gotten used to their presence. Like all riders, he didn't have to like it, but he tolerated it because it was mandatory. The two personal bodyguards, Ruggero and Lorenzo Forni, were quiet, alert and trained personally by Emilio. The newcomers, two young men, Elie didn't know, which would have made him very unhappy, except that Emilio's presence meant he personally vouched for them.

Elie, when he'd first gotten out of the military, had applied to be a bodyguard. He had thought to stop being a rider for the Archambault family. He'd been forced to disclose his background to Emilio. Once Emilio turned the information over to Stefano, Stefano asked him to become a rider for Chicago. That was how he had made his way into the Ferraro family. He knew from firsthand experience that neither Emilio nor Stefano tolerated slackers in any of their businesses.

The four bodyguards closed around Elie and Brielle as they walked up to the doors of the hotel.

"I'm sorry I didn't have time to allow for you to interview the new bodyguards for your bride, Elie. We can do that when she's had a few days to settle in. She can sit in on the interview as well." Emilio attempted a smile, which didn't quite make it to his dark eyes. He was a very serious man as a rule, although quite capable of joking with those he felt very comfortable with. It was clear he knew someone had put out a contract on Elie's life. Emilio would take that very seriously.

"Thanks, Emilio. This is Brielle. Brielle, Emilio, the Ferraro family head of security. Any order he gives, we all obey. Even Stefano."

Emilio uttered a low sound that could have been either a throat clearing or a growl. Elie shot him a quick glance of reprimand. He was trying to get it across to his new wife that certain rules had to be obeyed, and one was having bodyguards. If she had recently really become a rider, then she had only just had them assigned to her, but more than likely, she wasn't used to them and would ignore her need for them.

Brielle seemed very independent. Much more so than he ever thought possible. The woman answering questions hadn't seemed quite so stubborn or liberated. She stated that respect was extremely important, but she had no problems following when her partner led if he was a righteous leader. Her behavior, so far, didn't quite mesh with the answers she had sworn were truthful ones.

Brielle offered Emilio a tentative smile. "Stefano didn't

seem a man who takes to orders easily. For that matter, Elie doesn't, either. If you're able to get either one of them to do what you need them to if their lives are in danger, you must be really good at your job." Her tone implied that Elie might be stubborn just to have his way in the face of death.

Emilio shot Elie an amused look over her head as he reached to open the door to the private conference room where the party was being held. "When their lives are in danger, not if," he corrected.

Brielle nearly stopped walking, but Elie put a hand on her back to keep her moving. He glared at Emilio.

"What do you mean, *when*? Riders get in and get out. We're never seen. Why would Elie ever be in danger?" Clearly the idea of Elie being in danger wasn't something she'd considered and she didn't like it.

There was a short silence. Brielle tipped her head back, her startling green eyes meeting Elie's. "Elie?" There was a little note of demand in her voice, one that he couldn't help but like. There was also fear for him. He liked that even more.

"Everyone is waiting on us," he hedged. "We can go into this when we're alone, *ma chérie*."

She looked as if she might argue with him but then she turned to look at the group of people waiting to greet them and she instantly subsided. The bodyguards moved away from them, deeming it safe in the room filled with members of the Ferraro family. Brielle actually moved closer to him, coming under his shoulder, so that he slipped his arm around her waist, drawing her into the heat of his body as he walked her across the room, once again trying to imagine what it must be like for her not to know a single person.

"Most everyone is a Ferraro or related by marriage," he whispered, hoping to ease some of her trepidation.

"I heard their family is enormous. Cousins in various locations, even overseas," she acknowledged.

"It is very large. Not just the riders. They appear to be quite close. The ones in this immediate part of the family are

close and the cousins that are riders and their bodyguards are close. I wouldn't want to be the person who thought to harm one of them." He traced the back of her hand with his thumb as they approached the table with the small wedding cake.

Stefano and Francesca waited for them, looking happy. Elie could tell that Stefano hadn't shared Brielle's determination to end the marriage before it began with anyone else, although those attending the ceremony had to have wondered at the exchange before the vows had taken place.

Elie presented Brielle to Francesca first. Stefano was the head of the family, but Francesca was the undisputed heart of the family. She had given birth to a baby girl just two months earlier, and as always, the entire family—including Elie— was treating her as if she was too fragile to walk across a room. Francesca simply ignored them all and stepped forward to take Brielle's hands and greeted her warmly.

"I'm so happy to meet you. At last, we have someone for our Elie. He's the most wonderful—and annoying—man in the world. Just like the rest of them." She tilted her head to give Stefano a loving smile. He came up behind her to wrap his arms around her waist and pull her back against him. "Elie will treat you as if you can't possibly stand on your own two feet without him, and yet expect you to run his household without a single hitch. And God help you if you get pregnant, but have no worries, we will surround you and protect you."

She wiggled her finger to encompass the women in the room. "From all the male idiocy that is everything Ferraro, Archambault and Saldi." She lifted her gaze until it found Dario, who stood looking complacent, draped against the wall to the left of them. "Dario, I include you in the Saldi family, just so you know." Leaning close, she lowered her voice, but made certain it would carry. "He is undoubtedly the worst of the chauvinists."

Dario raised an eyebrow. "I take that as a compliment, Francesca."

"You would, Dario."

"And I think you're insulting me, Francesca," Vittorio said. He had his arm around his wife's waist as he came up on Brielle's side. "I'm Vittorio, one of Stefano's brothers. This is Grace, my wife." There was softness both in his voice and on his face when he introduced his wife. "We live on the lake close to Val and Emmanuelle, my baby sister."

For the first time, Brielle seemed to relax a bit, smiling at Francesca and then Vittorio and Grace. "I really do need to thank Emmanuelle for standing up for me." She turned her attention to Grace. "Is he chauvinistic?"

"No, he doesn't believe he is superior to women in any way, which is the definition of a male chauvinist," Grace denied.

"Dario isn't one, either," Francesca said. "Although he really likes to pretend he is. He knows we all have brains and can keep up with him. He's just very protective, like they all are."

"Sheesh, Francesca," Dario said. "Stefano, you're giving her too much freedom these days. You might want to rethink your plan to let her run wild the way you do."

Even Elie had to laugh. He swept Brielle even closer. "Stefano could no more let his beloved Francesca run wild than he would allow a criminal loose on our streets."

"Are you prone to running wild, Francesca?" Brielle asked.

There was a note of mischief in her voice. Elie found he liked that. Her natural personality seemed to be coming out surrounded by the women in the Ferraro family.

"I would if I could," Francesca admitted. "I've decided to use my position in the family to lead as a rebel. I've been giving it a lot of thought and I need to start with Emmanuelle. She's the most likely to listen to me. Emmanuelle and Nicoletta."

"I'd be willing to listen," Brielle said. "Rebellion always did sound good to me. In my family, I was always the one to follow all the rules and my sister was the rule breaker, although it was okay that she did."

Why was it Elie didn't know that? The matchmaking questionnaire hadn't covered personal home life and how they'd

grown up. It should have. That sort of information would help to give insight into what baggage each respondent carried.

He wanted to know every single thing about her childhood. Why her father wasn't with her. Was it really because she hadn't begged Elie to marry her? Would a father disown his daughter over something like that? His gaze went from Brielle's soft profile to the rugged angles and planes of Stefano's face. Elie couldn't imagine Stefano disowning his daughter over anything, let alone a demand that she plead with a man to marry her. If anything, if a man hurt his daughter, that man might not wake up in the morning.

"I don't think you need to lead any rebellions," Stefano said, lowering his head so he could bite Francesca's earlobe.

She gave a little yelp and turned her head to glare at him. "I think it's a necessity. You're getting too bossy for words. Let this be a lesson to you, Brielle. You give that man of yours an inch, he's going to take a mile."

"Walk away from Francesca now, Elie," Valentino advised. "I don't know what's gotten into our sweet girl, but you can't afford to let her talk utter nonsense to your woman. I'm hauling Emme out of here as fast as possible."

Dario gave a snort of derision, even going so far as rolling his eyes. "You're pussy whipped, Saldi, just like the rest of these Ferraro men. They talk a good game but they can't help themselves. One little whine and it's over."

"I told you he was the worst," Francesca said, not even wincing at his language. "We've tried our best to civilize him for polite company but he's very resistant."

"It's only because he's on that dating app all the time now." Emmanuelle gave him up without a qualm.

"What?" Grace spun around to stare at Dario. "You're on a *dating* app?"

Another couple joined them, Ricco and his wife, Mariko. Ricco pulled out a chair for his wife and nodded toward Francesca.

"Let's sit down so Francesca will," Elie whispered to Brielle, effectively stopping any protest.

"Your dress is so beautiful," Mariko said. "I'm Mariko, Ricco's wife. I have to admit, I find it very shocking that Dario is on a dating app. I love him dearly, but I'm not certain the world is ready for him to be dating." Her voice was extremely soft and nonjudgmental.

Dario looked up from his phone and scowled at her. "Woman, how can you look and sound so sweet and say something like that?"

Elie found himself fascinated with Brielle's genuine smile as he escorted her to their place at the oblong table amid the laughter. The moment they were seated, Stefano pulled out the chair beside Brielle to allow Francesca to sit and he immediately dropped into the one beside her. That seemed to be a signal for the rest of the family to come to the table.

"Mariko is extraordinarily sweet," Elie confirmed. "She's married to Ricco, and she isn't given to even minor rebellions. Giovanni and Sasha are seated beside them. Sasha would lead the charge right beside Francesca so I'm not certain the two of you can ever be great friends."

Dario nodded approvingly. "At last. A take-charge man. Val, you need to take notes. It's most likely too late. Emmanuelle's wrapped you around her little finger, but you could try to rein that woman in."

"I'm erasing that app if you keep it up, Dario," Emmanuelle threatened. "Don't you give Val any more ideas. He's quite enough to deal with as it is. You used to be silent—as in never speaking. When did that change and why?"

"I thought annoying you would be more fun."

"Sit your ass in a chair, Dario," Stefano said, "before I have to put your name back at the top of the hit list."

Emmanuelle tossed her hair over her shoulder and sank into a chair, her hand in the crook of her husband's arm. "This is Valentino, my husband, Brielle. And Dario is actually quite nice, but he likes to pretend he's a badass."

"Thank you for your help today," Brielle said. "Dario isn't a badass?"

Her accent was adorable the way she said *badass*. Elie was

born and raised in France. His mother was American, a distant relative of the Ferraro family, but his father had been an Archambault through and through. Elie, apparently, had an accent; at least that was what Emmanuelle told him. The years he'd spent in the service and with her family might have dulled it, but the accent was still there. That didn't take away his joy of hearing Brielle speak with hers.

"No, he's just a wannabe badass. He stands around looking mean and grim so everyone thinks he's one," Emme said. "That's how he gets women to date him."

Laughter went around the table. Food was being taken off plates from the middle of the table at an alarming rate. Elie had known the Ferraro family for years and they could eat a tremendous amount of food. He caught up Brielle's plate and began to scoop the pasta dish he knew was really good onto it.

"Salad," she whispered. "Or just the carrots and broccoli."

"The pasta is amazing. Taviano's specialty. He'd be hurt if you didn't at least try a little, Brielle." What had she done? Stopped eating so she could get thin? He wanted *all* of her curves back. They'd talk about that when they were alone—or with Stefano.

She looked down the table and Taviano raised his hand with a grin. "I hope you enjoy it, Brielle. Welcome to the *famiglia*. This is Nicoletta, my wife." Taviano raised his voice. "Dario, the pasta is going fast. Francesca baked the bread herself. You don't get your ass to the table, we aren't saving anything for you."

Dario heaved a huge sigh and made his way to the table, pushing his phone into his pocket. "Seriously, Taviano? Think before you take on the family from hell, Brielle. I was dragged into this through no fault of my own, but the food is delicious and they're an endless source of amusement when I don't have to save their lives."

Brielle smiled at him. "Do you have to do that a lot, Dario? Save their lives, I mean?"

She took a cautious bite of the pasta. Elie watched as she

took her time, savoring as she chewed. He hoped he would be able to persuade her to eat a lot of meals with the Ferraros.

"Yep. Sadly. They're impossible, as you can tell from the crap they talk. I spend most of my time saving them from the enemies they make just by opening their mouths."

Another burst of laughter went around the table.

CHAPTER THREE

You have a lovely family," Brielle told Stefano. "You're a very lucky man."

"I am," he agreed. "Are you still determined to break your agreement, Brielle?"

For a moment she hesitated, pressing her lips together. Elie's breath caught in his lungs, hoping she would decide against going through with her protest. She inclined her head. "Yes. I feel I have no choice."

Stefano waved her toward a chair in the office he'd taken the two of them up to in his private elevator. Instead of going to the chair, Brielle paced across the room, her movements flowing and fluid as befitting a shadow rider. She was both feminine and graceful in her elegant wedding gown. The veil was gone, revealing the wealth of blond hair she had pinned up in an intricate and stylish figure eight, taming the wild mass he had remembered vividly from when she'd sat so rigidly on Jean-Claude's couch in the sitting room.

Brielle stared out the window to the street below instead

of facing them. "I had thought I would be speaking with you in private."

"That would hardly be fair to your partner. He entered into this agreement in good faith and provided you with full disclosure. The things you learned about him are extremely private and nobody but his partner has the right to know."

Brielle flushed a dull pink, but she didn't turn, refusing to look at either of them.

"At any time, once your lawyer presented you with the papers to sign the marriage agreement, you could have checked his name but you didn't. I find that . . . strange."

There was no accusation in Stefano's voice, but Elie felt guilty anyway. He hadn't bothered to check his wife's name, either. Indifference? That was what Stefano's statement to Brielle implied. Had he been indifferent? He'd been upset. Uncomfortable with the fact that he'd married a woman he knew he shouldn't be with. It was wrong. It felt wrong because he was supposed to be married to Brielle. He didn't want to face the stranger until he absolutely had to. Had Brielle felt the same? Curious, he waited, like Stefano, standing by the desk for her to comply with the request to take a seat.

Elie admired the way Brielle straightened her shoulders before she finally turned to face the two men. There was determination in her expression. She didn't like the fact that he was in the room when she pleaded her case, but she wasn't going to let his presence stop her. With great dignity she crossed the room to the chair Elie had pulled out for her. Seating herself, she folded her hands in her lap. Elie took the chair beside hers and Stefano sat behind his desk on the opposite side.

"For accuracy, I'll record the conversation, but we can destroy the recording, Brielle, at the end of the meeting, depending on the outcome," Stefano said. "I need you to state your name, birth date and the reason you are here—the termination of your agreement to enter into a marriage with Elie Archambault. Elie, you do the same, stating that you don't wish to

allow Brielle out of the agreement. She will speak first, stating all her reasons why she wants out of the arrangements. You remain silent during her time to speak. Then you can offer a rebuttal and ask questions. Is that clear to both of you?"

Brielle's voice was low but firm as she followed Stefano's instructions. Elie didn't think that was a good idea. He would have preferred a little hesitancy. When it was his turn, he made certain to sound decisive and very calm. He was an Archambault. They were famous for keeping their cool under any circumstance. He had been a notorious hothead in his youth, but he had grown far past that and he wanted that on the record.

Brielle twisted her fingers together so tight, they were white. Elie had to resist putting his hand over hers to still the nervous gesture and comfort her.

"Forgive me, but I have to tell you this from the very beginning or it will not make sense to you," Brielle said.

"I have all night if that is what it takes," Stefano said, shifting back in his chair and steepling his fingers, his eyes on her face.

"In France, the Archambault family is very famous, not just among riders, but everywhere they go. I imagine it is much the same as your family here. They appear in all the magazines and they are quite handsome. There is much gossip about them."

Brielle pressed her thumb very tightly into her palm, steadfastly avoiding Elie's gaze. "My sister and I bought every magazine any of the Archambaults were in. My parents were certain Fayette would be a perfect match for one of them. She was an excellent rider and they carefully studied all the bachelors in the family. Fayette was groomed to become the wife of an Archambault almost from birth."

She raised her gaze to Stefano's, looking shy and a little apprehensive as if he might judge her family harshly. "Fayette is really quite beautiful and an excellent rider. She's tall and could easily have been a runway model had she chosen to be. She was asked dozens of times but turned down the offers. Her times in the shadows were ridiculously fast, so much better

than mine. She had her heart set on Elie and went to all the clubs he frequented. She told me how he often danced with her and . . ."

She broke off and pressed her lips together, for the first time glancing at Elie, that sweet rose color creeping up her neck and into her face.

Elie remained silent, very aware of Stefano's decree. He wanted to defend himself, but he also didn't want to take the chance of Brielle shutting down. Clearly, it was extremely difficult for her to offer her testimony to the two men—and he could see why. It was very personal.

"Fayette explained the sexual practices that Elie preferred in the clubs," Brielle settled on. Her voice dropped to a whisper.

Stefano held up his hand. "I'm sorry, but you need to be specific. Your sister had to have been very specific with you in order for you to want to break your given word."

The color deepened. She ducked her head. "Yes. She said he was into exhibitionism, bondage and pain, all while sharing his women. Sometimes he wanted more than one woman at the same time or to have his partner service several men at the same time."

Stefano's gaze flicked to Elie's face, but Elie made absolutely certain to stay expressionless. He could see why his woman wouldn't want anything to do with him.

"My parents spent a great deal of money and time on my sister's education in order to make certain she had every advantage and she would be the perfect wife for an Archambault. She had tutors in academics as well as for her physical capabilities."

Again, Stefano held up his hand. "Were you given these same opportunities?"

Brielle's color deepened even more. "You see my size. I'm nowhere near my sister's abilities when it comes to riding the shadows. I have to fight my weight all the time. She has a much faster metabolism and she's taller by quite a few inches."

This time, she staunchly avoided Elie's gaze. "I'm younger

than Fayette by seven years. My parents weren't expecting me to come along. I was a bit of a disappointment to them. Academically, I exceeded expectations, but I fell far short in terms of looks, riding shadows and just about every other way. My parents didn't have the money to waste and I understood that."

There was no bitterness in her voice at all. She had accepted everything her parents and sister told her. It had most likely been told to her from the time she was a young child, how important Fayette was, and how unimportant she was.

"Fayette was excited that Elie was paying her so much attention at the clubs. They weren't dating formally. He didn't come to the house and pick her up, but he met her at the various clubs and had sex with her often. She was certain a marriage proposal was going to happen very soon. She didn't tell our father, only that she'd bumped into Elie a few times and he seemed to be interested. Our mother had passed away two years prior, but Father was quite excited, certain Elie would be enamored."

Brielle's lip trembled for a moment and she pressed her fingers to it briefly before she once again rested both hands in her lap. "You can imagine their shock and horror when Jean-Claude Archambault sent for me, making his intentions clear—that he wanted Elie to marry me, not Fayette. Fayette wasn't mentioned at all. My father and Fayette accused me of sneaking out and meeting Elie behind their backs. They were certain I had done something to call attention to myself. In the end, I had to go to the meeting, because one doesn't say no to a meeting with Jean-Claude Archambault."

Elie knew that was the truth. Not even he had dared to turn down the meeting when Jean-Claude had called him to come to his home, and he'd been furious. He'd wanted to tell the head of the family to go fuck himself, but instead, when he heard whom they were insisting he marry, he knew they had invaded his privacy. He knew they had been spying on him and caught him having fantasies he should never have been having of a too-young girl. He'd struck out like the arrogant ass he'd been at that age, saying disgusting things

against the girl, trying to prove to himself—and to Jean-Claude—that the family knew nothing about him and his fantasies.

"I intended to point out to Jean-Claude that he had the wrong Couture sister. That Fayette was the perfect wife for Elie and that they already knew one another intimately, so it would be impossible for me to consider marriage to him. Elie made it abundantly clear he had no desire to marry me."

Stefano held up his hand. Knots suddenly formed in Elie's gut. The one person he respected above all others was Stefano. He knew what the next question was going to be and he was very ashamed of what he'd said.

"Do you remember Elie's reasons for not wanting to marry you?"

Brielle swallowed almost convulsively. She nodded. "It's been difficult to forget them, although I have to admit, he probably did me a service. First, Jean-Claude told him I was eighteen and a virgin, but had good genes, the best for producing riders. I was a rider but couldn't cut it. Elie sounded quite furious when he told Jean-Claude that he wasn't about to be saddled with a little child that didn't know the first thing about sex and would faint at the things he would demand of me."

Her chin went up. "He told Jean-Claude my breasts and hips were too big, and once I had a child, I'd be a cow for certain, that I was well on my way in that department already. He pointed out he wasn't in the least attracted to me, and what did Jean-Claude want him to do? Close his eyes the entire time he fucked me?"

There was a short silence when Brielle finished speaking. What the hell else was there to say? It was really the only truthful thing said as far as Elie was concerned and it was bad enough. Still, he waited. Not saying a word.

"What happened, Brielle?" Stefano pushed.

"I went home. I told my father and Fayette I wasn't going to marry Elie and she could have him if she wanted him. My father was furious since I didn't convince Jean-Claude to accept Fayette in my place. Fayette sobbed for hours, and in the

end, my father demanded I find Elie and plead with him to marry me or Fayette. I refused. He threw me out. I walked out and took a job as a nanny for a good friend's mother in Spain."

That was why he couldn't find her. Why his letters kept coming back unopened. Elie cursed under his breath. Damn her father. Damn Fayette. Damn him for being a complete ass and not standing up to Jean-Claude the way he should have instead of hurting the one person who mattered to him.

"You can see why it is impossible for me to marry this man," Brielle concluded.

"I haven't heard from Elie yet, Brielle. That is only one side of the story. There are always two sides. Given what Brielle has revealed, Elie, do you want to end this right now and give your consent to allowing her out of the marriage?"

"Absolutely not." Elie poured conviction into his voice. He leaned toward Stefano. "I never met Fayette Couture until she opened her door when I went looking for Brielle right before I made up my mind to enter into an arranged marriage. I had to fill out the same questionnaire as Brielle did, stating my preferences for sexual practices and I had to swear to the honesty of those practices. The computer matches the two subjects as closely as possible. I'm a shadow rider and I live by my word. I don't share women. I don't do threesomes, or practice anything else other than bondage and I do that with my partner and no one else. I am dominant in sexual practices. Fayette lied to Brielle about everything. I never touched her, kissed her or fucked her and that's the God's honest truth."

"But—"

Stefano held up his hand. "You have to give Elie the courtesy of hearing him out, Brielle, just as he did you. What you were saying couldn't have been easy for him to hear, just as this isn't easy for you."

"I did say those terrible things to Jean-Claude, not because they were true, but because I was so angry with him for running my life, taking my childhood away from me, my family, and dictating every aspect of my life to the point I wasn't even there when my father died. More, I had noticed Brielle when

she was underage working in the café I frequented. She was gorgeous. I knew I shouldn't be looking at her, especially since I was older and I already had certain sexual preferences. I couldn't stop myself."

Elie pressed his hand to his chest, remembering that moment when he first heard the sound of her voice. "She asked me what I wanted to drink and just the sound of her voice opened up something in me that had been so closed off, but I didn't understand then what it was."

Stefano held up his hand, frowning. "No one ever talked to you about what would happen when you found the right person?"

Elie shook his head and then pressed his hand to his temple, ashamed he had to confess not only to Brielle, but to Stefano, the one man he respected above all others. "I began to make certain I knew her shifts and I would go to her place of work. When our shadows touched, there was a sexual jolt that was unbelievable, but more, I could see our shadows knotting together. I always made certain I stood where our shadows touched. At first, I did it because I was addicted to the rush. But then I wanted to tie us together—to have a connection to someone. Not just to anyone—to her. She began to matter to me. Jean-Claude found out about her and what I was doing. I felt like he took the one good, decent thing I had in my life and ripped it away."

Elie forced himself to look at Brielle. "I honestly loved the way you looked with your curves. I said those things to strike out at Jean-Claude, not you. I didn't know you were anywhere around. It was idiocy on my part. I was young and hitting out at the great Jean-Claude Archambault. As for saying the things about sex, I played right into Fayette's hands. I didn't feel the family had any right to judge me when I felt abandoned by them and yet used at the same time."

He had. What other conclusion could Brielle have drawn besides believing that Fayette was telling the absolute truth? She had no reason to think her sister was lying. He knew there was that same raw hurt in his voice he felt every time

he let that door open on his childhood. He hadn't been physically abused—he'd been dangerous even at a young age and
any trainer recognized that trait in him. He had been emo-
tionally abused, but he hadn't recognized that fact until he'd
grown older and realized he had no idea what a childhood
was—or how to act in a family relationship or any other kind.
No one had ever loved him—not as a child and not as an
adult. Like other women, Fayette and her family had regarded
him as a prize.

Elie suspected that he had revealed all of his feelings to
Stefano in that brief exchange. He held himself straight, although he was ashamed that he hurt Brielle. "I struck out at
Jean-Claude, but the way I did it was wrong. I still feared his
power," he admitted. "I didn't know how to express the many
ways he, the family and the council had made my childhood
a nightmare. I felt they shaped me into something monstrous
I could never recover from. They left me with no softer side,
no way to know how to be a husband or father. Then he had
the gall to tell me I was going to marry an innocent girl—*my*
girl. It was tantamount to sentencing her to live with someone
cruel and brutal. Worse, I knew they all knew I'd been
stalking her and tying her shadow to mine."

That moment of recognition of just how cruel and ugly he
found himself in those days washed over him. He pressed his
fingers above his eyes, effectively shading his expression
briefly from Stefano. He'd been an arrogant prick, so full of
himself. Worse even than the Archambault family realized,
but he did. He knew what he was and he had grown to despise
himself. When he'd walked into Jean-Claude's sitting room
to see Brielle on the couch, holding herself so still, her inno-
cence shining through, he felt more the monster than ever.
He was the devil to her angel. He was *such* a prick. What he
wasn't was any of the things her sister had accused him of. He
had enough sins without Fayette lying about him.

Elie cleared his throat. "I tried to apologize to Brielle. To
explain to her. I loved the way she looked. I knew we were
meant to be together. The vicious things I said had nothing to

do with her and everything to do with me. When I couldn't get her to open her door and listen, or read my letters, I thought time might help and I came to the United States. I had hoped to finally have some kind of a relationship with my mother, but she had no interest."

He avoided looking at Brielle. Whether she believed Fayette had lied or not, she was much like Emmanuelle in that she was compassionate. He didn't want her pity. He wanted a lot of things from her, but pity wasn't one of them. Truthfully, a part of him was holding on to his anger at her. He recognized that he was and that he would have to admit that to Stefano if he was going to be honest and disclose everything to the man who would judge his fate.

Mon Dieu. Shadow Riders and the sacred, rigid rules they all had to live by. He would like to be deceptive in this one thing—that he was angry with Brielle for never giving him a chance to explain his side of things to her—but ever since leaving France, he had always strived to be as honorable as he could be. It was all he had left that he could like about himself. The one trait that had gained him entrance into the Ferraro family—the code Stefano held them all to.

"Once again, I tried to contact Brielle. When I didn't get a response, I joined the service. I continued to ride the shadows and work on my speed and keep maps in my head because it was so ingrained in me, but to be honest, I had no intention of continuing as a rider for the Archambault family. I thought I might stay in the service." He fell silent.

Stefano took over. "You were a member of an elite strike team."

Elie had not disclosed that particular bit of information to anyone, not even Stefano. He had admitted he had been trained as a Green Beret and served for a short time in that capacity, but he hadn't gone any further in discussing his career in the Delta unit. He said nothing. Stefano hadn't exactly asked. He'd made it a statement. The Ferraros, like the Archambaults, had superb investigators able to ferret out anyone's secrets.

"You left the service though, why?"

Elie had the discipline to hold himself very still. He'd needed his woman. He wanted to find her and plead his case. He'd worked on himself in those intervening years. Tried to find reasons for her to want to be with him. She had been dropped from the shadow riding program and maybe she would be happy with his choice to leave—although he still couldn't step away from riding the shadows and practicing every day.

"I was injured. I could have stayed, but I left to find Brielle," he admitted. "I wanted to plead my case again. I wasn't quite as young or as arrogant as when we first met. I thought she would hear the truth in my voice and know I had really worked to be someone different for her, someone better than who I was when we first met."

Stefano nodded. "But you didn't find her. Why didn't you use the Archambaults' investigators?"

"I wanted nothing to do with that family." Elie tried not to allow the old feelings of loathing to show in his voice. That angry, helpless fury belonged in his youth, not to the man he'd become. Holding grudges and letting his emotions control him wouldn't show Brielle he'd grown in character. He'd shut the door on the Archambaults and become a Ferraro as best he could, taking on as many of Stefano's traits as possible. "I should have swallowed my pride and gone to them, but I didn't think of it. I went back to Chicago and made my way to Emilio and asked for a job as a bodyguard."

"Emilio immediately turned over your résumé to me and I jumped at the chance to add you to our roster once I had you investigated. I did talk to Jean-Claude and he disclosed what had happened."

Elie didn't comment. He was always polite when the Archambaults came to Chicago on business. Always. He conducted himself the way a Ferraro would. He would never let Stefano down, no matter his ongoing opinion of the council members.

"I reached out to Brielle one last time before I resigned

myself to entering into an arranged marriage. She had disappeared, and I knew that if she followed the dictates of the council, and there was a good chance that she would, she would have already accepted a husband. She was getting to the age where they would insist she marry and produce children for them." Again, he had to work to keep bitterness out of his voice.

"How did you reach out to her?" Stefano asked.

"I went to see her father. I was told by his housekeeper that he was unavailable. I went to see Fayette. She met me at the door, all smiles when she thought I was there to see her. When I asked her questions about Brielle, she nearly slammed the door in my face after telling me her sister had disgraced the family by running off with a non-rider from another country and no one had heard from her. I could hear she was lying, but I also knew she wouldn't tell me anything. I left and returned to the States."

"Were you angry with Brielle?" Stefano's voice was very quiet.

There was silence in the room. The clock ticked. Stefano had dropped that question in very seamlessly as if it was just like any of the other questions. Why would he think Elie would be angry?

"I should have added, and are you still angry with her?"

Elie knew he should have answered immediately instead of hesitating. The knots in his belly tightened. He fucking wasn't going to give her up. She was sitting right next to him, the scent of her filling his lungs, making him crazy. If he could take back one thing in his life, roll back one single mistake, he would go back in time, muzzle the arrogant ass he used to be, and instead of insulting and rejecting Brielle, he'd marry her on the spot.

"Yes, I was angry with her. Brielle was condemning me to live with a woman I would never really love fully, even if I came to respect and admire her. That woman would always know, deep down, I didn't love her. My shadow crossed hers in Jean-Claude's sitting room, and even if she hadn't known all those times before when she was too young that she was

and they felt they'd found a perfect match for Elie, especially considering his interest in you."

"Why did you request to leave the program?" Elie asked her directly.

She stiffened. "Do I have to answer that question?"

"I was going to ask it myself," Stefano said, "but yes, he has the right to ask any questions, just as you have the right to ask him what you want to know."

Brielle remained silent for so long, Elie was certain she was going to defy Stefano and not answer, but eventually she twisted her fingers together until they were white. "It makes me sick when I'm in the shadows. I can force myself to overcome it, but I thought, since my sister could represent our family, I wouldn't need to force myself to keep going in. I was afraid if my team leader sent me in with a partner, I might compromise them."

"Yet you decided to train again," Stefano persisted. "Why?"

Elie was nearly a full head and shoulders above his new wife. It was easy enough to see her sneak a quick glance his way. She was extremely uncomfortable answering these questions in front of him.

"I wanted to change who I was. I felt like a child afraid of life when I left for Spain. I didn't want to be that person anymore. Although it was hurtful, I was used to rejection from my father and sister. Even the things Elie said about my looks were nothing that hadn't been said before. The difference was, I decided to do something about it. I decided since I was going to Spain, I could have a brand-new beginning and explore the things I was interested in."

"Why would you want to look like a fragile twig a man could snap in half when you had the perfect body with real curves, Brielle?" Elie demanded. "Fayette is not a beautiful woman. She looks like a coat hanger."

"Like the models you have hanging on your arm all the time?" Brielle retaliated.

"I don't date models," Elie hissed, his voice lower than ever, a bad sign with him. Anyone who knew him well would

recognize the signs in him. "If you had bothered to keep in touch instead of holding on to a grievance that happened *years* ago, you would have known. I'm not the only one to blame here, Brielle. By holding on to your anger at me, you would have condemned four people to a lifetime of misery."

"I wasn't holding on to a *grievance* over your comment on my weight, Elie. It wasn't as if I hadn't heard it all my life. Don't think you were that important. I went to Spain because I wanted to change my life and do whatever the hell I wanted to do for myself. Not you. Not my family. For *me*."

Elie had to admit, he was rather proud of her for that, even if it had been too fucking long for them to be apart.

Stefano held up his hand. "We are going to finish this very important conversation about shadow riding before getting into anything else. I send out the riders in Chicago, Brielle. If you were to join the roster, I would have to know you were fit. Your times are impressive. You certainly look as if you would be a huge asset to us. You asked to be trained by the riders in Spain and they agreed after looking at your training records and consulting with the council. You never disclosed to anyone that you quit because being in the shadows made you ill, did you?"

Brielle shook her head. "I didn't feel there was a need to. The family in Spain agreed to train me and I finished my training with no incident. The council approved me as a shadow rider." There was a hint of pride in her tone.

"You didn't answer the question," Elie stated. "Do you get sick traveling in the shadows?"

Brielle hesitated and Elie wanted to shake her. Riders *died* in the shadow tubes. Even experienced riders could have problems.

"Yes, but I can handle it. I don't want my husband to be ashamed of me because he thinks the mother of his children can't carry out assignments the way other riders can. I'm more than capable. I've learned how to manage being ill. I just am careful that I don't take the chance of compromising any other rider."

Elie couldn't sit there calmly. He was out of the chair, shoving it back and pacing across the office so he didn't grab her and shake some sense into her. "Do you even hear yourself? You know it's dangerous or you wouldn't be worried about protecting another rider, Brielle. Do you have any idea how many riders we've lost to the tubes, even riders who weren't sick or disoriented because they were sick? I've brought out four shadow riders myself, Brielle. It took me hours to find their bodies. I had to carry them back to their families."

He shoved his hands in his pockets and stared out the window at the city below, trying not to think of those riders, all relatively experienced. The thought of Brielle going in sick . . . He shook his head. "If your husband doesn't respect you whether you go into the shadows or not, you shouldn't be married to him. And you damn well shouldn't be going into the shadows no matter how good of a rider you are, if you get sick."

Stefano leaned his elbows onto the desk and placed his chin onto his hands, looking closely at Brielle. "Unfortunately, I'm in complete agreement with Elie. I'm unwilling to take a chance with your life. It's unsafe for you to do anything but travel in the shadows and that's accompanied by an experienced rider, not taking a job as an assassin, Brielle."

Her stubborn chin went up and Elie knew he was going to bite that chin sometime soon when he had her all to himself. She stirred up things in him that might be dark, but they weren't ugly. If anything, she managed to bring his darker practices veering away from where he'd thought he needed to go with a woman he wouldn't be attracted to the way he was to Brielle.

"I trained very hard," she disagreed.

"I can see that by these reports," Stefano said, holding up the thick papers. "You have amazing stats, but I'm not willing to risk your life, Brielle. Every shadow rider is important, whether they can work as assassins or in another capacity. You carry the genetics we desperately need."

Elie's breath hissed out between his teeth. "I don't see her

as a brood mare, Stefano. That's how the council sees her. That's how the Archambaults see her."

"I'm stating a fact, Elie. We're all aware we don't like that we live under rules or that we need to have children. You agreed to an arranged marriage to produce children. Twice now, in fact. After losing you, the Archambaults did take a hard look at their practices of raising their riders, and they are revising some of those practices. It's too late for you, but you're the catalyst for what hopefully will ensure better family relationships for future generations."

Elie hoped it was true, because as it was, he hadn't had *any* family relationships.

"It's been a difficult time for all of us, trying to figure out how to train the next generation, keep them safe, and yet provide a loving family for them," Stefano admitted. "I've struggled with balancing the needs of the rider community since Francesca and I had our first child. I know he has to be trained and yet I don't want his life to be one of just duty." He studied Brielle's averted face. "I can't in good conscience allow you to take your place on the roster when I know riding the shadows can make you sick, Brielle."

"It doesn't happen every single time," she countered. "Maybe you could send someone out with me to monitor me a few times."

"Because you know you're good at hiding that shit when you need to." Elie once again took the chair beside her. "You had to have been in order to make it through training. How often do you get sick?"

She scowled at him, her eyes deepening in color so the green blazed into a deep emerald. He resisted the urge to wrap his palm around the nape of her neck and drag her close to him so he could take her mouth and see if the heat in her eyes transferred to the scorching-hot flames that had caught fire when he'd kissed her in the chapel.

Brielle glanced at Stefano to see if he was going to allow the question to stand. He remained silent—waiting. "Every damn time and I *handle* it."

Elie couldn't help himself. He framed her face with his very large hands, forcing her to look at him, as he leaned his head down so his forehead nearly touched hers. His eyes blazed with a warning deliberately. "I don't give a damn if you handle it, Brielle. You will not be going into the shadows and risking your life needlessly. Do you understand? I forbid it. You can be as fucking angry at me as you want to be, but you aren't risking your life."

Brielle snapped her head back and he released her. She glared at Stefano. "Do you see what I would have to put up with? He thinks he can tell me what to do and I'll just do it." She switched her glare to Elie. "That is not happening."

He arched an eyebrow. "Really? Shall I bring out the papers you so meticulously filled out? So honestly? I had them printed out and laminated just so there wouldn't be any confusion. I was honest and I trust that you were. You knew exactly what you were getting when you agreed to marry me."

"That was before I knew it was you."

Stefano burst out laughing. "I think we're done here. The rest, you two are going to have to figure out on your own. It's very clear to me, Brielle, that your parents and sister lied to you about your sister's abilities in the shadows. She isn't a better rider. Whatever her motives for lying about Elie, she certainly was never with him. The Archambaults investigated your family thoroughly before they ever approached your father and you about a possible marriage between you and Elie. They would have known had Elie ever been with Fayette."

Stefano pushed the report toward Brielle. "We also conducted our own investigation into you and your family when we found out who Elie was going to marry. We would have shut it down if we didn't think you were a good match for him."

"You didn't tell me you were investigating my future wife," Elie said. He wasn't certain he knew how to feel about that.

"I protect *famiglia*, Elie, and you are that to me. My investigators are very thorough. Elie and Fayette were never together in or out of the clubs, Brielle. Fayette lied to you. You

have nothing on which to base your objections to this marriage and I cannot release you from your given word. I am ultimately responsible for the shadow riders in Chicago and I can't take a chance on risking your life knowing the tubes make you ill. You can read the combined reports of both the Archambault and the Ferraro investigations at your leisure."

"But . . ." Brielle's voice trailed off and she glanced up at Elie's face.

He stood up, wearing his stone expression when he wanted to grin at Stefano. This was a solemn occasion and he couldn't look smug, even if he felt it. Brielle had been dealt a few blows. Still, there was a part of him that felt she was prepared for those blows, that it didn't surprise her to learn that Fayette had lied about Elie.

Stefano stood as well. Brielle continued to sit. For the first time, instead of looking defiant, she looked frightened. Elie held out his hand to her. She pressed her lips together.

"The house is outside the city, on the lake, Brielle," Elie said. "It takes a bit of time to get there. Thank you, Stefano, for sorting this matter out for us. I appreciate you taking the time."

Stefano came around the desk. "I suggest you continue to talk things out. Communication is imperative between you going forward. And, Elie, don't forget you need to have bodyguards on you both when you're not locked in with a security system. Make your bride very aware that is an absolute law she will be living with at all times."

Elie inclined his head. "I am not about to forget anything regarding her safety." He was fully aware that the reminder was more for him than for his bride.

CHAPTER FOUR

Brielle didn't say one word on the long ride to Elie's house. She didn't know what to say. She was exhausted from the long flight and the shocking culmination of her arranged marriage. Never, in a million years, had she expected she would be married to Elie Archambault. She'd gone to great lengths to ensure she would never see him again.

She'd left her beloved country, France, and gone to Spain in order to get away from Elie and his apologies. She hadn't been running from the things he'd said about her body, although of course his cruel, cutting words had hurt, but she was used to being belittled in worse ways by her parents and sister.

She'd sat on Jean-Claude's couch, in his sitting room, burning with embarrassment that the Archambaults had vetted her, investigating her like some prize heifer, and then summoned her to be looked over by their prize bull. Elie's unmitigated rejection stung, but then she'd gone there to reject him and all things Archambault. Let Fayette and her parents have them.

How was she going to explain that to Stefano or Elie? Thank God they didn't ask the right questions and force her to confess her real reasons for not wanting to be married to Elie, but now she was in this terrible situation and she was too tired to figure out how to get out of it. Or even if she wanted to. That was the worst of it. What if she didn't really want to get out of it?

It was too late anyway. He knew things about her she'd never wanted him to know. He was the one person on earth she hadn't wanted to know the sexual preferences she'd answered so honestly about herself. There was so much more—the more she'd planned on confessing to her new husband if he was a good man and treated her right.

Fayette had told her so many lies. Brielle had reached a point she didn't believe anyone. It was just that—what possible reason could Elie have for lying? She was no treasure, no prize. If Elie had a hidden agenda, she couldn't see what it could be. Stefano Ferraro could hear lies even if she doubted herself. He had believed Elie. Now she had to resign herself to being married to him. First, she had to figure out how she felt about it and the revelations he had given to Stefano. She was just too tired to know how to feel anything at all.

Had he really stalked her? She certainly had stalked him. How could she not know he was doing the same thing? She had noticed he came into both of the places where she worked frequently, but she hadn't noticed he paid her a lot of attention. He had apologized a million times to her, and he had told her he thought she was beautiful. She sent every letter back and eventually never received them because she'd gone to Spain. She didn't dare be tempted by him. He was the one man she didn't want to give her secrets to. Now here she was, married to him. And he was the kind of man who would never leave things alone. He'd find out every single secret she had.

She must have dozed off in the car because, the next thing she knew, he was waking her and she found herself stumbling a little as she made her way into a large, two-story

house. Blinking sleepily, she did her best to take in the high ceilings and stone fireplace but he kept her moving toward the master bedroom and bath.

The thought of their wedding night had her heart suddenly beating out of control. She didn't think she could handle the idea of physical intimacy between them, not as tired as she was. He opened a door for her and gestured.

"Master bath. Get ready for bed, Brielle. You look like you're going to fall over any minute."

She nodded and pulled her gown in after her so she could close the door behind her. It would be such a relief to finally take off the wedding dress. It had been comfortable when she'd first put it on, but now it felt heavy, as if it weighed a ton. The moment she was out of it, she was going to take a long, hot shower, or better yet, soak in that luxurious tub that had bath oils sitting on the edge of it.

She reached behind her in an attempt to undo the very tiny buttons that ran up the back of the dress. It was impossible to slide them from the cleverly hidden loops crocheted into the tulle. No matter what she did, she couldn't free herself from the dress. She wanted to collapse on the beige and white splotched tiles and just cry. That would look lovely when Elie came to get her—and he would. She was certain of it. He would come to claim his prize heifer. Laughter bubbled up, a bit of hysteria she couldn't quite repress with two fingers to her lips.

Brielle stared at herself in the large mirror. She looked terrible, but then she always did when she was around Elie Archambault. She told herself it didn't matter. He preferred tall, rail-thin models, not extremely petite women who had to fight to keep every extra pound from their already hourglass figures.

Elie had put on his questionnaire that it didn't matter what his intended bride looked like, but she knew he had a preference. He was photographed for years going to charity events and fund-raisers, coming out of nightclubs and hotels, with

the same type of woman on his arm. Models and actresses, all interchangeable as far as Brielle was concerned. Not one of them was under five foot seven. Not a single one.

She stared at her too-pale face in the mirror. She was desperate to take a bath in the very deep tub. Its elaborate silver faucet had all kinds of extensions coming out of it that she probably couldn't get to work, but she didn't care. She longed to immerse her bone-weary body in hot water and just forget everything for a few minutes—especially forget that she had a husband just outside the door waiting for her. A husband who was going to find out her deepest, darkest secrets that shamed her more than she'd already been shamed.

She'd like to pretend she didn't want him to see her body, but she honestly didn't care. What mattered was him *never* finding out all the things she hid from the world. She wanted to cry. To scream. Mostly, she wanted out of the damn wedding dress. Emmanuelle had gotten her into it, but Brielle hadn't considered how she would be getting out of it. She thought to rip it down the front, but that seemed . . . wrong.

"Brielle, you're going to have to come out of there sometime. You can't sleep on the bathroom floor."

She nearly jumped out of her skin. Elie's voice startled her. It wasn't that he spoke loudly; in fact, his voice was incredibly low, a blend of velvet and raw sex. The sound stroked along her nerve endings and brought her body to life in spite of the fact that she was so exhausted. That frightened her. She hated that he could have so much control over her when she already felt so out of control.

Brielle took a deep cleansing breath and forced herself to calm down. For years, she had worked hard to become self-confident, to become her own person. She wasn't going to let this marriage to Elie Archambault destroy her hard-won confidence. If she wasn't so exhausted, she might be able to come up with better ideas, but right now, there was only one way out for her and she was going to act like it was no big deal.

She had no choice; she was going to have to ask him for

help. Could the day get any more humiliating? She closed her eyes for a moment and then, straightening her shoulders and lifting her chin, went to the door.

"I'll admit I'm so tired that sleeping on the bathroom floor is a possibility at this point, but I'd like a bath, so I'll sleep there in very hot water if you show me how to use that complicated silver faucet. The big holdup is my dress."

"Your dress?" Elie echoed. He came into her line of sight. His hair still gleamed with beads from the shower. The drops clung to the ends of his hair. His eyes were so dark, they appeared to be nearly black. He had the kind of face that was chiseled granite, beautifully detailed with rugged lines and planes. An aristocratic nose and defined mouth that could be sensual or cruel, maybe both at the same time.

His shoulders were very wide, although he was so well proportioned, it was difficult to notice at first, but there was no escaping the fact that he had muscles that went on forever from his thick chest down to his impressive abs, which led lower into the loose towel hitched around his hips.

She didn't look like that on her best day after six months' worth of salads and six-hour workouts six days a week. A little groan of despair slipped out and she turned away from him.

"What is it, Brielle?" He came into the room and she stepped back to make way for him.

The master bath was spacious, mostly white tile above her head and on the walls, adding to the feeling of space, but Elie managed to dominate the entire room the moment he stepped inside. It was as though he sucked all the available air out of it, so she couldn't breathe—or maybe she needed to just not look at him.

She focused on the tub, trying not to make a total fool of herself. "I'm just really tired, so exhausted I can't think. I'm sure there's a way for me to get out of the dress without asking you for help, but I couldn't think of it."

"*Bébé*, there is no need for you to be upset about asking for help. I don't mind in the least."

Elie crossed to the tub and thankfully worked the faucet,

making sense out of the complicated knobs. At once steam began to rise as water flowed into the deep bath. He beckoned her to him.

"Come here and turn around."

Elie sat on the edge of the tub, his thighs spread wide, leaving very little to the imagination. The towel didn't hide much and he didn't seem to care. He didn't ask again, just sat there with the steam rising behind him and those dark eyes fixed on her face.

Heart pounding, she obeyed, albeit slower than she would have liked. It was very daunting to force herself to be so close to him when he wore nothing but a towel and he was going to undo the buttons of her wedding dress. She'd had far too many fantasies about this man.

She had little resistance against Elie Archambault. She had known that the moment his shadow had collided with hers. If she was honest, even before that, when she'd spoken with him in the café and later in the restaurant. How many times? She had read every article and collected every magazine she could find that featured him in it. When he was photographed coming out of the kink clubs, Brielle found her imagination running wild and she was always at the center of the fantasy with Elie as her dominant.

Brielle was terrified he could read her mind. Could an Archambault do that? Did they have that kind of psychic gift? All riders had gifts. She couldn't control the blush that spread over her body so she kept her head down as she approached him and turned her back to him the moment she got close.

Elie wrapped his arm around her waist and drew her between his thighs. Thankfully, her dress was A-lined and had enough material to give her a bit of a respite so she didn't feel his bare skin against her, but that didn't stop the brush of flames as his knuckles touched her back when he began threading the buttons through the loops, allowing the material to part.

She hadn't worn a bra because it was built into the dress. She worked out and dieted carefully, but she still had a

more-than-generous butt. It was there no matter what she did. Firm yes, but still generous. And she did have breasts no matter what Elie had implied earlier. The fact that she did always made her look two sizes bigger than she was. In spite of what she was told, that was not the first place she lost weight. Her butt and breasts were always the last place.

Great. The moment Elie had the dress opened all the way down the back, he would see she wasn't at all what he was used to. A small groan escaped before she could stop it. She was just too tired to censor the way she needed to.

"*Ma femme*, talk to me. What are you so worried about?"

He reached up and pulled the dress from her shoulders. She caught at it to keep it from falling from her breasts.

"You can't wear your dress in the bathtub, Brielle." There was a hint of amusement in his voice. "I'm not going to assault you when you're this damn tired. Let me take off the dress and get you in the bath."

He was going to see her naked body sooner or later. It wasn't as if she could hide from him forever. She might as well get it over with. It wasn't as if she really cared that much, did she? He'd apologized to her there in Jean-Claude's sitting room. He'd written her so many letters of apology. He'd made it clear both to Stefano and to her that he had been attracted to her long before the Archambault family insisted they marry. Why did she have such a problem?

She dropped her hands and allowed him to peel the wedding gown from her body, leaving her in a barely there thong, garter, stockings and heels.

"Your heels add another three inches?" There was laughter in his voice.

"Not three," she denied, casting a quick look over her shoulder.

She shouldn't have looked at him. He skimmed his hands down her back and then shaped her bottom, cradling her firm cheeks, his thumbs sliding over her skin. Just the touch, skin on skin, sent electricity snapping through her nerve endings

and arching over her, a deluge of flames falling like sheets of fire to envelop her in a scorching heat.

"Three," he affirmed. "Don't move." His breath bathed her ear in warmth as he spoke.

She could see him in the mirror as he stood up slowly behind her, his much larger frame towering above her. Elie reached around her and took her hands in his, turning her body halfway so she was facing the large sink with the giant mirror.

"Look how truly beautiful you are, Brielle. I've regretted the ugly callous and very untrue things you overheard me say to Jean-Claude every single day since I told those lies. No one, for me, will ever compare to your beauty. You have to be able to hear the honesty in my voice. I know you're afraid of this marriage, but I swear to you, I'll make you happy. I know what you need and I can give you those things. I want to be the man to give you everything you ever need or want."

She shivered. He had no idea and she hadn't been courageous enough—or idiot enough—to admit to her real needs. The cravings that ran deep and would eventually begin to gnaw at her. His voice alone could trigger that hunger inside her and he didn't even know it.

He placed her hands on the marble surface and then very gently put the flat of his palm between her shoulder blades and applied pressure until she bent over.

She'd dreamt of just such an encounter with him. How did he know? How could he? In nothing but stockings and heels, in a steamy room with Elie commanding her every move. Her entire body trembled.

"That's my girl," he murmured. His hands slid from the nape of her neck all the way down her spine to her bottom. "Stay still for me while I get your clothes off."

Once more, he cradled her cheeks and then began stroking and kneading the firm flesh. He took his time exploring, literally following the curve around the sides and down around the bottom and in between, separating each cheek, using his thumbs and fingers to slowly trace the lines of her body as if

memorizing them. Then he crouched down, his hands running down the backs of her legs to her high heels. Very gently, he untied the bows and removed first the left one and then the right. When she stepped out of them, he held each foot in his hand for a moment and stroked the sole before setting it on the floor. She was definitely three inches shorter without the heels.

Elie nudged her legs apart and reached up to unsnap the silk stockings from the garters, slowly rolling them down her legs. There was nothing hurried about his movements. She found herself shaking so badly, she could barely hold herself up. His every action was purely sensual and yet, at the same time, almost casual. Everywhere he touched, it felt like a flame on her skin, a brand of ownership.

This time, as he removed the stocking from her right leg, he placed her foot on his thigh, up high so she felt the scorching heat emanating from his groin. His fingers kneaded the sole of her foot and moved over the top of her foot and ankle before placing it on the floor at least a shoulder width apart from her other leg. Then he lifted her left foot and repeated the same action.

Her entire body reacted to the way he undressed her. She could barely breathe, air moving raggedly through her lungs. Her breasts felt heavy and achy. Her nipples were hard pebbles, standing stiffly, pulsing and hot with need. Her sex felt as if he'd lit a match to her. She was slick, her thong soaked. She told herself she would not be embarrassed. He was deliberately seducing her and he was good at seduction. If she got nothing else from her marriage, at least she hoped to get outstanding sex.

"You're moving," Elie reprimanded softly. His hands paused at the tiny string that was her thong. "I believe I told you not to move."

"I know," she whispered. "It's much more difficult than I thought it would be."

He was silent, his fingers curled around the band of her panties. She closed her eyes and tried not to groan when she

realized the meaning he might construe from her simple explanation. Why had she spoken at all? She needed to keep her mouth closed, not blurt out anything at all. She already had made a big enough fool of herself.

She didn't realize tears were leaking out of her eyes until she felt the wetness on her arm where she rested her head. A shudder went through her body. She didn't know how to feel. Just not like this. Needing him. Wanting him. Terrified he'd discover her secrets and she'd be humiliated and unable to ever live with herself.

"Shh, *bébé*, everything is going to be all right. I take care of what's mine. And you've always been mine. Always, Brielle. You were meant for me. And I was always meant to be your man."

Elie leaned forward and pressed his mouth to the back of her knee and then reached for the silver knobs on the faucet to turn them off. Instantly, the loss of sound seemed to magnify her labored breathing. Her breath seemed to saw raggedly in and out of her lungs while she couldn't hear a sound coming from Elie. It was only his touch that allowed her to know he was there.

He would know she was crying. How could he not? She was such a mess while he was in complete control. She wanted to collapse onto the floor right on top of her useless wedding gown—the one she'd chosen with such care to give herself some much-needed confidence. Now what did she have? Nothing. She had nothing at all.

Another sob welled up, nearly choking her. She pushed her knuckles into her mouth. She wanted to go home. To France. But she didn't have a home to go to. She didn't have a family. She didn't have *anyone*. She only had her pride and she was fast losing that.

"You're going to be safe with me, Brielle," Elie assured her, his voice coming out of the silence. Low. Like the stroke of velvet on her skin.

She detested that she reacted to that velvet note in his voice. That was part of the reason she hadn't wanted to go

through with the marriage. She'd heard him giving instructions on more than one occasion, and from the moment she'd heard his voice, soft and compelling, she hadn't been able to think of anything else. Her body had refused to react sexually to anyone else.

Very slowly, Elie drew her soaked panties over her hips and down her legs, tapping each foot to silently command her to lift so he could remove the scrap of underwear, leaving her completely naked. He stood up with his casual, fluid grace, as silent as any jungle cat, but when he rose, his body slid along hers, a ripple of sleek, powerful muscles and hot skin. He helped her to straighten.

"Let's get you into the bathtub. You're exhausted, Brielle. You'd been traveling for hours and then had to go through a marriage ceremony to a man you want nothing to do with."

He turned her in his arms, keeping her body close to his, wiping her tears with the pads of his fingers, his touch tender, as if she were an infant—or someone he cared about. She wanted to protest that it wasn't true she didn't want anything to do with him—but that would be a lie and he would hear it. He would know. She was confused and ashamed. She knew they wouldn't work. It didn't matter if the shadows or the computer matched them—they wouldn't work. She would have her heart torn out and she'd had enough of that for a lifetime.

Another sob escaped and he pressed her face against his chest, his palm cupping the back of her head. "Ssh, *bébé*, you just need to sleep. We'll work everything out. You're overwhelmed right now."

She was. She was overwhelmed and her body was so sensitive and aware of him, it was insane. His hands fit around her waist, fingers biting into her as he lifted her carefully into the bathtub as if she were made of porcelain and might shatter into a million pieces at any moment. She sank down into the heat of the steamy water, grateful the tub was so deep, the water went to the very curve of her breasts.

Elie reached over her to get the pillow that lay in a wooden and steel-mesh tray that hooked over the tub. When he did,

his entire package slipped free from the opening of the towel wrapped around his hips and was right there in front of her face. In front of her lips. She had only to lean forward a scant two inches and she could touch him with her tongue.

She had seen cocks before. They weren't the prettiest things in the world as far as she was concerned, but his was different. And his was fully erect. As in *fully*. He was thick and long, the vein dark, the shaft pulsing with life. The broad head appeared velvet soft and there were small pearly drops on the surface she wanted to taste. Her mouth actually watered. She'd dreamt of him so many times. Had had so many fantasies. She'd never imagined him like this.

When he eased back, the pillow in his hand, his balls swayed, drawing her attention. Her gaze centered on his groin, the way he was so unashamed. Uninhibited. He yanked at the towel and tossed it aside as if it was an annoyance.

"Scoot down here, Brielle, so you can lean back and rest your head against the pillow."

She heard him, but in all honesty, she really didn't comprehend what he was saying. She was too busy memorizing the look of him. There was something really wrong with her that she was so fascinated with his physical endowments. Already, her body reacted, legs moving restlessly beneath the water, her sex clenching. Her breasts felt heavy and aching. She detested that she was like that when she didn't even know him—or like him.

But that was a lie, too. She did know him. She knew almost everything she could about him, and what she didn't, she'd made up. She'd wanted this man and only this man. She was obsessed with him.

Elie crouched down beside the tub, removing temptation from her sight. Cupping her chin in his palm, he lifted her head, forcing her to look at him. "Brielle." His thumb whispered across the bottom of her chin in the lightest of touches. She felt that brush like a brand. Her stomach did a slow somersault. "Enough." His voice was very firm. Commanding. "You're going to lay your head back against the pillow. I'm turning off the

lights and will just have the candles lit. If you fall asleep, no worries. I'll dry you off and carry you to bed."

She had the same sexual reaction to his commanding voice that she did his velvet voice. That was how far gone she was. How could she have confessed that to Stefano Ferraro? Even if she had been alone with him, she knew she never would have told him all of her reasons for wanting out of her contract. There were things about her character she had learned early on that had shocked and mystified her. That truly horrified and humiliated her.

In Spain, she'd gone into counseling in order to try to understand why she was the way she was. On some level, she knew her family had programmed her to feel submissive. They also made her feel desperate to be loved. To be wanted. But that had little to do with her reactions to a voice. She had heard the voice before she ever saw the man.

She'd worked in a very high-end restaurant during the evenings and a café during the day. Elie frequented both places with his models and actresses. He often came into the restaurant with a group of his friends, and occupied one of the rooms reserved for their best customers. She didn't serve in those rooms as a rule; only those with seniority were allowed as the money earned was more than generous.

Obediently she leaned back against the tub wall and allowed her head to fall against the pillow. Once he'd turned off the lights, she felt safe enough to ask questions.

"Is there a guest room I could sleep in tonight?" Deliberately, she closed her eyes so she wouldn't have to look at his face, just in case she made him angry.

Elie lit candles. She knew because she heard the scratch of the match and then smelled the apple-cinnamon scent.

"We have two guest bedrooms, neither of which you'll be sleeping in, Brielle. I expect my wife to sleep with me. I think that was made very clear in the questionnaire sent to you with all my replies. I have a strong sex drive. I intend to give you time to get used to us, but that doesn't mean I don't want you close to me. I sleep nude and expect you to as well."

She didn't protest because he had made that abundantly clear. "You said you liked sexy night things."

"Not to sleep in," he corrected. "When we play. I'll let you know when I want you to wear something by laying it on the bed. I have no problem telling you what I want from you."

A little shiver of awareness crept down her spine. He was close to her again, sitting on the side of the tub, his eyes on her. She could feel the way he stared at her. Just knowing his gaze was on her made her body come to life all over again, when it hadn't had time to settle. His hand spanned her throat, making her jump, and then his finger traced a line from her throat over the swell of her right breast to her nipple hiding beneath the water.

Her breath caught in her throat and her eyes flew open. He wasn't looking at her face to judge her reaction, but at her body. In spite of the heat, goose bumps rose on her skin. The burning between her legs increased. Her nipple tightened when he tugged and then flicked at the sensitive bud. His actions seemed casual, almost idle, yet he didn't look away from her breast.

"I'm not a man who forgives easily, Brielle."

Her heart jerked hard in her chest. She wanted to draw her legs up to her chest and make herself very small. He'd spent years trying to apologize to her and now he was fully aware she'd gone to Jean-Claude's to tell him she wasn't going to marry Elie. In fact, she was going to do her best to persuade the Archambaults to allow Fayette to take her place. Elie had no idea how just the thought of Fayette with Elie destroyed her, but she still had gone there with that intention. She couldn't blame Elie for holding a grudge against her. He'd admitted to Stefano he was angry with her.

Brielle pressed her lips together, aware, as the silence stretched between them, that Elie expected some sort of reaction from her. "From the things you said to Stefano about your relationship with the Archambaults, I did get that."

"I have no wish to ever work as an Archambault rider again. I don't want our children to ride the shadows as

Archambaults. I want them to grow up as Ferraros, in that family, knowing love and feeling it. I expect the two of us to raise them together and teach them what they need to know ourselves. I appreciate that you trained as a rider and that you're as good as you are because you can pass that to our children, but if you have hopes that they will ride as Archambaults, they will not."

His voice was lower than ever. At no time did he look up at her. Instead, he traced the underside of her breast and then moved to her left one, seemingly fascinated by the rounded curves as they floated just beneath the surface.

"Elie, I didn't expect to marry you so that was never a thought," she assured him. It took effort not to squirm away from his touch and to keep her breath from catching in her lungs.

"While I might have respect for the Archambaults as riders, I don't for the way they treat their children. Saying that, Brielle, I have a thousand times more respect for them than I do your parents or sister for what they put you through and I don't know the half of it . . . yet. You will tell me. I insist on it. You won't leave anything out. They lied to you about practically everything important your entire life. That is not to be forgiven. Not by me. At some point, your father may decide because you married me, that he is entitled to money or something else from you. He is not. Neither is your sister. They disowned you. That will stand."

For the first time, his gaze lifted to meet hers. The impact was so intense, she felt it straight through her body like an arrow. Elie was the most compelling man she'd ever met. She couldn't look away from his dark eyes. Shadows from the two large flickering candles fell across his face, giving him the appearance of mystery.

"Do you understand?"

She nodded.

"I mean what I say. This is one thing we are not going to argue over. You will not go behind my back or there will be severe repercussions. I have no sympathy for a man who

would choose one child over another to the point he would lie and deliberately neglect her the way he did you. As for your sister, she is so jealous of you, she is unstable. I will take no chances with your safety."

No one had ever stuck up for her and she wasn't exactly sure what to say or do. She wasn't even sure if she believed him. His speech was the last thing she'd expected of him.

He held her gaze until she felt as if he could see inside her. She had too many secrets, and in the end, she took the coward's way out and let her lashes fall.

"Fayette never held a job in her life. You began working when you were very young. Why?"

"I liked working." Working got her out of the house. There was always more work at home. Her parents had let their staff go in order to use the money to pay for all the things they needed for Fayette. Her clothes, her car, her endless classes to shape her into the perfect wife for an Archambault. She couldn't be expected to do household chores.

"That is not answering the question." His hand spanned her throat again, very lightly, so her heart beat into his palm. "I can hear lies, *ma petite mariée*," he reminded when she hesitated.

She opened her eyes to glare at him. "I have no intention of lying to you. I was considering whether or not I wanted to answer because it's personal."

His smile didn't reach his eyes. Instead, it made him look like a great jungle cat about to pounce on her. "Our agreement was to tell the other what was asked of us. We both thought communication was extremely important in arrangements such as ours."

She had an unexpected urge to splash water all over his incredibly handsome face. "I did my part to pay the bills at home. There were endless bills. Fayette's training to become the wife of an Archambault wasn't cheap. We all sacrificed in order to give her that opportunity. We had no one to cook or clean."

"Other than you," he corrected.

She shrugged. "That's true, I did both, but I like to cook. Then my mother got sick. She needed treatment, therapy and medicine. My father quit work to take her to the doctor and hospital and be with her. That meant I had to work more to cover the bills for Fayette."

"What did Fayette do to help? Did she care for your mother?"

"Sick people make Fayette ill," Brielle said.

"I see. So, she continued to be a drain on the family's income even though your mother was seriously ill and your father quit work."

"Elie, she was going to marry an Archambault. Your family members are extremely wealthy and would provide for my parents later in their lives. She was an investment for them. That's how they looked at it."

"Did you believe she would look after your parents if she married an Archambault?"

No one had ever asked her that. She'd considered that question on several occasions. Her sister hadn't helped with her mother at all, not even when it became evident that their mother wasn't going to live very long. That had alarmed Brielle. She had decided she would have to find a way to take care of her father in his old age if Fayette refused.

"Brielle?" Elie prompted.

"I'll admit, I was concerned. She's incredibly selfish. My parents raised her that way. They expected nothing from her so she gave them nothing. She didn't seem to care whether or not my parents had enough to eat as long as she got her beauty products and new clothes. If I tried to talk to her, she would pretend to get hysterical and go running to Papa. She was very manipulative and could turn on the waterworks at will."

Elie leaned over the water to brush a kiss onto the top of her head. "I know you don't like talking about your family, but I wanted to know why you were working so much when you were so young. I couldn't help but notice this beautiful young girl every time I would go into the café with my friends. I began frequenting that particular café, in the hopes of

catching a glimpse of you even though I knew better. It was wrong of me when I was so much older, especially when I began to compromise your shadow."

"You really did notice me?" Brielle's stomach seemed to drop right out of her body. He had never once let on. He'd come in often and not one single time had she ever caught him looking her way.

"How could I not notice you? I made it my business to find out who you were, which was what called you to Jean-Claude's attention in the first place. You were the only shadow rider I'd shown any interest in. He probably was jumping up and down for joy thinking he finally had me cornered. That was one of the reasons I was so furious. The council interfered in every aspect of my life. At the time, I believed they had taken me from my parents, not that my parents had given me up voluntarily. I should have known. You were special. Mine alone. No one was supposed to know about you. I felt like I hadn't protected you from them and they were the enemy."

He got up and paced away from the bathtub. The master bath was very spacious, and with only the candlelight illuminating the room, it was difficult to follow his progress. The candles were in tall pedestal holders about three feet high, positioned at either end of the tub, so the flickering light didn't quite reach all the corners of the room.

Brielle sat up straight, catching the pillow and replacing it in the tray extending from one side to the other of the tub. She watched him, frowning a little. "What do you mean, your parents gave you up voluntarily?"

"As you know, riders are sent to other families to train as they get older. Archambaults are sent away immediately if they show great promise and if their parents agree. My parents agreed. They wanted to be alone together. I didn't go back for holidays or any other time. They visited me occasionally, but rarely for more than a few hours or a day. I blamed that entirely on the council, not them. It was only after my father died and I tried to establish a relationship with my mother that I realized she wanted nothing to do with me."

He turned back to her, a humorless smile on his face. It didn't come close to reaching his eyes. "So, you see, Brielle, I'm used to not being wanted. You deciding to call off our arrangement when you found out who you were tying yourself to wasn't as shocking as you might have thought it was. I don't blame you for it and you don't have to be afraid of retribution. I don't expect love from you, but I do demand respect and for you to keep your word."

How could his parents not want him? At least her parents had the excuse of a first child they wanted with all their hearts. They had no interest in a second one. But Elie was talented, intelligent, gorgeous and everything any parent could be proud of. It made no sense that his parents wouldn't want him.

"You weren't the reason I wanted out of the arrangement, Elie," she admitted. "How do I let the water out of this bathtub? I'm so exhausted and the water's getting cold."

His gaze drifted over her face a little moodily and then he came right to the edge of the tub again, leaning down to open the drain before helping her to stand. "Was it for some other reason than the bullshit lying Fayette did about me?"

She should have let well enough alone and not let compassion for him rule her good sense. She just didn't make good decisions around him. Shivering, she made an attempt to step over the side of the tub. It was very high. Too high. Elie had to catch her around the waist and lift her over the edge. Immediately he sank down and pulled her between his thighs.

"Answer me."

"I don't want to answer you." Brielle used her snippiest voice.

He began to dry her off with a warm towel. "That's too bad, *bébé*, because now I'm very interested. Was there another reason?"

"As a matter of fact, there was another reason besides my lying sister. As if that wasn't a good enough reason right there."

"It wasn't a good enough reason and you know it wasn't because, eventually, you figured out she was lying."

That was true. Sort of true. "I wasn't sure what parts were

true and what wasn't. You frequented the clubs and there were all kinds of articles written up about you and then you said those things to Jean-Claude that seemed to reference kinky sex so I thought she could be semi-telling the truth."

"You knew she lied," he reiterated and stood up, once more towering over her.

Brielle sighed. "I want to go to bed and just stop talking for at least a year."

To her shock, he laughed. "I'll just bet you do. Finish getting ready and come to bed. We can talk about this tomorrow."

CHAPTER FIVE

Brielle woke up gasping for breath, her body desperate, needy, crying out for fulfillment. She'd had this erotic dream dozens of times, but not in such vivid, colorful detail. Her brain couldn't quite distinguish between reality and fantasy. It seemed as though she was lying in bed with Elie's naked body coiled tight around hers. He had one knee in between her thighs and his cock nestled between her butt cheeks. He moved—or she did—it had to be him because the rocking of the hips was gentle when she was frantic and his cock wasn't hitting the spots she needed him to touch.

That was so like him. He always tormented her. Made her beg him for what she wanted most. She bucked against him, but that gentle rocking never changed rhythm. He was that in control. His arm was a weight around her, one hand cupping her breast. Her nipple was buried in his palm rather than between his fingers. There was no satisfying hard pinch. He wasn't talking dirty to her. Why wasn't he murmuring in her ear with that velvet, commanding voice?

Reality began to seep into erotica and she fought to calm

her breathing and still her body, sending up silent prayers to the universe that she hadn't been moaning or begging him aloud. As erotic dreams went—and she was used to them now—this one topped the others by a mile. She couldn't quite slow her breathing, no matter how hard she tried. Having Elie's hard body wrapped so tightly around hers didn't help in the least.

She wanted to ease out from under him just to be able to give her body a little respite, but she knew if she did, Elie would wake up instantly. He'd be aware of her heightened sexual state and that would be one more humiliation to add to the long list she already had going. She lay quietly, staring up at the ceiling, counting her heartbeats, contemplating what she was going to do.

She was married to Elie freaking Archambault. The man of her fantasies. It was one thing to fantasize over a gorgeous man, so clearly experienced in everything she had tried to learn to be, but clearly was *not*. It was another thing to actually have Elie in her bed. Had he been a complete stranger, she was confident she could have handled anything demanded of her.

Brielle had researched everything she had been sexually drawn to very carefully. She was the queen of research. There were few who could match her on a computer. If she had a strong psychic instinct, it was following a trail on a computer. The moment her fingers touched a keyboard, she seemed to know which direction she needed to go and how to get there. She might be an emotional person, but she understood the logic of a computer.

She had learned where to go to get the physical experience, which turned out to be more like a scientific exploration until she realized all she had to do was add Elie Archambault into the fantasy of whatever scene she was exploring and she would manage to find excitement in it.

"*Bébé*, can't you sleep?" Elie stirred, his voice a little husky with sleep. He didn't remove his hand from her breast. Instead, his thumb brushed along the lower curve, instantly causing every nerve ending to flare back to total awareness

when her body had just begun to settle down. The sound of his voice, that soft velvet mixing with the dark rasp of sleep, added to the intoxicating, addictive and all-too-enthralling sensations pouring over her in the darkness.

"My mind is all over the place." That was the truth. She hoped he didn't question her any further. She wasn't going to admit her body was on fire. She willed him to go to sleep. Didn't men just turn over and go to sleep?

He shifted back, just his torso, keeping his hips and groin firmly pressed against her backside. His knee remained between her thighs. She should have been happy when he took his hand from her breast, but she wasn't. She found having him cup the weight of her in his hand was sexy. It didn't matter that her body was on fire just lying next to him. The feeling of her nipple pressed tightly into the center of his palm added to the flames burning between her legs, and she craved that feeling.

His hands went to her shoulders and he began a slow massage. His fingers were strong, digging into the knots of tension in her neck and shoulders. "Relax, Brielle, and just go back to sleep. Everything is going to be all right."

His breath was warm against her ear as he leaned in to whisper to her. When he leaned close, his cock, hard and erect between the cheeks of her buttocks, jerked and pulsed. It was all she could do not to groan. His girth felt enormous, as if he was stretching the tender skin between her cheeks. She tried not to imagine what it would be like to have him inside her, stretching the walls of her sheath. The craving for him grew in spite of her determination to separate fantasy from reality. Because right at this moment, reality was feeling dangerously close to her greatest fantasy.

"Listen to the sound of the lake, the way the waves hit the shore." Once more his voice seemed to come out of the night. "It's really soothing. Can you hear it?"

Brielle made an effort to hear past the thunder of blood in her ears. She pushed air through her lungs and made her body relax as she listened for the sounds he had pointed out to her.

The lake. She knew his home was on a lake; he'd told her so as they drove into the large garage. He'd promised to show her the house and grounds in the morning. She was just too tired to take everything in. She knew he had boats and piers and docks and other things she knew little about, but that he said she would enjoy.

The sounds of the waves lapping at the shore were soothing. Rushing forward and receding. A rhythm that was peaceful there in the dark. She concentrated on that sound and the amazing feeling he produced with the unexpected massage. The strength in his fingers kneading the hard knots in her neck and pursuing the ones in her shoulders and down her spine began to help her relax.

Elie wasn't anything like she expected him to be and that only made things worse. It really bothered her that he believed no one could want or love him and that even his parents hadn't. She *did* want him; that was the trouble. Elie Archambault was fearless. She was a coward. She didn't mind a stranger finding out every dark, humiliating secret she had. She didn't mind a stranger cheating on her. A stranger couldn't rip out her heart. Or destroy her. She hadn't built her dreams around a stranger. She'd built them around Elie Archambault. It wasn't his fault—it was hers.

Eventually, the heat from Elie's body, the strength in his fingers easing the tension out of her and the rhythmic waves lulled her back to sleep. When she awoke, the sun was up and Elie was gone from the bed. She was still surrounded by him. His masculine scent was everywhere. On the charcoal-gray sheets and pillows. On the dark chocolate comforter that was folded at the end of the bed.

Brielle sat up and took a good look around the room. It was a man's room, although the potential was there to be something extraordinary for both of them—if he allowed her to change anything. Directly across from the bed was a floor-to-ceiling stone fireplace. Above her head, the beams appeared to be very solid and hand-hewn from reclaimed wood. The ceiling was white between the rustic beams.

The floor was hardwood and a bank of windows that stretched nearly from the ceiling to the floor took up one entire wall. The windows looked out over a forest of trees in the distance. Two swivel chairs sat at the end of the bed facing the fireplace, both gray in color. There was a short gray dresser on one side of the fireplace with a screen on top of it. On the other side of the fireplace was another dresser with a long deep box on top of it. Otherwise, the very large, spacious room appeared to be empty.

Brielle went to her knees in the bed and inspected the room much more closely, paying attention to the windows and walls. He had nothing on the walls, not even a painting, with the exception of her answers to the sexual questions asked of her by the program for their arranged marriage. Her answers had been laminated and were hung on the wall above the headboard of the bed. His answers had been laminated and were there as well.

She crawled up to the wrought iron headboard to take a closer look at the two multipage documents collated and attached together by a set of rings. Hers were red rings. His were black rings. The rings were attached to the wall. He'd said they were in a frame, and they were, although they could be easily removed to look through. Just seeing what he'd underlined in red made her blush. Hopefully, no one came into their bedroom. *Ever.* She slid her hands along the ornate headboard and stilled when she realized what she was running into. The twisted spokes of the headboard held several different types of cuffs.

Gasping, Brielle pulled her hands away and turned her attention to the same ornate footboard. Several types of cuffs were on the spokes there as well. She found herself blushing and just like that her body had gone damp. Hopping off the bed as though it had burned her, she backed away from it. Every time she thought she was safe from thinking about Elie and sex, she found herself totally consumed by the thought.

It had been their wedding night. Elie had been as hard as a rock. No man had that hard of an erection without wanting

sex. She'd been exhausted. That had to mean he would be eager to consummate their marriage at any time. That thought was both exhilarating and terrifying. The terror only added to the thrill. Everything about Elie Archambault had always garnered intense emotions in her.

She abandoned scouting out the room and made her way to the master bath. She remembered it being very spacious from the evening before. Her wedding dress was no longer on the floor. She didn't remember picking it up. She wasn't a neat freak, but she was someone who kept a clean house and didn't expect others to wait on her or pick up after her.

Elie's scent lingered in the master bath, where he'd clearly showered earlier. There was no escaping him. She stepped into the large shower stall, designed for two people. She was able to figure out the silver faucets and all the jets positioned for a much taller person. Her favorite shower gel, shampoo and conditioner were there.

Brielle's heart gave an odd little twist in her chest. Elie must have put away her things while she slept. Had he put *everything* away? A hot blush seared her cheeks at the thought of Elie unpacking her suitcases and discovering the things she'd brought with her. She should have checked the closet and drawers before she stepped under the water. She hurried to finish showering and washing her hair, and had barely dried off before wrapping her hair in a towel and rushing back into the master bedroom.

The large walk-in closet held her dresses and skirts, all hung neatly on one side. Elie's suits and shirts hung on the other side. The closet could fit two rooms of her apartment easily inside it. She resisted touching Elie's shirts, but couldn't help the little flutter of excitement at the sight of his clothes hanging in such close proximity to hers.

Her shoes and boots were on a rack, not that she had very many pairs. She didn't spend her money on shoes. She had a pair for work, a pair for riding shadows and her cute boots for going out. That was pretty much the extent of her shoe collection. She approached the drawers in the dresser with slow

steps. She couldn't say the same about her lingerie. If there was one place she spent too much money, it would be there.

She stood in front of the dresser and opened the top drawer slowly. Sure enough, her lacy boy shorts were stacked neatly. The lavender cachets were even placed neatly inside the drawer with them. She peeled the pale blue silky ones from the top and pulled them up her legs and over her hips. Her blue jeans were in the third drawer down. She chose one of the oldest pairs because they were soft and molded to her figure immediately.

The carved wooden box on top of the dresser was intriguing, and after donning a lacy bra, she flipped open the box and just stood there staring at the contents. A gasp escaped and she stepped back, even as a flood of damp heat sent her into another dangerous spin of need. Her toys. She had brought several with her, choosing to be daring, determined that she would start her new life with confidence as a sexual partner to an adventurous man.

The blush spread over her entire body. There were more toys in the wooden chest than she'd purchased. She wasn't certain what a couple were or even how they were used. Lying right on top of the numerous toys was a note written in a neat, masculine scrawl. She took it out to read it.

Mon petit jouet très sale, you will no longer play alone with these toys. Until we are playing together and I am calling you mon petit jouet très sale, and give you permission, you will not touch them. I will decide when you may use them.

He was calling her "my dirty little sex toy." The blush deepened all over her body. She thrust the note back into the box and slammed the lid down. Why in the world did she go hot all over at the thought of him calling her his dirty little sex toy in person? Or directing her to use one of the toys while he watched? Or him using one of them on her? She wanted him to talk dirty to her. She needed him to. It was a craving she would never get over. She really was in trouble once he found out how responsive she was just at the thought of him commanding her.

The worst of it was, she didn't just want kinky sex with him.

That wouldn't be enough for her. She knew that. She knew she'd be in trouble right away. She already was. That was why the things her sister said about him had hurt so much. Hastily pulling out a very feminine pale peach fitted blouse with tiny pearl buttons, she quickly donned her pair of boots and made her way out of the bedroom to explore the house and get herself a cup of coffee.

The house was enormous. Not that she could get lost. Maybe if she went upstairs, but not downstairs. It was just that the ceilings were high and impressive with those rough-hewn beams. The craftsmanship was stunning.

The great room was gorgeous, combining elegant with rustic, modern with historic. She was coming to see how Elie would appreciate the combination of the hardwood floors, extraordinary high ceilings with the antique European chandeliers and the beautiful windows, which maximized not only the light but the views. The stone fireplace was regal and definitely a focal point.

Comfortable couches faced each other in front of the fireplace with an oval, polished wooden, glass-topped coffee table between them. A full bar was to the left of the fireplace, the cabinets behind it and above it filled with liquor bottles and all kinds of bar glasses. A white-and-gray rug covered the hardwood floor between the two couches, delineating the space.

Her favorite part of the room was a cozy conversation seating area comprised of four dove-gray chairs set in a circle with a small round table in the center just in front of three of the great room's five large windows. The chairs sat on the hardwood floor rather than the rug. Two smaller windows above the five large ones provided even more light.

The great room flowed directly into a dining area that housed a large round table with eight overstuffed chairs set around it. Another half-dozen windows graced the expansive dining room walls, providing extraordinary views of the lake and glimpses of the woods as well as letting in even more natural light.

Brielle found herself smiling. She could definitely live there.

The house was beautiful and spacious. From the dining room, she wandered directly into the kitchen. The floor plan was open so it was easy to see that anyone cooking could visit with guests in the great room or the dining room. The door to the back patio was open in invitation and she could see Elie outside, sitting at a table, coffee mug in hand while he talked on his phone. He had a frown on his face, his expression very serious.

She poured herself a cup of coffee without exploring the kitchen, one of the rooms she would have otherwise been the most interested in, but she didn't want to miss whatever was putting that expression on Elie's usually difficult-to-read face. Bracing herself, she sauntered out and gave him a quick smile as he looked up.

Immediately, Elie told whoever was on the other end that he had to go and ended the call. His gaze collided with hers, then drifted over her with that hint of possession and raw desire that sent her stomach into a riot of conflicting emotions.

"I thought you might sleep much later. How are you feeling?"

"Much better. I found the coffee." She held up the mug, thankful to have something to put in front of her like a shield. "The house is so beautiful, Elie. I love everything about it."

He nodded, his brief smile already fading. "We own the piers as well as the boats. Do you know how to drive a boat?"

She shook her head. "I can catch on though. I'm a fairly fast learner." She walked around the exposed aggregate river rock patio, trying not to appear nervous. The terrace had quite an impressive view overlooking the lake. The table with the umbrella where Elie was seated was round and made of wrought iron. Four chairs surrounded it. Across from it was a larger rectangle table made of cement with chairs around it as well. Just a step down was grass with a large round fire pit in the middle of it. Trees shaded their side of the lake, planted in large rounded beds at the end of the landscaping overlooking the retaining wall. The lake was beautiful, and even with the choppy waves, it was peaceful.

"Come sit down and drink your coffee with me."

She didn't want to look at Elie, not when he was so gorgeous and sexy, especially first thing in the morning. Okay, all the time. "It's just there's so much to see."

"Brielle, come here."

He was using that voice. Smooth velvet over steel. Her heart pounded. She turned her head first, a cautious action to see if she dared face him. Her stomach somersaulted. Why did he have to look like he did? Her gaze collided with his. Those dark eyes were so compelling. Reluctantly, she forced herself to cross the patio to the table.

Elie didn't give her the chance to take the chair directly across from him. He held out the one closest to him, so that she would have a view of the lake. She sank into it, placing the mug of coffee on the table in front of her.

He bent his head toward hers, blotting out everything around her with his wide shoulders and thick chest. Then his mouth was on hers, his lips gentle, barely skimming hers, but it felt like the lick of a flame. She gasped and one large palm curled around the nape of her neck, while the other curved around her throat, tilting her head back to give him better access as he took full advantage, kissing her with a slow, purposeful building heat that fast went from smoldering to scorching.

Brielle's brain fogged. Her body went into meltdown, an instant response, electricity running along her nerve endings, crackling with life, like little lightning strikes running all the way from her breasts to her sex, straight to her clit. There was no thinking, only reacting, only kissing him back, surrendering. Giving herself wholly to him.

Elie's kiss was gentle. Tender even. Filled with fire. With possession. With hunger. He wasn't rough at all, but the hint was there in that edge of hunger. In the dark lust stark in his eyes when he lifted his head and his gaze roamed her face with satisfaction.

The fingers surrounding her throat slid lower to stroke the bare skin exposed by the open buttons of her blouse. The pads

of his fingers rasped across the swell of her breasts. Immediately her nipples were little hot points of flames begging for his attention. Blood pounded in her clit.

Her gaze dropped from his to the front of his trousers. The bulge there was satisfactory, hard and thick, pressed tight against the immaculate pinstriped material. At least she wasn't alone in her reaction. She licked her lips, her mouth salivating. She wondered what he would do if she lowered his zipper and tried to swallow him down the way she did in all her fantasies.

She was too shy to follow through, but she hoped he would at least want to consummate their marriage. She felt desperate for him. Elie brushed a kiss on top of her head and slid into the chair beside her. As he did, he removed the towel she'd wound around her hair like a turban. Her hair fell in spirals and ringlets down her back.

"Why do you have your hair wrapped up in a towel? It will dry fast in this heat."

She held out her hand for the towel, annoyed that she couldn't quite control the trembling. She was still shivering with need. "My hair is really thick and wavy. In this humidity, it will get frizzy. I'll need to put tons of product in it to manage any kind of decent hairstyle."

"Your natural hair is beautiful." He tucked the towel on the other side of him.

"I appreciate you thinking that, but it won't be once the humidity gets to it. Really, Elie, if I keep my hair in a towel, I can deal with it later." She was reasonably proud of her voice. It didn't shake nearly as bad as her insides. She wrapped her hands around her coffee mug and stared at the lake. They really did have a wonderful view.

"For me, would you just this once let it go natural? No one is around. You can always put it up and get it wet again tomorrow morning."

When he asked in that low, gentle voice, how could she possibly resist? It wasn't that big of a deal and he'd see what a complete fiasco her hair would become. It could grow enough

for six people and frizz so she looked silly. But he was right—she could put it up or braid it.

"Sure. As long as no one else is coming around. I'm feeling as if I made a bit of a fool of myself yesterday. Facing your friends isn't going to be so easy." She flicked him a quick glance from under her lashes. "I'm sure you noticed how attractive all those women are."

"The Ferraro women?"

Elie very casually cupped the side of her face, which made her almost drop her coffee mug. She'd just gotten the courage to raise it halfway to her lips, believing she wouldn't spill the contents all over the table. His thumb slid over her lips.

"Not a single one of those women is more attractive than you. In any case, no one heard anything said when we were talking in the middle of the aisle. Stefano is bound to secrecy by the oath of his office as head of the riders of Chicago. He can't even talk to Francesca about anything said between us. You have nothing to worry about, Brielle."

The pad of his thumb caressed her lips one last time and then slipped away, leaving her heart beating a little bit too fast. She was too aware of him, and this close, she couldn't quite breathe right.

Elie leaned back in his chair. "Have you thought about what you want to do other than ride shadows?"

She lifted her chin at him. "You're really serious about me not taking rotations, aren't you? I worked very hard to become a rider, Elie. My times are good. I can keep any map in my head. I never lose my way. I have no problem with technique. I would be an asset to the Chicago riders and I know riders are needed here."

His eyes took on an ominous glint. "I'm well aware you worked hard, Brielle. I have no doubt you're an excellent rider. You seem to excel at anything you put your mind to." He leaned close to her and took possession of her hand, threading his fingers through hers. "If I didn't care, maybe it would be easy to say go ahead, but unfortunately for you, I do care about your safety. I'm not willing to take chances with your life and

neither is Stefano. You may not be aware of this, but he lost a brother in the shadows."

His thumb slid over her inner wrist before pulling her hand to his mouth. He regarded her over the top of her knuckles with his compelling dark brown eyes. "So, do you have anything else you're really interested in?"

She didn't like being in the shadows, but she'd carry out her responsibilities as a rider if she was needed, although there were other jobs she knew were imperative to make shadow riding go smoothly. At the top were the greeters. Everyone in the shadow rider community knew the Ferraro family was hurting for greeters.

The structure of the international shadow riders was designed with two things in mind: success in business and family survival. The families were split in order to ensure survival. Different factions with psychic gifts specialized in areas to further the family businesses. The shadow rider code of honor was extremely strict, but not necessarily legal. If someone wanted or needed help, they would first request a meeting with what the family termed "greeters."

Brielle knew she could never be a greeter. Most greeters were former shadow riders. Or they were family members born as human lie detectors. All meetings with potential clients were taken in person—no exceptions. The greeters would chat casually with the client, asking about anything but what their purpose for the visit was. Every person had a natural rhythm, breathing, heartbeat, inflections in their voice when speaking. Once patterns were established and recognizable through casual conversation, the greeter would ask the potential client to explain why they had come. Then they simply listened to the petition for aid without comment. Because they made no promises and said very little, it was virtually impossible to trap them if the potential client was really an undercover cop.

Brielle knew the Ferraro family had lost the last of their greeters when they had lost the matriarch of their family. They had aunts and uncles who were filling in, but if her brand-new

husband expected her to do that job, it wasn't happening. She had a faulty lie detector, thanks to her family. She wasn't about to risk shadow riders' lives when she couldn't trust herself to discern truth from lie.

"I can't ever be a greeter, Elie. I know Stefano's family needs one, but my parents and Fayette screwed me up when it comes to recognizing lies one hundred percent of the time. I just don't have the kind of faith needed in myself."

Elie's teeth scraped at her knuckles, sending a million butterfly wings soaring. "I asked what you were really interested in doing, Brielle. What you're most passionate about."

Him. She was most passionate about him. She couldn't say that and embarrass herself. She wasn't going to give away the fact that she'd been daydreaming about him since she was thirteen and having erotic dreams about him as soon as she was old enough to discover what *erotic* meant. It was a struggle to keep the color from creeping up her neck into her face.

"I'm really, really good on a keyboard. Better than in the shadows. I've always had this ability to track anything down on a computer." She could hear the difference in her voice, although she tried to suppress her excitement. She wasn't boasting. It was the truth. In fact, she was downplaying how good she was.

She saw interest leap into his eyes. He placed their joined hands under his jaw and rubbed back and forth so his bristles skimmed over her sensitive skin.

"Can you do investigative work? Find criminals without raising suspicion that they're being tracked?"

"You mean like the investigators do for our families before they send the riders out?"

No riders were ever sent out before two sets of investigators had thoroughly checked out the crime committed and the criminal accused of executing it. She'd already checked and she knew Stefano had two teams of investigators. They were really good, too. Not as good as she was, but excellent. He didn't need her.

"Exactly like that, yes. You'd have to be equally good."

"I'm better." She was. And she could hack into any computer—even the most secure—given time.

"How are you at bookkeeping?"

"That's a strange question."

"The job I have in mind has investigative bookwork as well as criminal work. You would have to be able to do both."

"Fortunately, I'm good at both." She found herself holding her breath. It seemed impossible that she could have just fallen into the perfect job. What would the Ferraro family need that their seemingly endless cousins couldn't provide?

"Emmanuelle married Valentino Saldi. I'm not certain if you're aware, but he is the acknowledged head of a very large territory in Chicago. In fact, Val and Emme are some of our closest neighbors here on the lake."

Brielle sipped at her mostly cold coffee. She didn't even care if her coffee was cold. She was too excited. A job. A real job. Was it protecting Emmanuelle Ferraro? Just give her anything at all to feel useful if she wasn't going to be taking rotations as a shadow rider. Brielle didn't want Elie to make up some position for her; she wanted something that made a difference. Something that would contribute toward aiding any of the shadow riders.

"Val appointed his cousin, Dario Bosco, to take over the territory vacated when Dario's father, Miceli Saldi, was killed. Miceli was involved in a human trafficking ring. Valentino and Dario spent over two years working together to shut it down. Miceli tried to take over Valentino's father's territory by attempting to murder Val, Dario and Giuseppi, Val's father. In the end, Val and Dario managed to escape with their lives and get Giuseppi out, but Val was wounded. Dario sent for Emme. Emme sent for Stefano. We all had to work to shut down the ring at that point."

Brielle frowned, trying to understand. "Val and Dario both head up a crime family, but they were against human trafficking?"

Elie nodded. "Val sacrificed everything, including his re-lationship with Emmanuelle, in order to try to shut it down. That was one thing that was always forbidden by his father and he was even more adamant that it would never happen in any part of his territory. Dario feels equally as strong. We knew we weren't going to get everyone, but we thought we'd get the main leaders that brought the ring into our territory."

Brielle couldn't take her gaze from Elie's face. He clearly was identifying with Val and Dario when he spoke about them and their territories. He was unhappy with the outcome of whatever had taken place.

"Valentino and Dario control the ports here now. Before, Miceli and the Caruso family did. They were the ones ship-ping out women and children and bringing them in."

Brielle's heart jumped. She sat up straighter. Was there such a thing as coincidences? Huge ones? She'd never be-lieved in them before, but here she was, married to a man she had wanted from the moment she laid eyes on him. She'd traced the disappearance of young women to several freighter ships that had made their way to Lake Michigan. She'd taken her evidence to the Spanish rider family for them to continue the investigation because she was about to be married. She hadn't heard whether or not they found anything more but it had only been a few short days.

"We thought we'd locked it down, but when interrogating Caruso, we learned he couldn't possibly have set up the ring and it was far bigger, more involved and better organized than we realized. It's definitely international and our ports are still being used. We don't know how. Someone here is betraying us. There is a hit out on Val, Dario and . . ." He hesitated.

Brielle's head went up alertly, her heart nearly stopping. If blood could run cold—hers did. "Not you. They wouldn't dare. If they dared to kill you, Elie, they would bring every Archambault in France down on them. No one would live through it. Don't they know that?" Her breath caught in her throat waiting for his answer. No one would dare go after the

most powerful family of shadow riders. It was sheer suicide. Her heart pounded so hard, she pressed her palm over it trying to calm herself before she had a heart attack.

"We figure the Ferraro family wasn't included on the hit list because whoever put out the contract fears them. They don't know they are shadow riders, of course, because no one does. They only know you don't fuck with them. They know I associate with the Ferraros, Val and Dario, but how would they know the reputation of an Archambault?"

She was silent, studying his face, wondering how she could make the world aware of the power of the Archambaults without giving them away. Everyone feared Ferraros, why not the Archambault family? "How can you be so calm about it, Elie? We could be sitting out here and someone could use a high-powered rifle and shoot you."

"They could try. We're going to find them. It isn't the first time someone wanted me dead. Or Val, or Dario. I just found out the night before the ceremony. We were already married or I would have put off the wedding until I took care of this so you would be safe."

"I'm not worried about me." She wasn't. She wasn't a threat to Elie's enemies. At least they didn't know she was. Not yet. "Tell me how you want me to help you. If you give me a place to start, I can track them."

"I want to think this through very carefully before we make a move. As for you working for Val and Dario, that's going to be only under certain circumstances. It would be extremely dangerous work."

She ignored the warning and obvious ploy at changing the subject. "Does Stefano know?"

Elie hesitated. "Emmanuelle knows, so I presume she would tell him."

Brielle scowled, her fingers tightening around his. "Elie, you can't take chances with your life like this. Having someone ruthless enough to be involved in human trafficking put a hit out on you is very serious. You have to know that. Human trafficking is a billion-dollar industry now and globally

one of the fastest-growing criminal enterprises. Whoever these people are, if you're threatening that kind of income, they'll do anything they can to remove you."

Elie leaned close to her, his dark eyes moving over her face a little too sharply. "Just how do you know all this, Brielle? When did you get involved in human trafficking? So much so that you can rattle off statistics?"

"Don't turn this around on me. I'm not the one with the hit out on me. You've already taken shadow riding away from me. Don't even try to take away my right to be just as concerned for my husband as he is for me." She jerked her hand away and stood up. "In fact, I'm uncomfortable sitting out here in the open. I think I'll go in and get a fresh cup of coffee. Do you have food in the kitchen? I can make us breakfast."

Elie stood up as well, towering over her as he followed her into the house. "You neglected to put down on that very detailed questionnaire, Brielle, that you have a bit of a temper. I noticed it when you stopped the ceremony. You might have confessed."

She glared at him over her shoulder. "Had I put that down, would it have deterred you?"

"Absolutely not." His voice dropped an octave, and he looked so sinful, she had to glance away. "I find your little fiery spurts of temper sexy as hell."

Feigning annoyance, she stomped into the kitchen, dumped her cold coffee in the sink and yanked open the refrigerator to survey her choices. Everything about Elie was sexy as hell. He was a walking temptation, yet he hadn't tried to consummate their marriage. She might have to hit him over the head with a frying pan soon if he didn't take action, especially if he had a hit out on him. What if they killed him before she became his official wife and she never got a chance to live out her fantasy? What then? She wanted to ask him that question and make him laugh, but she was too upset with his stupid, macho, cavalier attitude.

"I'm going to tell Stefano myself," she decided, pulling out eggs and cheese.

"We can discuss that further after we eat." He reached around her to add several containers of presliced vegetables to the cheese and eggs she had set on the cutting board in the center island.

"Let's talk about the possibility of you working for Val and Dario in the capacity of an investigator. They have a young man already working with them. They trust him completely and he's really good at what he does, but he's overworked. The problem you're going to run into, Brielle, and I have to know you can handle it, is that most of the things Val and Dario do are illegal. You have to be okay with that. You can never repeat anything you hear or see in their meetings. It would get us both killed."

She flicked him a quick glance while she looked through the drawers and cabinets to familiarize herself with where everything was kept. "The rules don't sound any different than those in the rider world."

"They aren't actually," he assured. "But as a rule, most of the time, our women are sheltered from seeing the brutal reality of our world."

Brielle paused as she placed a bowl on the center island and met his gaze. "I took quite a few rotations as a rider, Elie. I'm an assassin. I think that's considered brutal by most standards."

He shrugged his shoulders. "Sometimes prisoners have to be taken in order to find out necessary information. Each family has had to interrogate those prisoners. Were you made aware of that?"

Brielle cracked open eggs into the bowl, keeping her head down in order to prevent him from reading her expression. Her hair was drying rapidly in the warm air, curling every which way in a chaotic riot of waves and spirals to fall around her face, helping to hide from him.

"Mmm." She whipped the eggs and then turned away from him to the stove, where she'd been readying the omelet pan.

"That doesn't really tell me anything." There was amusement in Elie's voice.

She wasn't exactly sure why that little masculine note of his made her want to smile. "Did those training me reveal that sometimes prisoners were taken under extraordinary circumstances? Yes. That was actually said. No one said what those circumstances were or what was done with the prisoner."

"But you had an idea," he prompted, handing her the vegetables.

"Yes. I'm pretty certain anyone with a brain could have figured it out, Elie, especially when the prisoner never resurfaced."

"When Val and Dario are hunting for a traitor, or they call a formal meeting, they are looking for something specific. The investigators will be listening and jamming cell phones, sometimes hacking into them. Whatever is seen or heard stays there. If a traitor is discovered, Brielle, it can go bad right there. You might witness the matter being taken care of. There can be no question of your loyalty. You can't agree to work for them and not be one hundred percent certain you can be loyal."

"Am I loyal to the Ferraro family or to the ones employing me, Elie? I'm not a spy, nor do I want to be. If I work for Val and Dario, then I work for them and my loyalty is to them. If I work for the Ferraro family, I tell Val and Dario up front and walk if there is a conflict." She worked quickly, making the first omelet and then sliding it onto a plate for him before starting the second one.

"Your first loyalty is always to me. You're a member of the Ferraro family because you're married to me. We make that clear when we offer your skills to them. If they don't want to take you up on them, or they want to lock you out of certain meetings, that's okay, too, if you really want the job. If they do interview you, Emmanuelle most likely will sit in on it, and don't expect her to be sweet. Val and Dario are her family and she's fiercely protective of them."

She smiled at him over her shoulder. "Elie." He was busy

putting silverware on the table. She waited for him to look at her. "You are, too. It's very clear that you consider Val and Dario family. I imagine Stefano does as well."

He nodded. "It's true, Brielle, but I'm not willing to take chances with your life. Val and Dario are hard, dangerous men. They don't know you yet. Until they do, we're going to be very careful."

She slid her omelet onto the plate and made her way to the dining table. She eyed the numerous windows with fresh eyes. When she'd first seen them, she loved the windows and the view. Now she was worried that a good sniper might shoot Elie while he ate his breakfast at the dining table. She studied the angles carefully. It would be a difficult shot. The table was positioned back from the windows.

"I forgot to tell you, I put your electronics in the office upstairs. I'll show you that after we're finished," Elie said. "And the airlines delivered your missing suitcase this morning. I told them to leave it on the front verandah. I didn't want anything disturbing your sleep."

Brielle's eyes clashed with his over the table in alarm. "Elie, I didn't know about your house. I had Stefano's hotel down as my address. I had his phone number as the number to call in case I lost luggage, which I did not. All of my suitcases were accounted for when Stefano's driver picked me up at the airport."

CHAPTER SIX

Stefano studied the suitcase from a very safe distance. "Looks exactly like every other piece of her luggage, Elie. It has her name on it, just like the rest of her luggage. The address of my hotel and the number we gave Brielle to use if there were any problems were on the luggage tag. Our people at the hotel believed the airlines were calling to report Brielle's missing bag was found so naturally your address was given so her luggage could be delivered here."

Elie was silent as he digested what that meant. No one knew his bride's name other than her lawyer and the members of the shadow rider international council. And the council only knew when both lawyers turned in a copy of the formally signed papers to the head of the council the night before their formal ceremony.

Vittorio approached the suitcase with the Ferraros' portable 3-D X-Ray Scan system. Setting the screen on one side of the suitcase, he set the small image cam on the other side and walked away. Taking out his iPad, he activated the system. Vittorio flicked his hand in the air, signaling to Stefano and

Elie to join him. That meant he had concluded there wasn't a remote detonator.

"Definitely a bomb," Vittorio said. "Rolling it would activate it. You can see the detonator is hooked in a very sloppy manner to the wheels. I'll take a few pictures and then retrieve my system before blowing the thing up."

Elie watched him work in silence for a few minutes, letting the breeze from the lake cool the heat of his skin.

"That suitcase is a live bomb, Elie," Stefano said, his voice quiet. Deadly. "You are not the intended target. Brielle is."

For one moment, Elie's temper welled up, shaking him, and then he pushed it down, getting himself under control. Who would want to kill her and why? He glanced across the expanse of rolling lawn down to the terraced landscape that led to the lake. She was there with Emmanuelle, Val, Dario and Elie's two personal protectors, Ruggero and Lorenzo Forni.

Brielle continued sending him anxious little glances, worried that he continually exposed himself to a sniper rifle. He wasn't as worried as she was. He'd spent a great deal of time checking to see what it would take to get a decent shot with a rifle. The shooter would have to be on the lake to take the shot, and that meant a boat in the water. He should have told Brielle instead of letting her worry about him. He thought it was sweet that she was concerned, when she'd been so adamant that she didn't want to marry him.

"You had her investigated," Elie said, aware Stefano watched him with hooded eyes. "You had the report in your hand last night."

"I did," Stefano admitted without a qualm. "Thoroughly. She doesn't have a single enemy that my investigators could find unless you count her family. That's always a possibility, although an ugly one to consider. But since someone is sending her bombs, we can't leave anything to chance. We'll have to take another, much deeper look at her family. I fear for her if it was her father or sister. She's taken quite a few blows in her life and still made something of herself. She'll make a good mother."

"She's had it very hard," Elie said. "I admire her. I want

her for a lot of reasons, Stefano. Not just because she's going to make a great mother."

Vittorio placed the X-Ray system in the back of his car and then approached them again. This time Giovanni was with him. They kept their backs to Brielle. Elie knew it was to prevent lip reading, something all riders were adept at doing.

"We're going to have to use the blast containment vessel and detonate it. We'll slip the case over it and just blow it."

"You're certain they don't have a remote detonator?" Stefano asked. "I don't want to lose either of you."

"We both studied the bomb," Giovanni said. "In any case, if they did, I think they would have used it. Elie has so many security measures on the property, they would have tripped over a wire by now. I think they're long gone. We know for certain the bomb is motion activated. They expected Brielle to wheel it inside."

Again, the sweep of anger washed over Elie and he waited for it to recede before he spoke. "Let's get this done. I appreciate all of you coming to help out." He made certain his tone was even and not one shred of his inner rage could spill out. It was one thing for him to be targeted, another for Brielle to be.

There were a few tense moments as Vittorio manipulated the blast containment vessel over the suitcase, careful to keep from touching the sides of the case, enclosing it completely.

"Setting it off now," Vittorio warned.

From the pictures taken with the 3-D X-Ray Scan system, they were certain the explosives they were dealing with were C-4. The bomb itself appeared to be crude, but effective.

The bomb was easily contained by the vessel. In fact, Elie found the explosion rather anticlimactic. If any of his neighbors saw the black smoke rising into the air, it dispersed fairly quickly. He owned the two parcels on either side of him and quite a few acres behind him with the lake in front. Valentino and Emmanuelle were his closest neighbors on one side and Vittorio on the other. Down from Valentino was Dario. He doubted if that black smoke rising upward in a steady stream for a few minutes before beginning to dissipate would be noticed.

Vittorio signaled that it was safe to approach the house once more. "We'll take care of the mess on your front porch when we leave, Elie," Vittorio assured him. "No one will be able to tell that this ever happened."

"I appreciate it," Elie said.

He went down the front walkway to meet his bride halfway, holding out his hand to Brielle as they walked together back to the house. He ignored everyone else, concentrating only on his wife. She clearly had no idea she had been the target, not him. As they went through the door, he transferred his hold to around her waist, bringing her closer to him.

"I should have told you, a sniper would have to be on the lake in order to get a shot at me. We'd see the boat. Stop worrying when we're inside. We have great security cameras that pick up movement on the water as well as all around the property. We get notifications sent to us when there's activity. I'll install the apps on your devices so you'll get them as well."

She nodded, her eyes portraying her anxiety. "How did they know to send the suitcase here?"

"They called the hotel and the front desk gave them this address."

She frowned but continued into the great room, where the comfortable couches and chairs faced one another. Stefano, Giovanni and Vittorio sat on one of the long sofas. Elie and Brielle took the love seat facing the two couches and fireplace while Dario and Valentino and Emmanuelle sat on the other couch. The various protection details remained by the doors both inside and outside the house.

"It seems we have a problem, Brielle," Stefano said. "That bomb was directed specifically at you, not Elie."

Brielle reacted with a swift intake of breath, trying to pull her hand from Elie's, but he had anticipated her withdrawal and refused to let her go. He tightened his fingers around hers and pressed his thigh closer. She had married him. They were a couple and they would face any problems head-on together.

"I had you thoroughly investigated the moment I learned your name. I have two teams of investigators and I'm

comfortable saying both are extremely good. They found nothing to indicate trouble. Most certainly not the sort of trouble that would result in a bomb delivered to your door."

Valentino chimed in. "Stefano requested that Bernado Macaluso also look into the woman Elie was to marry and turn the report over to him. I, of course, cooperated."

Emmanuelle and Dario both looked at him. It was clear they hadn't known.

"There was nothing in Bernado's report, either, to raise a red flag, Brielle, yet someone definitely is trying to kill you," Stefano persisted. "You must have some idea why."

The room was silent while the Ferraros and Valentino and Dario paid close attention to Brielle. Elie knew they were watching her body, her every expression. All of them were adept at reading the least little hint of untruth or evasion. She began to rub her index finger along her thigh, her eyebrows drawing together.

"Enemies who might want to kill me?" She repeated it aloud, her accent twisting the words together. She sounded thoughtful. "I took my share of rotations but every one of them was clean. Nothing could be traced back to the family or to me personally. I wore gloves as well as additional fake fingerprints. I braid my hair tight and wear a skull cap to keep any hair from possibly shedding."

She sounded as though she was musing out loud, going through possibilities, so no one interrupted her train of thought. "Before I left Spain, I was independently tracking several freighters bound for Lake Michigan that I suspected carried women and children kidnapped from various locations. I turned over the information I had to the Ignazio investigators before coming here because I knew I wouldn't be able to follow up. What they did with it, I don't know."

Valentino hitched forward. "You were following the trail of human traffickers from where?"

"I was in Barcelona. I kept coming across the disappearance of very young women, and children, I should say young boys and girls and women. It bothered me. No one seemed to

be really looking for them. Or they had no idea where to start. I began to look for a common denominator, a place most were taken. I followed various leads but most were dead ends. Then I got lucky when a couple of kids talked to me."

"They saw you?" Dario asked.

"No, I was much more careful than that. I was always behind my computer screen. It's hard to get to me when I'm on my computer. Even if someone set a trap, I'd know."

To Elie, she sounded very certain of herself. She definitely had confidence when it came to her computer skills. He glanced at Valentino and Dario, who shared a look and then one with Emmanuelle.

"You're positive, Brielle," Stefano asked. "If someone knew you were onto them by tracking you on your computer . . ."

"I would put my skills up against your investigators', Stefano, or Mr. Saldi's. There is no way I was discovered through my computer. As for what happened after I turned over my work to the Ignazio investigators, I have no idea, but they would have taken my name off the report I gave them. It was extremely detailed. I'm a rider and all riders are protected."

That was so but . . . Elie didn't necessarily believe in leaving anything to chance. He knew there were corrupt people in every occupation. He was an Archambault whether he wanted to admit it or not, and Archambaults policed the entire shadow rider community for a reason. They were needed. Even shadow riders were human.

His gaze flicked to Emmanuelle. Only a handful of people—Stefano, Val, Dario and the Archambaults—knew Emme's mother had taken out a contract on her daughter's life. She'd tried to have her killed and intended to continue until it was done. Only the Archambaults could bring justice to a shadow rider and they did so. Elie hadn't been the one to carry out the execution, but even so, he didn't want Emmanuelle ever to find out. Stefano had requested that the sentence be carried out under the radar and Eloisa Ferraro's death be attributed to a brain aneurysm. That cause of death was believable and no one, least of all Emmanuelle, had questioned it.

"Call me Val, Brielle," Valentino said. "Traffickers would go after you if they thought you were in any way interfering with them. Especially if you somehow were able to identify them."

"You had to have gotten the names of the freighters," Dario added.

"Did you manage to get the name of any of these people?" Val asked.

"This isn't an interrogation," Emmanuelle interrupted before Elie could. "Brielle, ignore them. They've been working on taking down a trafficking ring for well over two years now. They thought they had removed it, only to discover they hadn't gotten it out of our territory. It came as somewhat of a shock."

"Not to mention," Stefano said, "a huge disappointment that someone we know has to be involved. We hear lies. We formed an alliance, but we still can't get the bastards. Now they're targeting Val, Dario, Elie and apparently you."

"I understand how all of you feel," Brielle said. "I just don't see how they would have gotten my name. Yes, I do have the names of the freighters. They're owned by the same companies. It was difficult to get to the actual owners' names. The freighters cross the ocean and rendezvous with smaller lake freighters to off-load their human cargo. The ownership of the larger cargo freighters was hidden under layers of shell corporations that I had to peel back like an onion. The owners are headquartered in New York."

Before Stefano could say anything, Valentino did. "Santoro. They're a big family out of New York City. Stay under the radar. Conduct a lot of business, but never call attention to themselves. Very well respected by all the families. To move on them would be dangerous unless we had undeniable proof—or absolutely no way for any blowback to come on us."

"We'd need undeniable proof before we could make a move," Stefano said.

"I could get it for you," Brielle said. "Seriously, I know I can."

"Before you do anything, Brielle, we have to find out who

put out a hit on you and why," Elie said. "I'm not taking any chances with your life."

"I'd like to pit her skills against my investigators'," Stefano said. "We might as well while we're figuring this out."

"I'd like to do the same," Valentino said.

Elie maintained no expression. Twice Emme had mentioned that Val and Dario wished they had a second computer person with skills similar to Bernado, but one they hired who would maintain loyalty to them. They had to rely solely on Bernado, something that was difficult for men like Val and Dario. They trusted Bernado—but it was always good to have a backup plan. It would be better if the two men came asking for Brielle to work for them than for Brielle to ask for a job. She'd be in a stronger bargaining position.

"Give her a day to get her devices set up," Elie advised.

"How can you be sure no one breached the security in your computer?" Stefano asked.

Brielle looked so outraged, Elie had to stifle a grin. That little flash of temper got to him every time. His woman was no pushover. Her chin rose and she leveled her gaze at Stefano, forgetting all about the fact that he was the leader of the Chicago shadow riders. And one of the most feared men in Chicago. Many equated him with Valentino Saldi—a man clearly not to cross.

"Seriously? I wasn't born yesterday, Mr. Ferraro."

Emmanuelle coughed behind her hand. Giovanni didn't bother to cover his snicker and Vittorio raised his eyebrow, shooting Elie a direct, telling look.

"You might pay attention to that streak right there, Elie," he warned.

"Close attention," Stefano added, rising.

"Oh, I am," Elie assured. "I'll see you out. Thanks for coming. I'll let you know when Brielle has her equipment set up." He led the three Ferraro brothers to the door. "Stefano, you might want to watch your phone over the next few days. She does have a bit of a temper. She might retaliate just to

prove a point. And, Vittorio, don't think she didn't catch your warning."

Vittorio laughed. "Stefano's comment stung. He's the one she's going to go after if she decides to prove a point."

Stefano shrugged. "I have very broad shoulders, but if she fucks with my phone, I expect you to punish that little hellcat."

"So far, she's been sweet," Elie said, managing to keep the grin off his face.

Everyone was intimidated by Stefano except Elie's sweet Brielle when the head of the Ferraro family challenged her computer skills. Elie made note that it would *never* be a good idea to do anything but praise his woman's skills on a computer. Since it wasn't his wheelhouse, that should be easy enough. He wasn't about to repeat Stefano's mistake.

Elie kept a straight face as he turned back to face his woman and their company. Brielle still had that little tilted chin that made him want to take a bite out of her. He had to will his cock not to react. Dario was giving him that knowing look that said he agreed with Stefano and Elie needed to tame his woman. Valentino lifted an eyebrow and sent him a mocking grin, but wisely kept his mouth shut since Emmanuelle was seated next to him.

"Sweet setup the Ferraros have for bomb detection," Val said. "We have something similar, so I'm always interested in anything new."

"Taviano is the genius in the family," Emmanuelle said. "Once Vittorio told him what he wanted, and showed him the various devices on the market, Taviano immediately came up with ones for under cars, larger vehicles and smaller things like suitcases. Vittorio and Taviano spent forever having fun designing the technology. Gee helped, too. They get together and you don't see them for weeks on end."

"I would have liked to get in on that," Val said. "Next time, let me know what they're doing, princess."

Elie found it interesting that Val had no worries about

being invited. Stefano had included Val and Dario in the family, making them so much a part of it that, like Elie, more and more they felt completely absorbed. Elie wanted that for Brielle. She needed a family and the Ferraros had a way of loving that was extraordinary. Noisy, sometimes annoying, always in one another's business, but tight, having one another's backs. To outsiders they appeared aloof and cold, dangerous and, like Valentino's family, perhaps like criminals. Behind closed doors, they were loving and funny. Careful of one another.

"We're going to get out of your hair since technically you're on your honeymoon," Emmanuelle said. She stood up, tugging on Val's hand. "Come on. We aren't staying," she added when he didn't move.

Val and Dario exchanged a long look. "Just give us a minute, babe," Val said.

Emmanuelle sighed. "Seriously, Val? Don't you remember what it was like? They want to be alone."

"I don't want that brother of yours to talk to her before we do."

Elie sank down beside Brielle, his thigh tight against hers, one hand sliding behind her neck, under the thick mass of wayward waves of curls and spirals going in every direction. Her hair was wild and he loved the look. She appeared untamed, not at all the sleek, sophisticated woman who had walked down the aisle toward him. She was more like the woman he'd first noticed and couldn't get out of his head. He wanted to unbutton her blouse just one more button, as well. There were already the shadows of the curves of her breasts showing beneath her blouse, just a hint, but he wanted more. Maybe a darker bra under that peach.

"What did you need to talk to me about?" Brielle asked.

Elie played with her ear, slipping the pad of his finger inside her ear and then tugging on her earlobe. He shifted his body just an inch, just enough that his shadow connected with hers. The moment their shadows collided, the sexual jolt was brutal.

Brielle gasped and looked up at him, her eyes dark with both desire and panic. Her thigh rubbed against his, her legs

moving restlessly as she tried to ease the burning between her legs. Her gaze dropped to the bulge pressing hard against the front of his trousers. He took her hand and brought her finger-tips to his mouth, biting down on the tips, slowly and gently at first, but increasing the pressure until there was a decided sting.

"Your computer skills," Val said. "We've been looking for someone to work for us, and if you really are able to match Bernado, we'd like to interview you for a job if you're looking for one. I know Stefano is going to try to grab you, but before you agree to work for him, at least hear us out."

Elie deliberately sucked her stinging fingers into the heat of his mouth and then pulled his hand down to his thigh. Up high. Very high. Toward the inside of his thigh so the tips of her fingers touched his bulging shaft. Using her fingers, he began to rub his shaft gently through the material of his trousers.

"I, um. I . . ." Crimson heat crept up Brielle's neck into her face. With her free hand she reached up to push at her wild mane of hair. The action lifted her breasts, thrusting them against the tiny buttons of her blouse.

Elie leaned in close, his much larger body effectively blocking out hers from the sight of the others in the room. "Valentino and Dario have been looking for someone to help them for a while now." He lowered his voice, putting his lips against her ear. "*Mon petit jouet très sale.*"

His fingers managed to ease open that offending top button and then swipe over the curve of her breasts. He wanted to curl his tongue over the hard peaks of her nipples. He called her his dirty little sex toy in his compelling voice on purpose, tempting her with dark fantasies. He wanted to see how she responded to him talking dirty to her with others around. "You'll give them a fair chance at hiring you, won't you?"

She nodded, clearly unable to speak, stark arousal in her vivid green eyes.

"She said yes, Valentino," Elie reported. "Now go away. We're on our honeymoon."

Dario made some sound that might have been a snicker.

Elie didn't look up. He heard the door close and immediately turned so that he faced her. "Open the buttons of that blouse. I'm very fond of it, *bébé*, and I don't want to tear it. I think it would look particularly nice with a dark bra under it. What do you think?"

His hands parted her thighs wide and massaged the inner muscles while he waited for her shaking hands to slip the buttons free.

Her eyes on his, she nodded.

"Answer me out loud, I want to hear the sound of your voice." He pushed a firm command behind the velvet over steel.

"Yes. I agree with you. It would look very nice."

"Then from now on, when you wear this blouse, a favorite of mine, you can wear your lacy black bra and leave the top three buttons open for me. It's so fucking sexy, Brielle. Take it off and fold it neatly. I like the house neat. Take your bra off as well."

He rose and walked across the room to the fireplace, keeping his eyes on her as she complied. She stood up as well, carefully removing the peach blouse and folding it, then looking around for a place to put it. He let her, enjoying the sight of her heavy breasts encased in the nude-colored bra. She walked to the kitchen counter, her hips swaying, and removed her bra right there. Once her breasts swung free, she glanced at the front door and then the banks of windows.

Elie knew what she was thinking. Their company had gone out, but no one had locked the door. He didn't alleviate her worry by mentioning there was an automatic lock. In her sexual preferences, she had stated quite plainly that she became very aroused at the idea of someone "catching" her naked or obeying her man.

"You're beautiful," he said. "And so damn hot right now. Get rid of the jeans and panties. We aren't going to need those, either."

A little shiver went through her body. Goose bumps rose on her skin as her hands dropped to the waistband of her

denim jeans. She slipped them over her hips and legs, taking them off and folding them. He noticed she only half turned, not wanting to give him a full view of her backside. That told him she didn't like the fact that she had an ass. He was already fond of that portion of her anatomy and she'd taken off a little too much of her curves to suit him.

He held his finger up and twirled it in the air. She glanced again at the long banks of windows and then at him, but her nipples were hard little peaks and the goose bumps were persistent on her skin. Her breathing was elevated. He knew when a woman was aroused, and his woman was very aroused.

He waited in silence, letting the tension build in the room. Very slowly, she complied with his request, turning in a circle for him to show off her body. His breath caught in his lungs. She might not think she was beautiful, but he did. She had gorgeous skin. That mane of wild hair gave him all kinds of ideas.

"Do you remember one of the first rules I put down that was extremely important to me as your husband, Brielle? I made certain to write it twice in the document I sent to you." He pitched his tone low as he approached her, making his advance a prowl, like a jungle cat stalking her on silent feet.

She shivered but nodded. He remained silent, waiting for her to realize her mistake. It took exactly two full minutes before she replied. "The first was you always led in the bedroom and I was to submit to anything you wanted. The second, you demanded respect at all times, especially when others were around. I represented you and could be as sassy as I wanted, but not in front of others, where I would make you look as if you had no control."

He trailed the pads of his fingers from her throat, between her breasts, down her belly to her mound. His foot slid between hers to push her feet apart and then his hand slid between her legs to find her entrance slick with heat. She'd answered the sexual questionnaire honestly. Everything he was doing, so far, was making her hot as hell, building her craving for him. He hoped it would continue to do so. Her

hips rocked forward as he flicked her clit and then circled it. He took his hand away and licked at his fingers, watching her eyes darken with need.

"Stefano Ferraro is head of the shadow riders in Chicago, isn't he, Brielle?" His voice dropped another octave.

He saw her instant comprehension. She bit at her lip, nodded and then swallowed. "Yes." Her answer was low.

"As such he is my boss, isn't he?"

"Yes." Now her voice was a whisper.

"He also is the acknowledged head of the Ferraro family, the family I explained carefully to you that took me in as their own. Is that not correct?"

"Yes."

"Knowing all that, you still disrespected him in front of his brothers and friends when he came at my call for help, didn't you?"

She moistened her lips. "Yes, Elie, but—"

"Don't make excuses. You disrespected him for no other reason than your ego, isn't that the truth?"

She was silent a moment and then she slowly nodded. "Yes."

He barely caught the admission. "Did you consider even once that he interrupted his day, risked his life and his brothers' lives to aid us?"

She blinked rapidly and shook her head. "No."

"Nor did you consider how you would make me look when you were so ungrateful, did you?" His hand slid up her thigh, and then between her legs once more, testing to make certain she had answered truthfully on her questionnaire. She widened her legs to give him better access, her breath coming in a ragged gasp as he slid his finger into her hot channel. She was tight and his cock jerked in anticipation.

"No, Elie," she whispered. "I didn't."

He pulled his hand away again. "There are consequences for your actions, aren't there? We both agreed on that, didn't we?"

A full-body shiver greeted his words. "Yes."

"Go to the window and place your palms flat on the last

lower pane. Press against the glass tight and push your ass out toward me. Keep your legs spread wide."

Brielle looked at the bank of windows and then back at him. With seeming reluctance, she made her way to the windows and then slowly bent down until she pressed her breasts flat against the glass with her palms on either side of her shoulders, down low, near the bottom half of the pane. At the same time, she widened her stance and pushed her bottom out.

Elie stayed very still just observing her. She liked what she was doing. Her pussy was swollen with need and so wet, it was nearly dripping. He'd been right to keep her wanting him. To drive her cravings up with all the touches, with stepping in and out of her shadow. He'd made certain to lie tight against her all night, to rub his thumbs over her nipples to keep them inflamed.

Her body bucked against his often during the night, and several times her hand had crept down, fingers moving in her body to try to relieve the ache in her sleep. He'd watched her for a few minutes, letting the tension in her build, before he'd firmly removed her fingers, sucking on them, tasting her spice and telling himself to wait, they would be better for it.

He had to have control in order for them to work as a couple. She needed certain things in their relationship. He'd read her answers over and over, read between the lines, and he'd been determined to make them work as a couple. Now that his wife was Brielle, more than ever, he was going to make their relationship work. She might think this was about sex, but he knew better. This was about giving her everything she needed or wanted. That meant staying in control even when he felt desperate—like now.

He padded across the room silently, making certain she didn't hear him coming up behind her. There was nothing more beautiful than the sight of his woman waiting for him, spread open, her pussy glistening, her rounded cheeks shuddering visibly, but the endorphins so jacked, the goose bumps had taken over her silky skin.

Deliberately, he pulled the leather belt from his trousers,

needed that kind of relationship. If he was entirely honest, he needed it as well. He liked games. He had learned them at a young age and those games had stayed with him so that he preferred his sex that way.

He believed the woman who had filled out the sexual questionnaire was absolutely perfect for him. Now that he knew she was Brielle, he wasn't so certain of taking her to the club with him as he had been before. He would have to think that through. He would have used the club to keep a sexual interest in a woman he didn't love, but he didn't need that with Brielle and he knew he never would.

Brielle was deliberately trying to entice him, using her body to seduce him into fucking her when she'd been punished. He didn't want her to think she was ever going to be in control. He'd lose her that way—and he wasn't going to lose her. He knew he was going to fall hard for Brielle. It was happening already.

CHAPTER SEVEN

Brielle paced back and forth, trying to get her body under control. She was on fire. *Fire*. There was no other way to put it. There was no hiding from Elie who she was or what she needed. She'd been so silly, disclosing so much about herself, thinking she was writing to a perfect stranger and telling him what she was like.

From the moment she learned about the wickedness going on in the clubs, her body had come alive. She had found ways to visit them, to see for herself what went on. Just watching had been such a turn-on when nothing had made her in the least bit aroused. Then she heard Elie's voice telling a woman what to do in that low, compelling voice of his and she'd had to go to the ladies' room. It had been her very first orgasm and it had been huge. He had only told the woman to behave herself.

After that she had erotic dreams of him giving her orders and punishing her if she didn't obey. Sometimes he would take her outdoors where they would almost get caught. He would force his cock down her throat in a club while the

music pounded around them and people danced. She would have multiple orgasms just fantasizing about him holding her in place but shielding her with his body even as he insisted she suck him dry. Other times, he would spank her with his belt. Still other times, his friends would come over to the house and into the bedroom while he had her handcuffed and her bottom presented. They would start a conversation with him, ignoring the fact that he spanked her with his belt. She liked when he was tender and gave her a million orgasms after he treated her as if she was his toy. That was all part of the fantasy. In every fantasy, her partner had been Elie.

Fortunately, she hadn't disclosed those fantasies to her potential husband. Only that she preferred to be submissive in the bedroom and she liked pain on a limited basis—a very limited basis. She agreed that she would be willing to try exhibitionism, bondage and a host of other things but she wrote down clear limits as well. Knife play was an absolute no. Cheating was an absolute no.

Under certain circumstances she had a very strong sex drive. Elie and anything to do with him were those circumstances. She couldn't stop shaking, but at the same time, the longer she waited for Elie, the more every nerve ending in her body was alive, begging for relief. What would he do next? The uncertainty was such a turn-on.

She stood in front of the one mirror in the master bedroom and stared at herself, for a moment unbelieving that the woman looking back at her could really be her. Her hair was wild, her skin flushed. She looked aroused, her full breasts jutting out, nipples stiffened into hard peaks. She turned slightly to catch a glimpse of the darker red staining the cheeks of her bottom. The heat had spread straight to her sex, making her channel throb and burn.

Brielle moved to the very large bed she'd been avoiding. Just looking at the various cuffs hooked to the decorative wrought-iron spindles on the headboard caused another flush of heat to spread through her body. At the same time her heart

accelerated. She'd said bondage. She glanced up at the sheets laminated and pinned to the wall right beside the bed with her answers on her sexual preferences.

She'd agreed to bondage but she'd also stated she wanted to get to know her partner. She had stated plainly she thought it necessary to be given the time to work up to trusting him before entering into that kind of play with him. Involuntarily, she reached up and touched one of the three scars on her body, running her finger over the faint reminder of her stupidity.

"Let me see."

She nearly jumped out of her skin. How could the man possibly sneak up on her that way? She had been trained like every shadow rider to know when there was danger, and Elie Archambault was a very dangerous man. Very slowly, to give herself time to get her breathing under control, she let go of the cuff and turned to face him.

"Elie." Just saying his name made her ache even more. Seeing him, barefoot, dressed only in his trousers, chest bare, heavy muscles rippling as he approached her in that stalking way he had, increased her hunger for him tenfold.

"Let me see," he repeated. This time his much larger hand reached out, fingers shackling her wrist, pulling her hand away from the upper curve of her left breast and holding her arm out and away so there was no hiding from him.

His gaze moved over her breasts. He frowned, stepping closer, leaning down, examining that faint white slash on the upper curve just on the side of her breast. The pad of his finger traced the mark and then his gaze lifted to hers.

"Do you have any other scars like this one?"

Before she could answer, he leaned down again and brushed his lips over the white slash that had hurt so bad when it first had ripped her open that she thought she might die. Just the touch of his lips, the feel of his tongue sliding along the slight dip where her skin had been gouged out, set butterflies soaring in her stomach. She lost her ability to speak. To breathe. To function. She was back in brain fog.

Elie straightened again, his dark, nearly black gaze meeting hers. "Brielle, focus for me. Do you have other scars made by a knife? Ones like this one?"

That low commanding voice snapped her out of her haze. She nodded and pulled at her hand. He let her wrist go and she pointed to another faint mark on her lower abdomen. "Here." That one had her screaming until her throat was so raw, she couldn't talk for hours. "And here." She pointed to the third and longest one. It had been the deepest cut on her body, right along her ribs, under her left breast.

"Crawl onto the bed, Brielle," Elie commanded. "Lie down on your back."

For the first time, there was an edge to that low, compelling tone. It was still velvet, rubbing over her skin like a caress, wrapping her up in sensual magic, but there was a rasp to it that added another layer.

She shivered, wondering why she reacted to his particular tone, why she needed to comply with everything he wanted from her. How, just by speaking, he could make her feel sexy even when he wasn't saying anything that had to do with sex.

Brielle crawled up onto the very wide bed, aware Elie watched her every move with that burning gaze locked onto her. The duvet was gray and very thick. Her knees and hands sank into the soft comforter as she made her way up toward the headboard. She felt wholly feminine, her hips and breasts swaying with every movement. In the center, she stopped, dipping her chest to the duvet first and then lowering her bottom before she rolled over to comply with his order.

She had deliberately gone all the way to the top of the bed. She was short and she knew her feet wouldn't reach the bottom of the bed and the footboard where the ankle cuffs were. She did trust Elie, but she didn't have confidence in herself yet. She still had nightmares and panic attacks. That was the last thing she wanted to have happen with Elie. What if he decided he didn't want to play in the bedroom? Or that she was too much work?

"Legs wide apart."

Elie stood at the bottom of the bed, his arms behind his back, his dark eyes drifting possessively over her. She liked that look on his face. It wasn't just that he regarded her with the look of someone who could be by turns objective or affectionate. Maybe more than affection. That was Elie's gift. He could make a woman believe she was special to him—real to him even as he made her his toy. One look or touch, one smile or just a word could bring a woman to her knees, make her want to do anything for him.

Brielle had watched him all those years. He hadn't even seen her, no matter what he said to her. She'd paid close attention to him and how the women reacted to him. He was so offhand, barely showing his dates any kindness and then suddenly bestowing his famous smile on them. Immediately the woman would fawn all over him. Brielle understood and felt sorry for his date. She knew the woman wouldn't last long; they never did. He had a pattern. What did that mean for her?

Elie caught her chin and turned her face toward him. "Tell me what you're thinking and don't lie to me."

The last thing she wanted to do was admit to him anything she'd just been thinking but they both had sworn they'd be honest. She veiled her eyes with her long lashes, her heart beating too fast. She knew he could see her pulse beating hard in her neck. His fingers were at her neck now, feeling it, counting her heartbeats.

"I'd rather not if you don't mind."

"I do mind. Tell me."

That was a strict order. "It's a little embarrassing and I know you aren't going to like all of it. I can't help the way I think, Elie."

He was silent. Waiting. She squirmed on the bed, realizing just how vulnerable she felt, completely naked, legs wide open, lying sprawled out while he was still clothed. That only made the flames burn hotter in her core and spread through her body like a wildfire out of control.

"I liked the way you looked at the bottom of the bed when you were looking at me," she admitted in a low tone. "You

have a way of making me feel like I really am your toy that you enjoy playing with, but at the same time, I'm your woman, the one you cherish and protect."

She hesitated, wanting to leave it there. She knew he could hear the truth in her voice. It was the truth, but . . . He remained silent as he stared down at her. His expression hadn't changed when she snuck a peek at him. He hadn't touched her. She sighed. It was uncanny how he knew there was more and he expected her to tell him.

"I remembered all the times you brought women into the café where I worked or the restaurant. They were always gorgeous models. Very famous women. They hung on your arm and stared up at you as if they were afraid to take their eyes off you. You treated them as if they were nothing most of the time but then you would suddenly smile at them or lean close and whisper to them and they would light up as if you had said they mattered to you. I knew you hadn't. I knew they didn't matter. I knew you would grow bored with them and drop them within a matter of weeks or even days. I felt sorry for them."

She hoped—sent up little prayers to the universe—that he wouldn't insist on any other revelations. She'd gone far enough.

Again, Elie stayed silent, but this time, his palm smoothed down her throat to the valley between her breasts and then to her belly. She tried not to suck in her breath in order to have a firmer stomach, but it was difficult when he had such a firm body and she still had that offending soft pooch she couldn't quite get rid of no matter how many crunches she did. His palm continued to glide lower over her mound, trailing the patch of blond curls until his fingers settled in her slick heat.

"You're very brave for telling me when you didn't want to. Finish, *bébé*." He whispered the command like temptation.

Those wicked fingers circled her clit, a whisper of a touch, a reward for her bravery. She knew it was. She wanted to push against his fingers, lift her hips into his hand, but instinctively, she knew he would step away from her fast if she did.

A flush started and consumed her from head to toe. She wished she could control the spread of heat, but it was impossible. She hoped he would put it down to the way he touched her and not what she'd been thinking. It was so difficult to confess. *So* difficult.

For a brief moment, she pressed her lips together, holding back the truth from him. She knew she couldn't look at him. Behind her eyes, tears burned too close. Swallowing the lump threatening to choke her, she forced the confession. "I couldn't help but think it was your pattern. The way you made women feel special so easily, as if you cared for them on one hand and yet could so quickly abandon them because you didn't really feel anything for them. They were really toys for you to play with. I had the thought that maybe you would abandon me, too, when you become bored with me."

He'd made a promise to her. He'd signed a contract stating he wouldn't cheat on her. He'd made that an absolute demand in his arrangement with her. During the ceremony, he had again made that same commitment before his chosen family, and then in Stefano's office, he had reiterated that he had vowed not to cheat. Would he think she had insulted him because of her wayward thoughts?

Brielle couldn't look at him. His hand moved up her body once again, sliding up her skin with surprising gentleness until he found the depression along her abdomen with the pads of his fingers. He explored, as if he were using Braille, getting to know her body by touch. Then he leaned down, his hair sweeping along her skin, the silky strands leaving flames crackling all over her. Then his mouth was there, gentle, like before, but when he kissed the scar, his lips felt scorching hot. His tongue slid along the white depression, a brand, claiming the spot for his own.

There was no way to stay still when that brand sank beneath her skin into her muscles and organs, into her bones. Her fingers curled into fists around the duvet as her hips bucked and a small needy moan escaped. Elie's palm pressed into her stomach, fingers spread wide, holding her down, as

he licked, kissed and nipped at that little wound. His teeth scraped back and forth, a rough caress, and then he bit down gently, which nearly sent her soaring. His tongue stroked, a rasp of velvet and soothing heat over the small sting.

Her legs shifted. She needed to rub them together to give herself some relief, but he smacked her inner thigh hard, his head coming up alertly, eyes blazing into hers. She subsided immediately.

Elie returned to his task, slowly using his mouth to kiss and nip his way until he found the deepest scar just under her left breast. He used the pad of his index finger to rub back and forth as if memorizing the shape and length of it. Then once more, he bent his head to administer a firestorm of kisses with his lips, tongue and teeth.

It was impossible to stay completely still, but she made every effort because she didn't want him to stop. It didn't matter if she had his attention now, and later, she might lose it. She would cross that bridge when she came to it.

That was her biggest fear. Her secret fear. She would fall in love with Elie Archambault. She had already been so obsessed with him over the years, and she knew, if she was with him, close like this, she would be completely wrapped up in him. Consumed by him. She was that kind of person. She surrendered everything she was. She'd told herself he wasn't real, only a fantasy she'd made up when she was little more than a child, but that hadn't stopped her. Now she was with him. Tied to him. Reality was better than any fantasy she'd dreamt up.

It was all she could do not to bury her fingers in his hair and hold him to her. Terror touched her mind. She hadn't been with him five minutes and she was already certain she would lose him. That had been part of what she had avoided telling Stefano, but now it was out in the open. She hadn't made the threat of losing him seem as certain as it was to her, or how shattering it would be to her, but at least she'd been honest.

Elie suddenly lifted his head and looked straight into her

eyes. "Was this knife play done with your consent? I noticed you emphasized no knife play and with bondage you were smart enough to say you wanted time to work on trust."

"I *never*, at any time, consented to knife play. I was adamant against it." She tried to keep any inflection out of her voice. She still felt guilty, as if what had been done to her was her fault because she was the way she was. "Once he had cuffs on me, he used the knife." Tears burned again and she tried not to think about the way it felt to have the blade go through her skin.

Elie gathered her to him, pulling her into his arms as he settled onto the side of the bed. She was shocked to find herself in his lap while he rocked her, one hand in her hair.

"Don't think about the way it felt, *mon petit ange*. There is no need. But I do insist you give me his name."

She pulled back to look at him. He was serious. Very serious if his expression was anything to go by. He looked every inch an Archambault.

"Elie, he doesn't matter. He was a member of a club I went to. I wanted to experience a few things to see if I liked them or not. He was there quite a bit and seemed to have a good reputation. No one ever said a bad word about him. He'd asked me to be with him quite a few times and I'd turned him down. I was a little afraid of him."

"Why?"

She didn't want to say he had a similar intensity to Elie without being compelling and sexy the way she found Elie.

"I know I should have stayed away from him. He gave me a bad feeling every time he approached me. It was just that he was so persistent. He clearly had been with the club a long time. I was embarrassed that I had no reason to give him for avoiding him and he asked me straight out in front of several other Doms why I was so reluctant to allow him to play."

Elie's fingers tightened on the nape of her neck and then began a slow massage. "When he did that, what was the reaction of the others?"

"They got up and left. I think one of them protested, but he kind of laughed. That made me even more embarrassed."

Elie brushed a kiss on her temple. "He had no right to do that to you and the others should have protected you. What happened next?"

"He told me to sit at the bar with him and go over my limits. I found myself following him to one of the rooms. Before I knew it, I had cuffs on and he had a knife out. He told me if I didn't shut up, he was going to gag me, that I deserved it for making him wait. He said I'd been teasing him for months." She wanted Elie to believe her. "It wasn't true. I didn't want anything to do with him."

"Tell me his name and the name of the club."

"It was a club in Barcelona called Fantasía Más Oscura. The Dom was called Master Serrano. I heard some of the men call him Izan."

"When you screamed, I hope the others came and rescued you." Elie made it a statement.

She nodded. "They did come. Serrano was angry with them and me. I never went back to the club and stayed far away from anyone I had met there. Once or twice, I thought I saw him when I was on the street coming out of a store, but I never could actually catch him and I'm really good in the shadows. Eventually, I had to put it down to being paranoid. I stayed in my apartment after that. I wanted to heal and I was already looking for the freighters. I'd agreed to an arranged marriage so I didn't think I ever had to worry about Serrano again."

"You don't," Elie stated firmly. "I'll take care of Serrano."

"Elie, just leave it alone. It's over with. The scars have healed." She could hear the unconscious plea in her voice.

"The trauma hasn't, Brielle. He very well could be doing that same thing to other women. No one has the right to touch you or any other woman without consent."

"But I went to the club specifically because I needed to alleviate . . ." She broke off, embarrassed, and then tried again. "Sometimes I reach this point and I need something." It was so

horrible to try to explain something to a man she wanted respect and eventually love from. Here she was, needing him to talk dirty to her. To spank her. She wished he would just let it go.

"This man was at fault, Brielle, not you. You told him no. No is no. You have no need to be ashamed because you went to a club and wanted to play. It was supposed to be safe. It should have been. This man took advantage and we don't know if he had something to do with the bomb that was sitting on our front porch. He warrants an investigation at the very least."

Brielle buried her face in his neck. "Investigation by the shadow riders?"

"Yes, and if he's up to no good, he'll be taken care of. If his crime is taking advantage of women at the clubs, I have friends who owe me favors. They would be more than happy to pay him a visit to make certain he knows that touching a woman who has said no is not okay. Your name will be kept out of it."

"Honestly, Elie." She sat up straight, forcing herself to look into his eyes. "I don't think that would deter him. He believes he has the right to do what he wants with a woman. I don't think what we do is . . ." She stumbled over what she wanted to say. She wanted to have a loving relationship with Elie, but she wanted to be free to play games with him in that relationship. The things she'd done in the club had been to learn about herself, but she'd considered them playing. She'd kept them in that context. She'd been very careful.

"I understand, *bébé*," Elie said and transferred her from his lap back to the middle of the bed. "He disrespects his partners and considers himself above them. He doesn't deserve the title of Dom, let alone the title of a partner."

He bent his head to the scar on her abdomen and pressed a kiss there even as he dropped his hands to the zipper of his trousers. Her heart nearly stopped and then began to beat wildly. When he lifted his dark eyes to hers, she saw tenderness mixed with heat. Mixed with stark desire. That fast, she

was his. One look. She'd never had anyone look at her with tenderness. She never thought anyone would.

Her breath caught in her throat. Her lungs felt raw, burning for air. He hadn't touched her yet, and just from that one look, she wanted to cry. He had gone from playing, treating her as his favorite toy, to treating her as someone cherished. She could see it in the expression on his face, in the beauty of his eyes. Brielle wasn't certain how to handle the emotions threatening to overwhelm her.

She wanted this from him—tenderness and caring—but if she lost it, she knew the loss would shatter her heart. Her gaze dropped from his to follow the path of his incredible abs. Who had abs like that? That led her to the sight of his very alive, straining cock.

"Elie," she whispered his name. He was beautiful when she'd never considered that part of men beautiful. Thick and pulsing, he looked as if he was sculpted in steel but sheathed in a velvet case with one strong purple vein running the length of that wide shaft. The broad head was smeared with enticing white drops that made her mouth water.

He widened her legs, kneeling between them so he could blanket her body slowly, laying his chest over hers. He was heavy, crushing her into the soft duvet, his skin scorching hot, chest mashing her breasts as he came down on top of her. Both hands settled into her hair, fisted there, holding her head still while he took her mouth.

Brielle expected rough. He gave her gentle. A slow, smoldering burn that had her entire insides shuddering with need. She ran out of air and he gave her his breath, breathing for both of them. She had never experienced anything so sensual or intimate.

One hand left her hair to anchor itself beside her head and the other slid to her throat. With infinite slowness, he eased his weight up just enough that she realized the thick duvet had given her enough of a cushion to keep his weight from completely crushing her. It didn't matter. She felt the

loss of his body imprinting on hers. All that heat. That rough against her silk. That male against female.

Elie stared down into her eyes with such intensity, she was mesmerized. Spellbound. Aware of every tiny detail of that moment. She felt his thumb brushing over the frantically beating pulse in the side of her neck. His palm completely surrounded her throat as if he might crush her at any moment. That only added to her excitement. His knees pressed tight against her thighs, keeping them wide apart so the air fanned the heat of her clenching entrance.

"I wanted you, Brielle. No one else. It was always you." He lowered his mouth and nipped at her lower lip. "Those women you saw me with? The ones you knew I wouldn't stay with? I made it clear to them from the start that I wasn't looking for a relationship. I had sex with them. Our time together wasn't exclusive. It was sex. I spelled it out before we had sex. During the time we were together. I never wanted them to think we were going to be together for any other reason."

His teeth tugged at her lower lip and then bit down until she felt a bite of pain. Instantly, he released her lip and his tongue soothed the sting. Her body reacted with that storm of flames rushing through her veins, settling low in her sex until she felt hot and needy. He held her body open so there was no chance of relief.

She didn't know how to feel about his revelation. If she could rely on her ability as a rider to hear truth, she would have to say he was being very truthful. When she looked into his eyes, there was that same tenderness that had been there before. He couldn't fake that, could he? If he could, he should go into acting.

"None of those women were shadow riders, *bébé*. I might not be happy with the way the Archambaults raised me, but I am a shadow rider and an Archambault. I believe in what we do. On some level, I knew I had already met the right woman destined for me. So, I was careful."

The right woman destined for him. Was that who she was?

What did that mean? So he could give the riders children? She wanted to look away from him. The hand around her throat was too large and kept her head in place. She wasn't wearing cuffs, but his large frame positioned the way it was prevented movement.

His lips were back, kissing each of her eyelids, then the tip of her nose, the corners of her mouth before settling on her lips. This time there was a demand in his kiss and she opened for him, unable to deny him anything.

His fingers stroked her breast as he kissed his way to the upper curve. "I assure you, Brielle, between us, there is no chance of boredom. I am very inventive. I have every intention of earning your trust. We made vows to communicate with one another. When I want something from you, I'll tell you. You promised to tell me."

She couldn't help but squirm a little. She had signed that paper saying she would ask for what she wanted or needed. She would talk things over with her partner. Unfortunately, that was extremely difficult for her.

His teeth nipped and then bit down with exquisite gentleness on her nipple. It wasn't quite painful, but just the anticipation had her catching her breath and bucking her hips. One of his hands was still wrapped around her throat, and when she arched her neck back, her pulse drummed into his palm.

"I know you have trouble expressing what you want, but we'll keep working at it." His tongue lapped at her nipple, sending flashes of heat through her body. "Communication is necessary in all relationships, but in one like ours, especially."

His mouth closed around her breast, sucked deep and hard, flattening her nipple to the roof of his mouth. The jolt was like lightning streaking through her body straight to her core, igniting a wildfire. Her nipple and clit had a straight line to each other. The harder he sucked, the more the conflagration built.

His hand slipped from her throat, stroked with infinite care over the curve over her right breast until his fingers

found her nipple. He rolled and tugged in time with the rhythm of his mouth pulling at her left breast. Then his fingers pinched down, gently at first, his teeth finding her left nipple to match the increasing clamp.

Elie lifted his head to watch her expression. His knees shifted, moving subtly up on her thighs, forcing them even wider apart. Because he'd started so gently and the increase in pressure was so slow, at first, she was mostly aware of the way her legs were so wide, her sex so completely open and exposed. She wasn't just damp. She was slick, even wet, once again desperate for him. Then the burn in her breasts turned to raging pinpoints of something between pain and pleasure. The fire was exactly what she loved, bordering on too much, but not nearly enough.

She found herself arching her back, thrusting her breasts at him, not certain if she wanted more or if she was trying to ease the ache. He let go of her right nipple first and slid his hand down her belly to her stiff, desperate clit. The blood pounded there. The moment he touched her, she nearly exploded. His teeth released her, but his fingers were exploring her slick entrance as his tongue licked at her nipples.

"You like that, don't you?"

"Yes."

"It isn't difficult to tell me what you like. Your body tells me, but I prefer to hear you say it. I want to know everything I do that makes you respond to me."

Hearing him talk made her respond to him in every way. He kissed his way down her belly, his tongue swirling in her belly button, and then paying attention once more to the scar there. She didn't know why, but that made her feel cared for and brought tears burning close. One hand settled in his hair. She didn't know if he would object and she almost pulled her hand back, but when he didn't say anything, she curled her fingers deeper, needing the connection.

Brielle couldn't take her eyes off Elie, afraid if she did, he might disappear. She might wake up to find this was one of her many erotic fantasies. Her breath exploded out of her

lungs when he looped her legs on his arms, forcing them wider still, and without any preamble settled his mouth on her, stabbing his tongue deep and flicking her clit with his finger, hard.

She screamed. She'd never screamed in pleasure in her life. Never. No matter what had been done to her. Her body detonated, shattered, came apart into a million pieces at the first piercing of his tongue and the flick of his finger against her clit.

He didn't wait for her to ease down as the orgasm rolled through her. He used his tongue, fingers and teeth to keep the powerful waves building in intensity. Brielle dug her fingernails into his shoulder and scalp, desperate for an anchor, for anything to keep her from soaring too high. She was afraid she might lose her sanity.

Colors flashed behind her eyes. There was a roaring in her ears. Her brain fogged. There was no way to breathe. Then he was moving again, looking up at her, smiling, even as her body was still convulsing with total pleasure and she could barely make him out as he casually wiped his glistening face on her thighs. She found that so sexy, her body just rolled right into another orgasm again, or maybe she hadn't stopped.

He knelt up between her legs, his cock in one hand, pressing the broad head to her slick entrance. Again, he didn't wait, but surged deep, his thick length driving through her shuddering folds, the friction almost unbearable. He was big, filling her, adding to the chaos in her mind. Then he began to move in her, long deep strokes that kept her off balance, kept building the inferno.

"Elie." There was no whispering his name. She was sobbing it.

"Right here, *bébé*." His fingers dug into her hips, urging her to keep up with his insane rhythm.

Brielle couldn't stop herself from matching the pace he set. The feeling was too good. At the same time, he was too deep, too thick, stretching her so there was a burning that

accompanied the streaks of lightning that rushed through her body as the tension coiled tighter and tighter. She didn't want him ever to stop, yet she was afraid to keep going.

One hand left her hip and he flicked her left nipple hard. A flash of fire roared in a straight line from her nipple to her clit. Her channel reacted with more shudders and deep in her belly the coil tightened. Elie slid his hand down to her hip again and continued to surge in and out of her with deep, hard strokes.

His gaze seemed riveted on the two of them coming together and then up to her eyes. "Look at me, Brielle," he commanded.

She felt a little lost in a haze of bliss. It was difficult to surface enough to do as he said, but she blinked to bring him entirely in focus.

"You're beautiful. Everything about you is beautiful. I'm grateful you're my wife." He bent his head slowly forward toward her chest. It wasn't easy. He had to lift her bottom to give himself the room. "Come for me hard. Give yourself to me."

His mouth was on her breast, the left one, his teeth clamping down on her nipple, the pressure hard this time. Fire erupted, engulfing her from the inside out and she did exactly as he demanded. Her body took over, her sheath gripping his cock with greedy muscles, powerful and eager, contracting and releasing, determined to milk every drop from him. She felt the hot spurts of his seed as he coated the walls of her channel, sending even more shuddering orgasms rolling through her body from her breasts to her thighs.

The aftershocks rocked her, so that she couldn't keep from crying out again. Elie was still for a few moments, breathing hard and then, once again, his body blanketed hers, pressing his chest over hers, giving her his weight. His hand slipped around her throat so that her pulse beat frantically into his palm.

Elie buried his face against her neck, and sank his teeth

into her shoulder. The pain moved through her, triggering another orgasm, so that her body clamped down on his cock. She felt the instant pulsing and throbbing as if he was still expanding, not shrinking, ready to leave her body. Her lungs burned with the need for air, but she didn't want him to move. Not yet. She struggled to breathe shallowly.

Elie brushed a kiss over the bite mark and then eased his weight off her chest the way he had before, by planting his hand in the bed beside her head. "I think it's official, Mrs. Archambault. There's no squirming out of the marriage now."

She wasn't certain she actually returned his smile. She'd never been so exhausted in her life. She did manage a nod and hoped that counted as an answer.

He rolled over. "Give me a minute, *bébé*, I'll get a washcloth and clean you up. When we both can move again, we can take a shower and use the Jacuzzi."

"I think I'm falling asleep."

His laughter was pitched low. "Go ahead, Brielle. We're on our honeymoon. No one expects us to surface for a few days. We're not on any schedule."

"You didn't plan anything?" That surprised her.

He ran his hand over her hip and down her thigh. "I had plans until I saw who I married. Then I decided spending time with my new wife was a much better idea."

Brielle liked his answer. She wanted time with him. As much as she could get.

"It's my job to keep us from ever getting bored with one another, Brielle. I don't plan on falling down on my job, so you don't need to worry about that anymore."

She pressed her lips together to keep from blurting out that just because he decreed she shouldn't worry didn't mean she could stop herself. "What happens when we have children and I don't look the same? Or we don't have as much freedom in the house to play the games we both enjoy?"

He sat up and looked down at her with dark, fathomless eyes. "I will love how you look after having my children. If you don't love how you look, we'll work on it together. As for

the games we enjoy, believe me, *bébé*, I very much look forward to the challenge of finding ways to continue playing under any and all circumstances."

He leaned over and kissed her. Thoroughly. Robbing her of both speech and breath, and then he sauntered out of the room to get a washcloth.

CHAPTER EIGHT

'm betting on my man, Bernado," Valentino said. He indicated the board Giovanni had set up in Dario's very large office. "Bernado has mad skills and even your teams can't possibly beat him, Stefano."

"Don't be so certain of that, Val," Stefano said. "Rigina and her sister Rosina Greco are my cousins and they're lightning fast and one hundred percent accurate on the computer. Accuracy counts. Your man has to be correct. He can't just make shit up, or guess when he's close to the answer."

Valentino burst out laughing. "Just how many cousins do you actually have, Stefano? It isn't like you don't have a big enough family as it is with all your siblings. You just have to show off with all those cousins." He gestured toward Dario. "I've got one."

Dario glanced up from where he was looking at his phone. "Stefano needs his fifty cousins. You only need me." He made the proclamation as if it was an edict they all should be aware of.

Emmanuelle nudged Ricco. "There you have it. Val only needs Dario. He makes up for all of you."

"Well," Ricco conceded, "that could be true. Dario does have that unfortunate reputation. My money's on the boys in the investigative world, Romano and Renato Greco. Stefano thinks the women, but I think the big brothers have this one."

"I thought that Rigina and Rosina assisted their brothers when it was needed, but they seemed to have taken over the investigative work more and more," Taviano said.

Emmanuelle raised an eyebrow and pretended to kick her brother in the shin. "You know perfectly well the two of them far exceeded the skills of their parents and brothers a long time ago and have been working on their own for some time."

Taviano indicated the white board that had been set up against the wall opposite the stone fireplace. One side of the enormous room was all glass. The double glass doors were framed in rustic wood and led out onto a balcony overlooking the lake. On either side of the doors were long windows, framed in the same matching wood as the doorframes. The floor was a dark hardwood and the very comfortable furniture was a chocolate brown. Long narrow windows were on either side of the floor-to-ceiling gray stone fireplace, but with the windows and the light rugs, the office was extremely bright.

"Are you betting on the girls with Stefano?" Taviano challenged his sister.

"I didn't say that." Emmanuelle shook her head. "I'm putting my money on Brielle."

Dario looked up, his gaze suddenly sharp. "What do you know that we don't?"

"Nothing. I just have a feeling. She had a lot of confidence in herself when it came to her computer skills."

"Ego is what you mean," Vittorio corrected. "Ego and sass. I'm taking the brothers. Romano and Renato."

Giovanni looked the board over carefully. "I'm backing the girls. They've never gotten anything wrong yet. They're lightning fast. Rigina and Rosina."

"Elie?" Stefano asked. "You have any thoughts on this? No one's going to tell your wife if you don't bet on her."

"Speak for yourself, Stefano," Giovanni said. "He'll never live it down."

"I'll be using this for blackmail forever," Taviano added. "The moment you put in your bet, we're all taking pictures of that board."

"Don't pay attention to them," Emmanuelle said. "I'll have Rigina hack their phones and wipe them clean."

"She can't do that," Ricco said with confidence.

"Don't be too sure," Valentino said. "Bernado can get into phones."

"Not all the time," Dario disagreed.

"In any case," Elie said, "I'm one hundred percent backing Brielle. Not because I'm worried any of you might rat on me, but because I'm taking your money. She's going to wipe up the floor with your investigators."

He poured confidence into his voice. He felt confident, so much so that he didn't look at the whiteboard as Brielle's name was written in as his vote, but he wandered over to the double doors to stare out over the balcony. Dario had a beautiful office. He'd been in Valentino's home many times, but never Dario's. It was . . . unexpected. Dario was a dark, dangerous man and those shadows clung to him. He didn't try to hide who he was; rather, he embraced the traits. The house reflected who he was, yet at the same time was open and unexpectedly bright with all the windows offsetting the dark wood in each room.

Elie had expected a small, cave-like house, not the huge home with elegant, custom features. Everything was in its place. He hadn't expected that, either. Now that he thought about it, the precise OCD elements made sense. Dario was a man demanding instant obedience. He had been responsible for Valentino's protection for a number of years during a very turbulent time when they couldn't trust anyone. They had relied solely on each other.

"That leaves you, Dario," Stefano said. "You haven't weighed in yet."

Dario walked across the large office to the back wall and stared at the board for a long while. "I've got a feeling about Brielle. She isn't a woman who insists on having her way in front of a group of strangers. You called it ego and sass, Vittorio, but if one of us insisted we were skilled enough to do something, would you have called it that?"

Vittorio frowned, giving the question honest consideration. "I doubt it. You have a point. If a man had done so, and I didn't know him, most likely I would have, especially if he was young. But one of you, no."

"Because he knows us," Ricco said. "That would make sense. He knows we don't brag."

"You thought she was bragging?" Dario asked. "I didn't hear bragging in her voice. I heard honesty."

"He wasn't there," Giovanni pointed out. "I was and I should have been paying more attention. To be honest, I thought it was funny that a little thing like her was defying Stefano."

"I didn't think it was so funny," Elie said. He couldn't keep the growl from his tone and he swung around just in time to catch Dario's dark glance. Their eyes met. Dario's eyes held comprehension. Elie shook his head slightly. They thought on two different levels. Elie knew they did. Dario might think they were close in the way they thought to handle their women, but they weren't. Elie didn't understand Dario's needs and he never would. He wouldn't ever judge him, but he didn't understand him.

"However honest Brielle thought she was being doesn't mean she's capable of beating our teams of investigators," Stefano said.

"Or Bernado," Valentino added.

"Perhaps not," Dario said. "But I'm putting my money on her."

That shocked the hell out of Elie. There was no inflection in Dario's voice, and he turned away from the board as Giovanni added Dario's name under Brielle's.

"You can't kill her if she loses," Emmanuelle said. "I mean it, Dario."

Dario shrugged. "Surely Elie took out a healthy insurance policy on her."

"I did," Elie said, deadpan, just to get a rise out of Emme. "The moment I saw who I was marrying. She's a pain in the ass."

"Elie." Emmanuelle flung herself into one of the low-slung swivel thick-cushioned chairs in front of the windows. "I can't believe you just said that."

"I insisted Valentino take out an enormous life insurance policy on you, Emme," Dario informed her. "Seeing as how I want to strangle you at least six times a day, I thought it best he has some compensation in case I can't restrain myself."

"Ha!" Emmanuelle narrowed her eyes and glared at Dario. "What makes you think you would win if you tried to strangle me? I'd kick your scrawny butt."

Dario was anything but scrawny. He was a man with wide shoulders, and muscles on his muscles. He didn't look bulky but he looked ripped—definitely able to handle himself.

"I did consider that," Dario said. "Or that if I managed to strangle you, I'd get back my status as the number one wanted man on your family's hit list." He poured satisfaction into his voice.

"I'd have to think that over," Stefano interrupted. "My brothers would want to vote. I do love my sister, but she's a pain in the ass. We want to strangle her six times a day, too. And you're family, Dario. Putting you back onto the list would be considered very poor taste, especially in the number one position."

"I earned that spot," Dario said.

"Wait a minute," Emmanuelle complained, throwing a dark pillow at her oldest brother. "I absolutely forbid you to humor Dario. He's probably really thought about strangling me."

Stefano picked the pillow out of the air, his face totally expressionless as he shot the pillow back at her. "Honey, every single person in this room has thought about strangling you, including your husband at one time or another."

Elie erupted into laughter with her brothers. A smirk flitted

across Dario's face and was gone. Elie knew Dario loved two people in the world—Valentino and Emmanuelle. He would give his life for Emmanuelle Ferraro Saldi whether he occasionally thought about strangling her or not.

Emmanuelle caught the pillow to her with a little pleased grin. "If that's true, then my mission in life is going very well. I wouldn't want any of you to be complacent and think you're getting everything your own way."

The Ferraro brothers laughed uproariously and Valentino joined them. A look of amusement flashed into Dario's dark eyes. Elie couldn't help wishing Brielle was there watching the way the family interacted. Like him, she didn't have the best model with her family, and seeing the Ferraros together always made him realize what he wanted for his wife and children.

Elie had made it a point to study Stefano and the way he treated his siblings, his wife and his children. Elie hoped both Valentino and Dario did the same. Neither man had much in the way of example of a really good, loving relationship. He knew Giuseppi, Valentino's adoptive father, had loved his wife, but he also loved his business and ruled with an iron fist. Val had grown up with the old-school ways of running the family business. Elie knew Val didn't run the business the same way, although Val was quite capable of ruthless behavior if it was needed. Dario certainly could—and did—handle that end. Now that Dario was running his own territory, Elie was trying to keep a closer eye on him, worried that his way of handling anyone stepping out of line might be more like Giuseppi's.

Elie didn't want Emmanuelle's loyalty ever to be caught between her family and her husband's family. He was absolutely certain Valentino would never place her in that position. He knew Dario loved her and was protective of her, but Dario was the most ruthless man he'd ever come across. He wasn't as certain of Dario as he'd like to be, but then he didn't know him as well. Val believed in him implicitly and that carried a lot of weight both with Elie and Stefano. At the

same time, Elie wasn't a trusting man and neither was Stefano. Until they knew Dario as well as Val, they would hold back just a bit and watch him. Dario was a shrewd man and easily read body language as well as registered every inflection and expression. Elie had no doubt that Dario was aware the Ferraros and Elie watched him carefully.

"I have to hand it to you, Dario," Vittorio said, "this is a great office. The space alone is amazing."

Taviano nodded and went straight to the double doors. "I like the balcony. Your view is incredible. I do my best thinking outside." He glanced back at Dario, seeking permission, and at Dario's nod, opened the doors. At once a cool breeze entered the room.

The flames in the fireplace flared so that the wood crackled behind the heavy chain screen. Taviano stepped outside. Dario and Elie followed him. On the balcony, Dario had two very comfortable chairs made of dark wicker with thick cushions in a chocolate-and-white stripe. Elie was coming to believe the color scheme reflected who Dario was. The chairs looked inviting. Certainly, the view was incredible.

Below, wild lavender grew in long rows over one section of the rolling hills. An emerald lawn rolled down the hill; lavender plants in rustic wood planter boxes framed the pathway leading the way to the lake. White sand covered the beach leading up to the water. Two boats sat in a covered boathouse situated between two long docks that jutted out into the lake.

"You not only have a great office, Dario, but a beautiful piece of property," Taviano said.

"I like it. Very remote. It has a full basement. Two office spaces. The other office is nearly as nice as this one. The property itself is a little over eighteen acres."

"You ever find yourself a woman, you'll have it made," Elie said, testing the waters.

Dario shrugged, his expression unreadable. "Never brought a woman here. Never needed to. Don't like anyone knowing the layout of my home. If I find a woman, she'll be safe here from everyone but me."

"She'll be safe from you," Elie said. "You find a woman and you know there's only the one, then you don't chance losing that."

"Should have said, she knows she's safe from everyone else. Don't want her to think she's safe from me. She's going to learn to do what she's told if she's mine. Can't live any other way and survive."

Elie heard the honesty in Dario's voice. There was a reason for his house to be beyond neat, with everything in its place. Dario was one of the few men Elie would not want to get a "kill" order on. Not just because he genuinely liked him and considered him family, but because he was one of the few men he might have trouble actually killing.

"You don't have to worry about her, Taviano," Dario continued. He stared out over the lake, no expression on his face or in his voice. "I can see by that look you think it's not a good idea for a woman to hook up with me. I don't think it's a good idea, either. The chances of me finding one I'm compatible with and would actually want in my life are close to zero. The chances she'd want to be in my life are even less." A faint smile lit the darkness in his eyes for a brief moment. "Then I have that interfering sister of yours. She'd bring my chances down to zero for certain."

"Emmanuelle wants to find you someone," Elie said. "She's keeping her eye open."

"Yeah, Valentino told me, but she looks in all the wrong places. She's not going to find a woman for me in a church."

Taviano burst out laughing. "Emme doesn't look in a church for women for you. No way."

"She might as well be looking there."

Elie had to laugh, too. "If she's looking, Dario, beware. She's a determined matchmaker."

"She doesn't like my dating apps. I keep them to annoy her."

"You show them to her every chance you get, Dario," Elie accused. "Emme has shared some of the worst ones with me. Those women are crazy."

"I know. I only let her see the really insane ones." Dario sounded happier than Elie had ever heard him, which made Taviano laugh all over again.

"You're good for my sister."

Dario turned away from the railing to look at Emmanuelle's brother. "Emme's good for us. For Val and me. She changed our lives just by being who she is."

Taviano nodded as he started back inside. "I know what you mean. She's Emme, Dario."

Elie knew what Taviano meant. He loved her, too. It was impossible not to. He wanted Emmanuelle to extend her magic to Brielle so she'd feel the acceptance of the entire Ferraro family the way he did—the way Val and Dario did.

"How long do you think this will take?" Giovanni asked as the three went back inside the office.

Dario closed the double doors and locked them. Elie watched him as he scanned the lake and boats carefully before turning back to those inside. He was always alert. He opened a panel, pressed a button and, outside, screens dropped down over all the windows. Those screens were see-through from inside the house but reflected light back toward the lake, making it impossible to see into the house. Still, Dario positioned his body between the windows and Valentino, remaining standing when most of the others were already seated. Dario was casual about it, never calling attention to himself, nearly fading into the background, something Elie would have thought impossible when so much light was pouring into the room from all the windows.

"I assigned them complex searches, one of which involves gaining access to finance books we've been wanting to look into. Those books will require tremendous skills and finesse to access. Obviously, if they get caught, they lose immediately," Stefano said. "There are three separate searches involving a crime that was committed. In each case the investigators were given the basic facts. They have to establish whether the crime was real, who was guilty, and if the party reporting the crime had a hidden agenda. The last search is on a crime family in

Los Angeles. We needed more information on them. We want to see who comes up with the most information the fastest."

"You don't think your investigators are going to have an advantage with two people versus one?" Valentino asked.

"Bernado really isn't in the hot seat, Val," Stefano said. "I wasn't planning on making this into a betting opportunity. That was Giovanni's idea, and you and Dario went along with it."

"Pitting Brielle against two sets of investigators who will be able to work twice as fast together hardly seems a fair test," Emmanuelle said.

"Yet you chose to put your money on Brielle," Ricco pointed out.

Phones began to light up throughout the room. Stefano frowned down as he read the incoming report. There was silence as each of them read the report thoroughly, going over and over it several times. Elie couldn't help the grin.

"Yeah," Emmanuelle said. "This is why I put my money on Brielle."

Their phones lit up again and right behind that alert came another. Rigina and Rosina and then Bernado checked in, sending their reports quickly followed by Romano and Renato. Again, silence descended on the room while everyone read the reports. This was the one on the books, finances Stefano's family was looking into. Each wanted to see how detailed the reports were. The win wasn't going to be based just on who was the fastest, but who had the most information and how accurate that information was.

Giovanni sighed as he stood and walked over to the white board. "Definitely a win for Brielle. Her report was accurate and had more details than the others. There were no red flags raised that our watchers could see."

"She was lightning fast on the financials," Val observed, with a quick look at Dario. "That's Bernado's forte. He does love to get into books."

Dario shrugged. "He did say he spends too much time looking around when he should get in and get out. That may have cost him."

Two hours later, their phones were lighting up again. This time, Rigina and Rosina sent in the first report on the criminal investigation, followed closely by Romano and Renato. The reports were concise and easy to read, both stating the crime had been committed. The one accused was indeed guilty, but the person bringing the plea for justice warranted deeper investigation. Bernado checked in next with exactly the same report. Brielle followed about ten minutes later. Her report was also concise. The crime had been committed. The accused was guilty. The person bringing the plea for justice not only was involved, but had plotted the murder and paid the guilty party for carrying out the murder. He had hired the defense attorney to get the guilty party off in order to ensure his silence, but he wanted him dead. She had evidence to back up her report.

Giovanni sighed. "The investigators would have gotten it right. Bernado would have as well. We can't fault Brielle for taking the time to actually do the work thoroughly."

"She came in dead last," Taviano pointed out.

"True," Stefano said, "but her report was thorough and complete. She has to be given the win."

"I don't know," Ricco argued. "All the others agreed the one bringing us the case needed more investigation. We didn't specify how much time was to be spent on each segment of the research."

Elie didn't weigh in. As far as he was concerned, his woman beat the others, hands down. He noticed Dario and Val weren't saying anything, either. They didn't care about the money being wagered; not that the Ferraros did, either. Dario and Val wanted to snatch Brielle up for her computer skills. Both men were looking at Stefano. He would recognize what an asset she would be. They would know it. They wanted to ensure they got to Brielle before Stefano had a chance to offer her a job. There was satisfaction in knowing they would come to her, not the other way around.

"You have to be fair," Vittorio said. "She went the distance.

She's a rider. She knows how important it is to have all the information. She wouldn't stop until she had it all."

"Rigina and Rosina know. That's their job. Same with Romano and Renato," Ricco pointed out. "They plainly clarified that it warranted more investigation."

Elie thought about what Vittorio had said. He was right, Brielle was a rider, but was that the reason she kept going when others stopped? He didn't think so. She had a gift. Her gift would drive her to continue, to follow the lead until she had the answers. He remained silent, even when Dario shot him a look expecting him to stand up for Brielle.

Elie didn't want to call attention to her gift. That was hers. He didn't understand how it worked. He wanted to know, but then he wanted to know everything about her. She intrigued him. They'd had two weeks alone together and it hadn't been nearly enough time. He didn't want to go back to work and leave her by herself in their home, even with personal protectors watching over her, as they were now. He'd been reluctant to agree to meet the others at Dario's home while she stayed behind to meet the challenge of who was fastest with a keyboard.

He had to resist the urge to send her a message, just to tell her he was proud of her. Had her parents even one time told her that? He was certain they hadn't. She'd spent a lot of time alone, reinventing her life, trying to make herself into someone confident after he'd contributed to tearing her down with his ridiculous and cruel remarks about her looks. The really insane thing was, he preferred her body type to the thin models he always dated. He had never wanted to take the chance of falling in love so he dated the complete opposite of who he was attracted to.

To distract himself, he paced around Dario's office, feeling a little like a caged animal. He preferred high ceilings and rooms that didn't have defined walls. He liked space, lots of it.

"Are you worried about her?" Emmanuelle asked softly, coming up beside him.

Over the last few years, Emme had become more than just his best friend. She was definitely the sibling he'd never had. They confided in each other and often talked over the things they most worried about. Elie was grateful that Val accepted him into their lives the way he did. He could as easily have insisted Emmanuelle put distance between them, although, knowing Emme, if Val had done that, she would have balked and more than likely walked away before she was married. She wasn't a woman to be told what to do.

"I don't like being away from her right now," Elie admitted. "I don't know if it's because someone clearly tried to kill her, or if I feel she needs reassurance that I want to be married to her."

"What's up with her family?"

"Her mother is dead, not that it would matter as far as anyone treating her better. Her parents wanted one child and when Fayette, her older sister, was born, she was declared a princess and then treated that way. No one was better or ever would be. From that day, they were devoted to giving her everything she could ever want to the point of driving them to the poorhouse. Fayette was so spoiled, she didn't care."

Emmanuelle nodded. "I've seen a few girls like that. They became so entitled, they didn't care if their entire family was drowning so long as they got everything they wanted."

"That's Fayette. She was groomed to be the wife of an Archambault. They studied my family and began to teach her everything they thought she should know in order to become compatible with one of the riders. They hired tutors and bought her clothes. Took her to the theater and had her run in social circles far above their own. She developed a habit of lying and they went along with it even though they had to have known she wasn't telling them the truth. She was a terrible rider because she was lazy and didn't want to work. She argued with the trainers. She believed she would marry an Archambault so why bother?"

"She doesn't sound like a nice person."

"Believe me, she isn't. Can you imagine someone like that

for a sister? When Brielle was born, she was unwanted from the beginning and raised to serve those in the household. She was made to work, bring the money home and provide Fayette with whatever she needed or wanted. Nothing Brielle did was good enough. She was told she wasn't good-looking."

Emmanuelle gasped. "Elie, she's gorgeous."

"I think so, and you do, but Brielle had a lifetime of her parents and sister telling her she was overweight and had a million other flaws. It's difficult to overcome that. Then I come along and hurl insults about her, which only added to her feelings of insecurity." There was pure regret in his voice. He didn't bother to hide it. Not from Emme. "I want her to feel welcomed by Stefano and your brothers, the way they welcomed me. I need for the women in the family to accept her and make her feel a part of them."

Emmanuelle smiled up at him. "I think we can do that, Elie."

Valentino came up behind her, sliding his arms around her waist. "We can do what, princess?" He nuzzled the top of her head with his chin.

Dario came up on the other side of her. "What have you committed us to now, *sorellina*?"

Elie had never heard Dario refer to Emme as *baby sister* before, nor had he heard the affection so blatant in his voice.

"Making certain Brielle feels a sense of family from all of us. Ferraros and Saldis."

"We can do that," Val said instantly. "Elie, no worries on that score. Brielle's your wife. That makes her family. I'm sure Stefano feels the same way."

Dario gave an exaggerated sigh. "Don't agree so fast, Val. Emme's going to have an ally. The other women stay out of our business. Elie's the only one who sticks his nose where it doesn't belong all the time, so much so, we had to make him an honorary Saldi just like the fuckin' Ferraros made him an honorary Ferraro. That means Brielle's going to be a pain in the ass right along with Emme."

Elie wasn't certain how to feel about Dario giving him a

bad time in that voice with absolutely no inflection. Dario rarely teased anyone, only Val and Emme, but somehow he'd managed to make it into that rare inner circle. He forced himself to keep a straight face when he wanted to break out into a huge smile.

"Brielle is a pain. She's got a lot of sass," Elie had to admit.

"As bad as Emmanuelle?" Valentino asked.

"Oh, yeah. Putting the two of them together might be courting disaster," Elie said.

Dario sighed. "I knew it. Anytime it seems as if Emme is doing some good deed, take another hard look at it, because she has an ulterior motive and you're bound to be the loser. Two of them will only double our chances of getting in harm's way."

Emmanuelle dusted her fingernails on her sleeve. "Nice to know you fear me, Dario, and you should be afraid."

Valentino burst out laughing. "You walked into that one, Dario."

"I guess I did." Dario gave Elie a faint grin as if he couldn't care less that Emmanuelle had gotten the better of him. "We'll take care of your wife, make her feel part of the family," he assured him.

Elie nodded, not certain what to say. Had Valentino reassured him, his response would have been easy, but Dario wasn't a man to include others in his circle, so having him suddenly admit Elie was part of those he considered "his" mattered. That put Brielle under Dario and Valentino's protection as well. That was huge.

"I love these floors, Dario," Emme said. "What kind of wood is this, or do you even know?"

That was Emmanuelle, causing a distraction when it was needed.

"Mahogany, you little snip. Are you implying I don't know everything there is to know about the house I bought?"

"I don't know why, Dario, but it didn't occur to me that you would be that interested in actual things like what the floor is

made out of. I knew you would know everything there was to know about entrances and exits and how the sun hits the house at what hour for security reasons," Emmanuelle confessed, "but things like whether you had granite countertops or mahogany floors is beyond anything I expected you to know. I don't know that kind of stuff about my own house."

Dario nudged her with his shoulder. "Yeah, well, babe, you know where the cutting boards are in the kitchen and I don't."

She burst out laughing. "You know exactly where they are. You know where everything is."

Elie loved her for her honesty. She really didn't know anything about floors and countertops and she readily admitted it after teasing Dario.

"The property came up for sale a few years back," Dario admitted. "Long before the break between Giuseppi and his brother Miceli. I bought it, but never moved into it. The house is a little over five thousand square feet. I renovated it, adding several security measures. There's a full basement, which was a huge draw for me. The three-car garage and boathouse were also something I could tie into security as well as the steel barn. At one time, the property was used as an operational lavender farm."

"That's why all the lavender," Emmanuelle said.

Dario nodded. "I snapped it up when it came on the market. It was right next to Val's property and you just never find a place like this one for sale on the lake. It's a long way outside of the city, but in order to keep you and Val safe, I have to be close anyway. Since he insisted on my taking this bullshit position in the family, taking over the territory, I needed a place close to you, so I could still eat with you and see to your security, but get away when you're driving me crazy."

Once more, Dario managed to sound annoyed with Emmanuelle, but Elie would never believe that tone again. He was coming to understand Dario.

Valentino heaved a sigh. "You need a housekeeper who will cook for you. You have a kickass kitchen."

"I have a cleaning crew. That's enough of an invasion. Emme can cook for me."

"You aren't my head of security. You have a huge territory to run."

"I'll always be your head of security. Your personal protectors will answer to me." Dario sounded bored.

Val's intense green eyes met Elie's over Emme's head. Val shook his head. "He's never going to change. He's got an entire territory to run, the one Miceli screwed up. He's putting it back together, finding out who he can trust and who he can't, but he's worried about my security, not his own. Do you have any idea how many death threats you get on the daily, Dario?"

Dario shrugged, his normal answer to anything he didn't want to answer aloud.

"Are you running these down, Emmanuelle?" Elie asked. "If you need help, when I'm not on the roster, I'll be more than happy to help."

"Would you? Val and Dario seem to inspire quite a lot of death threats, especially now that they've taken over running the businesses. Everyone knows they're close."

"Emmanuelle," Valentino cautioned.

She pushed away from him. "I'm head of *both* your security. Don't give me any trouble. I could use Elie's help."

"Elie isn't the point. Dario and I told you, until we know who is behind the threats . . ."

Phones began to go off, saving Emme from her husband's lecture, which she clearly was going to ignore anyway. Elie glanced down to see Brielle had sent in her last report. This was the information on the criminal family in Los Angeles that Stefano had requested.

Stefano had appeared to randomly choose one of the crime families to gather specific data on, but in actuality, Emmanuelle had requested Stefano to choose the Colombo family. She wanted them investigated, but she didn't want to ask Bernado to investigate. She knew he would immediately tell Val and Dario she had put in the request. She wanted her own investigator, one that was loyal to her. One she could

count on to report to her first, not Val or Dario. She wanted Brielle.

She'd been careful not to ask for specific information relating to anything that would tip her husband or Dario off that she suspected the Colombo family had anything to do with a number of the recent threats against them. This was more of a probe for data concerning how to gain entry into their lives, homes and places of businesses as well as their favorite places to eat. She had been very careful not to ask for anything connecting them to the Chicago business.

Brielle's report, as before, was very thorough. Elie read it over carefully, with a sense of alarm. There was an underlying impression he got that Brielle had delved deeper than she had been instructed to go, which shouldn't have surprised him. She hadn't included anything in the report that hadn't been asked for, but he had a gut feeling she might know more about the Colombo crime family than was good for her. Maybe it wasn't such a good idea for her to be an investigator for Dario and Valentino. His gut, as a rule, usually saved his ass.

The phones began to light up all over the place, as report after report came in, one after the other. There was satisfaction in knowing that his wife had been first, thorough and every bit as good as she'd said.

"Not bragging, Vittorio," he murmured. "But it looks like my wife kicked ass." He grinned at the others. "I'm heading home. You can transfer my winnings into my account. I believe I'm sharing with Dario and Emme."

CHAPTER NINE

Brielle frowned at her computer screen, pushing aside the small bowl of grapes she'd brought up from the kitchen once she'd finished the "test" that Stefano had devised for her. He'd pitted her against the other investigators. She had no idea how she did, and right at that moment, she didn't care. One of the crazy compulsions she couldn't ignore was fully on her. When it happened, she couldn't eat or sleep until she followed it all the way to the end.

She had a feeling about the Colombo crime family in Los Angeles. There had been a reason that particular family had been singled out. Stefano had indicated he'd chosen them at random and he'd made it very clear that none of the investigators were to go beyond what he'd specified in their searches. Just the fact that he'd made that one of the rules set off alarms in her head.

She stared at the screen and the information she'd dug up. Alfredo Colombo, the head of the Los Angeles crime family, was in his sixties. He and his wife, Bianca, had been together for over forty years in an arranged marriage that seemed to

work out, although he cheated on her. Dino, his oldest son, was forty and married. Jerico was thirty-three and still a bachelor. Alfredo's daughter, Elisa, was twenty-eight and married with three children. Like her parents, hers had been an arranged marriage. Alfredo's youngest son, Mano, was twenty-three years old and single.

The three sons worked in the family business. The daughter's marriage to a man with a large territory in Los Angeles had solidified an alliance between the two families. Or at least that was what the marriage *appeared* to have done. Brielle knew appearances could be deceiving.

She typed in several commands that got her nowhere and sat thinking, wondering why she couldn't let it go. Something just seemed "off" to her. She knew quite a bit about each member of the family now. What they liked to eat, and what they were allergic to. What their favorite sports were. She knew the entire layout of each of their homes. The list went on and on. She knew too much about each of them.

She sat back in her chair, looking around her at the spacious office. She wasn't certain she would really call this room an office. It was the most extravagant office she'd ever been in. Just like the rest of the house, the office was all hardwood floors, rustic beams and walls of windows overlooking spectacular lake views. She envisioned adding a thick, plush pile rug she could curl her toes in on cold winter days. Already, Elie's house felt like home to her.

Brielle stood up to stretch and wandered across the gleaming floor to the thick windows to stare out to the lake below her. The lake had a strong chop today. Brielle watched two small powerboats bobbing up and down on the swells as they crossed the lake in the distance. She frowned as she watched them plowing through the waves. Something nagged at her, something to do with the boats.

Going back to her laptop, she sank back down into her very comfortable chair and switched her gaze to the stone fireplace. Like the fireplace in the great room, it was also gas rather than wood burning. She brought up the latest information on the last

Colombo family member she'd been working on in Los Angeles. Dino Colombo. He ran the business in the harbor.

Los Angeles. The port. She tapped her finger on her lower lip and once more looked out to the boats as they moved farther away from the house across the expanse of choppy water. In New York's Santoro crime family, the oldest son, Carlo, also ran the business in the harbor. In Barcelona, where she had first begun to suspect the existence of an active human trafficking ring because of all the missing children and teens, there was also a port.

"A tie-in with ports," she murmured aloud. "What about the freighters? The Santoro family ultimately owns them. They clearly are shipping to smaller ports like the ones here on Lake Michigan, but what are they shipping to the larger ports? Or are the larger ports, like Barcelona, supplying and then off-loading to smaller ports? What other smaller ports would they be using?"

She stared at her screen for a few more minutes and then leapt up to pace across the hardwood floor to the window. Outside, the sky began to appear troubled with dark clouds forming over the choppy waters. The clouds appeared blue and a deep purple, with breakout orange as the sun set dramatically, streaking red-orange beneath the clouds and reflecting on the water and sand.

Waves raced in angry succession toward the shore, rolling over before reaching the sand, the force creating loud slaps as the water folded over on itself. The wind hit the long stalks of grass growing along the shore, rushing through them so they bowed, first one way and then the next, a carpet of dancing green.

She was on the verge of a major discovery. She could feel it, that same buildup of tension in her stomach as she saw reflected outside in the churning water of the lake. Out of all the crime families to choose from, why had Stefano chosen the Colombo family to be investigated? He could have chosen gangs. Or bookies. Anyone in the world. Why them?

Brielle rushed back to her laptop to break into Dino Colombo's private email account. She didn't expect to find anything incriminating there. He wasn't an idiot. In fact, by all accounts, he was a very intelligent man. She'd taken a look at the ledgers kept on port business and they appeared to be in order. She wasn't going to get anywhere fast by going through his books. *But* . . . she knew from looking at his correspondence that she would find a way into his computer. That was all she needed. A way in.

He was a wine connoisseur—or thought he was. He had a buyer who regularly sent him offers for his favorites. One such offer was already in his mailbox unopened. She appropriated the email, attached her program to it quickly and replaced it, knowing Dino would open it because he opened every single one of the emails sent from that buyer. She had only to wait. Antsy now that she knew she was so close, she logged off and set her laptop aside.

She needed to do some stretches and run on the treadmill for a short while, then find more fruit to snack on. Hopefully, when she came back, she'd be in. She glanced out the window at the lake and the beautiful, brooding sky one last time as she retreated. Just inside the door, she stopped abruptly. The two boats she'd been watching earlier were racing across the waves, this time coming straight toward the back of the house to the two piers.

The boats didn't look as if they were having any trouble handling the crashing waves and the choppy water was far rougher than it had been earlier. Without hesitation, she raced out of the office, pulling out her cell phone and hitting Elie's name as she ran. He picked up right away. She continued down the stairs, taking two at time.

"Elie, two boats coming this way fast. I don't like the look of it. Heading down to get the guards inside."

"I'll warn them, you stay inside."

"Already headed out back," she said. She was at the hall entryway. She knew one guard had stationed himself out

back and she was going there first. "Warn the front guard." She hung up on Elie and texted the guard out back to get inside even as she ran to the kitchen to exit that way, calling to him.

She yanked open the door, and the guard—a younger cousin of the Ferraro family named Leone Palagonia—shoved her back as the sound of gunfire erupted. He had his back to her and he returned fire. She yanked on his jacket, pulling him into the kitchen and slamming the door closed. Immediately she hit the security lock that dropped into place all the plates that supposedly protected the windows and doors from bullets and blasts.

Brielle turned and ran toward the front entrance, where Raimondo Abatangelo, another younger cousin of the Ferraro family, was assigned to guard her. He was already in the house and coming toward her. His gaze moved over her quickly and then to his cousin. Relief flashed over his face and then was gone.

"Elie doesn't want us to do anything unless they manage to get into the house. He's very certain that won't happen, but he'd like you to go to the safe room, Brielle," Leone said.

Brielle gave him her fiercest scowl. "I'm a rider, Leone. I can step into a shadow and I'll be gone. You're in far more danger than I am. I want to see who we're facing, not act like some fainting damsel in distress."

Raimondo coughed into his elbow and exchanged a quick look with Leone, who turned his head away, but not before she caught the faint grin he exchanged with his cousin. Her phone growled at her. If she didn't answer the growl, it would turn into a roar. She'd programmed that to be the ringtone for Elie's text messages because he reminded her of a saber-toothed tiger sometimes. Or a caveman.

She glanced down to read his message. You aren't in the safe room, are you?

She counted to ten before she answered. A slow ten. Not yet. I want to get a good look at these jokers first. You said the house is secure and I believe you. I'm getting a picture for you.

Leone and Raimondo will protect me. That was a line of crap. She intended to protect them.

Sheesh. She knew all riders were assigned personal protectors. Leone and Raimondo were Stefano's first cousins. They were sweet, too. Both of them. She liked them, even though she felt it was silly to waste either one of them on her. She'd been told in no uncertain terms she wasn't going to be utilized as a rider. That meant the Ferraros should free up these men to protect other shadow riders.

If Elie really insisted she needed a bodyguard, she'd accept one, but not one of Stefano's elite guards. That was just plain silly. And a waste. Besides, Leone and Raimondo were just too sweet to be put in a position of taking a bullet for her. She wasn't at all comfortable with that.

The tiger growled again. Somehow the sound managed to be increasingly scary. I'm on the way. Val and Dario are as well. We can get all the photographs and information necessary ourselves. They've called for a cleaning crew. Wouldn't want anyone to shoot the wrong person. Stefano is informing Leone and Raimondo now, giving them instructions.

She wanted to do her own growling. She should be able to give her personal protectors instructions, not someone off the premises. How would Stefano know what to do when he isn't even here?

Brielle clenched her teeth as she made her way back into the kitchen, ignoring Leone's call to her. If they were going to insist she go to a safe room, she wasn't going to make it easy on them, at least not until she had her picture and her laptop. Neither man wanted to put his hands on her. That was a distinct disadvantage to them. She could have stepped into a shadow and she would have gotten away with anything, but she was willing to play fair as long as she could.

"What the hell, Brielle?" Raimondo demanded. "You need to stay away from there."

"I'm getting a few pictures and then my laptop. I can figure out who they are, Rai. That's what I do." She kept her voice

calm and decisive. "It will only take a few seconds. Then I'll head to the safe room and you can lock me in if it makes you feel better."

"It will keep Elie from beating the shit out of us," Leone said.

"Well, don't slow me down then," Brielle said. "And just so you know, Elie isn't really as mean as he likes everyone to think he is."

She moved through the spacious kitchen with its hardwood floors, white cabinets, white marble counters and the double sliding glass doors surrounded by rustic wood that matched the overhead hand-hewn beams. Outside, on the patio, two five-man teams were in the act of consulting with their team leaders in an effort to find a way through the house's defenses.

"They obviously thought, with so much glass, it would be easier to gain entry," Leone said. "The man in the blue is the team leader. He's got a layout of the house." He fit binoculars to his eyes to bring the document closer. "It's newer, looks like they bribed someone Elie paid to make changes."

"He wouldn't have shown security changes," Raimondo declared. "Emilio and our crews handled all of that. Whatever printout he has doesn't show anything of use to him."

"It shows enough," Brielle contradicted. "He had the safe room built downstairs off the master bedroom and another one upstairs. He also created space in between the walls. That was done by carpenters. Whoever took that money for the blueprints knew the location of the safe rooms."

"She's right about that," Leone admitted. He immediately sent the information to Elie. "Who would be stupid enough to cross the Ferraro family, the Saldis and Dario Bosco?"

Brielle took as many photographs as she could, zooming in to get the individual faces as clearly as possible. At first, the men weren't aware of being observed because the three of them were hanging back in the shadows of the kitchen. Once one of the men noticed them, one of the team leaders walked right up to the sliding glass door, took out a gun and

held it up to the height of Brielle's forehead. He pulled the trigger repeatedly.

She smiled at him, held her phone up and snapped his photograph repeatedly. Then she sent the picture to every Ferraro she knew before sending it to Elie, Val and Dario. She held up her phone to show a picture of Stefano walking her down the aisle to Elie and she smiled again, pointed to the shooter and made the age-old gesture of someone cutting a throat—namely his.

Once she was done, Brielle turned and walked out of the kitchen. "I'll just be a minute. I'm running upstairs to get my laptop. Even if they know where the safe room is and they break into the house, I would assume they can't get into it, right? Or would I be safer in a shadow?"

Leone texted Elie immediately, frowning as he and Raimondo closed ranks behind her, so none of the would-be assassins could even think of getting a shot at Brielle. She shook her head, but kept walking around the long counter that would take her out of sight of the sliding glass doors.

"Do you think the picture of me with Stefano scared him a little bit?"

"It should. I'd be afraid of messing with Ferraros. Everyone knows that's a death sentence. They just don't understand how it happens," Raimondo said.

"The Archambaults are the acknowledged fastest and deadliest riders in the world," Brielle said. "I don't understand why they aren't feared throughout the world in the same way the Ferraros are. It's never made sense to me. None of the other families are as feared as the Ferraros."

Leone shrugged. "You'd have to ask the council that question. Or Stefano. Even Elie might be able to tell you. I certainly can't. I do know outsiders are afraid of the Ferraros because they believe them to be a crime family, they just don't understand how they work. Only that if you cross them, you don't live through it."

Once back in the office, Brielle sent another message to Elie. She didn't want to take her equipment apart if she didn't

need to. I sent pictures to your phone. I sent the team leader to Stefano, his brothers and M as well as Val and Dario, just to warn him we had friends.

Am outside now. M's with me. Val and Dario are nearly here. They're coming through a private drive unseen. We asked the Ferraros to pass on this one.

Brielle's heart jumped. She left her laptop on her desk and went to the huge glass wall overlooking the lake to look down at the patio below. The intruders had spread out. Most had donned climbing gear and were moving around to various positions, clearly planning to scale the outside walls.

She paid attention to the way the shadows fell across the grass. The large ominous cloud had grown, throwing a dark, brooding mass of purple and blue into the sky. Shadows fell across the grasses on the shore and the rolling lawn leading to the patio, striping it in places and putting blotches in others. One of the stripes led straight to an intruder as he stepped close to the stone fireplace. He placed one hand on it and then a foot. A figure much shorter than he was shimmered to life directly behind him. Emmanuelle raised her arms, her hands catching him perfectly on his jaw and skull as she snapped his neck. She lowered his body to the ground and was gone.

At the same time, not more than six feet away, a much taller shadow emerged from the closed umbrella's shadow on the patio. He was directly behind a second intruder, his hands already in position, snapping the neck and lowering him to the ground. Between Emmanuelle and Elie, it took under two minutes to dispatch eight of the ten men. They were like machines, Elie moving so fast, he was a blur. Brielle had never seen an Archambault in action and it was amazing to watch. She could barely see him as he moved from his target to the shadow and out again. Some of the time, she didn't actually spot him until the body dropped.

The two team leaders were the only ones spared. Brielle had identified the first one wearing blue. The second one wore an identical shirt in the same color of deep blue. When the two men realized their team members were lying on the

patio instead of climbing up the side of the house behind them, they rappelled down and ran toward the pier, where their boats were tied.

Valentino and Dario stood between them and their intended getaway. With the two crime bosses stood the men who insisted on protecting them.

"I suggest you drop your weapons, gentlemen," Val said, his voice low and smooth.

Both men did so immediately. Brielle watched as Val's and Dario's guards took possession of the guns and then, not very politely, took the men to the ground and did a very thorough search for more weapons. Once they were certain they had secured the intruders' arsenal, they secured their captives' hands behind their backs and yanked them up, directing them none too gently toward the corner of the house, where she could no longer see them.

Brielle assumed the prisoners were taken to a car parked out of her sight, near the private drive between the two homes. She made a note to inspect it the first chance she got in the morning. Right now, there was nothing she could do. Leone and Raimondo had already gone downstairs.

Waking her laptop, she brought up Dino Colombo's email. A surge of adrenaline swept through her. He'd taken the bait and opened the email from his wine buyer. Her little program allowed her to worm her way into his computer and look around his hard drive without tripping his firewalls.

Having done so many of these searches before, she knew to wait until her body's responses calmed so she could follow her natural reaction. There was a small bar in the office with a refrigerator stocked with her favorite mineral water. That little detail had been in the many things she had been asked to include in the sheets of personal information she had sent when she'd written to the man she had been matched with. She had been a little shocked that he cared enough to supply the fridge with the water she preferred.

Once she had settled, she began to search Dino's computer, allowing her brain and fingers to connect in the way

they did, not conscious thought so much as a flowing path that led her to the information she was seeking. If she overthought things, or tried to put herself too much in the way, it always took her far longer to get answers. But letting that natural connection flow through her seemed to always get her to the results she needed.

Unlike most of the men she investigated, Dino didn't have tons of porn on his computer. He didn't appear to have a mistress. He sent little notes to his wife often, as well as gifts. Brielle took a sip of water when she felt the familiar jolt that led her to open the little file with the interesting name. It appeared to be a playlist of songs. **Friends in Low Places.**

Her heart gave a little jump. There were four pictures there. Valentino. Dario. Elie. And one of her. That was all. No text. Just the four pictures. She brought up Elie's photograph as she took another sip of water and sat back in her chair to study it. Where had it been taken? She could trace it back and also find who originally sent it to Dino.

"Nice picture, baby."

Elie's voice nearly made her jump out of her skin. She hadn't even heard him come in. That was one of the things that made her a lousy shadow rider. She should be aware of her surroundings at all times, but she got so deep into her investigations, she was in another world.

"I didn't hear you come in."

"I noticed. What are you doing?"

There was no censure in his voice. It was that same low, almost caressing tone, the one that brushed over her skin like velvet, but she got the feeling she was in trouble.

"Following up on the Colombo family. I just had this feeling about them when I was investigating them. Sometimes that happens." She couldn't stop the eagerness that crept into her tone. "There's a connection between Barcelona, New York and Los Angeles, Elie, and the way they're using the freighters out at sea and then bringing them into smaller ports." The words tumbled over one another, a bad habit when she was

trying to explain something and she was certain the other person wouldn't listen to her.

Elie swept her hair off her left shoulder and pressed a kiss to her neck. "We need to get you a large whiteboard in here so you can connect all the dots for me."

Her breath left her lungs in a long rush. He wasn't arguing with her or dismissing her. That felt good.

"Why do you have my picture on the screen?"

"I found your picture, Valentino's and Dario's in a file on Dino Colombo's computer." She didn't mention hers, but then, she didn't lie. "I was just about to backtrack and find out who sent the pictures. Whoever did was most likely behind ordering the hits on the three of you. If not them, I'll keep going until I find out who."

"Is there a danger to you? Will he be able to find you?"

Elie rested one hand on the desk right next to her laptop. She had the feeling he would shut down her computer in an instant if she told him Dino could find her.

"I have warnings set up and would know the moment someone was aware I was in their computer or if anyone was hunting me." She used her most confident voice, mostly because she was confident. She knew what she was doing and she always took precautions. No matter how excited she was, or how close she was to her target, she never skimped on safety. She had to admit, she was far better on the computer than as a shadow rider.

"You hungry?"

She hadn't given food a thought. "I've been eating fruit."

"A few grapes are not what I'm talking about. I'll make us sandwiches and bring them up. By then, maybe you'll know a little more. Leone and Raimondo can bring up the whiteboard while I'm getting us dinner. Then I'll send everyone home and lock up the house."

"Val and Dario took those men with them." She made it a statement, but she kept her gaze locked with Elie's.

He nodded. "They had a few questions. They weren't here

to kill me, Brielle. They were here to kill you. The bomb was sent here to kill you. Val and Dario are very good at extracting answers from reluctant men. If they don't get what they want, I'll join them and I'll get the answers, because no one is going to kill my wife."

She liked the emphasis he placed on that so she just nodded and watched the way he walked out. He reminded her so much of a large predatory cat stalking through a jungle. Turning back to her screen, she began to search for the original sender of the photograph as well as who took it.

She barely noticed when Leone and Raimondo came and went, too busy writing in a separate document her findings and then doing the same with the pictures of Valentino and Dario, just to be certain. She closed the file titled **Friends in Low Places** and began a search for anything that looked like it could be similar.

Brielle found a second file that easily could have been a playlist. **Hear Me Roar.** Seriously? That didn't quite mesh with Dino Colombo. She opened the file and once again her heart gave a little jolt.

These were one-line texts. **Erase # heart emoji.**
Erase # female French bulldog male French bulldog.
Erase # devil fighter

Again, she sank back in her chair and took a sip of water. Someone had issued the order to kill the four of them. *All* four of them. That meant that her investigation in Barcelona hadn't been separate from Valentino's and Dario's initial one in the United States. She'd just started in a different place. She would have to tell Elie the truth, that she'd found her picture in that file as well. He wouldn't be happy with her for not confessing it immediately.

She sighed, printed out the text file and closed it and did a search for another file that contained any similar title. **When the Ships Come In.**

The moment she saw the title, she got that spark of electricity that zinged like lightning through her veins. She knew immediately what she would find. This was what she'd been

looking for all along. Sure enough, it was all there. Times. Dates. Transfers from one freighter to another and the coordinates where the transfers would take place. She had the names of the freighters and the ports they originated from.

Trying to still the trembling in her body, she pressed print. It was going to take a while. A long while. There were pages and pages of data. She went in reverse order, just in case, the latest to the oldest. Elie would want to know when the freighters would be coming to the ports and off-loading any victims and where.

She reached for the bottle of water only to be shocked when Elie's hand got to it first. He unscrewed the cap and handed it to her.

"You hit the jackpot." He indicated the screen.

"I believe I did," she agreed. "He's getting his orders from Riccardo and Carlo Santoro out of New York. Riccardo only chimed in once. All other correspondence has been through Carlo. He sent the pictures of the three of you. Riccardo had to send one of the freighter times when Carlo wasn't available. He mistakenly sent it from his personal email and then copied and pasted it into his 'encrypted' one."

She chewed on the side of her bottom lip before taking another sip of the water, avoiding his eyes.

"You may as well tell me, Brielle. You're going to anyway. The longer you wait, the more agitated you get."

That was true. She didn't know why she felt so guilty holding anything back from him. He was holding things back from her. She was certain he'd gotten news from Val or Dario. Probably from Emmanuelle, telling him things the two prisoners had coughed up. It was early, but she had studied Dario. He looked as if he could take apart a man and put him back together with his arms and legs on backward if he wanted to. If he was interrogating her, she'd tell him everything he wanted to know before he even started torturing her.

"Dino had four photographs in the file titled 'Friends in Low Places.' I was the fourth photograph."

Brielle raised her gaze to Elie's. His expression was utterly

inscrutable. He didn't say anything, just kept those dark eyes fixed on her. She sighed.

"He had another file titled 'Hear Me Roar.' I printed it out. Basically, it said to erase the heart, or Valentine. I would guess that would be Valentino. The female French bulldog and the male French bulldog, I would presume that would be us, and the devil fighter. I can only guess that one to be Dario." She indicated the paper in the printer. "I have it for you."

Again, he remained silent. Waiting. He knew she'd traced those photos to their origins. Someone had sent them to Dino in order to identify the targets.

"Santoro provided the photographs of Valentino and Dario. A man by the name of Carmine Catani, who works in Dario's organization, provided the photo of you. I haven't had time to go after him yet, but that's next on my list. I have to keep going on Colombo."

"Are you stalling?"

Brielle shook her head, because she wasn't. Her words were tumbling over one another again. She was talking too fast, trying to tell him everything at once. "My photograph was sent to Carlo Santoro by Izan Serrano. Serrano apparently works for the local mafia *famiglia* in Barcelona. Who knew the Toselli family in Barcelona would have such close ties with New York? Santoro's son, Carlo, is married to Valeria, the daughter of Arnau Toselli of the mafia family in Barcelona. They have two children together."

"You picked the wrong damn city to train in," Elie said.

"I did."

"And then you decide you have to frequent an underground kink club where you meet a man who probably finds women for the trafficking ring. He plays in the club, and sets up a few women to disappear."

"Great. I was one of those women."

Elie shook his head. "No, I don't think you were, Brielle. I think you were *his* woman, the one he wanted for himself and you kept sliding away. He has an ego. Then you investigated the freighters and he's involved with the Toselli family

and they're tied to the extremely powerful family in New York. He had to wonder if you played him."

She chewed on her lower lip. "How could he possibly find out I was investigating the freighters? No one could have found me, Elie. I'm too careful." The printer shut down and she closed the file and backed out of Dino's email. She'd been in it too long. The file had been unexpectedly large.

She put the screen down on her laptop, rising when he held out his hand to her. "I'm serious, Elie, there's no way anyone would have discovered me through my investigation."

Elie indicated the small table for two set up in front of the fireplace. He'd placed their sandwiches on plates and indicated for her to eat. There was a small bowl of fruit she found much more tempting, although her sandwich was an open avocado and cheese, which she usually liked. It was just that she wasn't very hungry. She still had a nagging feeling Elie wasn't very happy with her and that bothered her.

"We're looking into how Izan could have discovered you investigated the freighters, or for that matter, the Santoro family in New York. After the way you performed today on your computer, no one believes you made mistakes, not that I did anyway." He gestured toward her open-faced sandwich. "You don't eat enough to keep a bird alive. Part of a shadow rider's training are the courses given in nutrition. I know they aren't given just to the men. I was trained mainly by Archambaults, but I can't believe the courses would be that much different."

She couldn't help making a face at the sandwich. She would have made it at him, but she was nervous the moment she was alone with him. He had a way about him of taking up an entire room with his presence. She'd always loved the way he could do that, walk in and just by making his entrance fill the room, but living with it was much more difficult than she'd anticipated.

Her body responded to him the moment she saw him. He made her heart beat faster every time she looked at him. Her lungs would burn for lack of air. Her sex clenched and went

damp. She hoped those things never went away. She knew a few of the older shadow rider women would talk of still having such reactions to their partners, and when they spoke of them, their eyes would light up and their faces would take on a glow. That had been her dream. Her dream had always included Elie Archambault.

"Brielle?"

She blinked, bringing him into focus. That was the problem when she was around him. She went off into her fantasy world instead of paying close attention the way she should. She was too over-the-top crazy about him. Two weeks in his company had just made her reactions worse.

"I'm listening." What had he asked her? She scrambled desperately to remember. She was really, really intelligent, but she always looked like such a fool around him. She wanted him to respect her work and yet every chance she had to impress him, she did this kind of thing, went off into her own mind. Oftentimes it was to puzzle out where she was going next in the investigation and other times it was to fantasize over him.

A slow smile lit his eyes. "Eat, *bébé*."

Nutrition classes. That was what he had been going on about. She pushed the sandwich around on the plate. "I did take the nutrition classes, Elie. All of them. Too many if you ask me." She lifted the corner of the toasted melted cheese sandwich to her mouth.

"So, you do know the importance of protein and carbohydrates to keep your stamina up."

She narrowed her eyes at him. "I passed the classes with no problems."

Elie's phone went off and he glanced down. "Cleaners are gone. Leone and Raimondo are taking off along with Ruggero and Lorenzo. We're locked in for the night."

Her heart jumped. She kept her eyes veiled with her lashes as she diligently ate her sandwich.

"Why didn't you tell me you had discovered your photograph along with Val, Dario and mine right away?"

She winced. His voice was casual. Too casual. She risked a quick look at him. There was no expression on his face, but he was watching her closely. She was absolutely certain he could read her like a book.

"I didn't have the answers yet." That was a partial truth. She knew Carlo Santoro had sent the picture to Dino Colombo, but how had Carlo acquired it? She recognized the large plants and pottery in the background of the photograph. The café was one of her favorite haunts. Small, a hidden gem, she studied there when she could. "I wanted to find them before I gave you the report."

He continued looking at her without speaking. She *detested* when he did that. She knew he wouldn't stop until she confessed everything to him. She took a sip of water to wash down the suddenly dry bite of sandwich sticking in her throat. She waited until her heart had settled down and she could swallow easily.

"I knew the investigation Val and Dario started here in the States had to be connected to what I was doing in Barcelona, but it didn't make sense that someone had identified me. You were already very protective. I thought if I could discover who had been the person to send the photograph to Santoro from Barcelona, then I'd be able to figure out how they managed to find out I was onto the freighters and the crime family in New York."

"But you had planned to tell me . . ." He paused. "Eventally."

Her breath left her lungs in a long rush. He wasn't in the least bit happy with her. "I planned to tell you right away, Elie. I *did* tell you right away."

CHAPTER TEN

Elie studied Brielle's face with that curious melting sensation he was becoming familiar with in his chest. All soft, all feminine with her long sweeping lashes, and beautifully shaped lips, yet she had a backbone of steel. He admired and respected her. They needed shadow riders, and by all accounts, she was an extremely good one, but on a keyboard, she had a gift that surpassed anything he'd ever seen. She was a treasure for many, many reasons and she clearly had no idea.

"Your idea of telling me immediately and mine are clearly two different things," he informed her, keeping his tone casual. She didn't need to know how hard he was falling for her yet. Not until he could figure out what she was holding back from him. She'd been growing more and more restless the last two weeks, although he'd felt they'd grown close.

Elie didn't yet know exactly what his wife needed from him, other than reassurance that he wasn't going anywhere. He didn't think words were going to convince her so much as showing her. He needed to figure out the things she needed and give them to her. For the first time in his life, he'd tasted

real terror when he'd seen the two teams of assassins storming his home with the sole purpose of killing his wife.

He had prepared for an attack on the house, but that didn't mean there weren't weak spots in his defenses. Stefano's family had gone over and over the security to find any holes, but there was always some point of entry they might have missed. It had never occurred to him he would be like Stefano was with Francesca, wanting—no, *needing*—to wrap Brielle up in a cocoon of safety, especially so quickly. He only knew he didn't like the fact that she'd been in danger and he hadn't been there to protect her, nor had the precautions necessary to ensure she would stay protected.

"I'm sorry, Elie." Brielle did look remorseful when she put down the second half of her sandwich and widened her vivid green eyes at him.

Her long lashes fluttered and his cock reacted with a hard jerk. The flames from the fireplace flickered and danced on the walls and spread across the hardwood floors so they gleamed lighter in places. The flames created shadows throughout the room so that moving slightly in any direction, just shifting in his chair, would connect the two of them together. It was dangerous to do so when he was already in a heightened state of desire for her.

"I do things in a certain order," she added, a little frown appearing, drawing her eyebrows closer together.

He loved watching the various expressions on her face as she puzzled things out. She fascinated him as no other woman had ever done.

"I have a pattern in the way I do things, Elie, and I suppose I follow it meticulously. When I hunt for information, it's intuitive more than brilliant. I'm not super smart. Quite a few riders have psychic gifts. I believe I have a psychic talent that allows me to hunt for the information I need and that's what makes me good on a keyboard, but I also have to follow where it leads me."

He wanted to lean forward and kiss her earnest little face. *Mon Dieu*, but she was beautiful. His heart felt almost too big

for his chest. His cock certainly pushed too hard against the confines of his trousers.

"I'm not sure how that would stop you from telling me your photograph was there along with ours, Brielle."

Brielle chewed on the side of her bottom lip, one of the habits he was coming to know that indicated she was very nervous. "You, Val and Dario were here in the United States. That meant the source, whoever sent your photographs, was here. The *reason* was also here in the States. I put my photo out of my mind because it didn't matter while I was working on uncovering who had provided the pictures of each of you. Someone had taken them and sent them to someone else before they were given to Dino Colombo. Once I found out Carlo Santoro had sent them to Dino Colombo, then I backtracked the photographs to the origins. I wanted to know who provided them."

That did make sense to him. He could see the way her mind would work, and there was the underlying ring of truth there, but on the other hand, he also heard one small note that was off. She might not even be aware of it, but she was uncomfortable and had been from the moment they had begun talking about her investigation.

"Brielle." He dropped his voice another octave. He had his own gifts. "Look at me. Not around the room. Look at me." He waited until her eyes met his and then he held her gaze. There was trepidation there. Yeah. He was right. She felt guilty. His little woman. He definitely was falling in love fast. He hadn't known he was capable of the real thing. He hadn't even known what the hell it was.

"Are you certain that's the only reason you didn't tell me about the photograph?"

He got the lash flutter. The lip bite. Her gaze didn't shift away, but she swallowed hard. "I don't know. I may have thought about it for a minute and discarded the idea."

They had promised each other honesty and she was giving that to him. "I came in when you had my photograph up. Had you just found the file? Were the other pictures right under it?"

She nodded her head slowly.

"We were talking about it right when you found it, before you had really started your investigation, and then I went downstairs to make us sandwiches."

She moistened her lips with the tip of her tongue and nodded again.

"You don't consider that a lie?"

Fire flashed in her eyes. "Absolutely not. I may have omitted telling you, but I didn't lie. And I had every intention of telling you later and I did, as soon as I tracked down the origins of all the photos. I could have waited until *way* later, but I didn't. You omit telling me all kinds of things, so don't you dare be self-righteous with me about that, Elie. If you get to do things in our marriage, then so do I."

Her chin went up and he couldn't stop himself this time. He leaned over, framed her face with his large hands to hold her still and used his teeth, nipping her soft skin until she yelped, her eyes darkening with a mixture of desire and temper. His tongue soothed the bite and then he kissed it before pulling back.

"I'm not certain now is the best time to defy me, *mon petit jouet sexuel*. We're alone for the night. Locked in. You committed several indiscretions we have yet to discuss, not to mention I was away from you and men determined to kidnap you came to our home. I didn't like the way that made me feel."

At his soft-spoken declaration and him putting her on notice by calling her his little sexual toy, goose bumps rose immediately, and beneath her blouse, her nipples peaked. He had been thinking she needed more than his gentler lovemaking, although she was very responsive every time he touched her. The restlessness she tried to hide was coming from need. From a craving. Just the way she responded to his voice, the way he called her his toy indicating they were about to play a very intense game, meant he was on the right track.

He straightened and indicated her sandwich. "Eat."

She made a face. "I ate half of it. I'll eat the fruit."

He wasn't going to argue. She loved fruit. She seemed to

prefer it for every meal as well as for snacks. He'd managed to get her to eat half her sandwich so he called it a victory. She worked out daily and trained with him just as if she was shadow riding. He was fine with that, preferring her to be ready at all times, just in case she ever needed to escape into the shadows, not to mention protect herself in a fight against an assailant. He just didn't want her workouts and lack of eating to be about fear of gaining weight.

"I don't omit telling you anything, Brielle. You need to ask me when you want to know something. You're a shadow rider, whether you're an active one or not. We made a promise to one another to communicate honestly. I didn't mean that you had to do all the communicating and I could keep things to myself. Do I hope that you don't have to witness certain things such as the torture of a prisoner to extract information that does, in fact, take place? Or that you want to know about it and I have to tell you details? I hope you don't ask me for that, but if you do, I would tell you. You're aware Dario and Val have two prisoners now. They're attempting to shut down a trafficking operation and they aren't above using any means to stop it. Sadly, seeing children in cages and what the traffickers were capable of doing to those unfortunate human beings, I think I'm in agreement with Val and Dario."

Elie didn't look away from her. "I might not be any better than Santoro or Colombo for my decision to stand with Dario and Val, but I can't take having so many children, teens and women taken on the whim of others for money or power or just to use and then kill when they like. It sickens me. As hard as the law enforcement agencies try, they can't seem to shut these people down."

The intense fire in her eyes softened to that admiration and passionate caring she seemed to reserve for him. She didn't realize she gave away so much when she looked at him. She didn't want to care about him, but for some reason she did. He knew it would take time to get an admission out of her, but they had time. He wanted to know everything about her. He had thought he was obsessed with her before; now he

knew what real obsession was. He loved every one of those little expressions chasing across her face and needed to know what each meant.

"You're so compassionate, Elie. I'm ashamed to say I didn't expect that of you, or Val or Dario, either. Dario scares the hell out of me, but I can tell he genuinely cares for Emmanuelle, Valentino and you."

"And Stefano, but he'd rather be boiled in oil than ever admit it," Elie said, strumming his thumb over her soft face.

"Why didn't you tell me about your photograph right away, *bébé*?" Elie asked, keeping his tone gentle, all the while stroking his thumb along her cheekbone and then down to feather the pads of his fingers along her jaw. He slipped the question in while she was feeling safe and open and very loving toward him.

"You were already upset with me for something. I could tell when you came in. I didn't want you to be more upset, and I knew you would be. I thought I could come up with who sent the photograph and maybe even a complete report and you'd be happier. At least, vaguely, in the back of my mind, that's what I was thinking. You came in when I just found them and I was shocked."

He dropped his hands from her face and sat back in his chair to keep from strangling her. "You're not sure why I would be upset that someone sent two teams to our home targeting you for assassination? After already trying and failing to kill you with a suitcase bomb?" There was no way to prevent the edge from creeping into his voice.

Brielle looked more nervous at his tone than she had before. She got up and accidentally stepped into one of the many flickering shadows the flames from the fireplace sent dancing across the room. The physical jolt was brutal. He stood up as well, grateful he'd changed from his suit to casual clothes, giving him some relief, although his trousers were suddenly more than snug on him when they usually were very roomy.

"Don't go over to your laptop and think you're going to do more work right now, Brielle. What you're going to do is

Brielle returned from the bathroom, standing in the doorway of the huge office with its two entire walls of glass. He almost wished it were daylight so she would be even more worried that someone could see in. He didn't want to tell her that the outside screens could reflect back light so no boats on the lake could possibly see into the house. She got a secret thrill of being "almost" on display without actually going that far. She didn't know if she really would like being caught, but the idea was sexually arousing to her. He liked giving her that. He meant it when he said he would never share his woman. But he wouldn't mind giving her the thrill of feeling as if someone accidentally caught a glimpse of her.

He made her wait nearly a full minute before he glanced up and then indicated the couch with a jerk of his chin. There was no need to say anything else. He'd already said enough. She walked on the hardwood floor over to the couch, her bare feet not even making a whisper of a sound. The sofa was one he particularly liked. It was long and dark brown, matching the darkest color in the rougher beams overhead. Overstuffed and yet still firm enough, it also was high backed, something important to him since he liked to sit back and be comfortable, not have his neck hanging over the edge of his chair.

The height of his couch gave his little bride a bit of trouble as she tried to keep her feet on the floor as she bent over the top of it. There was no possible way. In order to do as he told her, she had to actually dangle her feet a few inches above the floor. The position wouldn't be comfortable after a few minutes. She had taken the middle of the sofa as he'd indicated, which gave her very little to hang on to.

Elie collected their dinner leftovers, left the door open and hurried down the stairs to change to his softer drawstring pants. He turned the air on to blow into the office, lowering the temperature significantly as he changed. He left his shirt open and gathered his toys for extended play, left a change of clothes for Brielle on the bed, a small bag of toys on the stairway, and brought the others into the office with him. He'd been gone only a few minutes, but he knew to her, it would seem

a very long time and she would only grow more excited with anticipation.

He received more texts from Val, keeping him abreast of the interrogation. They lost one of the two men and didn't expect the other to give them anything else. He sent them a quick message informing them of Brielle's investigation and what she'd uncovered and that he expected she would uncover much more in the morning.

Dario, through Val, wanted to know why she wasn't working on it right then. Val added a few laughing emojis. Elie sent spanking emojis and added the words *big trouble*. Dario said he wanted to talk to Brielle about working for them, and if she was tied up, all to the better. He didn't care if she was naked or not. He saw naked women all the time. Elie sent the finger to Val's phone and told him to give Dario that message. He got a lot of laughing faces and red flames for jealousy back.

He thought about Dario's message for a long while and what he'd said. Dario ran an underground kink club. His brand of kink was far different than Elie's but Elie wasn't a man to judge. He knew Dario wasn't, either. The more he thought about it, the more he decided he would give his little Brielle a very scary thrill. He texted Dario directly. It took a few minutes for Dario to answer him back, but eventually, the answer got to him.

He put his phone on the side table and walked around the sofa so she would catch a brief glimpse of him as he carried the small duffel bag with him. He set it a distance from the front of the couch, so if she lifted her head, she could see him removing items. He took out a bottle of lube and a jeweled plug without looking at her. She gasped and it was all he could do not to grin. She had carefully avoided the subject of her ass and all activity in the area. She was watching him, all right. The next thing he removed was a very thin rod. He laid that aside and then walked around to her exposed bottom.

"You didn't go into the safe room when you were told to do so, Brielle." He kept his voice low, velvet soft. Very casual.

Rubbing her left cheek gently, he kept his gaze on her pale skin. She had skin that marked so beautifully.

He dipped his fingers into her pussy to find her heat. She was already so wet for him. So ready. She definitely loved this type of play. The uncertainty of it. She never knew what he might do, and for Brielle, that was half the fun.

He continued to rub and knead her bottom, soothing her even as he occasionally teased her pussy and clit with his fingers. "I had your guards tell you to go to the safe room and you deliberately disobeyed them, didn't you?"

"They aren't—"

He smacked her hard with his palm, the print of his hand blooming bright red. "That requires a simple yes or no from you, *mon jouet sexuel*. I don't want to hear any other words coming from your mouth unless I ask for them. Is that understood? I don't need empty excuses."

"Yes," she whispered.

He went back to rubbing and kneading her buttocks and then dipping his fingers into that incredible heat, bringing her need up higher. "I told you to go to the safe room and you completely disregarded my order and instead went to the glass door and taunted the assassins, didn't you?" He lowered his voice even more, using his compelling, persuasive velvet tone that made her shiver and caused those goose bumps to rise everywhere.

"Yes."

He could barely hear her. There was no defiance in her now, only a need, bordering on desperate. She was very responsive to him, so much more than any woman had ever been.

"Do you think I ordered you to the safe room to control you?"

"No." She nearly lifted her head, but at the last moment stayed still.

He continued that slow rub to keep soothing her. She was being very good for him, even though he could tell she was becoming more fearful the longer he questioned her. She was also aware each time his fingers dipped into the

heated liquid and painted a line between her cheeks, lingering along that little forbidden star. She tensed but relaxed the moment he rubbed and kneaded her buttocks again.

"Did you think I gave you the order to show your guards I was controlling you?" He walked around the couch just far enough that she could catch a glimpse of his hands.

"No."

He caught her face in one hand and turned it toward him, forcing her green eyes to meet his. "I'm going to ask a yes or no question, Brielle. This is the discussion we're having on the subject."

He held up the plug and tube of lube. Her eyes widened, looked very nervous. She bit her lower lip, this time her teeth biting down hard.

"If you say yes, you will not be taking it back, but you will trust me enough to take care of you. I want you to be aware I will not be disappointed if at this time you say no and we can revisit the idea at a later date. First reaction, *mon bijou*, just say one way or the other."

Her eyes searched his for a long moment and then she took a deep breath. He felt triumph, but didn't allow it to show on his face. Having his little bride trust him when he hadn't yet showed her that he was making her the center of his world only made him fall all the deeper for her.

"Yes."

Elie brushed her lips with his, his heart turning over. He shouldn't have kissed her. Technically, this was supposed to be a punishment, but he couldn't stop himself. It didn't matter that she enjoyed the shit out of her supposed chastisements; he had a role to play and he was excellent at it, just apparently, not at that moment when she was being so brave.

He lowered her head gently and once more walked around to the other side of the sofa, out of her sight, ensuring he made no sound as he rounded the arms of the couch. He waited to touch her, drawing out the suspense. The sound of the storm breaking over the house could be heard, filling the silence. Rain beat heavily on the roof. The waves on the lake, loud and

angry, were rough as they slapped at the shore. That same building fury began to catch hold in his blood, pounding a rhythmic beat, slow at first, but gradually, as the wind grew in force, so did the storm in him.

He lubed the plug generously and then plunged two fingers into her pussy. She cried out and pushed back onto his hand, trying to ride him. He let her as he coated her little forbidden hole with the lube and slowly began to push the plug inside. It was a smaller plug, contoured for her, but wide enough to cause her to be just a little uncomfortable. The plug also heated and vibrated. It was a wonderful toy for his sweet little *bébé. Mon Dieu*, but she was beautiful, and so perfect in every way for him.

She started to squirm, trying to wiggle away, and he immediately removed his fingers and smacked her left cheek hard, all the while still applying a steady pressure with the plug. The sight of that jeweled, bright green plug, already glowing, slowly being swallowed, was sexy.

She made a sound, a moan, somewhere between pleasure and pain, and he fucked her with his fingers again, and pulled the plug back a tiny bit only to push it deeper.

"So sexy, *mon petit jouet très sale.* You should see the way your body begs for the plug, just the way you'll beg for my cock. You can't wait to take me there, can you, *bébé*?"

Deliberately, he slowed his fingers down, sliding them from her pussy, trailing them over her clit, flicking hard so she cried out, and then removing them altogether.

"Yes," she whispered.

"Yes, what? Answer me in a full sentence." He was relentless. After all, this was a punishment and she was enjoying it far too much.

"Yes, I can't wait to take your cock there."

He flicked her clit again and shoved the plug all the way in, at the same time pushing two fingers deep in her entrance. Instantly he was flooded with hot liquid. She cried out, her hips bucking.

"You're so hungry for my cock."

He laughed and began to pepper her bottom with hard smacks. He loved spanking her with his hands. The way her body responded, the way her skin turned color, the moans and pleas for more, all of it drove the blood to his groin, and made him hotter than hell. He warmed her up slowly, enjoying the way her skin turned color, matching his rhythm to the wild storm, listening carefully to her little cries and paying close attention to the signs her body gave him. He wanted her close, very close, but he wasn't going to allow her to get off. Not yet. She had a long night ahead of her.

Elie waited until Brielle's body was coiled tight and she was shaking before he halted the spanking and stepped back, reaching for her shoulders to pull her into a standing position. He had to hold her up, she was so weak with arousal. He wrapped his arm around her waist and allowed her to lean on him, his mouth on the side of her neck and then sliding up to her ear.

"You were very naughty today, *mon petit jouet très sale.* You shocked me with your wanton disobedience several times." His teeth nipped her earlobe as he walked her across the room to the table where they'd eaten their dinner.

He'd always, always been calm and cool when he'd played sexual games, but he found he had to work at keeping his heart from accelerating as he indicated the higher tabletop. "You're going to lie facedown and I'm going to administer the cane to your very pretty ass."

She gasped and swung her head around to look up at him, her eyes wide with shock. He nodded, keeping his expression implacable. He wouldn't cuff her, and if she said no, it was no. She didn't. She took a deep breath and glanced at the thin cane lying on the small end table and then back at him. Her breathing changed, turning raspy, her eyes growing dark with the combination of lust and trepidation he was familiar with in her. Elie could see she wanted that cane desperately. At the same time, she feared it. The idea of it heightened every one of her senses, so that she could barely breathe.

He brought her to the edge of the table and indicated for

her to climb on. She did so, hands and knees, giving him a good view of her very wet pussy and the jeweled plug in her ass. He could barely stand the material containing his monster of a cock. Every brush of fabric against his straining shaft and the broad, sensitive head sent hot blood coursing through him and filling his groin until he thought he'd burst.

"I won't harm you, Brielle, but this will leave marks on you. You'll feel it for a day or two. Do you still want to go through with your punishment?"

Brielle looked back at him, a haughty look on her face as if he'd challenged her, which wasn't his intent. He could see visibly the endorphins running wild, the goose bumps rising, her entire body flushed. She might look haughty, but the anticipation was all about the expectation of what she was going to experience.

"Yes."

She stretched out and the higher table gave him much better control. It was her first time with a cane and he had no intention of hurting her or causing her not to want to ever have him use the cane on her again. He needed to introduce it to her slowly. That meant keeping light strokes on her buttocks only.

He warmed her bottom again by using his palm and then slid a tiny little button vibrator over her clit. The remote he had set up worked the plug and button in opposite rhythms. He started them out slow. She gripped the edges of the table.

"You need to keep your ass cheeks relaxed, *bébe*, or this is going to hurt like hell." She would think it would anyway.

The first lick of fire came with a flick of his wrist, the rattan striking across her buttocks. He didn't lift immediately, allowing the rod to settle into her skin, an almost intimate experience. The compression felt like a sharp, blazing sting and then, as he slowly lifted the cane from her bottom and her nerves were allowed to decompress, the pain was like a fiery, white-hot line. It took a moment to process and she bit back a cry and clenched her cheeks.

"What did I tell you, *mon petit jouet trés sale*?" He rubbed

the streak with the pad of his thumb and then gently smacked each cheek with his palm. "Relax."

He waited until she obeyed him and immediately laid another stroke across her bottom, just under the first one. He was careful not to increase the intensity. As he lifted the cane away from her bottom, he upped the speed to medium on the vibrators. She sobbed his name, her hips bucking. He waited, rubbing her bottom, letting her get right there. So close. Abruptly, he turned off the vibrators.

"No. Elie. No. Please."

"Did you think your punishment was over, *ma belle*?"

She shivered deliciously as he rubbed her bottom one more time until she relaxed. He delivered the last stroke with just a little more strength, not much, enough to add to the line of fire streaking across her bottom. The vibration had to have been felt through her ass and pussy. The sting would be remembered and she would feel that fire when she sat. He hadn't given her the distraction of the vibrators and she gripped the table until he thought she might rip it apart. A long moaning cry escaped but she didn't try to get away.

Elie couldn't help but be proud of her. He put the cane down and took the tube of arnica cream from the small bag he'd left on the chair and rubbed it into the three dark, angry lines on her buttocks.

"We're going downstairs, just to the bottom of the stairs to the foyer between kitchen and side entrance. Can you walk?" He helped her off the table and let her rest against him while he gave her a bottle of cool water to drink. Her legs were very shaky. He kept his arm wrapped securely around her waist. "Tell me when you think you can make it down the stairs. Do you need the bathroom first?"

She shook her head and indicated the stairs. He didn't waste time. He turned the vibrators on low. She gasped and looked up at him, shaking her head. There was no way his little woman was getting off on that low of a setting. It would only drive her crazy and they both knew it. He was merciless, keeping her moving down the stairs.

The space in the foyer was very large and he had placed a wide rustic cabinet against one wall. The cabinet was made of rough-hewn bluish-gray wood. It was extremely strong, wide and long. What had intrigued him the most when he'd first discovered it were the dips carved into the edges of the top all the way around, dips that were the width of a neck or ankles. The railing on his stairs was made of iron and the chest had iron rings fastened into each of the heavy timbers making up the corners, the only decorations. There weren't even knobs to open it. The doors slid open. The cabinet looked perfect sitting in the spot just across from the stairs and the door to the master bedroom.

Brielle shivered when he returned, the goose bumps on her skin telling him she was more than ready for him. Her eyes begged him for relief, but she knew better than to say anything. She waited in silence, her gaze on the jewelry in his hand.

He leaned into her and sucked her right breast into his mouth hard, teasing her nipple with his tongue and then catching it with his teeth, pulling back, elongating it until she hissed. "I had these made just for you, with those eyes of yours. I never thought I'd have a chance to use them. I'll admit it pissed me off that you held a grudge all those years, *ma femme*. Turns out, all that time, you wanted me and were afraid of what we'd do together. Look at the time we wasted."

He held the clover clamp up so she could see the vivid emeralds dotting the large grips on each clamp. The chain looped from one clamp to the other and then down to her clit where the other large grip was equally dotted with emerald green. He clamped her right nipple and allowed the heavy weight of the grip to drop over her full breast, pulling the clover tighter. She gasped at the fiery pinch and immediately went still. He kept his smile to himself. His special clamps did quite a lot, just as the plug in her cute little ass did. He clamped her left breast and then crouched low to remove the vibrating button. Her clit was already engorged and ready for the clover clamp. Brielle did more than hiss. A soft cry

escaped when he allowed the grip to drop and the clover tightened with wicked force.

Elie brushed his fingers along her entrance just to make certain she was enjoying everything he was doing to her. He didn't want to go too far in their game. It was all about her being sexually excited. Gripping her arm, he guided her to the cabinet. "You're going to climb on top of that and lie on your back with your neck in that slot in the center so your head hangs off the edge. Both ankles will be locked in the dips right on the edges. I've pulled the cabinet just out enough from the wall that your wrists can fit down into the iron rings. You can grip them, but you are not to take them out for any reason. I don't care if you think the house is on fire. Do you understand me? Not for any reason at all unless I give you permission." He poured command into his tone. She needed to want to obey no matter what happened, have that uppermost in her mind.

"Yes. I understand." She nodded, meeting his eyes. Hers were filled with excitement. Apprehension. Pure lust. She was getting to that mindless place she seemed to need at times and he wanted to give her.

Elie helped her up onto the top of the cabinet. When she lay out, thighs wide apart, even as small as she was, her knees were slightly bent and he could see her pussy lips gleaming. She was so ready. She tried to stay still, but already she squirmed a little, and each time she did, those clamps tightened painfully and the hard wood rubbed unforgivingly against the cane stripes.

The cabinet was the perfect height for his woman to give him head. That was another thing he'd noticed about that cabinet top and he'd wondered if the maker had created it with that express purpose in mind.

The wood didn't have any give at all against the plug or the cane marks. The cabinet top was just rough enough to scrape against her sore bottom every time she moved. She couldn't help moving when he kicked up the vibrations in her butt plug and then added heat. That would only tighten those clamps

more. He would be getting the relief she so desperately wanted, and she would be the one giving it to him.

He stepped close to the cabinet and pulled the drawstring on his lightweight pants, kicking them aside before he reached for the remote that commanded the clamps on her nipples and clit. The clamps ran on a program. Vibrations. Heat. A tingling of electricity with ever-changing intensity. The same program synced up with her butt plug.

Her head was hanging low, her lips close to his straining cock. Her tongue touched her lips, wetting them in anticipation. He was brutally in need, already pulsing and weeping. Using both hands on either side of her jaw, he pressed with his thumbs, opening her mouth without preamble and pushing his cock into that hot, wet haven.

"Suck, *mon petit jouet très sale*. Suck hard. Worship your cock."

The sight of her struggling to get her full lips to stretch around his girth and take him down added to the raging lust coursing through his veins, turning his blood scorching hot until his hunger for her was impossible to control.

She couldn't use her hands and was looking up at him with those green eyes of hers, her tits heaving, the clamps tightening around her nipples and clit while the vibrations ran through her body like a river of pain and pleasure.

The phone he'd set beside him played a short tune and he glanced at it, let her have air and then shoved his cock back into her mouth, beginning a quick shallow fuck while he dictated aloud. "Kitchen sliders unlocked. Not finished with my very naughty toy yet. We're in the foyer. You can wait in kitchen or dining room."

Brielle gasped and started to pull back. Elie gripped her hair and shoved his cock deeper. "Don't you dare stop. You stop and we start all over again. You're going to take me down your throat and swallow every single drop."

The slider in the kitchen opened and closed. They both could hear it clearly. Elie had deliberately lit dim nightlights in the kitchen and one just past them on the upper stairs. The

foyer itself was shadowed, but not completely dark. The kitchen was very large, and if Dario walked straight in from the sliding glass doors toward the stove, he would be able to look toward the foyer and stairs, into those shadows. Elie had checked to see if Brielle would be seen on the cabinet top, but just her silhouette would show.

Brielle's answers had indicated she considered she was into safe exhibitionism, that it added to the thrill of her playing games, so Elie was testing the waters. He knew Dario would be respectful of her, and if Elie signaled to leave to another room, the man would leave instantly.

Elie kicked up the programs on the clamps and plug another level, wanting the heat, vibration and electrical rounds to distract her and tease her body to new heights of hunger. The program was designed to sense when she was close to an orgasm and back off before she could get there. He captured her jaws again and focused on her eyes, compelling her to look at him. He found it sexier than hell to have her play the part of his toy for him.

In this position, with her head back, it opened her throat and he took advantage, pushing his cock deeper, feeling that tight squeeze grasp his shaft. The sensitive head was all the way in her throat, and he stroked the bump through her skin, stroked that broad, flared cock head, all the while watching her eyes turn liquid and her hips buck. Her breasts rose as if she fought herself to try to find air, but she didn't release the iron rings.

He pulled back enough to allow her to take a breath, and just as Dario sauntered fully into the kitchen, Elie pumped his cock deeper into her throat. "You can do this, *ma chatte*." He didn't give her time to think about controlling her gag reflex; he pushed right past it, seeking that paradise. He did step slightly to one side, just a slight turn, forcing her head to turn with him, so her eyes could shift toward the kitchen in trepidation when she became aware they weren't completely alone.

He pulled his cock back again, barely giving her time to

breathe, and this time, went all the way, balls deep, feeling the hot well of semen churning. Soon. He didn't want it to end yet. Not yet. Not when her mouth was giving this to him. Not when her pussy was wetter than he'd ever seen it and her hips were bucking and squirming. When she was moaning, nearly sobbing around his cock, even as stuffed full as she was.

Dario leaned against the counter. "You need a crop to slap her pussy, Elie. She'd bring you off better."

"Yeah, I've got one ready," he replied calmly.

Elie pulled back and plunged into her mouth again, down her throat. They'd set up the dialogue ahead of time, wanting Brielle to think Dario might really be able to see her. Elie caught up the long-handled crop with the small tongue of flat leather. As he surged into her throat, feeling the semen beginning to rise like Mount Vesuvius, he flicked the crop, landing the tongue perfectly on her pussy with a hard slap. Her entire body shook. Shuddered. Her knees came up. Spread farther apart. Her throat clamped down around his cock, squeezing hard as she swallowed convulsively, constricting around him like a python.

Elie slapped again, this time directly on the clover clamp over her clit, shaking the steel, causing it to tighten more. Her entire body shook, hips rising and falling, pussy opening and closing. Her throat reacted a second time, swallowing and squeezing as his cock erupted like a fountain. Hot semen blasted down her throat. He stroked her throat and jaw over and over as his cock jerked and jerked in an ecstasy of sheer pleasure.

"Swallow it down. All of it. Every single drop. That's it, *petit jouet*." He felt cross-eyed and weak as he pulled his cock back, but he wasn't about to let her see that no matter what. He had to play his part. "Now lick me clean. All of me. Balls, too. You were a bad girl all over again, coming without permission. Don't think I didn't notice."

Now that she was coming back from the high of sexual pleasure, as she cleaned him with her delicate little tongue, she was very aware of the shadowy image of the other man

in their kitchen lounging so casually against the counter. Dario had actually given Elie a suggestion that Elie had followed. She had broken Elie's rule and had an orgasm because of it.

Elie watched her closely, aware of her reaction, of her body's reaction. She still seemed to feel safe with the distance and the darkness. There were the telltale endorphins covering her skin, and as he stepped around the cabinet to look down at her, he could see she was still in a state of arousal. That was extremely satisfying.

CHAPTER ELEVEN

Elie took his time dragging his thin cotton pants on and tightening the drawstring while Brielle struggled to control her raging body. She was so aroused, more than he'd ever seen her at any other time. He trailed his fingers down her cheek and then her breast.

"I've got to take these off you, *bébé*, you've been wearing them too long," Elie said, tugging casually on the chain, lifting her breasts slightly.

She cried out and writhed on the cabinet top. Her hips bucked. He patted her pussy lips as he made his way to the end of the cabinet. Her knees were still up and her body was shaking. He shut down the programs on the vibrators and her legs sagged. He ran his hands down her thighs to her calves and then massaged the tension from her muscles. "Turn your hips this way, Brielle."

She was going to be very reluctant to do that. Every movement now would tighten the clover clamps more and she was beyond sensitive. This was what she lived for though. They

both knew it. She couldn't lift her head and he hadn't helped her shift down on the table so she could rest fully on it yet. He wanted her breasts jutting up the way they were, sexy as sin, swaying with every ragged breath she took.

He waited, listening to the music of her breathing sawing in and out of her burning lungs as she slowly complied with his request. "Legs wide, *mon petit jouet*. Breathe deep." He stroked the inside of her thigh, knowing when the blood rushed back from that tight pinch, she would feel it like nothing else. Even the fire of the cane wouldn't compare for her in that single moment.

She gingerly spread her thighs and he leaned close, inhaling her intoxicating scent. Just smelling her sent hot blood rushing back into his cock. *Mon Dieu*, but he loved their games. Two weeks with her and already he was beginning to know every little sign her body gave him. He rubbed her mound and used two fingers to tease her entrance. He had no intention of yanking the clover clamp off her clit. She needed to work up to that. This time, he opened the grip, allowing her clit freedom. As it was, there was a brief moment and then she cried out, gasping, one foot nearly flying into the air.

He leaned into her and covered her clit with his mouth, sucking the inflamed little button deep, soothing it with his tongue, waiting for her to calm, to realize his hand had moved up to her breast and was kneading and stroking and then catching hold of the grip and pulling it free from her left nipple while he sucked at her clit. Her cry was more of a scream but the hot liquid flooding his mouth told him she wanted more.

Elie pulled his mouth from her clit. "*Mon petit jouet très sale*, you really love this." He pressed a kiss to the inside of each thigh and then up her belly to the underside of her breast, the one he knew had a throbbing nipple. Licking at it, he drew the hot little point into his mouth and sucked while his hand stroked and kneaded her right breast. She tried to squirm away from his hand and he slapped her breast with his

palm in warning, striking close to the clover clamp. She stilled instantly. That didn't deter him from punishing her by just catching the grip and pulling it away from her nipple.

She did scream. Loud. He didn't move from her left breast to her right with his mouth but his hand traveled to her pussy to see how wet she was. She was aroused beyond belief. He sucked on her left nipple and then flicked her right one with his thumb and finger before straightening.

"We have company. I believe Dario wants to speak to us about your work. Go into the bedroom and put on what I laid out on the bed for you. *Everything* I laid out. Don't keep us waiting. I think he's been patient enough. If you'd obeyed me in the first place, we wouldn't have had to keep our guest waiting at all."

Elie was gentle as he helped her sit up on the cabinet top. She was definitely shaky and he gave her several minutes to orient herself.

"You need to drink water before you try to walk, *bébé*," he reminded. "I'll go with you into the bedroom."

"I can make it," she said, eyeing the distance, keeping her gaze steadily away from the kitchen and Dario.

Sitting up seemed to make her feel much more exposed. She didn't seem to realize he was standing solidly between her and their guest and that Dario was staring studiously down at the screen of his phone.

Elie put his hands on her waist and helped her from the cabinet so she was leaning on him instead of the wood. "If you want to stop, you come out dressed in something else, Brielle. I won't be disappointed. You never disappoint me." He brushed a kiss on top of her head.

She pressed her face against his chest for a brief moment. "You give me . . . everything. More than everything I could ever ask for, Elie. You seem to understand me when I don't understand myself."

The little break in her voice turned his heart over. She really had a difficult time accepting this side of herself, although the craving in her ran deep. He needed to find a way

to let her know he would love her all the more for that part of her. He couldn't break role to assure her, that would have to come later, when he was giving her aftercare, but he wanted to pull her into his arms and hold her to him. Steeling himself, he turned her toward their bedroom, and when she took a step away from him, he smacked her hard right over the three cane stripes and the jeweled butt plug. She yelped and threw him an indignant glare over her shoulder as she walked very gingerly to their room.

Elie joined Dario in the kitchen and indicated they should go into the great room, where the stone fireplace and their couches were. There was also the "cozy circle" Brielle preferred with the four really comfortable chairs around the copper coffee table. He had a plan to continue their little game of punishment for her indiscretion.

Elie was learning Brielle's limits. He suspected she was learning them as well. He preferred they learn them in the safety of their home and with someone he trusted implicitly. He knew no matter what happened, Dario would respect her and never humiliate her or judge her for her choices. Had he done so, Elie knew, as did Dario, that Elie would defend her with his life.

He indicated one of the long couches in front of the fireplace and then turned the logs on low. There was a large round coffee table separating the two couches. Elie made certain it was placed exactly in position between where he would sit with Brielle and where Dario had seated himself across from him. He studied the flames from the fireplace and turned them even lower until they were nearly off.

Placing a long pillow on the floor just to the right of where his feet would be, he once more studied the position to ensure Brielle would be safe from exposure.

Dario shook his head. "That woman of yours is spoiled already. Mine disobeyed me like that, she wouldn't be smiling right about now. Your woman is practically purring."

"I like mine purring, Dario. I want her happy, healthy and to want to be with me. How do you want your woman to be?"

Dario leaned forward and looked Elie straight in the eye. It was disconcerting to stare into those dark pits of hell. "Alive, Elie. If I ever really managed to find a woman that was mine alone, I would want to know I could keep her alive. That would be a full-time job with what I do. I've got so many people who want me dead, she'd be my number one vulnerability. You know damn well, Emme is Val's and Brielle is yours. If someone wants to screw with you, they don't have to kill you, they just have to take her from you and fuck her up. That's worse than killing you. I can't ever afford to allow myself to feel for a woman the way you do. You can tell yourself that you don't love her already, but it's obvious you're already falling down that rabbit hole. It's bad enough that I care about that dumb fuck Val. Or Emme. Or . . ." Dario trailed off.

Elie knew Dario was right. He had never considered he would feel that way about any woman, but he'd built up his fantasies of Brielle over the years they were separated. The times their shadows had connected had tied them together. When he'd gone to the places Brielle worked, his shadow had crossed with hers often and he'd felt the sexual rush, so much so that he'd gone back again and again, addicted to the feeling. He'd been sexually enthralled with his date for a few hours because of it, but that had tied him closer to Brielle without his knowledge.

"Dario, the only way you're ever going to claim a woman is if you see one you find attractive already, then you realize she has the shadow you're searching for and there's some advantage she can give you. Only then will you allow your shadow to cross with hers to see what happens. The jolt will send rockets through you both and you won't know what hit you."

Dario didn't deny it. He shrugged. "Yeah, I get that the shadow thing can mess with control. I've seen it with all of you riders and even Val. You know me, Elie. At least you know me better than most men do. I'm rigid when it comes to

control. I have too many demons not to be. Never going to have a woman of my own, I already know that." He shrugged again like it didn't matter.

"You don't know that."

"I do know because I have a standard now. I know what kind of woman I have to have and I would never take less. I've got Emme. She accepts me just the way I am. Doesn't care that I'm a freak and a monster. She loves me and I feel that every day. I see her and now I see your woman. She's worth something, Elie. Don't fuckin' let her walk all over you when she's in danger. She's like Emme. She thinks she's a warrior, but she's soft inside. I can spot that a mile away. Even though I know that's what I want and need, I'd tear up a woman like that."

Dario glanced up at the same time Elie did, both aware as Brielle padded through the open dining area to the great room toward them. She moved in silence, a stark contrast to the storm seething outside, the rain hitting the roof and windows angrily, a dark tempest raging violently.

She wore the short little robe he'd left on the bed, the one he'd found in her luggage when he'd put her clothes away for her on their wedding night. She'd been exhausted and he'd thought to help her, but ended up intrigued with her choice of clothing. The robe was a filmy concoction of smoke gray and pale rose, the two colors swirling together as if paint had been mixed and dumped on the thin, stretchy material. The thin fabric could be transparent in the right circumstances, like when it stretched over the sweet curve of her ass cheeks or the alluring temptation of her breasts.

The robe was held together with a single tie at her waist, relying on the stretch of the fabric to keep the gaps closed. Elie had instructed her not to wear anything he hadn't put on the bed. He hadn't included underwear. Each step she took, the little robe would open just a tiny bit at the bottom, flashing him a brief glimpse of the very top of her inner thigh. She kept her arms at her sides, not attempting to cover up, knowing he would send her back to start all over if she did.

"*Bébé*, I left the pillow on the floor. Would you mind moving it before you sit down? Just to the edge of the conversation area will do."

Brielle glanced at him from under her lashes and then at Dario. Dario didn't look away this time. He looked hard. Dangerous. Every bit the man he was. He was probably the scariest man Elie had ever run across. She inclined her head like the little princess she was. He should have known she would have the grace of royalty as well. She remained sideways to both sofas, allowing the flickering flames to play over her face and the front of her robe. With the grace and skill of a shadow rider, she crouched low and caught the edges of the long pillow and then straightened, backing to the area where the cozy circle of chairs was. She simply dropped the pillow on the floor beside the nearest chair.

Elie wanted to laugh at Dario's raised eyebrow. Both of the men knew Brielle was still playing Elie's little toy, but she had totally outsmarted him with her flowing grace. He had the remote and he hadn't used it on her. He could have. She still wore the jeweled butt plug. The shock of the thing vibrating at just the right moment would have interrupted her little performance, but he was just too proud of her to take her perceived victory from her.

He patted his lap when she would have seated herself a little distance from him on the same sofa. Pressing her lips together, she curled her body sideways onto his, trying to turn away from the flames. Elie didn't allow it. His much larger and stronger hands caught at her hips and straightened her so she was straddling his thighs and facing Dario.

"Dario has a business proposition for you, *bébé*. I realize it's late, and you aren't dressed appropriately, but the matter is pressing and he caught us in the middle of your punishment." Deliberately, Elie pushed the tangle of wild, out-of-control waves and spirals of curls cascading down her back away from her neck so he could bite down on her soft skin. She shivered, reacting instantly. He loved that she was always so receptive to his touch.

Brielle tipped her head back just as he knew she would, resting against his shoulder to offer him her bare neck. That slight change in her body thrust her full breasts against the pale smoke-and-rose robe. Elie ran his fingernails very gently along her bare thigh, all the way to her buttocks. Back and forth, as though he wasn't aware of what he was doing, but he knew he was bringing every nerve ending to life and that small movement would center her entire attention right back on her hunger and need to climax. Right on him. She needed release and he was very skilled at keeping her on edge.

"You're extremely good with your investigations," Dario said. "Did Elie tell you that you won the competition?"

"No, but I didn't ask." Brielle's voice was low. Shaky. She curled her fingers around Elie's wrist as if she might try to still his fingers as they moved up and down her thigh, but she only rested her hand there.

"Why wouldn't you ask? You spent a good deal of the day working to prove you were faster at getting information than the others. Wouldn't you want to know if you were?"

Dario leaned forward, both hands around his phone, his dark eyes boring into Brielle's as he wholly focused on her. Elie had seen him look like this when he was interrogating a prisoner. Compelling. Utterly focused. Dangerously so. A relentless, merciless pursuit for answers. Voice soft. That low rasp he had that only added to the effect of warning the one he questioned they might be in the room with a predator, not a human. As looks went, it was extremely intimidating.

"I get caught up in what I'm investigating, and the last one, the one on the Colombo crime family in Los Angeles, nagged at me when I was looking into them. Stefano had set boundaries we weren't to go beyond. That didn't seem to fit with a normal investigation. When we're looking into someone, you want to know everything there is to know about them so there aren't any surprises."

"So, you disobeyed the order." Dario's voice dropped an octave. The lines in his face deepened. The flickering firelight played over him for just a moment, revealing his extremely

handsome features, the cruel set of his mouth, and the flames of hell burning in his dark, pitiless eyes.

"I'm an investigator. Of course I did. I would never allow anyone to walk into a bad situation because I didn't do my job. I went a little deeper before I sent the report." Brielle's voice strengthened.

When talking about the love of her work, her passion showed. She moved her body against Elie restlessly, leaning into his fingernails, her bottom rubbing along his thighs like a little cat. She was distracted by Dario, her body reacting naturally to the stimulation, while her mind struggled to answer honestly.

"The consensus was that you did win. You were thorough in every report and you were fast. There were times when others were faster, but then your report held more information than two-man teams'. Valentino and I have need of someone with your talents. On the other hand, you don't seem to follow direction very well. Not even your man's."

Brielle tensed, not liking the implication that she might make Elie look bad in front of his friend. Elie soothed her, bringing his fingernails gently up the sides of her body over the robe, along her rib cage and the sides of her breasts. She had such beautiful breasts. So full. She thought they were too full, but Elie loved the way the soft, perfect flesh flared out from the side, giving him access as he ran his fingers up her body and stroked her breasts with his fingernails as he had her thighs.

"Your tenaciousness is what most likely makes you a great investigator, but with what I do, if you don't follow orders, you could put your nose in the wrong place and it could get you killed. I wouldn't know what you had done because I didn't give my approval. I couldn't take the necessary steps to ensure you were safe." Dario's stare refused to allow her to look away from him. "I won't lie to you about what I do. You have to know what you would be getting into. The people who work for me have to be loyal to us. If they aren't, they don't live long. It's that simple."

Brielle's teeth bit down on the side of her lower lip and she chewed on that spot for a moment. More little goose bumps began to rise on her skin, an automatic response to the way Elie was running his nails so gently back and forth along the sides of her breasts and dipping underneath and then back up.

Elie bent his head to her bare neck, lips to her ear. "Be *ma petite chatte, bébé,* I do find it sexy when you rub against me the way you do." He followed the wicked enticement with a bite on her earlobe, his teeth closing on the thin skin and pulling back for a moment before releasing her.

She arched her back more for him, an automatic response to his command, rubbing her back along his chest, doing the same with her bottom along his thighs. He widened his thighs just a scant inch, forcing her thighs apart at the same time. The stretchy robe was accommodating. He decided the robe was going to be one of his favorite pieces of clothing. His hand slipped around her breast to find the opening. Her skin was smooth. So damn soft.

"I'm not sure what you're saying, Dario," Elie said, sounding all business. "You want my wife to work exclusively for you and her loyalty should belong to you but you're aware I'm a rider and, by extension, an adopted member of the Ferraro family. So, my first loyalty has to go to them. You can't exactly ask my wife to divide her loyalties between the families. That wouldn't be fair to her."

His fingernails very, very gently ran over the top of the curves of her breasts. He brushed little strokes tracing the curve down around her nipple as if painting. The fabric of the robe stretched over the back of his hand, rubbing with every slow, subtle movement. Brielle shivered. He wished he had put the clamps on her before he sent her to dress in the robe. They would have been perfect under the stretchy fabric. He would save that idea for another evening.

"I wouldn't ask your wife to divide her loyalty like that. I have another investigator, Elie. Bernado is a good man and has never once done a single thing to indicate that he might ever turn on us. Having said that, you know me. Valentino is

the man I trust one hundred percent. After him, I don't know. I like to hedge my bets, so to speak."

"There's a man by the name of Carmine Catani in your organization," Brielle said, her fingernails suddenly digging into Elie's thigh. "Dario, I should have told you right away. I haven't had a chance to investigate him so I shoved him into a corner of my mind, but he definitely is betraying you. He sent the photograph of Elie to Santoro."

There was a small silence while Dario continued to hold her gaze. His face seemed to harden even more, settling into even crueler lines. "Did you forget to tell me because you knew I would kill him for his betrayal?"

"No, he sent *Elie's* photograph. I would have gone after him myself."

Elie heard the absolute honesty in her voice. It took discipline not to tense beneath her. She was a rider and every bit as capable as any shadow rider of targeting a man for justice. In her mind, anyone threatening Elie was fair game, just as he believed that anyone threatening Brielle was. His woman wasn't going to hunt Carmine Catani. He had to make that absolutely clear to her.

He made a mental note to make it a priority to go into the shadows with her and see just how sick she really was when she entered the tubes. Truthfully, it was hell on the body. In the little time he'd had with her, Elie had come to know Brielle very well. And one thing she absolutely didn't do was complain. For her ever to have said anything about getting sick riding the shadows meant she was *really* sick when she was in the portals.

Dario couldn't fail to hear the honesty in her voice when she declared she would have gone after Carmine Catani. He'd spent far too long interrogating prisoners and knew truth when he heard it. Dario simply nodded. "Knowing what we do, would you have problems conducting investigations for us?"

"No. Unless your intention is to harm innocent people."

Dario sat back. "I think you would find working for Valentino and me much more exciting than for Stefano. He, no doubt,

will offer you a job. He's got two other teams working for him. We've got one man and a shit load of work. If you're interested, we'll draw up the proposal with the salary and the four of us will sit down and come up with a plan that will work for all of us."

Her chin rose. Elie nearly smiled. He knew right away what she was going protest. It was her job and she didn't think Elie needed to be there. He widened his thighs just a bit more and hit the remote on the plug, so that it pulsed and danced, heating as well. At the same time, his fingers on her breast found her nipple and pinched down like the clamps had. A slow burn that kept getting hotter.

Brielle gasped and squirmed, arching back against him, grinding her bottom against his lap, and lifting her hips. Elie was very grateful he'd studied all the angles ahead of time. The extremely large pottery bowl he'd found that went so well on the coffee table, with the thick, concrete-looking base, was finally good for something. It was large enough to hide his woman's lower body in the throes of her arousal.

When Dario stood, turning to leave, she suddenly seemed aware of her exposure, even in the dim light, but she didn't try to close her legs or pull the robe down to cover her gleaming pussy. Her body undulated, hips bucking in time to the rhythm of the plug and squeeze of his fingers. Her head fell back on Elie's shoulder, tossing from side to side.

If Dario could see anything in the dim light as he strode to the door, he didn't acknowledge it; he just called out to Elie he'd text a date when Valentino could meet with them.

Elie didn't reply. He widened his thighs even more. "Did you like that, *mon petit jouet très sale*? Someone watching us? Seeing how beautiful you are when you're aroused? And obedient? When you're my toy? Does it make you even hotter?" He bit down on that little sweet spot on her neck that made her shiver. "Do you think he saw the plug in your ass when you arched your back and rubbed like a little pussycat all over my chest?"

She nodded her head. "Yes. I liked it. It was crazy wild."

The more he talked dirty to her, the more she bucked her hips, frantic for release. Twice he kept her hand from straying between her legs. "You don't get to say when you get off. I say. This was a punishment. Dario thinks I'm too easy on you because you enjoy this so much, but you don't like it when you don't get what you want, do you, *bébé*?"

He heard her swift intake of breath, the realization that he might really deprive her of release after all the buildup of sexual need.

"Elie, please. I learned my lesson."

She was so far gone, he doubted she could even tell him what that lesson was at this point. He guided her off his lap and had her bend over the side of the couch, placing her hands in the cushions. She was so short. That placed her little ass right in front of him. He was grateful for the hearth she could stand on.

"I'm tempted to remove your little jewel and fuck you in the ass for your shocking behavior," he said as he dropped the drawstring pants and kicked them aside. At her gasp, he kicked the plug up another notch and watched the frenzied movement as it seemed to pound away inside her forbidden hole.

"Elie." She sounded nervous.

She was slick and hot and he didn't need to worry about getting her ready. He simply lodged the broad head of his cock in her entrance, caught her hips and slammed home. Hard. Deep. She was always tight, the friction nearly unbearable when he first entered her. Now, with the plug, there was almost no room at all. His cock felt as if it was being strangled in a silken vise. His fingers dug into her hips, dragging her back into him as he surged forward, driving through her tight folds, again and again.

It was exquisite torture for both of them. He felt every tiny movement of her body, the way the muscles clamped around him, sucking and gripping. Tongues seemed to lap at him, millions of them, wet and wild, streaking white lightning through his body and down his spine. Lights burst behind his

eyes. Her breath sawed in and out of her lungs almost in time to the pulsing dance of the plug as it pounded a counter rhythm in her ass, matching the hammering of his driving cock.

He felt the boiling and churning in his balls, the tension rising, and did his best to stop it. He didn't want this to end. Brielle sobbed his name in growing pleas of desperation, adding to the feral way he felt, primitive, bordering on savage and out of control. She pushed back into him, just as wild as he was.

Then her body shuddered. Seized. Clamped down with vicious force, a powerful storm of pure fire that took him with her. Lightning seemed to fork through his veins and spread through his entire body. Her scorching-hot tunnel squeezed down on his shaft, a tight fist, determined to milk him dry, twisting and grasping greedily, shooting fiery streaks through him until he couldn't think straight, until he was mindless, somewhere else, burning in a fire of heaven—or hell. Or both. He wanted to stay there forever.

His cock pulsed and jerked, coating her inner walls with rope after rope of his seed. Each time he thought he couldn't give her any more, she managed to wring more out of him. The aftershocks were nearly as powerful as the orgasms rolling through her. He collapsed over her back, his arms around her waist to hold her to him, his cock buried as deep as he could possibly be. She lay over the arm of the couch, breathing raggedly. Neither spoke for the longest time. He managed to reach down and fish around for his pants so he could get the remote and stop the plug from moving, realizing the frantic movements were continuing to trigger the shocking waves in her body.

"Taking it out, *bébé*. Take a deep breath," he warned her and grasped the jeweled toy and pulled steadily. Her body didn't want to give it up at first, and the movement triggered all kinds of powerful waves and aftershocks he received the benefit of. His cock was rewarded with a fresh bath of liquid fire.

Elie closed his eyes and savored the feeling of sharing

her body. Whenever he was in her, whether he took her slow and easy, loving and gentle, or hot as hades, he always found himself reluctant to leave her. As much as he wanted to be selfish and stay inside her as long as possible, she needed care. They'd been playing a long time and her body had to be sore. He also wanted her to feel his love for her—his acceptance and joy in this side of her. She hadn't fully come to accept or understand the need she had of playing this way yet. He didn't want her to be embarrassed. He wanted her to feel loved.

"Let me take care of you, Brielle." He helped her to straighten up slowly. "Are you dizzy?"

She shook her head, but leaned into him. Elie waited until he knew he was steady and then he swept her into his arms. She stiffened for just a moment before relaxing against his chest. He'd noticed she'd done that before when he'd picked her up.

"Do you think I'm going to drop you?" He carried her through to the master bath. There was the slightest edge of humor to his voice. Sitting on the wide edge of the tub, he started the bath for her, pouring in oil and salts to help with any bruising and soreness. It was easy enough with his longer arms to hook a pillow and attach it to the end of the sloped tub to rest her head. He also lit two of the large round candles on the tall pillars he'd bought specifically because, in her preferences, she said she liked taking baths by candlelight.

When the tub was filled, Elie wrapped his arms securely around her and lowered her into the hot water. She hissed as the water closed over her sore body, but she leaned her head onto his chest, eyes closed.

"That feels good. Stings a little, but still good," she murmured. Her voice was low enough that he had to strain to hear.

"We've got to talk about tonight, Brielle," Elie said, brushing kisses into the wild mass of hair she'd secured to the top of her head. All those crazy curls made him want to pull that knot free and let her hair tumble around her face and down

her back. "I want to know how you felt. I know how your body did, but how did you feel?"

Brielle didn't reply right away. He was used to the way she thought things over. "Having someone 'almost' see us was really hot, just the way I fantasized. It actually was crazy hot, but I know I wouldn't like being at a club or in a public place. As it was, even though my body definitely was frantic for sex, I wanted more darkness. More shadows."

He rubbed her arms gently, grateful Brielle was able to communicate clearly with him on anything to do with their sexual relationship. At first, when she was so adamant that she didn't want to marry him, he was worried that it was because of this—they both liked kink and she didn't want him to know. That wasn't the case; she was open and honest with him.

"I'm not certain I want to do it again very soon," she said. "One thing I did like was the shock of not knowing he was going to just walk in on us. That he might see us in the hall while I was going down on you. That was especially hot, that he just might stroll all the way in. When we were talking in the great room, my body was on fire and I couldn't follow the conversation very well, or what exactly was happening around me, but I was uncomfortable because he was so close." She tipped her head up, her eyes meeting his. "Is it going to bother you if I can't bring myself to go to the clubs and be on display like that?"

"I had already made up my mind I was never taking you to a club. Not ever." He dropped another kiss on her forehead as satisfaction gleamed in her green eyes. "I didn't mind Dario in the kitchen, because I knew he actually couldn't see us. I'd studied the angle and made certain the lights were just right. Giving you what you wanted was the goal. That and testing both of our limits. That, I think, was mine."

"He really couldn't see us?"

"Just a darker shadow if he strained. The cabinet is set back against that far wall. I asked him to stay by the counter, which he did. I made sure to test every position before I allowed him to come over."

She nuzzled his chest with her chin. "You always make me feel safe."

"You are safe with me. I've told you repeatedly, you will *always* be safe with me." He rubbed his chin on top of her head, the bristles along his jaw catching in her curls. "The scene in the great room went too far for me. There was no way to control the fire. It was as low as I could make it. Every now and then the flames flared up and I wasn't certain how much of you Dario could actually see and I didn't like that feeling. So, we won't be doing that again unless I've set up a better-controlled scene."

She snuggled closer into him. "I'm glad we're on the same page, and I'm glad it won't bother you that I wouldn't be comfortable at the clubs, exposed like that. You always had such a reputation. I didn't think I could keep up with you."

"I didn't really give a damn about anything, Brielle. I was a very young man, hot-tempered, angry, acting out. That was a time in my life I'm not so proud of."

"I watched you all the time," she murmured, her voice drowsy.

That particular tone of hers was one he was partial to. "I despised the Archambaults so much back then," he admitted. "They treated me as if I wasn't a person at all. I was simply an asset to them, one they could dictate to and move around like a little marionette on strings. I had no home, no base, no one to talk to. I realized very early on that not one single person cared about me as a person, only what I could do for them as a rider. Everything became about how fast I was. And then it was, could I get any faster? I told you this, I shouldn't repeat myself. I don't want to sound like I'm whining."

"Talking about your childhood and the way you grew up isn't whining, Elie," Brielle said. "I want to hear it."

"Sometimes, you were the only thing that got me through a day. I detested my life once I realized I didn't matter to a single person. The Archambaults scheduled every minute of my day, insisting I take so many rotations and then train younger riders when I wasn't working. I started going to the clubs out of

defiance, and then I did it because that kind of sex became addicting and it was one place I was in complete control."

Brielle rubbed her palm up and down his thigh, as if she could soothe away the terrible hurt his younger self had felt in those days. Rage had been his constant companion. "They wanted to dictate how I could live. They wanted my genetics passed on. They discussed this all without consulting me. I wasn't important enough to discuss it with."

Brielle traced little patterns along his thigh. "I had no idea that such an important family would treat one of its own family members and best riders that way. I'm so sorry, Elie. I know what it's like to feel alone."

"I know you do, Brielle." He brushed a kiss on top of her head. "I swear, *bébé*, I didn't know I was compromising you when you were so young by tangling your shadow with mine. I know you're uncomfortable that you enjoy kink . . ."

"I need it," she admitted in a low voice.

He was so damn proud of her. He kissed her temple. "I do, too. There's nothing wrong with us, Brielle. We just have to make sure we check in with each other all the time. You always need to let me know if you don't want to do something. If I take something too far."

"I will. Keep talking to me about the Archambaults."

He let her get away with shifting the subject back to him.

"Stefano says they've changed how they do things because I refused to return to them and made my home here instead." He laughed softly. "They did get their way when the computer matched us together in spite of you refusing to marry me. Not that I want our children to experience anything like I did when they train."

"What if they have problems in the shadows the way I do? That can be genetic, Elie. No one has ever looked into it, but it's highly likely I could pass that on to our children."

He shrugged. "Then our children will find other jobs that are equally useful to our family just as you've done. I do want to go with you and see just how ill you get when you're in the shadows."

The moment he made the declaration, as casual as it was, she tensed. "That's not necessary, honey. I said I would rather take an investigator's job. I won't go into the shadows unless it's absolutely crucial."

"It's necessary to me, Brielle," he said firmly. "I need to see for myself how difficult it is for you. In an emergency, I'll want you to use the shadows to escape. If we have children, I'd expect you to take them into the shadows to get them out of harm's way while I hunted our enemies."

"You don't ever have to worry on that score, Elie," Brielle returned. There was absolute steel in her voice. "Not only can I promise our children will be safe, but I'd hunt with you."

He sighed and tugged on the mass of wild curls. "You're a little bloodthirsty thing, aren't you? I find you sexy as hell, Brielle, but you're going to have to rein it in. Dario and Valentino will be very bad influences on you if you go to work for them. It's bad enough having the Ferraros around you."

She gave him her little undignified giggle that slipped out every now and then and tugged on his heartstrings. Once she'd sobered, she pressed her head back against his chest. "In some ways, I felt as if I had to protect my parents and Fayette, even at a young age. They had already gone through so much of their resources by the time I was able to know what was going on that I knew my mother was embarrassed to entertain in the house."

Elie tightened his arms around her. "Baby, I love that you're so fierce, but we need to have an agreement that you're going to let me handle the crazies of the world and you'll point me to them. I like teamwork. Having you be a big part of that is important to me, but knowing you're safe is also important to me."

"You didn't specify on the application that you didn't want a shadow rider, Elie."

He listened to the nuances of her voice. She was carefully neutral. No inflections whatsoever.

"That's true, Brielle. I'm ashamed to say when I thought I was marrying a stranger, I didn't think it would matter to me

if she went into the shadows and took rotations. I figured it would be all to the good, actually. I'd have time to get used to her and she would me. But you aren't a stranger. I've had years of thinking about you. Worrying about you. Being pissed as hell at you." He emphasized that with a bite to her shoulder and not a particularly gentle one, either.

Brielle yelped, but Elie continued.

"You matter to me; you always have. I don't want to chance losing you. What I feel for you isn't all about our connection with the shadows, although truthfully, every chance I get, just like I did back when you were a kid, I still tie you to me more and more."

"You do?" There was a hopeful note in her voice. She ducked her head, burying it on his chest so he couldn't see her face, but he heard that note in her voice that told him maybe she actually could care a little bit about him, too.

"Of course I do. You damn well nearly stopped our wedding right in front of the priest and all the Ferraros. If I could have, I would have spent all night with our shadows tangling together, just so it would have been impossible for you to even think of leaving me."

"I'm sorry, Elie. I was so terrified when I realized it was you." Her voice was whisper soft, brushing over his skin like the touch of fingers.

"Why? It wasn't about me knowing you were into kink, *ma belle*. You aren't in the least embarrassed. You already knew I was. You aren't inhibited. A little shy at first with experimenting, but you're ready to please me when I ask, so your hesitation had nothing to do with sex. On some level you knew Fayette lied to you about me. At the very least, you would have asked me yourself. You have integrity. Even if you don't entirely trust yourself to hear truth, I think you would have known if I had lied to you."

Brielle remained silent, shaking her head. Her body had gone tense, when before she was completely relaxed. He stroked caresses along her arms and hips in an effort to comfort her. She even gave an involuntary shake of her head.

"*Bébé*, you trust me with your body. When are you going to trust me with your heart?" He asked the question softly, aching for both of them. His heart was already involved. All those years of thinking about her, despising the fact that he'd hurt her because he'd been young and stupid and so angry that the Archambaults had stolen his childhood and made him an object rather than a human being. But in reality, hadn't her parents done the same to her? She'd turned out compassionate and warm.

"I'm afraid, Elie." Her voice was a mere thread of sound. "I'm all or nothing. If you shattered me, I'd never be able to put myself back together."

He heard the raw truth in the admission and it humbled him. He'd protected his heart for so long against everyone, never realizing until Stefano showed him a man could be strong and still love his family fiercely. Somehow, Brielle had slipped inside him, even when she wasn't present. Had she been real all along, or was she his fantasy? He was as terrified as she was to make that huge leap of faith.

"It's the same for both of us, Brielle. You aren't alone in that particular fear."

CHAPTER TWELVE

"Hello, Dino," Elie greeted softly. "I heard you were looking for me."

Dino Colombo whirled around to stare at him, shocked that Elie Archambault would show up in the middle of the night in his private locked office. In his home—his gated home—the one with his security force all around him. He was also very aware his father and mother were in the house as well. They had come to visit and were spending the night in the guest suite just one story below his office.

"Move away from your desk," Elie instructed in a clear, concise and very low voice. "Normally, I would have simply killed you and let it go at that, but I thought maybe we could talk this out. I know your desk is equipped with an alarm button and several weapons. If you reach for either, it will be the last move you ever make. Know that at this moment, every member of your family has a member of my family visiting them, including your wife. Make the wrong move and they will all be wiped out. I suggest you very quietly take the chair out in the middle of the room facing me."

Dino glared at him. "You don't know who you're screwing with, Archambault." He pushed off the edge of his desk, took three strides and dropped into the chair that had mysteriously been set up in the center of his office.

Elie let silence stretch between them for a few moments. Then he smiled. The smile didn't touch his eyes and was rather cruel. "I know everything there is to know about you. When we send assassins, we make certain our investigators don't fuck up. You take orders like any good little minion, so you didn't bother to check Valentino, Dario or me out for yourself. You took the word of your good friend Carlo Santoro in New York. Unfortunately for you, he fucked up royally. He was so careful not to give the order to touch a Ferraro. There's a reason for that, Dino. No one ever touches them because once that happens, retaliation is swift and brutal."

Dino did his best to look bored. "Just because you know Santoro's name doesn't mean shit. And everyone who's anyone knows you don't fuck with the Ferraros."

"Valentino Saldi is married to Emmanuelle Ferraro, the youngest and only girl in the Chicago Ferraro family."

Dino straightened in his chair, looking as if Elie had struck him. "That's not possible."

Stefano moved out of the shadows and sat on the edge of the desk, folding his arms across his chest. "She's my baby sister." His hooded eyes burned a hole right through Dino's shocked gaze.

Dino began to shake his head and sputter.

Elie took out a photograph and slapped it into Dino's large hand. "Take a look at that. My bride walking down the aisle to me. Brielle Couture. Recognize the man walking her down the aisle?"

Dino's big fingers nearly crushed the picture as he looked at the man in the suit, so clearly Stefano Ferraro. "I'm sorry, Mr. Ferraro, I didn't know."

"Look at me, not him," Elie said quietly. "Brielle is married to me. First you gave the order to kill her. When that didn't happen, you sent two teams, first with the order to kill her, then

at the last minute it was changed to kidnap her. You're part of an international human trafficking ring. Who gave that order to you that she was to be kidnapped, not killed? Understand, Dino, the lives of your entire family are at stake."

"The order came from Carlo Santoro at the last minute. The Santoro family is tied to the Toselli family in Barcelona through marriage," Dino supplied. He tried to sound arrogant, as if just the name *Toselli* would scare Elie and Stefano.

Elie was well aware of those ties, thanks to his brilliant wife. At one time, the Toselli family had ruled parts of Sicily, Italy and Spain with an iron fist. No one moved without their say-so. They were so powerful, they had ties to governments and certainly law enforcement. Most notably, they were tied to the drug cartels of South America.

Eventually, other families in Sicily and Italy went to war when the Tosellis in those regions tried to bite into their territories. The feuds went on for quite a long while. Unbeknownst to the Tosellis, the Ferraros were enlisted to aid one of the smaller Italian families, and with no explanation, the Italian family became the undisputed ruler of the territory. Little by little the Toselli family lost ground. Recently, they had begun to come back in strength, building their power again, both through drugs and human trafficking. He should have known the Toselli family was involved.

Both the Ferraro and the Archambault families had their investigators tracing how Brielle's name had gotten back to the Toselli family to put her on a hit list. She had turned her findings over to the investigators of the rider family in Barcelona. None of them could conceive of a rider on the payroll of the Toselli family, but the shadow riders weren't taking any chances.

Elie studied Dino's face for a long time, allowing the man to see he wasn't impressed. "You don't seem to understand we can get to anyone and no one ever knows we were there. That includes the Toselli family. How did they know Brielle investigated them?"

Dino shrugged. "I have no idea. I just got the order from

Carlo. You'd have to ask him." He smirked. "He's in New York in case you want to go see him."

"I intend to do just that. I don't think you have anything else to tell me that I don't already know." Elie didn't move from his chair. "You're not too smart, Dino. You should have done your homework before you targeted my wife. You would have known the Archambault family is no one to fuck around with. We police the Ferraros. And messing with Valentino Saldi and Dario Bosco? Are you out of your mind? You have to know their reputations. They will skin you alive. I might have promised to keep your family alive, but they aren't nearly as nice as I am."

"I told you what you wanted to know. Get the fuck out."

Elie arched an eyebrow. "Did you think you'd live through the night after you tried to have my wife killed? I promised to let your family live, not you, you son of bitch."

Behind Dino, Stefano grasped the man's head in his hands, in the age-old traditional manner of the kill. He yanked in one fluid motion, breaking the neck easily. "We didn't get anything new."

"Not really, just confirmation of everything Brielle already told us. Let's get back to the jet. There's a party going on with the LA cousins and we can't leave until Ricco, Mariko, Giovanni and Sasha return. We'll head for New York."

Stefano stepped into a shadow and Elie selected a second one. At once, his body felt as if it were being torn apart, the skin flying from his bones as the tube shot him through it with unbelievable speed. The shadow took him down the stairs and through the great room and under the door, nearly spitting him out before he could halt in the mouth of the portal, waiting for his body to orient while he looked for the next shadow to step into.

All riders kept maps of cities in their heads. He knew the route to the airport and made his way back without hesitation. Used to riding the shadows, he chose the smaller feeder tubes that were extremely fast, so much so that oftentimes they could

make an experienced rider ill, but he wanted to get back to the plane and go over all the reports sent in from the investigators.

Leone Palagonia and Raimondo Abatangelo, Brielle's two bodyguards, had been trained by Emilio Greco, Stefano's cousin and head of security. Elie had received training as a personal protector from him and knew firsthand how thorough he was. Few could surpass him when it came to training his men. Elie knew his wife was not only protected by the two men, but the security of the house had been reviewed by Emilio as well as the Ferraro family. He should be satisfied that she was safe, as long as she was there, but for some reason, he had this nagging feeling in his gut he couldn't quite get rid of.

The truth was, he preferred to watch over her himself. He couldn't very well insist she travel with him through the shadows when he'd told her he didn't want her going into them unless it was absolutely necessary. Stefano had the time to go with him to seek out Dino Colombo. He wasn't very happy that his brother-in-law had been targeted and he was more than willing to make that known. Elie knew Stefano didn't want Emmanuelle to go after the Colombo family or the Santoro family unaided, which she was more than capable of doing.

Elie waited until the pilot for the Ferraro aircraft had opened the door and stood at the top of the stairs as if he needed fresh air. The pilot, Franco Mancini, had thrown on overhead lighting, casting shadows up the stairs so Stefano could slip inside and then Elie. Once both men were inside and out of sight due to the covered windows, Franco stamped around a little and then came back inside, closing the door.

"Text the others and tell them to cut it short and come back when they can make a graceful exit," Stefano ordered. "Use code, Franco."

Franco nodded. He turned and went back up front. Elie picked up one of the reports from Stefano's investigators. "You read this already?"

"Haven't had the chance. They just came in. I had Franco

print them out for us. Didn't want to put it on our phones. We can burn these." Stefano picked up the second copy.

There was silence while they both hurriedly read through the reports. Elie swore under his breath. "They thought this was acceptable? I'll be paying them a visit."

Stefano glanced up. "Elie, I understand you're pissed. I am, too. In all fairness, the report Brielle handed over to the Ignazio investigators didn't have anything at all to do with the shadow riders or any case they were on. The investigators were most likely overworked as it was and, not knowing what to do, handed Brielle's report over to Interpol. They removed her name to protect her, but when an Interpol agent followed up and wanted to know who had turned in the work to know how credible it was, they were given her identity."

"Which was absolutely wrong," Elie pointed out. "Nor did they warn her they were going to and they didn't tell her they'd done it."

"No, they didn't, but you can't just go after them. You have to go through channels."

"I'm an Archambault, Stefano. I *am* the channel you go through."

Stefano gave him a faint grin. "I notice how you make that work for you when you want to, Elie."

"What's the point of having the cursed name if I can't use it to my advantage once in a while?" Elie continued to scan the document. "If Brielle's report was passed around to several departments, any corrupt agent could have discovered her name once it was attached to it."

"That was my thought as well," Stefano agreed.

"I don't like that the Ignazio investigators simply handed out her information," Elie said. "It's possible one of them was bribed."

Stefano nodded. "Or threatened. The Toselli family plays rough, although if an investigator is threatened, they merely have to go to a rider and the threat should be handled immediately. The council would sanction any kind of retaliation and an investigator would know that."

"So, they were careless, or they took a bribe. Either one is not good."

Stefano flashed a faint smile. "I thought my brothers were bad, but you've taken on all my worst traits and have the arrogance and savagery of the Archambaults. When we head for Barcelona, Elie, I might just give you so much work, you won't be able to come."

Elie couldn't help but laugh at the empty threat. "We'll see."

"You're sure about your woman." It was a statement of fact.

Elie inclined his head. "Absolutely."

"I can see it in you. Almost from the moment you laid eyes on her in the chapel, definitely in my office. There was resolve in you like I've never seen before. You weren't about to let her slip away from you. Did you ever find out the real reason she didn't want to stay married to you? Because she's one hundred percent attracted to you. I'd say she might even have genuine feelings for you. She's far too intelligent to believe the bullshit her sister spewed for too long. At least she had to question it."

"I think the problem is she does have genuine feelings for me and that scares the hell out of her. Neither one of us has a very good track record when it comes to family loving us. That translates to a lot of insecurities. She can relate through sex, and her intellect, but she fears handing over her heart to me. I can't really blame her."

"You making certain there's no chance of losing her?"

Elie knew his smile was ruthless. "I've tied her shadow so tight to mine, I'm surprised it can breathe with all the knots I've tangled in it. Every moment we're together, I add more. I think I'll be doing that until the day we both die."

Stefano nodded approvingly. "I do the same with Francesca. She's my world. I'm not so easy to live with and I never will be. She knew that going into our marriage, but knowing it and living with it are two different things. I try to remember what she has to live with so no matter what, when we clash, I force myself to listen to her. I can be terrified for her safety, and that's what makes me the craziest, but I still listen. She

needs me to hear and acknowledge her point of view. I can't always give her exactly what she wants, but I do my best to come close."

"I hear what you're saying, Stefano," Elie said. He did hear. It was just that . . . "Brielle has a different personality than Francesca."

Francesca was the heart of the Ferraro family. Even Dario had to acknowledge that. He'd fallen a little bit under her spell whether he wanted to admit it or not. She was sweet and compassionate, traits Brielle had in abundance, but Brielle was also a fierce warrior and she would go her own way in an instant.

"Brielle will defy me the moment she thinks I'm in danger or you're in danger or anyone else. She won't think twice. She's got a wild streak in her, one I love, but one that could definitely get her in trouble. I think from the beginning that was half the attraction to her, back when I noticed her in the places she worked. She was too young and I was all about defying the Archambaults. I've got my personality and she's got hers and we're bound to clash in all-out wars."

Stefano poured Elie a drink of whiskey, handing him the crystal glass and then pouring one for himself. "Maybe, if you allow it to go that far, Elie, but you're the one in control. She likes it that way and that's your one advantage. It's up to you to keep that advantage. You have to know her so well that you anticipate what she's going to do before she does it. How she's going to react to any given piece of information. If you know ahead of time her reactions, you can prevent arguments and stop the behaviors that could possibly get her killed."

Elie turned Stefano's advice over and over in his mind as he took a drink. Stefano was definitely right about Brielle. She preferred Elie to lead and be a strong lead. She wanted a partnership, but if he gave direction, she took it immediately. For one moment, she had thought to object because he had included himself in the meeting with Dario and Valentino when she would interview with them for a job, but she backed down when he just continued as if the matter had been settled.

"I didn't expect to feel so much for her so fast. It's . . . disconcerting. I mean, I knew I was obsessed with her, and had fantasies, but I had no idea I was even capable of feeling so damn deeply for anyone the way I do her."

Stefano laughed. "I understand completely. When I first met Francesca, believe me, I had no idea I was going to fall so damn hard or fast. It was terrifying. Still is."

Stefano, at least, had his siblings before he found Francesca. Elie had no one. Not a single person who cared about him enough to call him family. No one had loved him until the Ferraros had entered his life. He hadn't the least idea what a relationship was until he met them. Now he had Brielle. He knew there was a part of him that was more than terrified of losing her. Everything was new to him. Mishandling Brielle would be heartbreaking.

"Emmanuelle asked me to check into the Colombo family," Stefano confessed suddenly. "I didn't just choose them randomly. She had a feeling about them."

"She didn't share with Valentino or Dario?" That had been evident during the betting. Neither man had raised an eyebrow. Dario hadn't mentioned Emme when they discussed the information they'd obtained from the two prisoners, either.

"What led her in that direction?"

"I have no idea. Emme always had intuition that led her to request the investigators to move in different directions. She was always correct. I put it down to a gift. We all have them. As to why she didn't say anything to her husband or Dario, I suspect, as part of their security, she intends to remove any threat to them without having either of them forbid her to do so. Val would never want her to go to New York, and Dario would lose his mind."

Stefano took another drink of his whiskey. This time, his smile reached his compelling blue eyes. "She thought I was bad watching over her. Now she has the two of them, her brothers and you. Serves her right for all those times she snuck out of the house."

"Can you imagine what Dario would be like if he found a

woman he wanted?" Elie asked. "I've tried, but my mind just doesn't go there."

All traces of a smile faded from Stefano's face. "I haven't allowed the investigators to delve too deep into his past; not that I think they'd find much. He's got his past buried deep if I'm right about him. Dario's very damaged. That kind of damage doesn't get fixed just because we love him. He feels deep loyalty for those he allows into his circle. Even love. So, he's capable. But he's also capable of shutting off all emotion and that isn't good. I think without Val, he could have gone an entirely different direction."

Elie agreed with Stefano's assessment of Dario. "He's a good man deep down. He makes the right choices. He has a code he lives by."

Stefano nodded. "Yes, I'll admit he does. And he loves our Emme fiercely. That makes me believe he could love a woman of his own, but if he found someone, I don't know if she could live with him, even if she loved him. He'd be difficult to love all the time. He'd make it difficult. He'd need her to prove her loyalty to him. He'd be worse than me with control and I'm pretty fucking bad. And there's his proclivity to kink. His club is renowned for it, and he makes no bones about how he plays. He doesn't care who knows how he is."

Elie was very aware of what Stefano was talking about. He enjoyed playing in the bedroom with Brielle. He had enjoyed going to the clubs. He had never been into any of the things Dario was into—and Dario wasn't playing. He lived that lifestyle and would expect his wife to live it as well. Yeah, Elie couldn't see a woman putting up with Dario forever. How could the man make it worth her while? He felt sad for Dario. Dario had to know there was little to no hope for him, but then, Elie had felt the same way and, somehow, he'd been granted a miracle.

"He's a strange man," Elie said. "But I like him. A lot."

"I do, too," Stefano admitted.

Franco returned from the cockpit. "The others are on their

way back. They've had quite the party with the cousins. Lots of pictures taken."

"That's good," Stefano approved. Photographs were what always kept the family safe. As long as the paparazzi photographed them at nightclubs and social events during the time deaths occurred, all riders were safe. No one could ever blame a Ferraro or any other shadow rider for a death in the community. All the LA cousins were accounted for at the club with their Chicago cousins. No one was the wiser that Stefano and Elie were in town. They both were supposedly back in Chicago with their wives.

As a rule, a rider rarely carried out an assassination in his own hometown. A rider came in from another city; that way, no suspicion could ever fall on those living close. A plane would arrive carrying cousins and they would all get together in a very public way. Behind the scenes, an assassination would take place, carried out by the unseen rider who had ridden the shadows to and from the plane just as Stefano and Elie had. That way, if the petitioner ever changed their mind and decided to go to law enforcement and confess they'd hired the Ferraros to carry out an assassination, there was no proof of such a thing.

Elie waited until Giovanni and his wife, Sasha, entered the plane, waving wildly at the Los Angeles cousins, who were yelling back to them to come again soon. Behind them, Mariko entered while Ricco, his hand on the small of her back, brought up the rear. Franco closed the door and the four newcomers turned to Stefano and Elie.

"Everything go all right?" Ricco asked, escorting his wife to one of the very comfortable leather chairs.

"No problems," Stefano assured. "Dino thought he was going to get away with putting out a hit on Val, Dario, Elie and Brielle without retaliation. I don't know why he would think we'd just have a little talk with him and walk out of there. Maybe shake his hand first."

"I'd like to be there when his father discovers him in the

morning and has to report his death to Riccardo Santoro," Elie said. "Santoro will beef up security around Carlo. He'll take Dino's death as a warning."

"It was a warning," Stefano said. "Although Carlo is going to die. My guess is, Santoro will ask for a meeting with Valentino and Dario. He won't try to hide he was behind the hits, but he'll blame them on the Toselli family and his ties with them."

"What will that accomplish?" Sasha asked. "That just sounds like he's admitting he tried to have Val and Dario killed. He is, isn't he? Isn't he the one who wants Brielle dead as well?"

Elie was never sure how much the Ferraro men told their wives. Mariko was a rider and took rotations alone. She was an excellent assassin. Sasha had never been trained, although she was deadly with rifles. She'd been raised on a ranch and she knew her way around weapons. She wasn't afraid of much and Elie knew she trained with the others and had asked Enrica, Emilo's sister, to train her as a personal protector. She was often left with Francesca, Grace and the children if there was an emergency, and she wanted every advantage should there be a need to protect them. It was obvious that she knew why they had come to Los Angeles.

"Santoro's used to making deals," Stefano answered. "He'll try to give Val and Dario a piece of the action. Hopefully, whatever he offers them will give us some insight into how he's running the trafficking operation. I wouldn't be surprised if Brielle already knows everything about it by the time we get home." There was an edge of humor to his voice.

"She's really that fast on a keyboard?" Mariko asked.

"Like lightning," Ricco said.

The engines were rumbling and Franco's voice came over the cabin's speakers, warning them they were about to take off. Ricco reached out almost causally to ensure Mariko had her seat belt fastened. Elie hid a smile. The gesture was so automatic, it was clear Ricco hadn't even thought about it. He'd seen Stefano do the same thing with Francesca each time

they were in a car or a plane. Sasha, however, did up her own seat belt and reached for Giovanni's hand.

Elie realized the very competent Mariko didn't mind Ricco's extra check because it was what Ricco needed, not her. Francesca didn't care that Stefano needed that extra check as well. The two women didn't feel as if it took anything away from them as women. They were giving something to their men. Sasha's man didn't need that same reassurance. Whatever he needed, she evidently provided. Every relationship, he realized, was different, depending on what each person needed or wanted.

"Brielle's accurate, too," Stefano said. "That ass Dario intends to scoop her up, doesn't he? Has he already tried to get her?"

Elie laughed. "That same night. Offered her adventure. Said you'd be trying to get her but you're more mundane and wouldn't let her branch out and fly like he would."

"That rat. I'm going to pay him a visit and see what kind of surprises I can leave for him to unravel. He won't be calling me mundane after that."

"Those weren't his *exact* words," Elie said, a little more cautious. He didn't want a war between Dario and Stefano, even a friendly one. "She has to hear their offer still."

The humor faded from Stefano's eyes. "You'll be with her." He made it an order.

"Of course. I know their rules, even for family. She isn't familiar with them. Emmanuelle would look after her."

"Would Emme be there? A part of the meeting?" Stefano asked. "She's Ferraro and Saldi, with ties to both families."

"Brielle is Ferraro," Elie said firmly. "My name is Archambault, but I'm still Ferraro and she's my wife. Our first loyalty lies with you. I made that very clear to Dario. I told him I would not allow her loyalties to be divided. He assured me they would never put her in that position."

"But they don't know Brielle, do they?" Stefano said quietly. "She'll say she won't go any further than Dario and Val direct her, but she has a gift. That gift compels her, Elie. When

there is compulsion involved, it is very difficult to stop. I doubt if Brielle will be able to overcome something she's been doing since she first touched a keyboard."

Elie feared Stefano was right. "That's why I'm going to the meeting. I want to lay down the rules if she wants to work for them."

"You want her to."

Elie inclined his head. "I think it would be good to have a pair of eyes other than Emme's there. I don't mean using Brielle as a spy. She wouldn't do that even if I asked her. She'd simply say she couldn't do that kind of work. I don't like Emme responsible for security without any of us backing her up. Val and Dario have made a lot of enemies, and before this is all finished, they'll make a lot more. They hold a large territory and it has important ports. Someone is always going to be looking to take it away if they make a misstep. The good news is, Val and Dario are family and they have us."

"Dario never wanted to be head of his own territory. Val forced it on him," Stefano said. "I think he's come to understand it's best that he stays in that position. Dario's asked two men he's known since his childhood to join him. They'll act as his personal protectors. Valentino knows them, but no one else does, including my investigators."

"That's impossible." Ricco frowned. "They were born somewhere. They have to have paperwork. If they have any kind of paperwork, there's a trail and our people can follow them."

"You would think," Stefano said.

The plane leveled out as they all sat in stunned silence.

"The paperwork is that good?" Giovanni ventured.

"It is," Stefano said. "At least, that's what Romano told me. He said no doubt it was forged for the two of them, but it was the best he'd ever seen, other than Dario's. They're supposedly from a small village in Sicily, but came here some years ago and have US citizenship. If any of this crap is to be believed, they received their citizenship at the same time, nine

years ago. They travel a lot, back and forth between here and Europe."

"You talked to Val about them?" Elie asked. "Because neither of them said anything to me about these men."

"They arrived just before we boarded the plane. Taviano sent a text to Franco along with photographs. Anyone new in Emme's world, we like to vet for her." Stefano indicated their phones as they started lighting up. "These are the men. As you can see, they are extremely intimidating. They aren't even trying to hide what they are."

Again, there was a short silence while they studied the faces of the two men Dario had brought into his organization. He had proclaimed to Elie he didn't trust anyone other than Valentino. But had he said that? What was it he said exactly? Who were these men to Dario? They had the same cold, killer eyes. The same detached, emotionless, stone expressions. Elie didn't want them around Brielle.

Knowing Brielle, the moment she realized the paperwork on the newcomers was forged, she would try to track their true identities with her keyboard. She wouldn't be able to resist. That was what Stefano had been talking about.

"Dario needs men he can trust in his organization. Val's spread too thin trying to protect both of them. Emme can't be in two places at one time. When I'm not taking a rotation for you, Stefano, I've been covering Dario. He insists the guards all cover Valentino and that leaves him completely vulnerable." Elie stayed concealed in the shadows most of the time. He wasn't about to leave Dario vulnerable during the day when so many of Miceli's old followers were still hidden within the organization just waiting for an opportunity to kill the new don.

"I just wish we knew more about them," Stefano said. "Dario knows us. He should have talked to us before he brought them on board."

Elie felt compelled to defend Dario. "He hasn't been around our family that long, Stefano. He's only known and trusted Valentino. He let Emmanuelle in recently. Through her, we became

his family and that's been a reluctant acceptance. But he's learning, just as I had to learn. It's a slow process. Give him a little time."

"I've got to agree with Elie, Stefano." Ricco unexpectedly backed him up. "We don't know Dario's past, but we know it had to be horrific and it didn't include much in the way of family or relationships."

The lines in Stefano's face deepened visibly, giving Elie insight into what it must be like to have the weight of not only an entire family on his shoulders, but the Chicago rider community. No outsiders had been allowed to know about shadow riders until Emmanuelle had married Valentino. She had never told her husband, never given him any information on her family, but he'd figured it out by watching her closely, and the Saldis had their own version of a shadow legacy. By Dario bringing in unknown men, men he hadn't discussed in advance with Stefano, he had inadvertently threatened the family and the community of shadow riders because those men would be with Dario at all times.

"Elie, I'm going to put this on you. You have a couple of days to straighten this out. Talk to him. Make certain he understands he needs to bring these sorts of decisions to me before he makes them. Any man that accompanies him around us needs to be vetted. Hopefully, Emmanuelle or Valentino has already explained to him the reasons and he understands."

Elie wasn't so certain Dario would understand. The Saldis operated an empire. They had for hundreds of years. Dario was part of that and he'd grown up with that legacy. They didn't bring outsiders in any more than the shadow riders did. The Saldis' criminal organization had been run on fear, intimidation and secrecy successfully. They stayed away from civilians for the most part, keeping their dealings with those in their world, building up their coffers with the sales of guns and drugs in the various countries where they held power. They had their hands in most deals, from laundering money to betting on just about anything.

Giuseppi Saldi, Valentino's adoptive father, had drawn the

line at human trafficking. It was a firm line, one with which his brother Miceli didn't agree. The power struggle had nearly cost Valentino his life. Val and Dario were still trying to find out how their ports were being used and who in their organization was aiding the traffickers. Just because the Ferraro family had come to the Saldi family's aid and they'd formed an alliance didn't mean Dario would think he had to answer to them or share all knowledge. Stefano certainly didn't think he had to share with the Saldis. How did one point that out tactfully to the head of the shadow riders?

"I'll talk to him." What else was there to say?

Ricco sent him a faint smile. He knew that conversation wasn't going to be an easy one and didn't envy Elie at all.

"Are the New York investigators working on the Santoros or are we keeping this in-house?" Giovanni asked.

Everyone on the plane fell silent again as they all looked to Stefano. His word was law as far as the family was concerned. No one, not even Emmanuelle, would go against him. He scowled and shook his head. "It's protocol to inform them if we're going to make a hit in their city. We have to use them for cover, just as we did our cousins in LA. I told Severino that we had investigated the Colombo family for Emmanuelle. We knew Dino had put a hit out on Valentino, Dario, Elie as well as Brielle. I told him we'd stumbled across the information during the contest between Brielle and the other investigators. Everything I said was true, including that Brielle continued to research after the contest was over because she had a 'hunch' just as Emmanuelle had."

Elie had met Severino Ferraro several times. He was head of the Los Angeles family of shadow riders. Very much like Stefano, he was respected by his siblings and all other riders. Stefano and Severino were very close. If Stefano asked Severino for a free ride in his city, he'd get it. As it was, Stefano had assured Severino that they'd done their homework and everything was in order.

"I turned over Brielle's initial report, including the damning photographs. I'm not about to ever put him in a position

of having to answer to the international council for us. He is fully aware that Emmanuelle is married to Valentino and that she is head of his security whether he approves or not. Which, by the way, he does not."

"I take it neither do you," Elie said.

"Do you?" Stefano challenged. "Do any of you?"

Sasha and Mariko exchanged a look and both raised their hands. "She's extremely intelligent," Sasha said. "And capable."

"She has gifts," Mariko added. "Talents others don't. They would go to waste if she sat at home. She would be unhappy, Stefano. She was born to be a rider and she's very good at what she does."

"I'm very aware of my sister's abilities. I had her train with Elie for a reason," Stefano said. His voice turned harsh.

Ricco's head snapped up and he sent his brother a warning look.

Stefano visibly made an effort to soften his voice. Again, Elie took note. "Valentino's world is different from ours, Mariko. My worry for Emme has nothing to do with her abilities and everything to do with the fact that loyalties aren't the same. They shift according to power and money in that world. She was raised with loyalty coming first. She's given that to Val and Dario. I believe Val returns that loyalty; most likely Dario does as well."

Elie didn't like the fact that now Stefano was questioning Dario's loyalty even to Emmanuelle. He hadn't ever thought that would happen. That made him uneasy. Dario was the backup for Leone and Raimondo. Val and Emme were out of town. Vittorio and Grace had gone to check out some site for one of Grace's events she planned for a charity, so they were on the other side of Chicago. He knew Taviano and Nicoletta were in the city visiting Lucia and Amo and weren't going to be around. Dario had agreed to be backup if it was needed, not that anyone thought for one evening there would be a problem. Now his gut nagged at him. There could be no communication because, technically, he was supposed to be in the

house with Brielle, just as Stefano was with Francesca at the Ferraro Hotel.

"Once we go to New York, I'll talk to Geno and tell him what Brielle discovered on the Santoro family and that we intend to take down that family. I can't very well go into his territory and not inform him."

Geno Ferraro was head of the family of shadow riders in New York. There were only three riders in New York. It was a very small group and at times the other cousins helped to fill their rotations when necessary. Geno, like Stefano and Severino, carried the weight of his siblings and the other riders on his shoulders, but he never shirked his duties. Elie knew him to be a good man. He didn't want to get him in trouble with the international council, either. It was a good thing they'd held the contest to see just how fast and accurate Brielle was on her keyboard, although at the time, Elie thought it rather silly.

CHAPTER THIRTEEN

Brielle stood at the windows of her office staring at the lake below. She had to admit, she loved the view and the spaciousness of the huge room. She could look down into the backyard and see the patio where she shared morning coffee and orange juice with Elie. They'd been together over a month now, and she still had to pinch herself every now and then to believe it was real.

Just the thought of Elie produced a full-body shiver. He enjoyed getting up very early, before the sun rose, to work out. She got up with him, because who wouldn't want to watch him work out, and she loved working out, too. They trained together. He was unbelievably fast and it brought her skills up quickly. Then they showered together. Most of the time, they had sex in the shower, or he would make love to her on the bed, or the dining room table before she prepared breakfast. He loved omelets. She preferred fruit. She prepared both for them.

Some mornings, he wouldn't initiate sex and the anticipation always made her body coil tighter and tighter as she cooked for the two of them. He liked touching her and he

always did while in the kitchen, which only added fuel to an already burning fire. Just thinking about Elie could make her body ache. He had a way of looking at her that made little flames lick at her skin. She found herself wanting to do anything for him, anything to keep that look of arousal in his eyes and those lines of carnal lust carved into his face when he looked at her.

Sometimes, in the morning when he pretended to be aloof, when he didn't touch her in the shower, but his cock was hard and he shook his head when she brushed her fingers along his thighs, her heart went wild at that controlled expression. She loved that as much as the one of total arousal. They would take their breakfast out to the patio and sit at the smaller, more intimate two-person table to eat. It was her favorite time. One of anticipation. Those times, he would tell her to wear his favorite robe. The smoke-and-rose one and nothing else.

This morning had been one of those times. The sun hadn't quite come up yet and it was quiet like it always was just before daybreak. Not dark. Not light. This morning the lake had been relatively peaceful. As she sat there at the table with Elie, she'd felt her body trembling. Waiting. Her entire focus was on Elie. She was aware of every single thing about him. Every movement. The way he brought his coffee cup to his mouth. The bites he took of his omelet. The oblong box sitting close to the coffeepot in the middle of the table. She knew what was in that box.

He watched her eat three of her strawberries and then beckoned her to him. Her nipples peaked and hot blood pounded through her veins. She wasn't wearing any panties or they would have been soaked. She stood and moved the two steps necessary to take her to him, trying to stay still and not squirm.

Elie smiled and opened her robe, pushing the fabric to the side so it framed her breasts. "You're so damned beautiful."

A part of her was thrilled when he gave her those compliments. She needed them. Not because she was vain, but because she was still building confidence that he really wanted

her as a woman. There was sincerity in his voice. He gave her that one hundred percent focus when he looked at her, as if he couldn't tear his gaze away. That added to the excitement building in her.

"Offer your breasts to me, *bébé*."

That had been new. Just that morning he was going to Los Angeles with Stefano and two of the Ferraro couples who would be meeting with cousins to go clubbing. Brielle shivered again and touched the curves of her breasts, remembering how she complied, cupping the soft weight of her breasts and lifting them toward his mouth.

It felt so decadent and sexy to be standing outside in the early morning hours in her short, nearly transparent robe offering her breasts to Elie with him fully clothed. Then his mouth was on her right breast and she arched back, wanting to sob his name, wanting to bury her fist in his hair and yank him closer. He used his tongue and teeth ruthlessly, sending fiery darts rushing through her bloodstream in every direction. The clamp closed on her nipple and the fire pulsed through her, a storm of desire that shook her.

"I thought sapphires this time to go with the lake. They're drops going from small to large and are surrounded by diamonds. When the sun rises, you'll be able to see how beautifully they shine."

She could feel the brush of the chain of sapphires against her ribs. It was nearly to her belly, it was so long. It was also heavier than the emerald clamps. Then his mouth on her left breast distracted her and she was arching back again and the sapphire chain swayed madly, the clover clamp pinching down along with the bite of his teeth. Exquisite fire burst through her nipples as the second chain of sapphires dropped to brush along her exposed skin.

Elie indicated for her to step back for a moment. He nodded approvingly. "I knew that would be perfect. Come here, *bébé*."

His voice alone had sent velvet brushing over her skin. She wanted him so much, but more than that, her heart lurched

dangerously. She was so afraid there was no going back. She had stepped off a cliff and was free-falling. What if he wasn't what she hoped and dreamed? What if he was all fantasy and no reality?

"*Mon petit ange*, you scare yourself by thinking too much. Stay in this moment, unless you want to stop and we'll go inside and sit together and talk about what you're most afraid of."

She didn't want to stop. Her fears were not going to be put to rest so easily, not with one or two talks. She had issues and would for a long time, perhaps her entire life. Right now, she was desperate for him, thinking of him, her body on fire. She shook her head.

"I want to continue, Elie." She had no idea how she managed to get the words out.

His fingers bit into her hip, urging her forward another step. His hand slipped between her thighs, forcing her to widen them. "More, Brielle. This is a newer piece and one I'm experimenting with. I'm not certain if I'll like it. I drew it and had it made. It looks gorgeous, but against your skin it should look even more so."

Elie lifted another chain from the box and hooked it between the two clamps. The chain was a little heavier than the one on the emerald clamps. It didn't hang quite as low, not even to her belly button. He took another long chain, this one made up of small gems that looked as if they could be sapphires matching the ones hanging from her nipples. The long chain extended to her clit, where it clamped, and then dropped, just as the ones on her nipples, small to large gems, surrounded by diamonds.

Elie's fingers slid into her slick heat and then massaged her inflamed clit. She tried to ride his hand, to press against his fingers when he flicked and thumped and added more hot blood to the little bud. The bite of the clamp sent a fire of agony and ecstasy shooting through her. Each movement of her body sent the little sapphire chain hanging down swaying, pinching the clamp tighter.

He wasn't finished. He caught up a last, much longer piece

of sapphire-decorated chain and attached it on either side to the long gem-studded one just above her mound. He stretched the chain around her hips and indicated for her to turn and place her hands on the table. Heart beating like mad, she did so. Very casually, he dipped his fingers in her slick entrance over and over and then coated between her cheeks and her forbidden star.

"Big breath, *bébé*." He pushed a plug into her without further warning.

It felt a little larger than the last one, but she hadn't expected it and he went smooth and steady, pushing until it was all the way in without stopping to give her a break. Two chains fell across her cheeks and the large chain settled around her hips, low. He indicated for her to step back again.

Now she was dressed in sapphires. It was outrageous and she hoped the gems weren't real. The weight of them felt real. She moved away from the table a few steps, gliding the way a rider would, almost floating with her footfalls, so she wouldn't sway too much. Each step made those chains sway so that fire streaked through her.

"Let your hair down for me, Brielle."

He sounded like temptation. Like sin. He was up to something and she loved when he was. She loved being his focus. Loved when he played his games with her. She wished she could see herself. She lifted her arms carefully, trying not to lift her breasts, an impossible feat. Pulling the scrunchie from her hair sent wild curls cascading in every direction.

Elie lifted his phone and began to take photographs of her. He walked around her, telling her to turn her head this way and that or lift her arms or push out her bottom so he could see the harness to show her later. She obliged him, certain the pictures were only for the two of them.

When he had finished, he placed his phone on the edge of his table facing outward and brought up his playlist. Taking her hand, he switched on the music, and led her down to the lawn. Positioning her in the center, he began to move in a slow rhythmic circle around her, his body swaying to the music.

She recognized the song and knew the dance intimately. Elie was an excellent dancer. She'd learned that because she'd watched him and knew he was so good. This was a rumba, a very sexy dance and one that could be done close and intimate, or he could do several sensual movements that were demanding, including high leg lifts and sharp turns, swivels, lifts, any number of intricate dance steps that would set the chains leaping and swirling right along with her body.

Brielle couldn't help the excitement coursing through her as he moved behind her and reached for her robe, peeling it down over her arms to remove it altogether, leaving her adorned in sapphires and diamonds. He swept the curls off her neck and kissed his way to her earlobe before taking her hand and extending her arm as he began to move to the music, leading her into the first of several dance steps.

The rumba Elie chose was extremely sensual, and he moved close to her, his hand gliding up her leg so that she lifted it high above her head and spun in a circle. Every chain seemed to bounce and the plug tightened along with the clamps. Fire burst through her as he bent her body back over his, and her arm went gracefully over her head like a ballerina posing. He lifted her easily and both legs wrapped backward around him. The hips never stopped moving in rumba, and while she was "riding" him, his hips continued to move because his feet, ankles, knees and legs generated perfect action.

He turned her toward him and closed them intimately together, enfolding her in his arms, keeping barely a scant half inch between her breasts and his chest. Their upper bodies barely moved as their lower bodies kept time to the rhythm of the sensual music. She matched him easily, but as he led her through more intricate footwork, the little dangling chains hanging from her nipples and off her clit swayed and danced with her. Every step sent more fire pulsing through every nerve ending in her body.

It was a heady experience, dancing in the dim light, with the sun just beginning to rise over the lake. His mouth was on

her neck, teeth biting, lips kissing, tongue soothing. Between the tugging and bites of the clamps, the hot blood roaring through her body and her desperate hunger rising, her mind seemed to melt until there was only Elie. Nothing else. No one else.

When the song ended, he tipped up her chin and his mouth descended on hers. His kisses were white-hot, sizzling through her veins. She wrapped her arms around his neck, uncaring that the movement sent another jolt through her body from her nipples to her clit. She was already insane for him. The fiery bite sent streaks through her body of both pain and pleasure, mixing the two in that way she couldn't quite divide.

He lifted his head. "Come, *mon petit chat sauvage*." He took her hand again and led her to the firepit. The circular pit was very large and made of thick cement walls. "Face the lake so you can see the sunrise."

He placed her hands firmly on the wall of the firepit, bending her over, his palm smoothing her cheeks and then kneading them. She pushed back into his hands, unable to stop herself. He seemed to know she was at her limit, her body shuddering and shivering, moans escaping almost continually. He simply unzipped his trousers with one hand to free himself and lodged the broad head of his cock in her slick entrance. As he did, he brushed the jewel-encrusted chain wrapped around her lower body, sending the little dangling gems swaying.

"When you make those sounds, Brielle, I actually feel lust washing down my spine in waves of heat." He didn't plunge into her fast and ferociously as her body demanded. "I'm looking at you with the first rays of the sun streaking down highlighting you, dressed only in my sapphire-and-diamond chains. I knew they would sparkle, come alive as the sun came up, just the way they are. What I didn't know was, along with the lust, would come this other, entirely unexpected emotion."

He didn't say what that emotion was and she was so far gone, so in need, that she couldn't ask him, even though she desperately wanted to.

He entered her slowly. "I wish you could watch the way

your body is swallowing mine. This is the most intimate, sacred moment between a man and a woman."

Simultaneously, reaching between her legs, with infinite care, he opened the grips on the clit clamp to remove it even as he pushed his cock through her tight folds. At first, she was unaware, his movements had been so slow and gentle, she hadn't noticed he'd touched the clamp, and his cock had entered her tight tunnel, filling her, giving her that necessary burning stretch she desperately hungered for.

Blood rushed back to her sensitive clit. A thousand nerve endings came to stark, vivid life at once, sending a firestorm of agony and ecstasy twisting together through her. She sobbed his name as her body detonated; a massive, powerful orgasm overtook her fast, flowing into a series of waves that rocked her body. Her hips bucked against him. Her breasts swayed, setting the chains of jewels dancing, triggering even more waves.

He pulled back and surged forward again, feeding her his cock right through her orgasms, but not with his usual aggressive, wild, out-of-control force he used when they played. Each stroke was a slow, burning entry, pushing through her tight, convulsing folds with deliberate care. She felt the way his hot blood pounded through the thick girth of his cock, stretching the tender tissues of her channel. She felt the heavy vein running along his shaft. She could count his heartbeats through his cock. In spite of the sapphire-and-diamond harness and clamps, every movement he made felt like love to her.

"Look at the sun coming up, *bébé*. That's us. That's the way we are together." He whispered it against the small of her back, bending over her, pressing a kiss there. "Are you looking, Brielle?"

She lifted her head and looked at the lake, at the first fiery rays of the sun. As she did, his cock moved in her harder. Deeper. The exquisite flame matched the crimson beauty of the sun, that sweep of color falling around the water, looking as if it was rising from it. She could barely think with his cock moving in her the way it was, not fast, but hard, driving

through her narrow tunnel, so deep until she felt his balls smacking against her cheeks.

His hot breath was still ragged against the small of her back as he leaned over her body, his arms around her, under hers. Another hard surge forward and the flames raced through her body. Simultaneously, her nipples became engorged with blood as he gently removed the clamps with the grips. The intensity of the fiery chaotic frenzy of signals being sent through her body sent stars dancing behind her eyes and her body once more erupted into a powerful series of orgasms. She muffled a scream, trying to stay on her feet.

Elie wrapped an arm around her waist and began to move hard and fast in her, using the other hand to work the plug between her cheeks in a counter rhythm, so that the orgasms continued rolling through her, building and building until she thought she might really go insane from pleasure. Then he was pulling the plug from her body, gripping her hips hard, pulling her into him as she pushed into him, so they were coming together like two wild animals. She felt the hot splash as ropes of his seed coated her inner walls. Her sheath bit down on his cock, greedy for more, hungry for every last drop he could give her.

They stayed bent over the firepit for a long while, breathing hard, trying to catch their breath while the sun climbed a little higher. As usual, it was Elie who had managed to pull himself upright first. "Thank you, *ma belle*. You make me feel as if I have a home. Someone to come back to."

He murmured the words so softly, she nearly hadn't caught them, especially since he was pulling out of her and the slide of his cock triggered delicious aftershocks and her breathing was ragged and loud in her ears. Unhooking the chain around her hips, he gathered up the jewelry.

"Sit for a minute." He tucked his cock away and retrieved her robe.

"Elie." She had to moisten her lips. "You do have a home and someone to come back to. You have a family. Me. I'm

your home and family. You're mine. We may be new, but . . ." She indicated the sunrise. "That's us."

He studied her face for a long time. She couldn't read him.

"Let's go in before the boats start coming out to play." He wrapped his arm around her, kissed her thoroughly, tucked her under his shoulder and walked her back to the house.

Brielle, we're starving," Raimondo yelled from the bottom of the stairs. "Are you ever going to come down here and fix us something to eat?"

His voice snapped Brielle out of her reverie. She put her fingertips on the window as she looked down at the firepit. What had Elie meant by an unexpected emotion? He'd made her sad to think he'd never had anyone to come home to. She didn't know how to keep her heart safe anymore. She loved everything about Elie Archambault. He was unexpectedly . . . vulnerable. The strange thing was, he didn't realize it. He was always in charge, something she liked and needed. At the same time, he needed her and she wanted that. Yearned for that. She *needed* him to need her every bit as desperately as she needed him.

It was important to her that not just anyone would do for him. She didn't want to be just a warm body for him. There were so many moments with him that told her she was so much more. She just wasn't certain if she was making too much of those times because she so desperately needed him to be falling for her.

"Brielle." Now Leone sounded impatient.

She had to smile. Her two boys. That was how she thought of them. She knew she wasn't supposed to think of her personal protectors that way, but she did. She had confidence in her ability to protect herself. She could slide into a shadow and disappear if she had to. They couldn't. She didn't want either of them "taking a bullet" for her. That was absurd. She disliked the idea on principle alone.

"Seriously? You just ate. I made you French toast and eggs." Not just any French toast and eggs, either. She'd given them fresh maple syrup and caramelized pears with fresh fruit. Along with that, she'd made eggs Benedict. The two had consumed both dishes without a scrap left on their plates. She didn't see how either man could possibly be hungry for the rest of the day.

"That was hours ago, Brielle. *Hours*," Leone complained. "You've been up there working. When you're working, you have no idea how much time goes by."

"She's not working," Raimondo said. "I wouldn't have interrupted her if she'd been working. She was at the window, staring out at the lake and mooning over Elie again. Really, Brielle, it's disgusting how often you blank out and lose it over that man."

She came partway down the stairs and glared at him. "I don't do that." She *did* do that. Sadly. But she wasn't admitting it. Her nipples were sore. Her clit was sore. Deliciously so. The material of her underwear, as soft as it was, rubbed, causing a delightful friction that kept reminding her of her early morning adventure with her surprisingly adventurous husband. He certainly came up with interesting ideas that she would never have thought of.

"*Hungry*," Leone reminded her.

Brielle burst out laughing. "You're impossible. I'm surprised the two of you can even fit into your clothes. You must have super-fast metabolisms. If I ate like you, I wouldn't be able to even walk on my treadmill."

"You could stand to put on a couple of pounds," Raimondo observed. "Not to say," he added hastily, "that you aren't filled out in the right places."

Leone coughed behind his hand. "Talk like that could get you shot. Elie might have this place wired. He's a jealous man."

Brielle rolled her eyes. "He is not." She made her way down the stairs to stand at the bottom, her hands on her hips. "The two of you just make crap up. You're the gossip team."

"You don't think Elie's the jealous type?" Leone's eyebrow went up.

"No, I don't. Jealousy is a really bad character flaw. It doesn't say nice things about a man at all. In fact, Leone, it means he doesn't have confidence in himself, which Elie has in abundance, maybe a little too much. And it also means he doesn't trust his partner." She flounced past him to go into the kitchen.

Leone exchanged a grin with Raimondo. "I see. No one would ever expect that Elie could possibly have a character flaw."

"Or that he wouldn't trust his hot-as-hell partner," Raimondo added.

"For your information, Raimondo, he does have the place wired, although not because he's the jealous type," Brielle said as she pulled the container of masarepa cornmeal from the pantry, measured out two cups and put the container away. She would have given anything to look at her bodyguard, but she worked fast, collecting the other ingredients to make the Venezuelan arepas, griddle-fried corn cakes she needed for what she wanted to serve.

"Wait. What? Why would Elie wire this place? You mean he's recording what we're saying? He just heard me call you hot as hell?"

She pressed her lips together as she worked, quickly mixing the dry ingredients together and then adding in water, milk and butter, kneading the dough until it was very smooth.

"For God's sake, Raimondo, you just said it again," Leone pointed out. "Now you're sweating. What an idiot."

"Why would he wire the place?"

Brielle covered the dough to give the cornmeal time to absorb some of the moisture. She turned to face the two men as she leaned against the counter. "Mice. We're overrun with the little rodents and he's tracking them." She said it without hesitation. "The audio has a special algorithm built into it to detect the sound of their little feet when they run across the floor so we can find their nest."

There was absolute silence. She put a heavy cast-iron skillet on the stove and then retrieved two tomatoes and the pulled pork she'd prepped the day before from the fridge, setting both

on the counter before she looked up. The two men were staring at her. "What?" She did her best to look innocent.

"I've never heard of that. Is that really a thing?" Leone asked suspiciously.

"If you've never had mice everywhere, why would you have heard of it?" she countered as she sliced the tomatoes and set them aside.

The two men exchanged another long look and then turned back to her. "You're full of shit," Raimondo accused her. "There aren't mice in this house. If there were, you'd be standing on a chair right now."

"You mean *you'd* be standing on a chair right now. I would still be cooking because I'm afraid of mice." She glanced at the clock, took the cover off the dough and began kneading it again. She spent some time on the job before once again covering the dough and glancing at the clock.

"What are you making?"

"Venezuelan arepas. They're a griddle-fried corn cake. Sweeter and a little milder than regular corn tortillas. You'll love the sandwiches, trust me. Let me do my thing."

"No mice in the house, right?" Leone said.

She laughed. "You boys are so easy."

"That's what I thought. And no wires."

"Not to my knowledge." She added a few drops of barbecue sauce to the pork and heated it on low in the oven.

"You took ten years off my life, Brielle," Raimondo accused.

"I'll make it up with dinner." She began shaping the arepas into round disks nearly an inch thick and a good three to three and a half inches wide. Once she had them made up, she heated a light amount of vegetable oil in the skillet and placed the arepas into the oil, turning the heat down to medium-low. She wanted them crispy brown on each side, but not over-cooked. It took only three to four minutes to brown on each side. She cooked all of them.

"I hope you really like these. They've always been a favorite of mine." She sliced open the arepas, spread them with

mayonnaise and then a generous helping of the pulled pork. She added lime, cilantro and garlic along with a slice of tomato. "Try that. If you don't like it, I can make you a regular sandwich with just the pork." She made herself a sandwich from the arepas and sat at the dining table with a bottle of water.

Leone had already wolfed his down. "Where do you learn to make this kind of thing, Brielle?"

"I like cooking. When I like something, I tend to spend a lot of time researching it and trying to find people who will help me learn the things I want to know. I'm fairly good at researching so I can usually get in touch with the right people pretty quickly. I don't like to waste my time."

"I watched how you made this. Stay there, I'm going to make a couple more." He got up and went to the counter to fix himself two more sandwiches.

Brielle smiled, shaking her head. It was a good thing she'd made plenty. They really could eat. Raimondo joined Leone in the kitchen, making more sandwiches for their dinner.

Shadows were lengthening outside. She liked this time of day, although she had a view of the gardens and trees, not so much the lake from the dining room. She could see the front of the house and all the surrounding landscaping. She and Elie spent so much time outside in the back on the patio watching the beauty of the lake that she had all but forgotten they had the other side.

Finishing her sandwich, she studied the trees as they swayed in the breeze. The leaves turned and spun like dancers, glittering as the last rays of the sun fell over them, showing the dazzling colors of fall. She found it mesmerizing to see one side of a leaf appear orange and the other side green or gold. Somewhere in that thick expanse of trees, on the property that Elie had purchased, there was a hidden road that ran between Dario's home and theirs. You needed a four-wheel drive to use it, but it had been built between the two properties recently.

Valentino and Emmanuelle's home lay on the other side of Dario's. If Brielle hadn't promised Elie she would stay put,

she would have been tempted to explore. She'd been here awhile now and hadn't really gone to see either place. Nor had she seen much of anything in Chicago for that matter. When she was with Elie, the isolation didn't bother her. She enjoyed just spending time with him, getting to know him. But when he was away, she wanted to begin establishing her own life. Go out, find little places she enjoyed going to on her own. She'd always been independent. She would have to talk to him about that.

"You're sighing. Loudly," Leone observed.

Raimondo cleared the dishes from the dining table. He shot her a quick, worried look. "What's up, babe?"

She shook her head. "I just need to start learning my way around the lake and my neighbors' properties. I'm looking at maps, of course, but it isn't the same thing as actually going places and seeing where everything is with my own eyes. Maps aren't always correct, especially if they're old."

"You have plenty of time," Leone said. "Are you planning on working from home? I thought you'd decided not to take rotations as a rider. At least, that was what Elie indicated."

Brielle wasn't certain why she felt ashamed in front of the two men. They were Ferraros. Cousins of the Ferraros, but Ferraros. Riders were guarded fiercely. They were considered the most necessary of all family members because they kept everyone safe. There were very few of them and they dedicated their entire lives to being riders. A rider rarely chose whom they were able to marry; they led a life of duty. They certainly didn't get to say they didn't want to take rotations when they were needed. Everyone knew all capable riders were needed.

Brielle looked down at her nails. She kept them short, rarely put on more than a clear color, although sometimes, she liked to paint them dark red when she was in a mood. She felt moody now, but she wasn't certain why. Once more, she looked outside. The sky was streaking with silver and gray through the blue. Clouds drifted closer as the wind picked up, making the leaves on the trees whirl a little faster. Some broke free to dip and spin their way to the ground.

"Elie said you were capable, trained as a rider, and would help out when they needed you, but you were lightning fast on a keyboard and could blow the socks off any investigator they had. Stefano backed him up on that." Leone leaned back in his chair as Raimondo rinsed the dishes and put them in the dishwasher. "To make a statement like that, you have to be extraordinary, because I know everyone thinks the Greco family is about as good as it gets."

Brielle pushed back her chair. The praise should have re-assured her, but she had a restless feeling that wouldn't let go. "There's always someone better, Leone. I wish I could say that wasn't true, but it is. No one should ever claim they're the best at anything. If you hear them say that, you know they're full of shit."

"It doesn't work that way if *other* people say you're the best at something," Raimondo objected, grinning at her. "Es-pecially women. Women have a tendency to tell the truth."

Leone groaned. "He's about to tell us a lie. A big one. Don't listen to anything he says."

Brielle gave them a distracted smile and wandered over closer to the fireplace to stare out the windows at the gather-ing clouds. Storms didn't usually make her so moody. She liked storms, especially when she could see them up close like she could when she was inside this house with its many windows, glass walls and expansive views.

The spinning and churning of the darker clouds were mes-merizing as they drifted overhead. The trees began to sway, reminding her of macabre stick dancers warming up before a performance. She had to smile at her odd fantasy.

She loved how beautiful it was here. She had lived in a city most of her life and she'd expected to live in the city of Chi-cago. She'd been surprised that Elie had purchased a property outside the city. She thought, without the constant sound of traffic, she might get anxious, but she found she enjoyed the peace. In any case, there were boats on the lake, the engines loud at times, rushing past their home occasionally. She liked to watch them. She'd never been around boats and lakes

before so it was all very intriguing. Elie promised her he would teach her how to drive a boat and she was looking forward to that.

"Are you paying any attention to what I say?" Raimondo demanded.

"No." She found herself really smiling.

Lights flickered along the tree leaves for a moment and then winked out. At least she thought she saw them. Inside, she went very still. "Leone, do we have cameras on the driveway?"

The long drive wound in and out of the trees. There was no huge fence to keep intruders out. With access from the lakeside, Elie had secured the house itself, rather than concentrating on trying to protect the entire property. Lights flickered again on the trees and then were gone. Someone was coming up the drive.

"Yes," Leone answered. "The car tripped the alarms a few moments ago and they sent us the information. It's an SUV, dark tinted windows. Rented. I've got the license number. I sent the details to Rigina and Rosina. They're working it now."

"You didn't think it would be a good idea to say something to me?" She kept resentment from her voice.

"I was about to suggest you change into riding clothes just to be safe. Also, to be prepared to go to the safe room. This time, you might actually do it, just so Elie doesn't replace us with Emilio and Enzo. You don't want that."

Rigina's report came back immediately. The man renting the car had come in on an international flight. His name was Asier Fredrick. He was an Interpol agent who'd spent the last eight years working for the National Central Bureau in Spain, mostly providing important data on international criminal organizations.

Brielle pressed her closed fist against her chest. She had turned in her report to the Ignazio investigators in Barcelona. They had turned over the report to Interpol and were supposed to have removed her name. Interpol had her name. It stood to reason they would want to talk to her in person.

"Brielle?" Leone put the onus on her.

She took a deep breath and made up her mind. She couldn't live her life afraid. She didn't need Elie holding her hand while she briefly told an agent the little she knew. She would only tell him what she'd actually written in her report—what she'd observed and what she'd managed to find out on her computer. She wouldn't include anything she'd discovered after she'd left her position in Barcelona, not without discussing that with Elie and Stefano first. She could always contact the agent again.

"I'll change quickly. One of you hang back unseen. I'll speak to him out in the open but close to the shadows. This little circle area works perfect for that." She indicated the sitting area adjacent to the sofas. It was one of her favorite places. There were four very comfortable armchairs centered around a single small table. The spot was between the dining area and the sofas, along a bank of windows. "Cover him at all times. Before he comes in, make certain Rigina and Rosina get facial recognition on him to confirm his identity."

CHAPTER FOURTEEN

Asier Fredrick was a short, stocky man with a handsome face and a charming smile. He immediately showed his identification to Leone, who blocked the door while he closely inspected the ID as if he hadn't already read the reports from the investigators.

"I wish to speak with Ms. Couture. Brielle Couture."

"It's Archambault. She's married," Leone corrected him. "Her name is Brielle Archambault."

"Yes, of course. I'm aware of her marriage." Fredrick looked around him at the front of the house and landscaping and woods behind them. "Beautiful home."

Leone stepped back to allow the agent entry. He followed Fredrick inside, closing the front door firmly and then engaging the remote to lock down the house. When he turned back, the agent was watching him closely, hooded eyes dark with suspicion.

"You did not return my passport."

"Welcome to my home," Brielle greeted him, forcing their

visitor to turn toward her. She stretched her arm past Fredrick to allow Leone to put the agent's ID into her hand. "What can I do for you, Mr. . . ." She glanced down at the ID. "Fredrick?"

"I was given access to a report you wrote on human traffickers in Barcelona. I've been collecting data on criminal activity in our city for a very long time and I've never seen such a concise and well-written report. I wanted to meet with you in person and see if you could add any details and discuss a few other things, if you don't mind. I won't take up much of your time. I certainly didn't mean to get here so late. My plane was delayed."

Brielle made a show of studying his passport once again and then she handed it back to him before indicating the circle of chairs. "Please make yourself comfortable. Would you care for anything to drink or eat? Coffee? Water? Something stronger?"

"Coffee would be fine." Fredrick glanced at Leone, clearly expecting him to get the coffee for them. Leone had moved back to give them a measure of privacy, but he wasn't leaving his charge alone with the man.

Leone went into the space by the stairs where he had a clear shot at Asier Fredrick from any angle. He didn't pretend to be anything but what he was—Brielle's personal protector.

"You didn't call to make an appointment." Brielle made it a statement, but she clearly expected the agent to give his reasons.

"I apologize for that. I've been . . . uneasy lately." He didn't say anything else.

While Fredrick chose a chair, Brielle collected two mugs, poured coffee and put cream and sugar on a tray.

She had changed into a charcoal pinstriped suit, just the trousers and jacket. The jacket fit snugly over her breasts and hugged her ribs and waist, but the material allowed for loose movement. Beneath the jacket she wore a tight bra, one that rubbed against her sore nipples, reminding her of Elie with

every movement. She'd hastily woven her hair in a tight braid and removed her engagement ring, leaving only the simple wedding band.

"Is your husband home?" Asier inquired, looking casually around the beautiful, rustic but elegant home.

She had known that was coming and had prepared an answer. "He actually just stepped out to visit our neighbor. He's not that far away if you need to speak with him. Dario most likely would accompany him here so they can get whatever business they have out of the way." She made a little face and sighed. "Dario has so many bodyguards, I can barely fit them all into my home. Not that I mind, it's just that they're *big*."

"It isn't necessary, and like I said, I don't wish to take up too much of your time."

She carried the tray to the table and took the seat closest to the shadows thrown from the lit sconces on the wall. "You've come a long way, Mr. Fredrick."

"Call me Asier."

"Asier, then. I'm Brielle." She poured and indicated his coffee mug. "I didn't know you were coming so I didn't have time to make espresso. You'll have to do with regular coffee, but the quality is good. Cream or sugar? Help yourself."

He took a sip and then added sugar. "I do like coffee sweet, although, you're right, the quality is very good. I'm just going to jump right in here and start asking questions, if you don't mind, Brielle. I have to admit, reading your report, I was astonished at the detail. The depth of information you provided rarely crosses my desk." He sat back in the chair, looking much less tense, the mug of coffee in his hand, his shrewd eyes studying her. "When did you become interested in investigating such a heinous crime?"

Brielle was happy to see him relaxing. That was the purpose of the more intimate circle with the very comfortable chairs. Outside, the sun had set and night was drawing a shroud around the house, the clouds obscuring any chance of a show of a sliver of the moon.

She had always loved storms and this one was coming in fast. She wished Elie was home already. She knew his plane was in the air. She'd been informed that Stefano and Elie were on their way back and maybe that was what made her so uneasy. She just couldn't quite put aside the little niggle of unease that kept haunting her.

She pulled her attention back to Asier Fredrick. "I was studying in Barcelona, working for the Ignacio family as their live-in nanny part-time." Clearly, he was already aware of that information. "I'm one of those people who notices small details. I like to study in small *cafeterías*. I began to notice that several young women who were regulars like me suddenly stopped coming in. I didn't think anything of it at first. People move away or find somewhere new to frequent, but one of the women was a friend of mine. I was concerned when she didn't show up for several days, and I went to her place. That's when I discovered she was missing. Once I realized she was missing, I started to notice missing persons signs everywhere. Children. Teens. I discreetly talked to some of the people on the street and around the parks, places they might have been taken. I heard that two young women who frequented a kink club had disappeared and I joined that as well. Once there, I was told a waitress who worked there had vanished. The list kept growing. The weird thing to me was that no one seemed to be doing anything about it."

Deliberately, Brielle took a sip of her coffee, watching him carefully over the rim. Asier Fredrick was definitely good at his job. He appeared to be even more relaxed, but he was paying very close attention to everything she said. He was also aware of Leone and the fact that her bodyguard had positioned himself where he had a clear shot at Fredrick, but the agent would have to make a cross-body shot to even get close to taking down Leone. It didn't seem to bother him that Leone never took his eyes off him. So far, the agent seemed unaware there was a second bodyguard covering them.

"We were paying attention, but we weren't collecting

enough information to give to our other agencies, until your report. Did you discuss this with anyone else? Your employers perhaps? A friend? Your new husband?"

She frowned and carefully placed her mug on the table. "Why would I do that? I would never put another person in danger, which was clear to me would happen. That was extremely sensitive material. My employers certainly wouldn't know what to do with something like that, neither would any of my friends. Why in the world would I tell my new husband I was investigating human trafficking in Barcelona? That would be absurd. I turned the report over to people I thought would get it into the right hands—yours—and I left the country. There wasn't anything more I could do."

Brielle was very careful of her tone. The agent wasn't a shadow rider who could hear lies, but in his line of work, he must question people often. He must have ways of knowing when they lied to him.

"So, that's the end of it for you? Your curiosity will not get the better of you and you won't try to follow up and see if you can find who took these women and children?"

Brielle sighed, and once more looked out the window at the spinning, dark clouds. She felt like those dark, ominous clouds were trying to tell her Elie wasn't safe. Her fingers itched to pull out her phone and text him. She would never break protocol just for reassurance. When had she become so needy?

"I'll admit I think about those lost children and women often. How could I not? But I'm not a trained police officer. I wouldn't know what to do even if I did find anything more. I didn't study criminalistics. I studied cooking. Languages."

"The report you prepared would say otherwise."

Brielle flung herself back in her chair, the perfect, comfortable chair that always soothed her, but didn't. Her stomach churned. She had the beginnings of a headache. She never should have allowed the agent into her house, not with Elie gone. She hadn't expected to have separation anxiety. How completely pathetic was that?

"I'm fast on a keyboard. I have good instincts, but I'm not

trained or anything. There are people who are amazing. I'm not one of them."

A rumble of thunder sounded far off. The clouds appeared heavier. Drooping, as if so full, they hung on the very tops of the trees, darker at the bottom. Twice she caught a little dazzling display of energy rippling along the edges of them. That energy normally invigorated her. Now she concentrated on her breathing, paying close attention to her guest and what he was saying, in order to keep her mind from the plane in the sky carrying her husband back to her.

"I work every day with the kind of people you are talking about. People, amazing on their computers, pursuing criminals by gathering information on them. Interpol's goal is to provide the greatest possible assistance to all law enforcement to prevent international crime. It's the one place that all data is shared between countries. We need people who can deliver thorough reports like the one you turned over to us."

Brielle was astonished. Shocked. For a moment she was speechless. She could only stare at the man in utter surprise. "Did you come here to offer me a job? Is that what you're doing in some strange roundabout way?"

"You didn't share your knowledge with anyone, which means you instinctively keep things confidential. You can work anywhere, you don't have to be in Barcelona. In spite of your denial, you and I both know you have excellent skills on a computer. Most hackers aren't trained in school. They're self-taught."

Color tinged her face. "I didn't say I was a hacker." She would never admit it, either. Was he trying to trip her up? She didn't think Interpol agents arrested hackers, but what did she know? She'd been hacking everything she could from the moment she'd first touched a keyboard. It had been instinctive, just the way writing her own programs had always been. She was so careful to set up alarms, to keep watch just in case someone noticed and tried to trace her. Mostly, in the beginning, it had been the challenge of it. The thrill. Then it was that compulsion that wouldn't let go of her. Now it was

because she knew what went on in the world and she was going to provide the shadow riders—herself included—with the best possible data there was available. She also was never going to make a mistake and kill an innocent person.

"No, you didn't say you were a hacker, but then one rarely ever admits to that." He calmly drank his coffee, now that he'd delivered the real reason he was there. "But not a single one of the men or women I asked to break into your computer was able to do so. What does that say about you, Brielle?"

"Only that I have excellent malware and virus protection on my computers and I keep it updated at all times." She looked him right in the eye. She'd written her own programs and she knew every single time anyone tried to break through her defenses. She immediately initiated an attack on their computer even as she shut down any ability to get into hers.

His eyebrow shot up. "Really? Funny that twice, when anyone got close to your computer, our computers were attacked with an unknown virus."

She maintained her innocent expression. "That's hardly my fault. And it isn't very nice that you would try to attack my computer when I sent in a thorough report and tried to help you." Brielle put just the right touch of indignation in her voice.

She didn't dare look at Leone. She knew if she did, both of them would burst out laughing. She wasn't going to confess to lawbreaking to an Interpol agent. Not ever. For any reason. Sheesh. And she had another job offer. At this rate, Elie would probably decide to be her manager.

She pressed a hand to her still-churning stomach. *Elie.* When had she first begun to need him so much? When she was that silly teenager, dreaming of him? When he would come into the cafés where she worked looking so handsome and unobtainable? Was that when it started? Or was it when her sister would come home and lie about him? Bragging about the underground clubs and lying about what she and Elie had done in them? Even back then, Brielle knew she had a proclivity in that direction, and she'd thought it perfect that

her fantasy lover did as well. Was that when Elie had become a necessity?

"What do you think, Brielle?" Asier persisted. "Would you be interested in working for Interpol?"

"In all honesty, I'd have to think about it. I'd also want to talk it over with my husband. Since I've been here, I've had two other job offers, both quite interesting."

Asier nodded and stood up. "Interpol could use someone with your skills." He pulled a card from his wallet. "If you decide the answer is yes, call this number and ask for me. There's a formal hiring process that has to be completed, but I can move it along faster."

For some reason, the dread in her stomach worsened. She glanced at Leone as she followed Asier across the hardwood floor. Her soft-soled boots didn't make any noise while the agent's shoes sounded overly loud, matching the drumbeat of the rain splattering against the windows and pounding on the roof. Her heartbeat found an alarming counterpoint.

Asier moved toward the front door, his card in hand even as Leone came out of the alcove where the cabinet was located in front of the stairs. Brielle walked Asier politely to the door as he explained the process of hiring to her. She knew she wasn't going to take the job, but she did find it fascinating that he had made the offer.

Asier turned to her as he opened the wide door made of thick, rough-hewn wood. To reinforce security, Elie had steel embedded down the middle of the thick, old-growth hardwood, a difficult task, but it was impossible to tell the wood had been tampered with. She loved the front door. The sound of the storm burst over them, as the wind sent a wild gust of rain at them. Fortunately, the porch was wide and the roof prevented them from getting soaked. The storm didn't seem to deter Asier from continuing his conversation.

"I must make a confession. My wife has a particular love of gardening. I took a couple of pictures of these bushes right around the front of your home." Asier indicated the hydrangeas

growing on either side of the stairs. He bent down toward the purple-colored bush, which was very wide and a good three feet tall.

"Brielle," Leone cautioned, coming up behind her.

The churning in her stomach exploded into a volcano of red flags everywhere. "Gun," she yelled, not even seeing one, but knowing. Just knowing. The lie was there. She heard it in the agent's voice. There was no wife, no gardening. The uneasiness she'd been feeling hadn't been because Elie was in the air in a storm. It was because she'd allowed an assassin into her home.

She half turned, keeping Asier in sight, trying to push Leone back into the house with one hand on his chest. Out of the corner of her eye, she saw shadowy figures directing orange-red streaks at them from every direction.

Something hot hit her hard in her upper right arm, tearing through her muscle and spinning her sideways with amazing force. At the same time, she felt another fiery pain lance her right thigh. Leone went down hard, half in and half out of the doorway. She would have toppled over him but didn't dare. Sheer will kept her on her feet. She leapt over him, landing on her good leg. Crouching, she reached down and caught at the back of his shirt and dragged with all her might, angling her body to try to take them both to the side of the door.

A bullet kissed her temple, streaking fire through her head and making her stomach lurch. For a moment her vision blurred. She kept dragging Leone. Then Raimondo was providing covering fire and pulling Leone inside as well. It was impossible to close the door, and a hysterical part of her made a note to tell Elie they needed an automatic door closer to smash that heavy door on intruders.

"Brielle, get to the safe room. They can't get in there. I can hold them off long enough for you to lock yourself in." Raimondo gave her the order in a steely voice.

She was assessing their situation the same as he was. They didn't have a chance. They couldn't get Leone into the safe room. Someone had to provide the covering fire in order for

her to make it—if she could. That would leave both men outside alone, with one down. They would both be killed.

"I'm a shadow rider, Raimondo. I'm not losing either of you."

She dove into the nearest shadow before he could point out she had three wounds. She wasn't going to think about it, or how the shadows would tear apart her body even more, spraying blood in every direction. She refused to allow the wild churning in her stomach to disorient her. There were two men's lives at stake, men she'd already grown fond of. She had to save them and she would.

The pull on her body was horrendous, as if all the flesh was being torn from her bones. Her eyes felt as if they'd been plucked from her skull. Her hair, although braided, seemed to be ripped from her head. She'd been scalped and there were only the bloodied remains of her open brain with the contents leaking out into those hideous tubes.

Normally, she prepared herself to go into the shadows. She meditated, breathed deeply, put herself in a state of being where her mind could accept the horrors and illusions of what happened to a rider during transport. The odd thing was, in spite of the disorienting sickness, the terrible fear and hallucination of sensations, she retained every map and grid of where she was and where she was going. She never lost sight of her mission and the determination to complete it. The danger came in *after*—when she was returning home. She no longer had that single important goal to get her through the horrors.

Brielle came up behind Asier first. He had the best angle on the door and was moving to get inside, leading the way. She snapped his neck fast, dropped him and was back in the tube, seeking her next target, a taller, swarthy man who trampled the pink hydrangeas on the right side of the stairs as he charged the door. She emerged from the shadow, gripped his skull and broke his neck fast, and stepped into a longer one that took her to their backup man.

She chose him because he had Raimondo pinned down.

She could clearly see the angle he had on the inside of the house. The drive was circular. The SUV was parked right beside the stairs and their backup man was on top of the vehicle with his rifle. If they were going to get that door closed, locked and able to keep the others out, she would have to take him out, but she needed to do it fast. Already, her body was giving out, growing weak fast.

Blood was spraying inside the tube from her wounds. She had no idea how bad they were but she was functioning so she doubted they could be too bad. Still, the inside of the shadow appeared reddish-black with blood, all along the curves and even overhead, slick with it. Her stomach was inside out, ripped out of her now, one of the worst illusions she sometimes had, adding to the sickness in her mind.

Taking a firm grip on herself, Brielle transferred quickly into the small shadow that had a slick tube, one that would take her very fast beyond the SUV if she wasn't alert and ready. As she sped past the large vehicle at breakneck speed, she stepped from one feeder tube to a narrow shadow she'd spotted running up the back corner of the SUV. That took her right to the roof.

She sent up a silent thanks to the universe that it was night and the clouds were dark because the moment she stepped out of the shadows, blood splattered across the roof. That wasn't an illusion. The blood was very real and appeared wet and nearly black as it fell on her target. He started to turn, but she was fast, one knee planted on his back as she gripped his head in her hands and smoothly ended his life.

A bullet hit the body as she dropped it and she leapt from the SUV into the nearest shadow created by the yard lights, one that hopefully would take her up to the house. Still, she felt another burn along her ribs as she heard the spray of automatic fire.

Where was their backup? Who was it? She couldn't remember. Her brain was glitching and her stomach was completely gone, left behind with intestines and entrails in a bloody mess in one of the tubes. She'd never find any of her insides and be able to put herself back together. There was too much blood in

her eyes to see where she was going. She didn't think she could make it back into the house. If she had to make an exchange, she wouldn't be able to. She'd lost too much blood and was too weak.

Brielle could only hope she'd done enough and Raimondo could get the door closed. Hopefully he'd called for their backup and the Ferraro surgeon for Leone. She knew every rider family had them. There was no calling an ambulance, not with active shooters and dead bodies outside their home. And not with riders in the air when they were supposed to be home with their wives. Stefano and Elie had to be protected at all costs, including her life.

The tube spat her out just inside the house. Raimondo caught her arm and jerked her all the way inside, slammed the door closed and locked the house down. Covered in blood, Brielle tried to help him by crawling across the hardwood floor away from the door, toward Leone. She couldn't see well enough to know whether he was alive or dead. He was so still.

Vaguely, as if a great distance away, she could hear Raimondo swearing. She knew she didn't have much time. She was a female rider, one able to produce children. He would save her life before Leone's. She wouldn't waste time trying to argue.

"Veins. Both of us." She managed a whisper. Her throat felt swollen. Maybe the tubes had managed to turn that part of her inside out as well. "Collapse." She knew it was a possibility. She was going to crash soon. If Raimondo didn't get a vein now, both she and Leone would be in trouble.

Her entire body was shaking uncontrollably. Raimondo was up and running across the room for the cabinet built into the wall where they stored medical equipment and arms. He slammed his palm against the hidden release and the door sprang open. Rushing back to her, he was on the floor beside her, swabbing the inside of her elbow and inserting a needle.

"Dario is backup. He's already here and taking out the rest of those bastards." They could hear the steady sound of gunfire. "God, Brielle, you're shot all to hell." He was inserting a needle

into Leone's veins as well. "Once Dario clears the way, we can get the surgeon in here. Don't you dare die on me, Brielle."

Dario was at the front door, demanding entrance. Raimondo looked up and saw him with two men he didn't know. He swore again and shook his head. He desperately needed help, but protocol demanded he know anyone entering the home. He didn't know the men with Dario. He caught up his phone and texted Dario even as he tried to assess which was the worst wound on Brielle.

"I can't let that dumb fuck in, Brielle, and he's threatening to cut my balls off if I don't. If you die, I think he really will."

She turned her head away from him, her stomach lurching. This was going to be bad. "Tell Elie . . ." She began vomiting. Not just a little vomiting, but gut-wrenching vomiting, as if the tubes weren't satisfied with taking her insides, her eyes and hair—they wanted every last bit they could get from her before she died.

Raimondo did his best to keep her head from landing in the mess she'd created. He wiped her face off multiple times and then tried to move her a couple of feet from the vomit. There was so much blood from both Leone and Brielle, she didn't see how they were ever going to get the floors clean.

Dario continued to pound on the door and it was beginning to hurt her head. Each knock sounded as if it vibrated through her skull. Raimondo looked up, clenching his teeth.

"Let him." She thought she managed at least those two words. She couldn't get a full sentence out. Surely Dario could save Leone. He didn't look as if he was breathing while Raimondo was trying to stem the bleeding on her from various places.

She hardly felt her body anywhere. There was no pain. Just. . . . "Cold." She couldn't stop shivering.

"Damn it, Brielle, don't do this." Raimondo glanced over his shoulder at the door, texted one-handed and waited for Dario's assent. The men with him backed off and Raimondo unlocked the door from his phone just long enough to allow Dario in before he locked out his bodyguards.

"What the fuck is wrong with you?" Dario snarled as he hastened across the room and dropped down beside Brielle. "You just going to let her die because I have men with me you don't know? What the hell happened to her? I've got her, you take care of Leone."

He was thorough in his examination, uncaring of modesty, tearing off her sleeve to look at the wound on her arm. Yanking down her trousers to look at the one on her thigh. Calling for more medical supplies. In the end, he cut off the jacket in order to attend the wound on her rib cage. He swore steadily as he found everywhere a bullet had bit into her.

Brielle's body began to shake violently. Dario caught her by the shoulders and glared down at her. "Don't you dare have a seizure. I'm not kidding around with you. I'm not like that pansy-ass husband of yours so don't you dare disobey me."

Dario took off his coat and laid it over her, leaving her leg exposed so he could work on her thigh. "What happened, Raimondo?"

"Interpol agent showed up." Raimondo's face remained turned away, desperately working on his partner. "He was legit, but clearly on someone's payroll." He looked toward the door as warning lights flashed. "Surgical team is here."

"You letting them in?" Dario asked, sarcasm dripping from his voice.

"Yeah, Dario," Raimondo snapped back. "They get in because they've been vetted, and in an emergency, I know who the fuck they are and who I can count on." He opened the door for the surgical team.

Dario immediately stepped back and apprised the surgeon of Brielle's wounds. She could hear him talking, although his voice was fading in and out. There was something important she had to say, to get them to understand, but it kept slipping away. Everything was so dark. Usually, she could see in the dark, but not tonight. Not with the blood seeping into her eyes and the smell of death all around her.

She was cold. Like ice inside. The shadows could do that to a rider. She'd heard of that syndrome. Riders coming out

of the shadows permanently damaged with ice in their lungs. Or had she just had nightmares? She was shaking uncontrollably. She knew she was, but she was detached from her body. Looking down at it.

"She's crashing. She's crashing."

She heard the voice as if from a great distance. She wanted to float away from all the blood. There was a giant pool of it spreading out under Leone and her. Leone's breathing was shallow. He was struggling, but at least he was alive. She had thought they'd lost him. She was thankful that she had acted fast enough.

She could see Dario bent over her, someone doing compressions on her chest, Dario breathing air into her mouth. What was it she was supposed to tell him? Her brain just didn't want to work. It was so important, too. She hovered above her body, looking down at the scene below her, the way everyone moved in a synchronized pattern as if they'd done such things a million times.

The surgeon gave calm instructions, and the nurses moved quickly and efficiently setting up his mobile operating area for him. They could have used Dario's men, but he didn't say a word; he just kept breathing when it was his turn to push air into her lungs. Then her heart caught the rhythm and she was forced to return to that freezing-cold body she was so disconnected with.

Dario sank back on his heels and glared at her. "Don't you do that again, Brielle."

"I'm going to second that," Raimondo said. "You took a few years off my life."

"Let's get her onto the table," Dr. Arnold instructed. "I have to find where she's bleeding internally and get it stopped."

Dario and Raimondo just picked her up and carried her to the table before the nurses who were sterilizing everything could sterilize them. If Brielle wasn't so frozen, she might have laughed. Always the bad boys. Suddenly, she remembered. It was important. She needed to tell someone. Ignoring the bags of fluids the nurses were hanging around the table,

the ones flowing into her arm, she forced herself to find her voice.

"Tell Elie . . . for me, he was always the one."

Dario swore. "Don't do that, Brielle. You'll tell him yourself. Just make up your damn mind you're going to stay alive. It's bullshit to quit breathing. It isn't that hard to keep it up."

He had no idea how difficult it was to draw in a breath. For some reason, it felt as if her lungs were frozen, blocked by great chunks of ice. She couldn't manage a smile for him, even though she wanted to. She was too tired. Her lashes fluttered, eyes closing again.

"Why is she doing that?" Raimondo asked. "You can't let her go to sleep."

"I'm putting her out," Dr. Arnold said. "I'm not about to dig through her body while she's awake. Go help my assistant with your friend. I'll be there as soon as I can."

Brielle was fading, but she wasn't out. She wanted someone to tell her how Leone was doing. Everyone was whispering since the doctor had arrived, everyone but Dario. Usually, he lounged against a wall, so quiet no one noticed him after a while. He wasn't quiet now. He was like prowling panther.

"Where the hell is Elie?" Dario hissed at Raimondo as they moved away from the dining area to huddle together, leaving the two medical teams to work on their patients. "I know he's supposed to be back soon. He's going to lose his shit when he sees this mess. I've got a cleanup crew coming for the bodies. They should be here any minute."

Raimondo glanced out the windows. Dario's bodyguards were back inside their vehicle, out of the rain and wind. "What's wrong with you? How could you bring unknown men with you in a lockdown situation? We could have lost both of them. I needed help, Dario, and I was counting on you."

"I wouldn't have brought anyone I didn't know and trust personally."

"That isn't the protocol. In a lockdown situation, when we're under attack, we have to follow procedure to the letter. All of us were counting on you."

"I came. Your enemies are dead because we killed them. Those men you don't trust helped me kill them, Raimondo. They put their lives on the line for perfect strangers."

"They put their lives on the line for you, not for us. I still didn't know them or what they might do, any more than I knew the legitimate Interpol agent who came to ask Brielle about a report she did. He appeared on the up-and-up as well. Stefano is going to eat you for breakfast for this fuckup if Elie doesn't do it first, and you deserve it."

Dario sighed. "I suppose you're right. It never occurred to me to have his people investigate them, or at least go talk to Stefano about them and introduce them to the family. I've always done whatever I want, particularly in matters of security. It's my business and I like to keep it that way."

Raimondo shrugged. "It is your business. But those men are your personal protectors, which means they travel everywhere with you. You attend Ferraro family functions. You're around Francesca. Stefano's children. Grace. Can you imagine Vittorio if some stranger was around his wife and he had no idea who that man was? These are protective men, just as you are. You would never allow that shit; why would they?"

He wasn't backing down an inch. Seeing Brielle covered in blood, crashing the way she had, being alone with two people he cared about, afraid he was going to lose both of them, had Raimondo angry with Dario all over again.

"I get your point. I wouldn't allow strangers around my family, especially if I had a woman of my own. So yeah, you did the right thing. I don't have to like it, but you're right."

"I could use a drink right now," Raimondo said, looking at Leone as the nurses crowded around him. "Hell, not just a drink, a whole damn bottle." The second doctor had arrived. Dr. Townsend had begun work on the young bodyguard. "Brielle told me to get a line in their veins. First thing out of her mouth. I was trying to stop them both from bleeding. Even in the shape she was in, she knew to do that in case they crashed."

"What the hell happened?"

Raimondo shrugged. "Everything looked fine. We vetted

him. He checked out. He was the real thing. We're going to have to make his death look like an ambush somewhere. I don't know, Stefano can figure it out." He put his head back against the wall and stared up at the ceiling. "He asked her questions. Nothing pointing to him lying to her. She didn't signal she thought anything was off. Neither did Leone. Then they walked to the front door. He said or did something that hit her wrong and she reacted fast. He pulled a gun from somewhere he'd hidden it outside. His men were everywhere, firing at Leone and Brielle, hitting both of them."

Raimondo wiped beads of sweat from his forehead. "She dragged Leone inside with my help, but when I told her to get into the safe room, she didn't; she went after them."

"These women," Dario said. "I told Elie she was like Emmanuelle. She may not be quite as outspoken as Emme, but she's going to go her own way when she thinks she's right, no matter what. She likes you too much, Raimondo. You're not mean enough."

Raimondo shot him a faint grin. "I hate to give you the bad news, Dario, but she likes you, too. All that snarling you do hasn't put her off much. She isn't very afraid of you."

"She should be."

"You're losing your reputation."

"Thankfully, only in your family circle. In my world, the mere mention of my name makes people hide in their homes and hope I pass by without stopping."

"Can you get more light in here?" Dr. Arnold snapped.

Raimondo got to his feet. "Coming right up." They had everything they needed. They could get lights. They had blood. Medical equipment. Surgeons on call. This was a rider family and they had the money necessary to support whatever was needed. They needed more manpower. Raimondo was going to talk to Stefano about that. He never wanted to face this situation alone again. It didn't matter that only a few minutes had gone by; he could have lost both Brielle and Leone in those minutes. There were others in the family who could be trusted to guard the riders and they needed them.

CHAPTER FIFTEEN

Elie paced back and forth across the floor, never too far from the large, four-poster bed where his wife sat pretending to look at her book. The Ferraro Hotel had luxury beds, but mostly, he cared about the tight security. They were staying there, he told Brielle, while their home was being cleaned of all the blood and evidence that she'd nearly been taken from him. They were really staying there until he could remove the threat to her. He was done with anyone trying to kill his wife.

"Honey, stop." Brielle put her book down and gave him a look that told him she was about to get up.

Elie pointed a finger at her and gave her a severe look that would have stopped an army. "Don't even think about it."

She sighed. "How long am I going to be confined to bed? The doctor said I was fine."

"No, that's not what he said, *mon petit monstre*. He said your other wounds were mostly superficial, but that you had to be very careful of the internal one for a while. No jarring.

No running or working out. Definitely no riding the shadows. But then, we had already discussed that, hadn't we?"

He couldn't look at her. If he did, his chest hurt like hell. He stalked over to the window and stared down at the view of the city. Every single time he thought about that moment when he walked into their home and saw what looked like a slaughterhouse, his wife on their dining room table, a surgeon operating on her, up to his elbows in her blood, he would nearly go to his knees. Nothing had ever come close to taking him out the way that had.

Stefano had been with him, the only reason he hadn't gone crazy and left for New York to kill every member of the Santoro family and then gone to Barcelona to go after the Toselli family. Anyone involved in the ordering of his wife's assassination was going to die. And he was going to find every last one of them, no matter what. When he needed answers, he could be every bit as driven and ruthless as Dario or Valentino.

Elie hadn't roared with rage. He hadn't said a damn thing. He stood in front of Raimondo and Dario, silently demanding answers. They both gave them to him. Raimondo clearly had done his best. He had followed protocol. Asier Fredrick had been a legitimate agent, checked out thoroughly by the investigators and identified by facial recognition software, not once but twice. He was a real agent. Unfortunately, there was now no question, he'd been on the Toselli payroll.

"Elie, are we ever going to talk about this?"

Were they? He didn't know if he could talk about it without losing his shit. How could he make her understand? She sat there looking so reasonable, sounding so reasonable, when there was absolutely no reason or understanding in the situation. She hadn't seen what he had. She hadn't felt what he had, but then again, she hadn't wanted their marriage from the beginning.

"Sure, *bébé*, we can talk about it. You can tell me why you chose to disobey direct instructions to save your life and get

your sweet little ass into the safe room for the second time. It isn't like we haven't discussed this, but you don't seem to give a damn what I think. Or what I care about."

Elie turned to face her, keeping his distance, back pressed to the wall, fingers curled into tight fists. His gaze drifted over her pale features. She looked a little shocked by his choice of words.

"Elie, of course I care what you think. I had to make a split-second decision. Leone was already down. Raimondo had no chance at all if I went into the safe room. The only way to get the door closed was for me to take out the men preventing us from doing so. It was instinct more than anything else. I just dove for the shadow."

Brielle even put one hand in the air as if that would deter his anger. He didn't feel anger at her. Or rage. That was reserved for those conspiring to kill her. He felt—hurt. Fear. No, terror. She was uncontrollable, just as Dario had said she was. Just as Stefano had said. Unlike Francesca, she didn't love him enough to give him what he needed, which was to know she would be alive and well when he returned from wherever he had gone.

"Did you ever once think of me, Brielle? What would happen to me if you didn't live?" He asked the questions in a low tone, knowing his voice shook, betraying the intensity of his emotions. She got it because she went very still. "You didn't, did you? When I stood before the priest in that chapel, knowing I was marrying you, I meant every damn word I said. I *meant* those vows. For the first time in my life, I thought maybe I would have someone of my own. Someone who would love me back. My own family. The two of us. I thought I could make you happy if you just gave me the chance."

Brielle's eyes went wide and she shook her head. "Elie."

"You would have left me with nothing. But then you never wanted to marry me. You made that very clear. Sex is great, isn't it? But you've never really wanted *me*. I should have taken you at your word instead of forcing you into something

you didn't want from the beginning. Maybe if I had, you wouldn't risk your life every time I turn around."

He could barely talk. His throat felt raw, and the lump in his throat was so large, he was choking on it. Was she deliberately putting her life at risk in an effort to escape him? He hadn't thought of that. He should never have insisted on their marriage. Was it too late to have Stefano let her out of it?

Brielle tossed back the covers and went up on her knees when he once again pointed at her and shook his head. She couldn't get near him. He didn't have control. That had deserted him the moment he saw her lying on that table covered in blood. He'd thrown out all the furniture. Every single piece of it. Had the floors sanded down. They were going to start over. He was uncertain if he could walk through the front door again. The thought of it made his stomach lurch.

"You don't understand, Elie. It was always you. Always. From the very first time I ever saw you, when I was still a teenager. I stalked you like some creeper. I did it so much, I was ashamed of myself, but I was obsessed. Fayette knew how much I wanted to be with you. That was why she made up all those stories. It was to hurt me. I never wanted another man. I never seriously considered another man."

Elie ran his fingers through his hair in agitation to keep from strangling her. She made no sense, but then she often didn't. "Brielle. If it was always me, why did you go to Jean-Claude's to say you couldn't marry me when you were eighteen?" He didn't believe her. He *couldn't* believe her, yet there was the ring of honesty in her voice.

"My father was counting on you marrying Fayette. I was terrified you would find out I was obsessing over you. My family was so awful and I didn't want you to think I was out for the money or prestige of marrying an Archambault. There were so many reasons. Your lovely comments on my body added to them."

"That makes no sense. What about in the chapel?" he demanded. He'd been shocked and elated to see that his bride

She bit down on the side of her lip, always a sign of nerves with her. "I apparently feel sensations on my nerve endings very easily; at least that was what one of the doctors said to me. When I go into the shadows, all my nerve endings become inflamed and my mind plays tricks on me. I start to hallucinate. When I'm on a mission, I'm very focused, so I don't have a problem. I complete the mission without a problem, but once it's done, then I have a difficult time keeping the hallucinations from merging with the sensations I'm feeling on my body because they're so intense and extreme."

He studied her averted face. She refused to look at him. She was telling him the truth, but not all of it. There was more, things she didn't want to admit to him, although he couldn't imagine what. That was bad enough.

"Are you aware Stefano lost his youngest brother, Ettore, in the shadows? Riders die in the shadows, Brielle. The sickness is very real, and once it takes hold, you can get turned around and never get out."

She nodded slowly, still not looking at him. "I'm very aware, Elie. It's terrifying."

"And yet, you persist on going in."

Her chin went up. "I'm a rider. I was born to ride the shadows."

He stalked across the room to the side of the bed, leaned over, planted a knee on the bed and caught her chin, forcing her to meet his eyes. "You were born to be with me. Not for the shadows to swallow you. Not for you to kill yourself saving your own damn personal protectors. To be with me. For us to be a family. To have children together. So you can be a mama bear or a little tigress for our children. That's why you were born, not to ride shadows. I'm not giving you up to them."

She blinked up at him, liquid gathering in her eyes, deepening the color to an emerald. "I really didn't think, Elie. I reacted. I don't know how to stop that reaction. I want to promise you it won't happen again, because I really want a life with you, but I don't know how, if something like that comes up again and then there's this weird thing that sometimes happens."

Again, she put her head down.

Elie sank down onto the edge of the bed. "Brielle, you have to be able to tell me anything. We established that communication between us is extremely important."

"You didn't tell me how you felt about me." She lifted her long lashes and gave him an accusing look.

He wanted to tell her it was because he was waiting for the perfect time. He'd certainly thought about it enough times. He had a lot of ideas. A rug in front of the fireplace in the great room, music low, no lights, just the flames from the fire. He had ideas. Lots of them. But that wouldn't be the truth and they'd promised each other the truth. If he expected honesty from her, he needed to give it.

He spread his fingers wide and looked down at his hands rather than at her. "For the first time in my life, Brielle, I was a coward. I didn't want to lose you by telling you I couldn't live without you. I didn't expect you to love me back. I expected rejection. I'd already had it from you and wasn't going to chance it again. You're *everything*. I don't know how else to put it."

"Elie." She whispered his name in her little accent, this time with love that ate at his heart, both melted and terrified him at the same time.

"I told myself I was finding the right moment, Brielle, but I was deceiving myself because I was too afraid of losing you. I was choosing to be a coward rather than risk losing you."

"You are anything but a coward."

He turned his head to look at her. Love could be damned overwhelming. "The same is true of you, Brielle. Just tell me. You've been afraid, just like I have. Let's be done with these secrets."

She took a deep breath. "It's just that it's rather humiliating. The pain thing I have. I guess it started from childhood. I don't like too much, but I have to have some in order to have an orgasm. I'm not a total exhibitionist, but yet the thought of it excites me. I'm a shadow rider, yet I'm not. I'm such a contradiction."

"A mystery," he corrected. "Mysteries are always the best because they keep a man on his toes."

She smiled at him but he could see she was still distressed. "There's pain in the shadows. And fear." She blurted it out and then just stopped and looked at him for condemnation.

Elie slid his hand up her back until his fingers settled on the nape of her neck in a slow massage to ease some of the tension out of her. "Don't you think I know how addicting the pain and even the fear can be for someone like you? That only makes riding the shadows more dangerous for you."

"I know. I did talk to the counselor about it before I went back into training. I was worried. I stayed in the classes for mental preparation and began going to the underground clubs hoping to find my limits and what I would like or wouldn't like. I thought doing those things would stop me from becoming addicted to the pain and fear of the unknown in the shadows."

"Did you go to a counselor in France or Spain?" He purposely kept any inflection out of his voice. He was an Archambault in that moment. His family policed the riders and every aspect of their system. If she had confessed to a counselor that she became violently ill in the shadows and that she feared she would become addicted to the pain and fear she got when riding, and the counselor allowed her, even recommended she continue, the counselor needed to be pulled.

"I went to the one in Spain. They only have one, a male counselor. I hesitated, at first, to go to him, but he was approved by the international council, so I made myself go."

"And you told him everything? How sick you got? What the doctor said about your body and the nerve endings inside the tubes?"

"I made myself be very honest, even about my need for pain. It was difficult, but I did it. I will admit, it was a little surprising when he suggested I continue to push through by taking the various classes. I also confessed I started going to the underground clubs in hopes that when I went into the shadows, I wouldn't have the reaction and he agreed it was a

good idea." She looked up at him. "It wasn't, Elie. I do fine for a while. I can make myself go a couple of weeks, three, four, but then I'm wound up, restless, moody. I start needing not only pain but that edge of fear and dominance."

He had already noticed she began to get edgy and needed him to initiate their sexual games. He had no problem with that. He didn't want her to think there was anything wrong with her, which she clearly did. What was wrong was risking her life in the shadows in order to find relief. The counselor should have known better than to allow her to continue.

"I *hated* the way I was, but I couldn't stop the cycle. I went for counseling, I took classes, I did everything I could, and then when I went back to shadow riding, I found myself delaying coming out of the tubes after my mission for as long as possible, just to get some relief, even though it was so horrible." She continued her confession in a low voice.

Elie didn't like the way she looked miserable and embarrassed. Humiliated even.

"There is nothing wrong with you, Brielle. You're the most wonderful, courageous women I've ever met. I love you exactly the way you are. What would I do if I didn't have you? You don't need to risk your life in the shadows when you have me. Your cravings match my own so perfectly."

He brushed a kiss in her hair. "But you can't do any more shadow riding." He made it a decree. "It's too dangerous."

"I did everything I could to stop, Elie, I really did. At the same time, I *am* a shadow rider, and I'm good at it. I was needed when Leone and Raimondo were in trouble and I instinctively acted."

Elie continued to massage her neck. "I would expect nothing less of you, *bébé*. You are incredibly courageous. I wish, at times, you were less so."

"I'm always terrified when I go into the shadows. I usually have time to meditate when I know I'm taking a rotation. I can prepare myself a little bit in advance."

"We really need to come to terms with this, Brielle. I can't come home to a slaughterhouse like that ever again. You nearly

died. It was your blood everywhere. Leone was bad, yes, but you were the one bleeding out. Dario and Raimondo performed CPR on you and kept you alive long enough for the surgical team to set up. Arnold had to find where you were bleeding and close it off."

His voice was strained all over again. He had to remove his hand in order to keep her from feeling the way his body tensed up all over again. The anger once again began to bubble up, seeping out of the well, escaping just enough to release the pressure cooker so he wouldn't explode. He slid off the bed and stalked over to the window, shoving his hands in his pockets.

Stefano had taken Dario to task for not following protocol and releasing the names of his personal protectors to the investigators to vet. Dario had admitted they were men he had known since his childhood and he was protecting their past. Stefano made it clear that if they were ever to be allowed around the family, they had to earn the same trust that Dario had. He also pointed out those few minutes could have cost Brielle and Leone their lives.

Dario had taken the dressing down from Stefano without a murmur, something Elie had never thought possible. Raimondo had sent for Nicoletta and Taviano, the two closest riders. They had come as soon as possible and they'd been horrified at the blood-soaked state of Elie's home.

The two riders had assisted Dario and Stefano in providing an adequate explanation for Asier Fredrick's untimely death. They made it appear like he'd been robbed after he left Elie and Brielle and was on his way back to the airport. As for the men who had traveled on the same plane with him but were never seen with him, they didn't bother creating a false narrative to explain their deaths. Those men had no association with Interpol. They were known associates of the Toselli family, according to Stefano's investigators. That made it easy. So Dario simply made them disappear.

Since Fredrick had died after he'd left Elie and Brielle's home, they had been prepared for the police to ask them questions. Fortunately, as they were relatively newly married, it

wasn't inconceivable that they were traveling around, Elie showing his bride the sights. They finally met with the police, Vinci, Stefano's lawyer, with them, in the Ferraro Hotel, where they were having a romantic getaway as they hadn't had a proper honeymoon yet.

"It wasn't like I planned it, Elie," she reiterated.

"Maybe you shouldn't have opened the door. I was supposed to be there with you. Isn't that the entire premise of shadow riders? I have to have an alibi when I'm out of town doing my job. You provide that alibi. I'm in this house with you. You never should have allowed the agent into our home in the first place. That was your first mistake and a direct violation of our rules." He swung around to face her again.

Brielle ducked her head, her wild mass of curls falling around her face. "I know. I'm used to being the rider, not that I'm making an excuse, Elie. I take responsibility for my actions and I know I have to face Stefano at some point for a disciplinary action."

Like hell she would. Being shot six times was enough discipline as far as Elie was concerned. Stefano wasn't going to take her to task. Elie could do it and no one else. She owed him an explanation. They would work out their problems between them.

"I've never been on the other side, the one providing the alibi. I just didn't consider until he actually was in the house what I was going to say if he asked about you."

"How was it possible you weren't alerted prior to him walking out the door?" That was something that really nagged at him. Her family had certainly made her question her belief in her ability to hear lies, but she had gained so much confidence in herself, he found it difficult to believe someone could sit with her and lie for an extended period of time and she wouldn't realize.

"I've gone over the conversation with him in my head numerous times. He never once said anything that could have been a lie. Not until he mentioned his wife and gardening. He didn't do that until he had the door open."

"He didn't raise any alarms prior to that?" He found that a little shocking.

"I was uneasy during the interview, but I put it down to you being away. There was a big storm and you were in an airplane, flying. I had all kinds of reasons for being uneasy. Even when he seemingly made the job offer, he only said that Interpol needed people like me, not that he did. He was already standing and walking to the door when he actually said something about helping me with the process and I just knew then. He kept up the commentary, bending down toward the bushes. He'd hidden his gun there. I tried to warn Leone, but he was throwing his body in front of mine. I remember pushing him, trying to get him inside the house."

Elie didn't want to hear any more. He knew Leone had gone down, taking the bullet meant for Brielle. The Tosellis were going to pay for that. They were going to pay dearly. The Archambault investigators, as well as the Ignazio family investigators in Spain, were also working to uncover information on the Toselli crime family and the ties to the Santoro family in New York and the Colombo family in Los Angeles.

At first, Elie and Stefano had planned to take care of the problem on their own, but the attack on Brielle had been too blatant and it was the third attempt on her life. She was a female shadow rider, married to another shadow rider. All shadow riders would rise up to find a way to track down those plotting to kill her and dispense justice. The Archambault family, in particular, was incensed. They had wanted the union, and in spite of Elie's reluctance to come back to France, he was a rider and carried the genetics they needed to continue the line.

Stefano's investigators were on it. Dario and Valentino's man, Bernado, was on it. The three crime families had no idea a storm of pure fire was coming after them and all because they thought themselves invincible—and invisible. They had no idea what true invisibility really was.

Stefano's cousins in New York and Los Angeles had their people working as well, while the riders watched the family

members, getting a feel for their daily movements. It was important to know the routine of everyone living in the main houses. They had the Ignazio riders watching the main members of the Toselli family for the same reason. It was never a good idea to rile up the riders and even the largest crime family in Spain was going to find that out.

Elie studied his wife's face. She really was getting to the point where she was going to rebel if he tried to keep her down much longer. The doctor hadn't decreed that she remain in bed. He was afraid for her. Terrified by the idea of losing her. Each morning he helped her shower, washing her hair for her, drying her off, helping her to dress and then putting her back in bed.

"Stefano and Francesca invited us to dinner tonight. Do you feel up to a crazy family night? The brothers will be there. It will be loud and noisy," he warned. "Most likely, Dario and Val will be there as well with Emme."

A small shadow crossed her face but she looked up at him eagerly, nodding. "I'd love that, Elie. Does everyone dress up, because I don't think I have anything dressy."

"No, *bébé*, when they're together, they're very casual. You have plenty of casual clothes here. I brought soft leggings that shouldn't hurt any of the wounds. The bandages are covering them, but we can ask the doc to check them before we go."

She shook her head. "No, nothing hurts, everything is fine. You changed my bandages this morning. There was no fresh bleeding. Really, Elie, I'm healing fast. I've always healed fast. When is the dinner? Are you sure it's all right for the two of us to go? Francesca won't mind two more dinner guests at the last minute?"

"Francesca never minds two more guests at the last minute. She expects it." He went to the bed and helped her slide to the side, pretending not to see her wince as she gingerly shifted around to sit on the edge of the bed. The bandage on her temple stood out starkly against her pale skin, making his heart ache more, even though the covering was so much smaller than it had been.

"She just gave birth, didn't she? Surely, she isn't cooking for a huge crowd? I could have helped her had I known. You know I love cooking, or would she be upset with someone else in her kitchen?"

His thumb slid over their wedding band on her finger. He stood directly in front of her, preventing her from sliding off the bed. "Francesca shares her kitchen with anyone who loves to cook, *ma chérie*." He continued to stare down at her, his thumb on her ring, until she lifted her gaze to meet his. "Brielle, do you have a problem with Emmanuelle?"

She blinked, her long lashes veiling the jeweled green of her eyes, but not before he caught the hint of guilt and uneasiness. She didn't lie to him. She sighed and squirmed a little. "I think it best if we don't go there, Elie. Sometimes it's just better to let things go. Emme is your friend and I'll get to know her. It isn't like I've had tons of time. When she's been around, she's been very sweet to me."

On some level, he'd felt the reservation between Brielle and the others. It wasn't a huge thing, because she didn't make it one, but it was there. She wasn't as natural and relaxed around others as she was when she was alone with him. When Emmanuelle was with them—which, granted, wasn't that often—Brielle was even more on guard.

"You know I think of Emme as a sibling, nothing more. She regards me the same way." He hoped Brielle listened to the ring of truth in his voice. It was there because it was the truth.

She nodded her head, but her eyes avoided his again.

"Brielle, look at me." He caught her stubborn little chin in a firm grip. "We are going to talk about this because it obviously bothers you. If Emmanuelle and I wanted to be together, don't you think we would have been?"

"You mean like at every charity ball? Every nightclub dancing together? The fund-raiser dinners? Skiing together? Sailing? The speculation for how many years on the inevitable engagement between the two well-suited, perfectly matched *beautiful* people? How many times was that written up?"

Brielle kept her voice low. There was no accusation, but yeah, she believed Emmanuelle and he had been far more than just friends. Maybe they were just friends and in his mind like "siblings," but he had forgotten she had kept track of him in the intervening years. She knew he had been around Emmanuelle.

"You believed I decided to go back to France and enter into an arranged marriage after she married Valentino Saldi, didn't you? That's why you were so adamant that you not be placed with anyone from Europe. You thought I didn't want to be in the States because of her."

She made a face. "Does it matter what I thought?"

"It matters and you know it does. I was never in love with Emme. She was never in love with me. There was no physical attraction between us. There never was. For Emmanuelle, it has always been Valentino. He's her one and only. For me, it has always been you."

Her smile was forced as she looked up at him and nodded. "I get that, Elie. I do. I'll work at a friendship with her."

He had no doubt that she would, but that didn't take the shadows from her eyes. He kept possession of her chin. "*Mon amour*, I'm asking you to tell me what is wrong. What is it about Emmanuelle Ferraro Saldi that puts those shadows in your eyes?"

Her small white teeth bit down on the corner of her lower lip. "Can't we just let it go, Elie? Please?"

"You make my heart ache, Brielle. I can't let this go because you matter to me. Anything that hurts you, and this does, needs to be addressed. I'm asking you to let me in."

"It just makes me ashamed. She's everything I'm not. It was there, in those photographs for the years you spent here with this family. She's a gorgeous woman. Over and over, in the articles or sometimes the headlines, it would say 'one of the most beautiful women in the world.' You can imagine how that made me feel in comparison. I already knew your opinion of me."

"I lied, Brielle," he reiterated softly. Firmly. "I wish I could

go back and unsay those untrue words. That's not how I ever saw you."

"Still, that reinforced how I felt about myself. Then there was her family. They clearly doted on her, just as you did. I was a throwaway. My family detested me. No matter how hard I worked for them, I meant nothing to them. She's a shadow rider and, by all accounts, a good one. No one tells her not to go into the shadows. If they did, she'd tell them to go to hell and you'd admire her for that reaction. You *do* admire her, Elie, for all the things you say you don't want me to do. She doesn't have a pain addiction. She's probably not addicted to anything. I'm nothing like her, and yet, she's your best friend. I can't compete with someone like her. I hate coming across as a jealous wife, and I'm not going to make a big deal out of your friendship with her. I won't. That's a promise. I already made the promise to myself and I can make it to you."

She looked so miserable, Elie wanted to put his arms around her to comfort her. Instead, he continued to stand firmly in front of her, his thumb sliding back and forth over her ring, reviewing carefully every word she'd said. Emmanuelle was beautiful, that was true. She did have a doting family. She was an excellent shadow rider and she'd tell anyone to go to hell if they tried to stop her from doing what she wanted to do. No, she didn't have a pain addiction. She didn't need a man like Elie in the bedroom. His best friend? She had been for a long while. When he wanted to share something, he had always thought to call Emme. Was it that way now? No. He could say with all honesty, his friendship with Brielle had superseded what he'd had with Emme.

Very slowly, he shook his head. "I don't see you as a jealous wife, Brielle. After the way you were raised, you have insecurities. That's natural. After the way I was raised, I'm going to have them, too. Neither of us were wanted in our homes or by the people who were supposed to love us. We're building our own family and sorting out what a relationship is. But, *bébé*, it's *our* relationship. Not Val and Emme's. It's *ours*. Emmanuelle

would never suit me. She didn't when I first met her and she doesn't now. Do I think she's a beautiful woman? Yes. She is. Do I look at you and think you're the most beautiful woman I've ever seen? Yes. Absolutely I do."

She shook her head. "Don't, Elie. That's not even close to being true."

"It is, Brielle. I've seen you in the morning when you first wake up, looking so vulnerable with those freckles scattered across your nose like angels have been kissing you. I've seen you desperate for me, looking at me with such trust it makes me feel like no one has ever made me feel. I've seen you a thousand ways, ways no one else has ever seen you, all of them gorgeous. You aren't made up for the paparazzi. You're mine. Here in our home. Laughing. Whispering with me on our pillow or in the bathtub. You're eating pizza. Or cooking me some amazing dinner with a little apron tied around a pair of jeans. You're so fucking beautiful, sometimes my heart can't take it."

Her vivid green gaze hadn't left his face the entire time he was talking. "You really do think so, don't you?"

He helped her slide off the bed. "Yeah, I do."

She walked gingerly to the clothes closet with him. He kept talking because he never wanted her to feel less around any woman. "As for her family, they do dote on her. She's the only girl and her brothers adore her. Her mother, however, despised her. It didn't affect her the same way our childhoods affected us though, because Emme has always had the benefit of older brothers and cousins who love her so much. You didn't have that, Brielle, and neither did I. I'm fully aware of what it means to be alone, what it feels like. I know you do, too. And I don't want that for you, ever again. I don't want that for me, either. Brielle Couture Archambault, you're my family. You're the center of my entire world. Hopefully, I'm the center of yours. The Ferraros have opened their hearts to us and taken us in. I'm all for that, but ultimately, it's going to be us, you and me, with our own family to join with theirs. That's the way I feel about that."

He reached into the closet to pull down the soft pale mint-green blouse she indicated. He liked the feminine tops she tended to pair with her blue jeans. The fabric was thin and shaped her body lovingly, resting easily against her skin without pressing or rubbing over the wound at her ribs or the surgical incisions where the doctor had gone in to find and stop her internal bleeding. The little buttons were darker green squares that looked to Elie like an invitation to open each one.

It was all he could do to keep his fingers from shaking as he carefully buttoned Brielle into her shirt. He'd been sleeping with his wife every night, holding her close, but careful not to aggravate any of her many wounds, and after the initial terror of nearly losing her had passed, the agony of holding her so close yet not being able to make love to her was driving him mad.

What the hell had Stefano done when Francesca was on bed rest prior to giving birth? Stefano never looked at other women and he had an incredibly healthy sex drive.

Elie had discovered that having Brielle's soft body right next to him was sheer torture when he couldn't make love to her. He was going to have to figure something out. Because not holding her close at night was out of the question. He was an inventive man. It was just that he was terrified of hurting her.

Feeling like the most tortured martyr in history, Elie helped Brielle step into lacy boy shorts that slid up and over her cheeks. He really loved the shape of her bottom. He found himself cupping her cheeks and rubbing them. She pushed back into him and he quickly found her leggings before his cock was too full and painful for him to be able to walk.

"You're going to get yourself in trouble."

"You started it."

He had. He couldn't deny it. "Let's talk about shadow riding and Emme's penchant for telling people to go to hell. I've told you how important you are to me. What it makes me feel like when your life is threatened. I'm a different man than Valentino. He and Emme have their own relationship and they've worked out what makes them happy. I can't take it when I think

there's a possibility I'll have to live without you. I may not have had you in my life for long, Brielle, but you've given me the first true happiness I've known. The first true sense of finally having a home. I don't want to go back to a life without you. Not ever. That has nothing to do with your ability in the shadows; it has everything to do with my issues. My fears and my needs."

Pulling up her leggings over the thick pad that covered the wound on her thigh was a little trickier than he had thought it would be. He paused to ensure he didn't jostle it before pulling them up over her hips and then slipping on her shoes while she kept one hand on his shoulder.

"It's your choice whether or not to fulfill my needs, just as it's always my choice to look after yours, which includes both of us having sexual cravings in the bedroom. I can't deal with you shadow riding. You already know that. If you tell me to go to hell, so be it, but then how long would we work? I honestly don't know, Brielle. How long would you be able to live with me if your passion was to ride the shadows and I told you to stop? That wouldn't work, either."

"Fortunately, my passion lies in another direction altogether."

Her fingers moved through his scalp, a whisper of a caress that trailed down his temple to his jaw. He felt her touch like a brand.

"That would be?" he prompted, just barely keeping his voice from shaking.

"Aside from you, my laptop. I do love the work I do on that."

"Good that you remembered to put me first. You are healing fast." He poured sensual threat into his voice.

She took her hair down, looked in the mirror and sighed. "There's no hope."

"I love your hair wild. It's beautiful." He touched one of the springy curls and leaned forward to kiss her neck. "Emme is not my best friend. She isn't the one I think of when I want someone to talk something over with. You are. That's the

reason you get those infuriating text messages when you're working. I get random thoughts and want to share."

Elie kissed her neck again, used his teeth to scrape back and forth and then sucked at her soft skin. "I'm going to get creative tonight. Think about that when we're at dinner."

CHAPTER SIXTEEN

The private elevator leading to Stefano and Francesca's penthouse apartment opened directly into their foyer. Brielle's breath caught in her throat. The penthouse was a gorgeous, elegant home, something straight out of a magazine.

"The entire upper floor is their home," Elie whispered in Brielle's ear. "With the family gathering so often, they might need the floor below as well."

Brielle couldn't help but laugh. "Especially when all of them start having children. Then again, he might just buy a lake house. Taviano already has one somewhere out there, and so does Vittorio. Nicoletta says she loves the house Taviano found near the lake." She wanted to bite her tongue. When she was nervous, she talked too much.

"Many of the older properties are beautiful. They've been in the same families for generations," he told her. "Dario discovered a working lavender farm and snapped it up."

She stopped right in the middle of the great room, ignoring the cream-colored couches and matching armchairs and

the grand piano. "Dario has a working lavender farm? He actually sells lavender? Are you kidding me?"

"It's a legitimate business. I'm not saying he doesn't ship dead bodies out with the lavender. The fragrance helps cover the smell."

Both hands on her hips, she glared up at his expressionless face. "Ha ha, very funny. I can't imagine Dario Bosco, badass crime lord, selling lavender for a living. If his enemies only knew, he might lose his bad boy image for good."

"I had to tell you. Once I found out his lips had been on yours, I didn't want you thinking he was a badass anymore. He has a reputation with the ladies."

"Mmm." Brielle tried on her dreamiest look. "I only remember his lips in a dream."

Elie's brows came together. "Is that so? In a dream?"

"I hovered above us and watched him. He appeared a little distracted. Not fully focused the way you are when your lips are on mine," she clarified.

Brielle decided she might have gone a little too far in teasing him when he got a wholly wicked smirk on his face. Elie was the master of evil planning. He had more ways to tease her sexually than she could ever conceive of. At least he didn't have any of his toys with him. That would have been horrible in a room filled with Ferraros she didn't know very well. It also would have been secretly thrilling if she believed she could have gotten away with it without anyone suspecting—which she doubted. The Ferraros were too perceptive.

It didn't take much for her to be aroused. She'd been too long without Elie. Now she was thinking about sex. Wondering what he was going to do. Or say. He would do something and he'd make her wait. Her heart accelerated. He always made her feel alive. When she was nervous, he turned her entire focus on him.

"Elie, be serious, does Dario actually run a lavender farm?"

He grinned at her, sweeping his arm around her waist and heading through the great room toward the sound of laughter.

Clearly, he knew exactly where he was going. "Yes, he does. I think he really runs it himself, too. He wouldn't admit it, if you came right out and asked, he'd probably give you his 'fuck you' look, or his 'shut up or you're dead' look, but Val believes he runs it himself. He has a manager, but he oversees it. Dario doesn't let much out of his hands."

Brielle didn't have time to admire the elegant features of Stefano and Francesca's home. The large dining area opened straight into the kitchen so it was one huge room. She recognized Taviano at the stove stirring what appeared to be spaghetti sauce in a commercial-size pot, while Emmanuelle was chopping vegetables at the center island. Both whirled around as Elie and Brielle entered.

"Oh, good, Brielle," Emmanuelle greeted her. "Francesca and Stefano had to step out for a few minutes. She forgot the baby had a checkup. They'll be right back, but the dinner is not going to be ready in time. She was going to whip up some dessert, which is not the forte of either of us. Nicoletta is having some kind of meeting with buyers or sellers for Lucia's Treasures and will be late, so no help there."

Elie looked outraged. He caught Brielle's elbow. "Are you seriously suggesting my wife, who, let me remind you, was shot six times less than two weeks ago, should help with the cooking the first time she comes to dinner?"

"Well . . ." Taviano paused for a moment. "Yeah. She's family. Brielle, you're tough, right? What's a few bullets? You can whip up one of your desserts Elie's always bragging about while you're sitting down, can't you? Elie can hand you anything you need. If we don't have it up here, they'll have it downstairs in the kitchens." He grinned at Elie, entirely unrepentant.

Brielle laughed, feeling much better. If she was busy, not just sitting around trying to think up things to say, she wouldn't chatter like an idiot. "As a matter of fact, Taviano, I'm very tough. A few bullets won't stop me from making a dessert. Let me look in the fridge and freezer and see what you have."

Taviano looked like his oldest brother, Stefano. He had the

same black hair that seemed artfully messy and the same blue eyes. His nose was straight, his jaw strong and covered in the signature Ferraro persistent darker shadow that helped, despite his sensual mouth, to make him look tough, confident and a bit arrogant.

"She's tough because I gave her the air right out of my lungs," Dario stated from where he was lounging against the wall.

Emme flung a knife at him. It lodged beside his left ear, the tip buried deep in the wall. Dario sighed and yanked it free. "You'll be the one over here mudding and painting, you little monster. Val, keep your woman under control."

"No woman is tough because you breathed your nasty air into her lungs," Emmanuelle declared.

"Actually," Brielle said sweetly as she scrubbed her hands. "Dario's breath smelled just like lavender. I think that's what brought me back. I was hovering above my body watching everything happening and then this lavender scent began calling to me. It was impossible to ignore. You know how lavender is, Emme. One feels so calm around lavender."

"You could use more lavender in your life, Emme. You're always wound up so tight," Elie said. "We should find out where to order some for you."

"It's really good for you." Brielle studied the contents of the fridge and then the freezer. "I can make little fresh peach or apricot soufflés if everyone likes them."

"That sounds delicious," Emmanuelle said. "Is it a lot of work? I'll lend you a hand when I finish chopping all the veggies—which Val or Dario could be doing for me, so I could help you." She looked up to glare at the two men.

"Lavender is supposed to be calming, Emme," Elie continued. "Dario, if your breath smells like lavender, maybe you should go breathe on the dragon and see if that calms her down. You have to get up close and personal so she gets the full effect of your sweet breath."

"I have a gun, Elie," Dario announced.

"Tell me what you need, Brielle, and I'll get it for you,"

Elie offered. "You can sit on the high-backed stool up by the counter."

"I'll need to be able to move around," she protested and then stopped at the look on his face. He'd brought her against his better judgment. She was in the kitchen working rather than in a bed. Cooperating with him might work in her favor. She gave him a smile. "Thanks, honey." She rattled off a quick list of everything she'd need.

Elie was fast and efficient, keeping out of Taviano and Emmanuelle's way as he maneuvered through the kitchen, getting all the ingredients and the necessary mixing bowls and utensils. Brielle loved watching him move. He had a panther-like quality to him, silent, muscles moving beneath his shirt. He was wearing casual clothes, but the tee stretching over his chest was a dark charcoal with thin, gray stripes. Somehow, his choice of clothing emphasized the predatory quality to his movements.

Emmanuelle looked up from where she was chopping vegetables with swift efficiency. "Seriously, Brielle, do you actually remember Dario and Raimondo doing CPR on you? How could you when your heart had stopped?"

Elie sighed. "Could we just not talk about this? Walking into my house and seeing my wife on that table with the surgeon up to his elbows in blood was the worst experience of my life." He fixed a stern eye on Brielle. "We aren't repeating it. Ever."

Taviano laughed. "Lay down the law, brother. I hear you loud and clear. Does your woman? My experience with women—which comes mostly from growing up with my sister, I'll admit—is they don't hear a thing we say to them."

"Or if they do hear," Dario corrected him, "they ignore you because they don't have to deal with the consequences of their actions." He didn't look up from his phone. "Or they believe their actions have no consequences."

Emmanuelle threw another knife at him. This one stuck very close to his shoulder—so close, it just missed his immaculate dark blue shirt.

"Getting a little too close," Valentino reprimanded her, striding across the room to yank the knife from the wall. "If his bodyguards were here, they might decide they have to protect him and then we'd be in a shoot-out."

"If I wanted to hit him with a knife, Val, I would have. I did consider putting it right through his chauvinistic heart," Emmanuelle declared.

"I'm not worried," Dario claimed. "She's crazy about me."

Brielle had already begun mixing her ingredients for her soufflé. She did her best not to laugh at the exchange between Emmanuelle and Dario. They did act like brother and sister, although a bit on the lethal side. Brielle thought Emmanuelle should have more ammunition if she didn't already have it.

Brielle had been ordered not to investigate Dario, especially his past. She'd ignored that order, knowing Dario and Val's man, Bernado, would never be able to track her computer, even if he tried. Everything she found on Dario had obviously been planted. It was good work, but most of it wasn't true. That frustrated the hell out of her and only made her want to dig deeper.

"Why didn't you tell me you run a thriving lavender farm, Dario?" she asked as she worked. She was careful to keep her head down, as if she was totally engrossed in what she was doing. "It's an actual legitimate business. How do you find the time to run such a large farm and still do all your other work?"

There was a small silence. She looked up at Dario. His dark eyes were on her. As usual, there was no expression on his face, but the darkness in his eyes sent a shiver through her body. The rhythmic chopping ceased altogether, telling her Emmanuelle was looking at Dario. She must have been to Dario's home numerous times, right? Was this such a huge secret she'd just given away?

She looked up at Elie, then back to Dario. "I'm sorry, Dario, was I not supposed to say anything? The only thing I remembered about that entire ordeal after I went down was the smell of lavender. I was calm because I knew you were

there and I kept trying to ask you to give Elie a message for me."

"A fucking bullshit message," Dario snapped. "If you'd died on me, I wouldn't have told him, that's how pissed I would have been."

"What message, *mon amour*?" Elie sent Dario a look that would have backed anyone else off.

The only way Brielle kept from smiling was to look down at her soufflé ingredients and begin work again. "I wanted him to tell you that you were always the one. He said to tell you myself, that it was bullshit to quit breathing. He had a few other choice things to say as well."

"I'll bet he did," Emmanuelle said.

"You scared the fucking hell out of him," Valentino snapped. "What did you expect?"

Brielle realized that was the truth. She'd scared them all. Somehow, she mattered to these people already, more than she ever had to her own blood relatives. "I suppose I did."

"Um, really?" Emmanuelle came to her rescue. "It wasn't like she planned to get shot. Valentino, I seem to recall that you were shot not too long ago. And, Dario, didn't you take a couple of bullets as well? Elie? I'm pretty certain you were in the military with Drago and Demetrio and they tell some tale of you being all heroic and getting shot up and having to leave the military, which is how you ended up in Chicago. They said they told you to come here and work with Emilio."

"Not the same thing, Emme," Taviano said.

The others nodded. Vittorio and Grace had come in, listening to the conversation. Vittorio pulled out a chair for Grace, seating her close to everyone, pulled a pitcher of fruit-flavored water from the refrigerator and placed a glass in front of his woman.

"Vittorio?" Taviano asked.

Brielle looked up at Vittorio and her breath caught in her throat. He was very tall with broad shoulders and extremely fit looking. He had the same extraordinary dark blue eyes the Ferraro men seemed to have.

"No." Emmanuelle held up her hand. "You don't get to weigh in. You are the most overprotective man in the world, with the exception of Stefano."

Brielle snuck a quick glance at Grace. She had bright red hair, pale skin, green eyes and was medium height with a slight build. She had a little smile on her face as she nodded her agreement with Emmanuelle's assessment of Vittorio.

Stefano strode in. He was carrying a baby in one arm. Beside him, a little boy held his free hand, but the boy pulled free and ran to Vittorio, who scooped him up immediately. Stefano had clearly heard his sister's description of him. "I don't accept that I could possibly come close to being the most overprotective man in the world, Emme."

"I want my niece," Grace said decisively.

Stefano looked at Vittorio. Brielle thought that was odd. Stefano was clearly looking for permission. Grace appeared almost defiant.

"My shoulder is doing far better. It's holding, Stefano. I'm not going to drop her."

"Gracie." Stefano's voice was loving. "I would never think you would drop our little Luciana. I was worried the shoulder was just beginning to really stay in place and didn't know if her weight would be too much." He crouched down beside the chair and offered the little bundle to Grace. "This injury has been such a journey for you. You never complain, but we all know how painful it is. The doctor told us if this replacement doesn't hold, there is nothing else they can do. We're just being cautious, you understand? Out of caring."

Vittorio stood behind Grace's chair, his free hand on her good shoulder, his nephew on his hip. "So many operations, *il mia gattina*, all of them failures. This is our last hope."

Grace nodded her head, but she bent over the little girl, her gaze fixed on the baby with longing. It was clear to Brielle that she wanted a child of her own. Most likely, the doctors didn't want her to get pregnant while her shoulder was healing. She would have to ask Elie about Grace's injury.

For now, however, it was nice that the spotlight was no

longer on her. She could make her soufflés and observe the family dynamics.

Crispino, Stefano and Francesca's son, was passed around the room from uncle to uncle, and that included Valentino and even Dario. Elie tossed him into the air and ran around the house with the boy on his back. Dario took him out of the room to play with him, but she noticed that Stefano trailed after them, seemingly to talk to Dario about an important issue.

Francesca wasn't nearly as nervous around Val or Dario as Brielle had expected her to be. In fact, she was genuinely warm and welcoming. She looked tired, and took the chair her husband pulled out for her right beside Grace. Ricco and Mariko arrived with Giovanni and Sasha. Nicoletta came in right behind them.

The room should have felt crowded, but it didn't. The dining table was long and seemed to accommodate all the chairs with space in between. The noise level went up, but if anything, it was all laughter. Brielle was introduced to the family. She would have been extremely shy but Elie stood right beside her and she continued to work on the soufflés, putting them in the little ramekins so they could bake in the oven.

She tried not to be nervous with all of them there. Everyone felt welcoming. It was just that there were so many of them. They worked together like a smoothly oiled machine as if they'd been doing it for so long, they didn't think about it. Dishes were put out on the table, along with silverware and wineglasses. Bottles of wine were opened. Angel hair pasta was put in large bowls and placed in the middle of either end of the table along with bowls of salad, the cooked vegetables and garlic bread. Taviano placed large bowls of hot spaghetti sauce on either end while Elie took the last of the ramekins out of the oven.

Stefano and Francesca put the baby down in the nursery while Mariko deftly tied a bib around Crispino and placed him in his high chair between Stefano's chair and Francesca's. Brielle found herself intrigued, but felt out of place by

the way the Ferraros interacted so easily with one another. Through it all, they kept up a running commentary, sharing news of their day, exchanging news of their households, just talking about their everyday lives. It was beautiful and poignant to her.

Brielle had always wanted a family. The Ferraros were the epitome of the big, loving Italian family she'd always read about. She didn't know how to be part of something like that. She couldn't relate to them. She found herself watching Elie. How had he managed to find his way into their lives? He seemed as if he'd always belonged. He laughed with them, teased, looked at ease. How had he managed when he'd been alone, the same as she had been?

Elie, sitting beside her, laughed at something Ricco said, something she missed because she was too busy concentrating on not getting up and running from the room. She swirled pasta on her fork, trying to look as natural as possible, wishing she had Elie's ability to keep from giving away her thoughts on her face.

His hand dropped to her thigh, his knuckles stroking back and forth. She looked up at him, but his focus was on Ricco and Giovanni. The two were talking racing and cars, subjects she knew nothing about. The others at the table seemed to be listening. Even Crispino seemed to know more than she did, leaning toward the speakers eagerly.

Elie's knuckles moved higher, settling between her legs, stroking light caresses from her mound to her entrance, then along her lips, tracing up to her clit. The breath left her lungs as he nudged her legs apart with his fist. All the while, he didn't miss a beat, keeping up his end of the conversation. The pasta dropped off her fork back onto her plate. She felt a little like Crispino, who was trying to eat on his own. He wanted no part of the adults feeding him, determined to be one of them, just as grown-up, and they let him.

Elie turned his knuckles and tormented her even more, sliding his fist sideways in between her lips, rocking his fist,

finding her sensitive spots and stroking them over and over, but so lightly, he only inflamed them, not giving her anything close to relief.

"Brielle?" Stefano's voice penetrated her Elie-induced fog brain.

She sat up straight and hoped no one noticed her heightened breathing and the color creeping under her skin. Elie withdrew his hand and sipped at the wine as though he was completely innocent.

She focused her entire attention on Stefano.

"Tell me you didn't already accept the job Val and Dario offered you, Brielle," Stefano said, clearly repeating himself. "If it's money, we can do better than they can."

Dario made a sound of derision but kept eating. Valentino rolled his eyes. "Everything isn't always about money, Stefano. Sometimes it's about interesting versus boring."

"Please tell me you are not calling our investigative work boring," Giovanni said.

"Well, actually I am." Val didn't deny it. "You already have two teams of investigators. What is Brielle going to do? Twiddle her thumbs? If she works for us, she's actually going to be doing what she loves. Chasing down leads, not getting the leftovers from your two lead teams."

"That's not what would happen, Brielle," Stefano objected. "Is that the line of crap they fed you? If you haven't yet given them your word, we need to sit down tonight and talk after dinner. We can throw their asses out and come up with a plan."

"Stefano," Francesca murmured. But she sounded on the verge of laughter.

"Asses," Crispino repeated. Loudly. He tossed pasta into the air. It landed in his curls.

"Far too late," Dario said before Brielle could respond. "I had to share lavender breath with her. Don't do that often and there's no going back. She owes me." He added more spaghetti sauce to the second helping of angel hair pasta he'd put on his plate without looking up.

There was silence and then Emmanuelle burst out laughing. The others followed suit. "Unfortunately, Stefano," Elie said, "Dario has a point. There's no going back from that."

"There's a story there I missed," Nicoletta said.

"Don't worry, I'll share," Taviano told her.

Brielle noticed no one reprimanded Crispino for his language. Stefano calmly removed the pasta from his hair. When the baby went to throw more into the air, Stefano took the plate.

"Are you finished, son?"

Crispino shook his head.

"Do we throw food?"

Crispino shook his head.

Stefano put the plate back in front of him and then leaned over and kissed his temple.

"Dario." Francesca's brows came together. "You aren't eating any of the vegetables. We can get a different recipe if you don't like this one. Is it all the spices?"

Dario scowled at her but he didn't reprimand her as Brielle knew he would her had she pointed out he wasn't eating something in front of others. Probably because Francesca exuded genuine concern that he might not like the recipe and she was willing to change it just for him. There was something about her that made others, Brielle included, want to protect her and please her at the same time. Not to mention Stefano might leap up and kill anyone who dared to swear at his wife. Brielle couldn't imagine even Dario crossing that line.

"I love the pasta and wanted seconds, Francesca. And I had quite a bit of the salad. Saw Brielle making that dessert so I was saving room."

Francesca smiled at him. "That makes sense. I just don't want to serve anything you don't care for."

Brielle waited until Dario looked at her and then she rolled her eyes. Emmanuelle did the same. Both women knew he didn't eat that many vegetables. Emmanuelle because she cooked for him and Brielle because Elie had told her Dario

was difficult when it came to food. He gave no indication that he noticed the two of them.

"Stefano, were you aware that Dario owns and operates a lavender farm?" Emmanuelle asked. "He totally runs it. Isn't that cool? That's why he always smells so good."

It was a taunt, pure and simple. Dario flicked his poisonous, vengeful gaze at her, but she appeared completely unfazed. At the very least, Brielle would have moved closer to Elie.

Elie spun pasta on his fork and took a bite. "He does, that's true. He found the best piece of property on the lake and snapped it up. I wish I'd found it."

"Had I known the owners were going to put it up for sale, I would have made a try for it," Val added. "It's a huge piece of land. Twenty acres if I remember correctly. I really covet that piece of property. The house is fantastic. You have quite a bit going on there, right, Dario?"

Brielle knew that was the men closing ranks, taking the focus off the lavender farm and putting it on the property.

"Main house has over five thousand square feet," Dario said. "Gives me plenty of room to roam around in. Couple of custom fieldstone fireplaces. The kitchen is a work of art for any cook. I would have bought it for the kitchen alone."

"Dario, do you cook?" Sasha asked.

"No, but I'm always holding out hope that there's a woman out there who cooks better than Emme. If that happens, I'm kidnapping her and tying her to the stove." He took another bite of the pasta. "Although it has occurred to me to kidnap Taviano. This is damn good sauce, Taviano."

"Damn good," Crispino repeated like a parrot.

Francesca's head turned sharply to look at her husband. He gave a little shake of his head. "*Bambina*. No reaction, remember? You were the one who cautioned me."

"I think I was wrong. Isn't it funny how he mimics all the bad words and not the good ones?"

Stefano laid his hand over hers. "It does feel that way at

times, doesn't it? We'll all try to do better with our language in front of him."

Around the table, the others solemnly nodded. Brielle loved that the family were in agreement for her. Giovanni sat back in his chair, pushing his plate toward the center of the table. Sasha did the same. She reached out and Giovanni took her hand. The sudden silence cued Brielle that the Ferraros realized the couple had something to tell them.

"I wanted to thank everyone, especially you, Francesca, for the kindness you showed to me when I lost Sandlin. I was so lost and you were giving birth under difficult circumstances, and you still reached out to me and were so loving and supportive. Thank you. All of you." She took a breath. "I know that was two months ago. I just couldn't talk about him until now. I miss my brother every single day. I had far more time with him than I ever expected to have. After the accident that caused his brain injury, the doctors told me he would only have a couple of months to live, but I had longer, and he got so he knew me. Maybe not as his younger sister, but he knew me. All of you helped so much to give him a better life. I can't thank you enough."

"You're family, Sasha," Stefano said. "Sandlin was our family."

The way Stefano made the statement with such authority in his quiet voice gave Brielle goose bumps. He made her a believer. Elie sounded like that. Suddenly, she realized he would speak with that same authority to their children and anyone they took into their family. She also realized she believed in him the way everyone sitting around the table believed in Stefano.

"Thank you for always treating us that way," Sasha said simply.

"Sasha and I have a little announcement," Giovanni said, threading his fingers through his wife's. "We waited to make certain she carried through the first trimester. Sasha and I are going to have a baby. We're pretty excited that Crispino and Luciana Cella are going to have a cousin nearly the same age."

Smiles broke out around the table. Stefano and Ricco

produced two very rare bottles of wine and sparkling grape drink for toasts. Brielle caught Grace looking down at her hands with a sad expression, but she recovered quickly and was beaming with joy for Sasha and Giovanni. Stefano, as head of the family, was the first to formally stand up and give the toast, followed by everyone around the table. Even Brielle was expected to say something. She did so, managing to wish the couple a healthy, happy baby.

Brielle was surprised when the men cleared the table, rinsing the dishes and putting them in the dishwasher rather than having the women do all the cleaning. Stefano was the first one up. Elie and Valentino began to serve the dessert to everyone and eventually Vittorio and Taviano helped. Nicoletta jumped up and grabbed extra whipped cream. The others laughed at her. She just laughed with them.

"You put that on everything," Ricco accused her.

"She does," Taviano said solemnly.

Everyone groaned. Nicoletta turned a shade of red and ignored them. It didn't stop her from swirling quite a lot of whipped cream on the apricot soufflé. She took a bite and moaned. "This is so good, Taviano. This is really good."

He leaned over and licked whipped cream from the corner of her mouth. "I took one of the peach ones so you could try both. If you insist on moaning like that, we're taking them home."

Another round of laughter and Nicoletta's blush deepened, but she took a bite of Taviano's soufflé and moaned again, causing him to kiss her with whipped cream still on her lips.

Brielle was waiting for Francesca's verdict. She hadn't had much time to come up with anything wonderful. Emmanuelle hadn't weighed in yet. Some people didn't like peaches or apricots. She'd made both just in case.

"You made this at the last minute out of nothing," Emmanuelle said. "Didn't she, Taviano? We just saw her and asked her to come in and whip something up. Good grief, Brielle, are you a chef? A bakery chef or something, because this is really good."

Under the table, Brielle reached for Elie's thigh. She had to make contact with him. She didn't know why it was so important that everyone like what she made, but it was. He shifted his weight slightly toward her. "Fantastic as usual, *bébé*."

"You should have hired her as a bakery chef, not as an investigator," Vittorio said.

"I'll hire you to work for my company," Grace offered. "We put on events, fund-raisers, weddings, huge events. We could use someone like you exclusively."

"She has a job," Valentino said decisively. "All of you quit trying to steal her away from us. It wasn't easy to get her."

"Actually, Brielle," Dario interrupted, and the table went silent. "This could have used a touch of lavender."

Everyone broke out into laughter again. Brielle couldn't help herself, Dario was so funny, even delivered in his straight-man voice. She laughed, but her gaze still strayed to Francesca and Stefano.

Francesca took a bite and exchanged a look with Stefano. She shook her head. "I really don't like to disagree with you, Dario, but I think it's rather perfect as it is. I have the apricot soufflé. Maybe you have the peach one."

"I have the peach one," Stefano said. "We could vote on it. If you lose, Dario, I get to hire her."

"In your wildest dreams, Ferraro," Valentino said.

Emmanuelle rolled her eyes. "Brielle is quite capable of speaking for herself. It doesn't matter what kind of voting you do. She's going to choose who she wants to work for."

"You're only saying that because you're married to Val and he *makes* you say that," Giovanni taunted.

"Just how could Val make me do anything I don't want to do?" Emmanuelle challenged.

"All of us know that one," Taviano said.

"That's easy," Ricco said at the same time.

"Just tell you no sex until you comply," Giovanni announced with a shrug of his shoulders. "Works on you every time."

"No sex. No sex," Crispino chanted, clapping his hands.

Francesca threw her arms into the air. "Stefano, are you coaching him behind my back?"

Stefano burst out laughing, leaned in and kissed his exasperated wife. "Even I couldn't get our son to say inappropriate things on cue, *bambina*."

"Valentino Saldi, did you tell my brothers you threaten to withhold sex from me if I don't do what you want me to do?" Emmanuelle sounded outraged, but she looked close to laughter.

"Why, no, Emmanuelle Saldi, I did not. Now, however, they know it's the truth."

Emmanuelle turned her head slowly to look at Dario. "You traitor. You scumbag traitor. I take you in and feed you to keep you from starving to death and you go behind my back and repeat *private* conversations to my awful brothers."

"Emme, a conversation isn't private if I'm there and half the neighborhood can hear you. You need to look up the word *private*. Besides, I lost a bet."

"You lost a bet and so you paid it off by telling my brothers that?"

Dario raised an eyebrow but didn't reply.

Emmanuelle glared at Stefano, who just grinned at her. "They are out of control. Completely out of control."

"I agree," Francesca said.

Stefano's smirk faded. He nodded and gave his brother a solemn look. "Clean it up, you're not two."

"I'm two," Crispino announced.

"Yes, you are and always getting me in trouble with that mouth of yours," Stefano said. "But I love you for it. What are we reading tonight?"

"The lion and the mouse."

"First in Italian and then in English," Stefano said.

Crispino nodded his head. "Then Mommy can sing to me."

"Yes, after we read a story."

"I can kiss baby sister."

"That's before we read," Stefano said firmly. "No stalling tonight."

Brielle felt Elie's hand tighten around hers. He was observing the exchange between Stefano and his son carefully. She realized Stefano was his only example of a man with his family. She was very glad they'd come to the dinner and she had the chance to see the entire Ferraro family together. If Elie had to choose a man to show him the way to treat his wife and children, Stefano was a good example to emulate.

On the way down to the floor where they were staying, Elie explained that Grace's shoulder had been shattered by a bullet when she stepped in to protect Vittorio. She had undergone so many surgeries and had pins, plates, bolts, cement, physical therapy and over time more surgeries, and now an actual shoulder replacement. Her muscles didn't want to hold the shoulder in place. This was their last effort.

"That makes me so sad for her. She's so sweet, Elie."

"The women in the Ferraro family are good women, Brielle. I hope you felt welcomed. They wanted you there tonight."

Elie's body crowded close to hers in the privacy of the elevator, his body heat keeping her warm. She wrapped her arms around his waist and leaned into him. Her body hurt in half a dozen places, but she ached for him. It seemed as if she'd been without him forever.

"Did the doctor clear me for sex?" She looked up at him hopefully, uncaring that she was the one asking. Uncaring what that said. He'd been teasing and he'd implied they might have sex, but she ached for him. On the other hand, the wound in her thigh felt raw and chafing under the constant movement of her leggings when she walked.

"Not quite yet, Brielle. Not actual sex," he clarified. "We can do a few other things, but Doc said we should wait another week at least."

That made her uneasy, especially since she knew Elie would be traveling in the shadows extensively again. Shadows always made riders horribly aroused. She nodded and when they returned to their room, she let him help her take her clothes off to get ready for bed. When she was ready, Elie

helped her onto the bed, but when she would have moved to the top, he stopped her with a wicked grin.

"I think I told you I had plans. We might not be able to have sex, but that doesn't mean we can't play. I intend to play for a long time, so you may as well get comfortable, *mon petit amor.*"

CHAPTER SEVENTEEN

From the shadows, Elie couldn't keep the amusement from his face when Riccardo Santoro's bodyguards approached Dario and Valentino to search them. Both men stopped them with just one look.

"Seriously? We were asked to come to see Riccardo. He knows we are armed," Val said. "That said, we didn't bring our protection detail, but we can leave. And, gentlemen, if you're stupid enough to point your weapons at us, you're going to start a war you can't possibly win even here on your home turf."

Riccardo Santoro came down the hall. A lean man with handsome features, graying hair and a smooth, easy smile, he waved his security back. "These men are invited guests. There is no need for this. Valentino, Dario, please come in. Val, I thought you might bring your wife with you."

Riccardo gestured down the wide, impressive hallway. It was a gallery filled with artwork from many of the masters. Beautiful paintings meant to impress. Valentino had an eye for

art and he made a show of looking. He took his time, giving Ricco and Stefano, who had entered the house when they did, plenty of room to find the shadows they needed to explore the huge mansion.

Riccardo thought he would have the upper hand in this meeting. He had always been good at reading his opponents. He believed, because Valentino and Dario were so much younger and had only recently taken over the Saldi territories, that he could come to a compromise with them. He also was certain he could convince them he wasn't responsible for the hits taken out on them—or Brielle.

Emmanuelle, Taviano and Mariko were following along with Dario, Elie and Valentino as their protection detail. In the shadows, they would be able to study every nuance of Riccardo's body language as well as every inflection of his voice. They would also have time to react if there was any kind of danger toward their charges.

Riccardo took them to a large round room overlooking the park. Deliberately, Dario wandered over to the windows to look down at the view. Val stood in the doorway, staring down the hall at the impressive paintings. He made certain the long shadows thrown by the overhead lighting to show-case the artwork provided a generous pathway to allow Elie and the other riders to slide into the room and lock into other shadows.

"Beautiful paintings, Riccardo," he acknowledged.

"My wife, Eva," he replied and came to stand beside Val. He smelled of cigars and depravity. "She's always loved art. When she was younger, she painted. The house always smelled of oil paints or acrylics. I learned to know the difference. In those young days, I didn't know anything about art, but because she loved it so much, I learned."

Val knew Riccardo Santoro *had* learned. He'd gotten into the business of ripping off collectors by selling fake originals to them. The copies he sold were so good, many experts couldn't tell the difference. Naturally, the original would first be stolen

from the museum so the illicit collectors would be duped into believing they'd bought the real thing. It was a clever scheme and he'd made a fortune.

Val stepped back and Riccardo closed the door. When Riccardo turned, he was shocked to see Elie Archambault standing beside Dario and Valentino. The crime lord blinked several times, but it was clear to Elie that he didn't want to acknowledge that he hadn't seen him walk down the hall with his other two guests. That would make him look weak and he couldn't afford that.

Valentino simply leaned against the wall, his gaze on Riccardo as if he were a cat watching a mouse. He was a Saldi, perhaps new to the throne, but he'd been raised by Giuseppi to hold on to what he had through sheer brute force if necessary. Though young, he had already made a name for himself, someone to walk very softly around. Valentino and Dario appeared supremely confident by leaving their security force outside the gates. Elie knew that move alone had shaken Riccardo just a bit. Now, with Elie appearing out of nowhere, Riccardo was more than shaken; he was confused.

Elie turned to the others. "Shall we get down to business? We wouldn't want our men to get nervous."

Riccardo's laugh betrayed his tension. He waved them to the chairs in front of his desk. Before either man could sit, Dario took several moments to examine the chairs, then nodded and stepped back without a word. Valentino sank into one and Elie the other. Dario moved back against the wall.

"Did you think I had a bomb under the chairs in my own home?" Riccardo demanded, striving to look as if it was a joke.

"The possibility occurred to us," Val answered for all three. "I'm not going to beat around the bush, Riccardo. We have evidence that your family, specifically your son Carlo, ordered a hit on Elie, Dario, Elie's wife and me. Brielle was nearly killed in the last attack on her. To say you stirred up a firestorm is an understatement. Both Elie and Brielle are connected to the

Ferraro family. I married into it. Emme, my wife, is demanding justice. You have no idea what that family is capable of. You can order all the hits in the world on them, but I will guarantee, your entire family, every man, woman and child, will be wiped out in a single night. You know their reputation."

Riccardo listened attentively, his expression sorrowful. "I hear you, Valentino. The situation is dire. I heard what happened to Dino Colombo. Killed in his home with his father and mother and wife right there. No one saw or heard anything. His security was intact. Nothing was caught on camera. The reputation of the Ferraro family is always something we take into consideration and we all strive to avoid any contact with them."

He sighed, looked down at his hands and then spread his fingers wide before looking up again. "I have an alliance with the Toselli family in Barcelona. My son Carlo is married to Arnau's daughter, Valeria. I have two grandchildren by them. They live here on the estate with me. My daughter Claudia is married to Arnau's son Guillem and they also have two children together. They live in Barcelona, where I can't protect them. Do you see my problem?"

In a gesture very reminiscent of Stefano, Valentino steepled his fingers and he looked over the top of them, one eyebrow raised. "No, Riccardo, I don't. Are you saying Toselli threatened your daughter and grandchildren? He forced you to do his bidding by trading Elie's wife and our lives for your daughter and grandchildren?"

Put like that, the head of the Santoro crime family would detest looking weak in front of Val and Dario. For just one moment anger darkened Riccardo's eyes, a resentment that promised retaliation toward Valentino, but was quickly gone. He had learned to school his features over the years of running his organization. Riccardo's gaze flicked to Elie, who didn't change expressions.

"In essence, yes." Riccardo nodded his head sorrowfully.

"You didn't think to take this to the council; you just made

the decision to order the hit on all of us?" Val's tone was mild, as if it mattered little that the man he faced had been responsible for the near death of Elie's wife.

"Not when my daughter is there in Barcelona and I can't get to her." Now Riccardo poured steel into his voice. "The attack on your wife was unfortunate, Elie. I tried to rescind the order, but I believe I was countermanded by Arnau Toselli himself. I don't know why."

Valentino looked at Elie, who shook his head. "You did rescind the order and it was countermanded by Toselli, but you're lying. You do know why he wants Brielle dead. I want to know the reason. It's in your best interests to tell me, Riccardo."

All pretense of civility evaporated in an instant. Riccardo Santoro dropped his mask of a sweet, aging senior trying to negotiate a settlement between families. He became the consummate crime boss, a man who had ruled his territory for years with an iron fist. His enemies had never been given quarter and never would.

He leaned toward Val, his eyes almost wild. "You are an upstart, just learning to lead. You know nothing at all. Did you think you could come into my home with your veiled threats and scare me? Out of respect for your father and uncle, I had thought to come to some kind of agreement between us, but you brought this man with you." He waved his arm toward Elie. "He is nothing. Not part of us and yet you treat him as family. His wife is a liability to us. *He* is a liability. The only thing we should be talking about is the matter between the Saldi family and the Santoro family."

There was a small silence. Elie was silent. His dark gaze moved over Riccardo Santoro. Then he smiled. "It wouldn't have mattered to me what you said anyway, you ignorant fatuous prick. You nearly killed my wife. As far as I'm concerned, you and your family as well as the Toselli family have earned everything coming to you and I intend to see that you get it." He stood up, his smile cruel. "Talk away, gentlemen. Just know, Santoro, that one by one, you'll see everything you love taken away before I take you last."

"You *dare* threaten me?" Riccardo Santoro demanded, standing up so violently that he knocked his chair back against the wall.

Ignoring the man's outrage, Elie opened the office door, back and shoulders straight, closing the door softly behind him. Swearing and red-faced with fury, Santoro stormed over to the door and yanked it open. There was no sign of Elie. He looked up and down the wide empty hallway, sputtering, then called for his security. They came at once, having been only a few feet from the office.

After a brief, furious interrogation from their boss, the guards insisted they hadn't seen Elie or anyone else emerge from the office. They vowed to sweep the house immediately and look at all the security tapes. Santoro turned back to Valentino and Dario. Neither man had moved.

"Who is that man?" Santoro demanded.

"I am certain I mentioned to you that the Ferraros have a very healthy respect for Elie's family." He waved that away. "We came here today out of respect for the years you have given to our organization." Val stood up. "Did you honestly think you could put out a hit on Dario and me and we would simply ignore it, Riccardo? Given your history, I would never believe this would be the end of it. You would continue to come after us."

"No, no. I am prepared to offer you a partnership. A very lucrative partnership, Valentino. You young people are so fast at making up your minds. There are always ways to fix these problems without bloodshed or going to war. Take advice from an old hand at this. Sit back down and listen to reason. You just were at war with your Uncle Miceli. How many men were lost? And, Dario? You are still in the process of weeding out the old guard. It is useless to continue to shed blood when we can come to terms."

Valentino made a show of reluctantly taking a seat. The more they heard, the more they learned. Riccardo Santoro believed himself invincible. He had already dismissed the threat Elie Archambault or the Ferraros might bring to his

family. He'd been in his position, one of strength, for far too long and he didn't believe anyone would seriously try to harm him or any member of his family.

"I believe you know why Brielle Archambault was put on the hit list," Val stated. He kept his voice low. He had a gift for compelling others to want to talk to him. He used it sparingly so no one ever questioned why they would suddenly offer him information they would otherwise never reveal. "Let's start there."

"She's nosy. She sent a report to Interpol giving specifics about our freighters. She even traced them to us. No one has ever connected us to those shipments before. But more than that, she apparently has 'confused' one of Toselli's most trusted men. Toselli wants her dead so there's no more confusion. He doesn't like his men being loyal to anyone but him."

Val nodded. "That's understandable. You can't have your men divide their loyalty."

Riccardo smiled at him. "I'm happy to hear you say that, Valentino. I knew you could be reasonable. These things can be worked out. Had we done so from the beginning, I assure you, this misunderstanding would never have occurred."

Val raised an eyebrow. "The 'misunderstanding' being the hits you put out on Dario and me."

Riccardo waved that away. "You have to understand the business is no longer what it used to be. We can't run around carrying guns and threatening people anymore. Everything is very different. Always you want to look good for the press. You can't ever afford to look as though you're dirty. You must appear to be a do-gooder. Be into charities. Have your wife be on all the boards for cancer—all the things that will make you look good. Anything to do with children. Sponsor the hell out of that crap. You're lucky, because you're getting in on the ground floor. I already had a reputation, but you're just starting out in the business. You can look clean. Legit."

Val watched the man come out from behind his desk, animated now that he had an audience. He perched on the end of his desk, facing the windows. "Look at it, Val. It can all

belong to you and Dario. Your generation. That's what I tell my son. Play your cards right. Get in on the ground floor. We've got the connections. We've got the ships. We already know what we're doing. Trafficking is a billion-dollar industry. *Billions.*"

There it was. He was going to offer them a deal. Val had been certain he would. It wouldn't occur to him, in spite of the war he'd started with Miceli, that Val would never take it. A man like Santoro was certain Valentino wanted the territory.

Riccardo waited for a reaction. Val kept all expression from his face. "I'm listening."

"We supply to Europe. They supply to us. We just swap the merchandise. The family in Europe has freighters and we have ours. We meet off the coast and off-load the merchandise to smaller freighters to take it to small ports where it's easy to smuggle it in. We already have the officials in place we need. It's a smooth operation. No one has come close to suspecting us."

"Until Brielle Archambault."

Riccardo waved his hand again. "A mosquito. Easily swatted. She'll be dead inside of twenty-four hours. We have eyes on her. At this moment, she's staying at the Ferraro Hotel in Chicago."

Val regarded him with his dark eyes. "And you believe you can kill her when she's surrounded by security right under the nose of Stefano Ferraro. Why would you think that?"

Riccardo laughed. "Two reasons. First, because, we're going to strike a deal and you have your brother-in-law in your pocket. Everyone knows he has one downfall and it's the women in his family. He'll do anything for his baby sister. That's how you got him under your thumb in the first place. And second, we've got someone in the Ferraro camp who owes a debt. He doesn't want his balls cut off and his entire family killed, so he'll do the job he's been instructed to do. Either way, she's dead by morning."

"What percentage of the business are you prepared to give each of us for your poor judgment in sending your very ineffective teams after us?" Val asked, getting down to it.

"We've taken the most risks, set everything up," Riccardo pointed out, hedging. "You'd both be coming in after we've smoothed the way."

"After you put out hits on both of us," Val reminded. "And you're clearly expecting me to share Stefano Ferraro with you, or at the very least, keep him on a leash when he wants to rip out your heart for murdering his little darling Brielle, which he will."

"*And* her asshole husband, Elie," Riccardo added.

"That's going to cost you, Riccardo," Valentino said. "You have no idea what I've gone through to bring home the Ferraro prize and keep it. I'm not going to hand that one over easily, especially to a man who put my name on a hit list. You come up with a proposal. A good one. I want to see that you can deliver what you promise. I see Brielle Archambault is dead in the morning, and I like your deal, we're in. If not, my brother-in-law is going to come calling."

He stood, this time making it clear he was leaving and nothing Riccardo had to say was going to deter him. Dario waited until Santoro opened the door politely for Valentino before he moved to cover Val's back. In the hallway, shadows zigzagged up and down, thrown by the various lights illuminating the art hanging in what was for all intents and purposes—a gallery.

The two men exited the home and went straight to their town car with the tinted windows. Valentino waited until they were nearly to the airport before he exchanged a long look with Dario. "Elie and Stefano are most likely tying up every investigator the riders—and we—have looking for the traitor Santoro has planted in Stefano's hotel."

Elie stood in the shadows just outside Carlo and Valeria's large sitting room, listening to the two of them and Riccardo as they boasted.

"My papa listened to your conversation with Saldi, just as you suggested," Valeria said. "He agrees that letting them

into the network is better than killing them if they can bring in the Ferraros. They have the ports as well. Papa wants the woman dead and he wants it done tonight. He has a large shipment of boys and girls both, all under thirteen. They'll bring in a huge sum of money. He doesn't want to ship until Brielle Archambault is dead."

She got up, poured drinks into tall glasses and handed one to her husband and another to her father-in-law. "You don't want to disappoint him. So much money to be made." She wrapped her arms around her husband's neck from behind him and rubbed his chest. "I love to see the cargo manifest when it says 'Full,' don't you, baby? When it says 'Doorknobs' or something silly like that? We know it's all about adding to our family's future."

Carlo patted her hands and then took a drink. "Yeah, love. No one is going to disappoint your papa. We want the bitch dead, too. She had no right to dig into our business. She's as good as gone. The order went out."

Valeria straightened, a satisfied smirk on her face. "Eva said you would take care of it." She sauntered over to the windows, her hips swaying. "She said you and Riccardo always take care of everything."

"I told you to have faith," Carlo said, his voice smug.

Elie took the shadow that led directly behind his chair and waited. Riders were renowned for their patience. Valeria had her back turned. It wouldn't be long before Riccardo looked away. Sure enough, his cell rang persistently. Elie was certain it was the first of the many bad news calls Riccardo Santoro, the untouchable crime lord of New York, was about to get.

The moment he turned away, phone to his ear, Elie stepped out of the shadows and grasped Carlo's skull between his hands. In one fluid motion he broke the man's neck, whispering, "Justice is served," under his breath as he stepped back into the shadows. Killing Carlo had taken less than a second.

Using the shadows in the room, Mariko stalked Valeria, waiting until the woman had leaned one slim hip against the wall and set her drink on the windowsill so she could pose

better for the men in the room. The light coming from the overhead chandelier softened her features and put shine in her hair. The shadows hid any flaws. She didn't realize the shadows also hid death coming directly at her from her right side.

"What do you mean, the money disappeared from the accounts?" Riccardo shouted into his phone. His face turned beet red. "All the accounts? That's impossible, Paulo. Money doesn't disappear. You find it. All of it. Right now. This has to be some kind of an error."

Valeria swung around, alarmed. Money was the reason she had married into this family. She was far from home, doing her father's bidding. Riccardo was swearing under his breath, staring at the cell phone in disbelief.

"Carlo, check the bank accounts," Riccardo ordered. "I'm going to check the safe downstairs." He turned back toward the center of the room.

Mariko stepped out of the shadow tube, grasping Valeria's head in a firm grip, breaking her neck in the smooth move the riders began learning from the age of two. She murmured the accepted phrase of justice served as she disappeared back into the shadows. She was gone before Riccardo realized his son's drink was in his lap and he was no longer alive.

"Carlo," he whispered and took a step forward. "Valeria, Carlo."

He heard the sound of Valeria's body crumpling to the floor behind him. Whirling around, Riccardo stared at his daughter-in-law's body, his features slack and uncomprehending. The phone rang again. He just stood there until it stopped ringing, his hand gripping the edge of his chair. On shaky legs he approached his son to feel for a pulse. A sound rose in the back of his throat, a protest, when he found no sign of life.

Gasping, he staggered from the room and headed up the stairs to go to his wife. She sat in her favorite chair facing the television set. It was on, but low, the way she liked it. He

could never hear it when she had the volume so low, but he didn't care for television so much, other than the news channels. She was staring at the news now, her mouth opened wide, one hand covering her lips to keep from screaming. When he came in, she pointed to the screen.

He read the captions easily. A series of explosions had rocked a fleet of freighters owned by the same company. Every freighter was completely destroyed. The entire crew of each freighter had been lost with the ships.

"Those are ours, Riccardo," she whispered. "They're saying the freighters were empty except for the crew. How can that be? Even the smallest freighters are lost along with the crews. The ships that weren't at sea were destroyed in the harbor and every member of the crew was found dead." She looked up at him, her eyes dazed with shock. "*Every* member of the crew was found dead. No one was alive. They all had broken necks."

His cell phone continued to ring until he forced himself to answer it. Paulo again. No, there was no money to be found in any of the bank accounts. They weren't frozen; they had been drained. Paulo was still trying to trace the money. And that wasn't all. There was no insurance on the freighters. None. Paulo couldn't explain what had happened with the insurance policies. It was as if they'd never been. There was no record of them in existence. Paulo had checked personally the moment he heard about the first explosion. Even the paper copies stored in the company safe had disappeared along with all cash.

"Find out what's going on, Paulo," Riccardo said. "Money doesn't vanish overnight. Neither do insurance policies. We're under attack by a very clever opponent." He turned his attention back to his wife. "When was the last time you checked the safe, Eva?"

"This morning. You know how my brother likes to have his fun. I have to pay cash for his little playmates. They never last long, either. He likes those boys so young." She rolled her eyes.

"I had to pay nearly twenty thousand for some little street urchin to keep him happy until our shipment gets in. That horrible girl, Brielle, delayed everything with her meddling."

Observing from the shadows, Elie felt his stomach drop. Eva had paid for a child just that morning. This was such a sick family, conscienceless, corrupt and depraved, living large off the backs of so many human beings, most young children. He knew Eva's brother Ezra lived on the estate, just as their son Enrico did with his wife and children. Enrico worked for his father as well. Their second daughter, Debora, had married into another family in Houston. Houston was a big port. Elie was going to make a point of checking them out. That would have to come later.

He didn't move. Didn't make a sound. He was fast and could strike with blurring speed. He had only to wait until Riccardo checked the safe. The vile crime lord wouldn't be able to stop himself. He'd lost too much already.

"Eva, call Enrico. Tell him to have security guards in the room with him at all times. Don't let him argue the point. In fact, he should bring Cinder here. I know the children are visiting her parents. Why they're allowed to go there, I don't know." He stalked across the room to a wood panel that looked as if it was seamless. "Her parents are idiots. That marriage didn't do a thing to further our family. Enrico thought he was so in love. Now look at him. He runs the clubs and takes extra care that he's the one ensuring any women we bring in know how to behave before we sell them."

"Cinder suits him, Riccardo," Eva replied, patience in her tone. "She doesn't mind him instructing the women as long as she gets to watch. She enjoys it. They have a better sex life."

"That's sick," he declared and slid the wooden panel back to reveal the thick wall of the safe. He immediately used an eye scan as well as his fingerprints to unlock it.

Mariko stepped out of the shadow behind Eva and dispatched her without making a sound. She stepped back into

the shadow and was out the door. Elie waited to ensure Riccardo was aware of more of his losses.

When Riccardo yanked open the door of the safe to stare into the cavernous space, he did so almost blankly. There was silence in the room other than the ticking of a clock. "Eva. The money was in this safe this morning. You said you removed twenty thousand to pay for some kid for Ezra? Did your brother know how to get into the safe?"

When his question was met with silence, he spun around. The sight of his wife, slumped in her chair, neck broken, just like their son and daughter-in-law, made him stagger back, his hand over his heart.

Catching up his cell phone, he punched in a number. Elie heard Val's voice come on telling his caller to leave a message. Riccardo snarled and nearly threw the phone.

Elie took the shadow out of the room and chose one that would take him to the rooms where Ezra Mendoza resided. The suite of rooms consisted of a bedroom, bathroom and sitting room. Ezra was lying back on his bed, completely nude. A boy of about eight sat huddled in the corner of the room, knees drawn up and head down, bruises and knots already forming on his body.

The boy wept quietly. He suddenly hiccupped loudly. Ezra threw a can of peanuts at him and yelled at him to shut up. The boy didn't respond or look up. Ezra leapt up, crossed the room immediately and grabbed the child by his hair, dragging him to the bathroom. Elie could see the bathtub was filled with water and Ezra clearly intended to push the child's head under.

Elie came out of the shadows just as Ezra reached the tub. Grasping Ezra's head, he wrenched, delivering the kill, and immediately stepped back into the shadows. For the first time in his life, he regretted the speed with which riders dispatched their targets. Because he wasn't certain that letting Ezra die so easily was actually justice. If anyone deserved to suffer before they died, Ezra Mendoza did. Then Elie was riding a

fast shadow, one that moved like greased lightning to Enrico's house.

He passed Riccardo, who was hurrying toward his son's home, using the shortcut through the garden. Enrico's house wasn't the big showcase his parents' was, but inside, it was quite luxurious. Cinder had a fur wrapped around her and was parading up and down in front of Enrico.

"We could have all the girls wrapped in furs and nothing else, do something entirely different for the auction. They could crawl onto the stage with tails and ears. Their handlers could be dressed in jungle gear or something like that. The music could be amped up, real exciting, maybe rap. We could get someone to write the lyrics we want. If we serve drinks and just edge them with that wonderful drug like we did last time, we could rake in so much money, Enrico. What do you think?"

Enrico drummed his fingers on the arm of his chair. "I think you are a genius, Cinder. Do you have ideas for the staging?"

Cinder tossed the mink to one side and rushed over to a small desk where she had a drawing pad laid out. "I do. I've been working on this idea for a few days. I thought you'd like it. Watching you at the club with those two girls, getting them to obey you, making them crawl to you, was so inspiring. I wanted to create something really special."

Elie came up behind Enrico. The man leaned forward in his chair, eyes on his wife. His breathing had changed. He was clearly aroused at the thought of the things Cinder had planned for the next auction and he couldn't wait to hear about it.

Elie came out of the shadow just as Mariko did. Enrico started to stand, seeing a woman emerge behind his wife, grasping her head in her hands. Elie had him in the death grip and wrenched. The pair died at the same time. Riccardo rushed into the room as the two bodies dropped to the floor.

Riccardo stared at them in horror and then he screamed. Swore revenge. Tried calling Valentino again, but only got

his voice mail. This time, he didn't seem to care if the feds were listening.

"Call them off, Val. Make them stop. They're killing everyone. I know it's them. Everyone is dead. My money is gone. My ships are gone. Everyone is dead. My sons. My wife. My . . ." He broke off.

Riccardo ignored Enrico's two security guards, who rushed in the room when they heard him yelling. Both went straight to the bodies and then looked at him with suspicion. Imbeciles. Where had they been when Archambault or Ferraro had become the devil and killed his sons? Screaming in fury, he pulled out his gun and shot both of the guards.

He hurried out. His parents lived on the property. The last of his family that could be alive, other than his grandchildren and two daughters. One daughter in Houston and one in Spain. At least they were both alive. Claudia, in Spain, was untouchable. No one would dare go near her. She was married to Guillem Toselli. Unless Guillem's father, Arnau, lost his mind and decided to kill Claudia in revenge for Valeria's death, Claudia was safe.

Riccardo's old man lived by the sword, had taught him everything he knew. He went to him often to discuss his business dealings. Riccardo had always admired his father. He loved his mother and the way she cared for his father. He got to the little cottage the pair had insisted was all they wanted, right in the middle of the garden.

There was no sound and his heart began to beat too fast. He knocked, but then just opened the door and went in the way he always did. His parents sat together in front of the television the way they always did, watching old reruns of sitcoms. He knew they were dead the moment he stepped into the room.

He dropped into a chair and began to rock back and forth, grief welling up.

A voice came from the shadows. Low. Hard. Cold. And familiar. "These people you love, Riccardo, that's just a small fraction of the way I love Brielle. You tried to take her from

me. This man you have in Stefano's hotel, the one you think will be able to get to her, will be dead before he gets anywhere close to her. And if you're counting on Toselli to exact revenge on your behalf, don't. He's about to experience the same thing you just have. No one goes after my wife and gets away with it."

"Archambault. You fucking bastard." Riccardo pulled out his gun and began to shoot in every direction. Bullets hit his mother and father, which made him scream. Fingers of steel closed around his wrist and the gun turned toward his head. He kept pulling the trigger. He couldn't stop himself, even though he knew he should. Bullets spat at him, into his jaw, his temple, his skull.

He slumped over and thought he heard someone say they had a plane to catch and needed to get out fast, the cops were on their way. He didn't know if he was alive or dead. Mostly, he was dead.

Elie took a fast tube to the airport and joined the other riders on the Ferraro jet. Franco Mancini had already filed their flight plan and they were in the air as soon as they were cleared for takeoff. The other riders had gone after the key members of Santoro's organization, taking out the ones who had dealt mainly with the trafficking business.

"Has there been word on any of the investigators uncovering the mole at the hotel?" Elie asked the moment he was seated.

"No one has found any evidence of money that shouldn't be in any account so far," Ricco reported. "That seems to be the first thing they always look for."

"There's no connection that anyone can find," Vittorio added, "not even a distant connection with the Santoro family by blood or marriage."

Elie could demand the plane put down in Chicago. He'd discussed going back with Val and Dario, but in the end, he had decided he would do better in Spain. The Toselli family was firmly entrenched in Spain and their tentacles were far-reaching. Stefano's security force was the best. Emmanuelle,

Valentino and Dario assured him they would watch over Brielle. And Brielle was no slouch when it came to self-defense. She was fierce, even if she was wounded. That was part of his worry, that she would try to protect everyone around her.

He pressed his fingers to his temples and tried not to think too much about her alone in their hotel room. Was she alone?

"Don't drive yourself crazy, Elie," Stefano advised. "It won't do you any good. Think of all the people you helped today. We spared Riccardo's grandchildren. Hopefully, they'll grow up outside of the business and have a chance to be happy. The young child was taken out by the child protection agency. The security guards will tell the cops that Riccardo was acting strange, muttering to himself and ignoring them. Security tapes will show him demanding to know where you went, that you just left the office. There was no evidence of you going into the house or leaving it. No security guard saw you. We made sure of that."

Elie nodded. "I stayed in the shadow, until Riccardo had closed the door to his office. I also made certain I could never be seen on any of the cameras. He does look like he was losing his mind."

"I've asked that Geno keep us apprised of what happens to that poor child given to Ezra," Mariko said. "I wanted to bring him home with us and just take care of him."

Ricco wrapped his arm around her. "I hate that you continually have to be exposed to the worst of human beings."

She smiled up at him. "But then I have you, Ricco. You turn everything around for me."

Elie realized that was what Brielle did for him. She'd done it in such a short time. Her laughter. The way she was in the kitchen, chattering with him while she prepared some amazing feast she didn't even consider was fantastic. She noticed his preferences. He liked to get up early and do his meditation and breathing to keep his lungs fit and mentally prepare for shadow riding. She always got up with him, or woke him even earlier than usual with her mouth on him, a very pleasant way to wake.

She noticed he preferred candles to lights at night, especially in the bathroom. She used candles. There were so many little things she did for him that he had never expected. He was utterly unused to being pampered. He had taken care of himself for years—right down to doing his own laundry. Part of that—he knew—was paranoia, not trusting anyone to get that close. Now there was Brielle. And he loved the way she pampered him.

"I don't want to lose her, Stefano. Not to some damn sleeper assassin that somehow slipped by us unnoticed. Why would he be working in your hotel?"

"That's a good question. Was Santoro targeting a Ferraro, or was that coincidence?"

"I don't believe in coincidence," Elie said.

"Neither do I," Stefano said.

CHAPTER EIGHTEEN

Brielle, what the hell are you doing?" Valentino demanded. "You're making me crazy. You're like a tiger in a really small cage pacing that way."

Brielle paused for a moment, sending him one emotion-laden look from under her lashes. "I think better when I'm moving and I need a bigger space. If you're going to make me stay in a really small room, then I have to pace."

"Doc says you're not supposed to be up," Dario intoned in his usual expressionless way.

"He did not." Brielle glared at him. "You just make things up, the same as Elie."

"This is not a really small room," Val objected, looking around at the large suite. "You're just trying to find a reason to go snooping around to find the mole. You're not a detective."

Emmanuelle sighed. "I think you're just frustrated, Brielle. Do you want to talk it out? Does that help?"

Brielle swept her hair out of her eyes, wincing, turning away from them in the hopes that none of them saw that it still hurt like hell if she moved wrong. The shoulder and her

temple weren't really that bad, but if she raised her arm without thinking and then hit her temple like an idiot, pain ripped through her and not in a good way. Really, it was her insides that hurt the worst. Well, that and her thigh.

"It isn't like I don't have a suspect," Brielle admitted and then instantly bit down hard on the side of her lower lip. She slapped her hand over her mouth. Stupid, stupid mistake.

Valentino turned around and Dario quit pretending to play with his phone. Not only did he stop pretending, he put it away. All the way away. In his pocket. His dark eyes had taken on the "look," the one that scared her a little bit.

"What the fuck, Brielle," Val snapped. "You have a suspect and you haven't said a word? You don't think sharing is a good idea?"

Brielle stepped away from Dario, crossing the room toward the nearest shadow, trying not to appear as if that was what she was doing. Dario seemed so menacing and Valentino didn't look much better.

"I misspoke. Sheesh, you two. You look like you're about to leap on me or something." How to play this off? They might not be able to hear lies, although she suspected they could. They knew body language. They interrogated people all the time. Emmanuelle definitely could hear lies. "I'm used to finding information immediately. This is a huge puzzle. I can't find a single link to the Santoro family with any employee here at the hotel. There are a lot of employees to go through, by the way."

"You're stalling," Val accused.

Dario didn't say anything. His soulless eyes didn't leave her face. She felt like he could see right into her. She took another step closer to the shadow, so close she felt the pull on her.

"Brielle, don't," Emmanuelle whispered. "The doctor *did* say the wound inside wouldn't hold. It's too dangerous. We're here to guard you, not hurt you. Why do you feel so threatened?"

Why did she? She knew they were there to protect her.

"Because she's lying her little ass off, that's why," Dario

said. "She does have a suspect and she doesn't want to name him—or her."

Dario was so right. She felt guilty and she knew the two men would be able to tell she was lying to them. Elie always knew. These men weren't shadow riders, but they were like Elie, very perceptive.

"Why wouldn't you want to tell us, Brielle?" Valentino asked. "We can't keep you alive if we don't have all the facts."

She pounced on that. "That's just it, Val. I don't have *any* facts. I don't have anything at all. No reason to be suspicious. I'm not going to chance naming an innocent person and be wrong. I'm an investigator. I deal in facts. I get suspicions and I follow those until I hit on trails that lead me to real facts. It's the only reason I'm good at my job."

There was a small silence. She knew her voice rang with truth because she was telling the absolute truth. She did have a suspect because the moment her fingers touched the keyboard, every instinct went in the direction of Stefano's chef's assistant. His name was Constantine Babell. He was forty-three years old, divorced and had lived in Chicago his entire life with the exception of the years he'd gone to culinary schools.

She'd tried every other employee she could input and her keyboard wanted her to go back to Babell. She followed him as far back as she could and there was no connection she could discover between Babell and the Santoro family. He had never been to New York. She couldn't find that he'd ever been near organized crime in his life. She'd checked for weaknesses. Prostitutes. For the possibility that he had used any part of Santoro's human trafficking operations. She'd checked his computer for porn. For any evidence he might be a pedophile. She'd found nothing.

"You could still tell us your suspicions so we could watch out for him," Val suggested. "We could have your security detail on the alert for him."

"See, that's just what I don't want. The man goes for a walk and someone shoots him."

"He wouldn't innocently be walking up here, Brielle," Val pointed out. "At least we know you suspect a man."

"Tell me and I'll watch him from the shadows," Emmanuelle declared. "That way, if he does anything he shouldn't, I can report back to you. Also, I can search his things."

"Fine, but, Dario and Val, don't you touch him until I know more about him or anyone else I suspect." She threw that in there just so they would think she had more than one suspect.

"He's worked for the Ferraro Hotel for seven years as the chef's main assistant. His name is Constantine Babell. Again, there is *nothing* to suggest he is involved with Santoro."

"What about the Colombo family?" Emmanuelle asked.

Her cousins had wiped out the Colombo organization in Los Angeles in the same way Elie and her family had taken down the Santoro family in New York along with all key personnel that had been involved in trafficking.

"Is there a tie between Constantine Babell and the Colombo family?"

Brielle resumed pacing. "I did think of that and checked. Babell was never near them that I could find, and believe me, I was thorough."

"The Toselli family in Barcelona?" Valentino suggested.

"No ties to them, either."

"Did he go to Spain at any time? They like to get their hooks into tourists," Dario said.

Brielle spun around and stared at him for a moment then she rushed over to the desk and her laptop. "He was in Spain. He attended a couple of culinary schools in Europe before returning to the States." She sucked the side of her lower lip into her mouth and bit down, chewing on it while she read through what she'd already found out about Babell's time in Europe.

"He spent two weeks in Barcelona with two other students. Okay, my man, let's see what you were up to while you were on your little vacay." Her fingers flew over the keyboard.

Almost at once, she felt she was on the right track. She didn't know how she could tell, but that feeling was there, as if she'd had a clogged artery and suddenly the passageway was wide open and her blood was flowing normally.

"I'm going to head down to the kitchen and check him out," Emmanuelle said.

Brielle didn't look up and gave a little wave of her hand. Emmanuelle crossed the room to her husband and gestured to Dario, who went to her. Brielle was aware of the three huddling together. That drew her out of her usual keyboard fog.

"Watch her close, you two. I think the shadows keep pulling at her. She can't go into them for any reason. If this chef's assistant comes after her, and she tries to go into the shadows, it would kill her for sure. That repair they did on her isn't close to healing. It would get torn apart and she'd bleed out before anyone could fix it. Please watch over her."

"No worries, princess," Val said, leaning down to brush a kiss on her lips. "No one is getting close to Brielle and she isn't getting close to the shadows. We gave our word to Elie."

"She's ours," Dario echoed. "Family. No one gets her."

Emmanuelle nodded, stepped into a shadow and was gone. For just one moment, Brielle had the urge to follow her, to find out in person just what Constantine Babell was up to. How was he going to try to kill her? Val was right; he couldn't just take the elevator to the upper floor to their private suite and expect to get past the multitude of security guards and then Valentino and Dario on top of them. Fortunately, her fingers kept typing even as her thoughts went a little chaotic.

Constantine had gone to Barcelona on holiday with two other students, Otto and Rupert Winslow, brothers he'd grown up next door to in Chicago who had gone to Spain on vacation and met him there. Otto and Rupert owned a thriving high-rise window-cleaning business together. Stefano used their company to keep the windows immaculate at his hotel, which their employees did.

Constantine was now forty-three years old. Otto, the older

of the Winslow brothers, was the same age, with Rupert only eighteen months behind. Constantine had been in Barcelona when he was twenty-three, so twenty years earlier. Finding out what three men did during a short vacation twenty years ago was going to be extremely difficult. She needed to find something that would connect one of them with the Toselli family.

She sat back in her chair and tapped her finger on the desktop as she ran through the possibilities in her mind. Three young men set free in a foreign country looking to have really good times. No one was around to be the word of caution. What would they do? Where would they go? Party hard. Drinking for sure. Women. Gambling maybe. Trying drugs?

What were the hotspots in the city back then? What were the names of the clubs where everyone partied? If you wanted to catch three young men in your web, where did you have a local woman bring them? One lead led to another. Even twenty years earlier, the Tosellis had had their hands in everything. Law enforcement looked the other way if tourists got robbed and went crying to the police.

"It appears that Constantine and two of his friends, Otto and Rupert Winslow, took a holiday together in Barcelona twenty years ago and partied hard in one of the Tosellis' many clubs. As young men do, they drank, danced and hooked up with women who took them to the back rooms and had their wicked way with them. They woke up in the street with no money and no passports. They went to the local police, but they were thrown in jail. It seems that one of the women they partied with was found dead, beaten to death. The youngest boy, Rupert, was covered in her blood, under his shirt and pants. She had his skin under her fingernails."

Again, Brielle sat back in her chair and studied the laptop screen, shaking her head slightly. "That is one big bunch of bull."

"Why would you say that?" Valentino asked, coming up behind her.

"First, there's no mention of it in the press. It would have

been big news. This woman isn't dead. Unless the tourist demanded to see her body, the Tosellis wouldn't have to produce her. They just make her look good for photographs and the report is written up over and over the same way. Here, I'll show you."

She got into the police files and found three photographs. Two were exactly the same, one appeared similar. She pulled up the police report. It was written up the same and signed by the same officer. "They didn't even bother to use new material. The tourist is terrified, and as soon as the rescuer comes to help them, they take whatever they can get in order to get out of the country and go home. The Tosellis 'clean up the mess' for them and in return ask for money or favors. The favor might be right away or come twenty years later. In this case, it appears, the favor has been called in."

"Why Constantine and not Rupert?"

"Rupert can't get to her," Dario said.

"How does Constantine think he's going to get to her?" Valentino asked. "Bring her a birthday cake when it isn't her birthday?"

"It would be the last thing he ever does," Dario said.

"This is so sad," Brielle said. "I feel sorry for the people the Toselli family traps and then uses. Everyone makes mistakes. Anyone can get drunk and do something dumb."

"That's why you have a sober friend looking out," Val pointed out.

She rolled her eyes. "Don't tell me you never did anything stupid, Val."

He laughed. "Sure I did. I lost Emme for a very long time. I never want to go through something like that again, but as for getting drunk and being dumb, no, can't say I ever did. I had Dario watching my back and I watched his."

Her insides ached. She thought maybe she could take a break and stretch out on the couch just for a minute and no one would make any cracks about it. She didn't stretch when she stood up, although ordinarily she did. Her belly felt too tight.

"I didn't have that growing up," she admitted. "In some ways, it was good. I learned to rely on myself."

"Is that why you have such a difficult time when anyone tells you to do something that might save your life?" Dario asked.

Her first reaction was to bristle like a porcupine, but then she tried to hear him and be fair. She did have a difficult time. Before Elie, she'd relied on her own judgment for everything.

"I suppose so. I never thought about it. I'm not deliberately being defiant or going in the opposite way someone's telling me to go, but I've always done what I thought best in the circumstances." She judged the distance to the sofa. It looked a long way off. Maybe it would be better to just sit down in the desk chair again, although it wasn't very comfortable.

"For instance, right now, you're pale and need to lie down, but you're pretending you're strong and don't want us to know you need to lie down, so you're going to sit back in the chair that's making you hurt," Dario said. "That's good judgment? Or defiance? What is that exactly?"

She sighed, tempted to give him the finger. "I hate looking weak all the time."

The two men exchanged a puzzled look. "Why would you think you look weak?"

"I don't know. I think I view myself that way because I'm not like Emmanuelle. I always wanted to be. She and one of Elie's cousins, Axelle, have always been held up as the gold standard in our business. I never met that standard, or even came close." She looked across the room at the sofa. It was really far away.

"Ask for help, Brielle," Dario said.

He was worse than Elie. He really was. He knew she was afraid to walk the distance to the sofa, but was he just going to come over and help her? No, he was going to make her ask for help. Maybe she really was too stubborn. And why could these men read her so easily?

"Has it occurred to either one of you that I barely know you and maybe it's a little difficult to ask for help from strangers?"

"We aren't strangers to you." Valentino dismissed the idea. "Now you're just stalling. You're family. You belong to Elie. We regard him as a brother. That makes you a sister."

"Elie is a pain-in-the-ass brother and you're worse," Dario pointed out. "He isn't going to like that you were so fucking stubborn, you would rather topple over than ask us to help you to the sofa."

Sweat had begun to bead on her forehead and trickle between her breasts. Little black dots began to float behind her eyes. "Fine. I would appreciate help in making it to the couch since I'm about to faint."

Dario and Val both jumped to either side of her. Val slid his arm around her waist, careful of where he put his hands, not wanting to hit any of the places a bullet had torn into her body.

Dario, muttering curses under his breath, gripped her with hard hands. "I don't envy Elie one minute. We should let the chef's assistant make his try. Maybe put poor Elie out of his misery."

"Dario," Val tried to sound harsh, but his voice was filled with laughter.

"I'm getting used to him," Brielle said. "He's scary when he's at a distance, but this close I can smell lavender all over him. Lavender has a calming effect. It's used for things like reducing stress, anxiety and even mild pain."

"Oh, for fuck's sake," Dario snapped as they helped her onto the sofa.

Brielle gratefully lay back. She definitely felt the stretch on her belly, telling her she'd been sitting too straight for far too long. She'd been warned that she had to be careful and take it slow. She wasn't to work long hours at a desk.

Valentino burst out laughing at her revelation that Dario wasn't in the least scary close-up. "We'd better take that into consideration when you're interrogating prisoners, Dario."

Dario gave him the finger.

"I think maybe it's just me, Val," Brielle said, closing her eyes against the light. It felt so good to be off her feet and just

lie down. "I used lavender all the time for anxiety and when I'd get so sick when I'd work." She was chattering because she was nervous. Talking too much, but she couldn't stop herself. "I found lavender was calming to me if I used it for aromatherapy or as oils in the bath. I probably conditioned myself to react that way. I honestly didn't mean to embarrass you, Dario."

She loved that he not only had a lavender farm but oversaw the running of it himself and that it was a legitimate business. He didn't taint it in any way. He didn't use it to launder money or for any purpose other than to sell the lavender to his whole-sale clients. Brielle found that was endearing.

She lifted her lashes, just to try to get a look at his expression, but Dario raised an eyebrow at her, his mask slipping easily back into place.

"I knew when I bought that farm, I would take some heat for it," he said before throwing himself into a chair in the casual way he had.

She lowered her lashes again, partially blocking out the light, but she was still able to see the two men. "Did you always intend to keep it going?"

"No. I bought the property because it was next to Val's. He needs looking after whether he wants to admit it or not."

Val made a sound of derision under his breath. "He likes to think that. It makes him feel needed and gives him the opportunity to be bossy."

"I'm good in that role."

"Which is why I handed Miceli's territory to you. Boss away, Dario."

Dario raised his middle finger to Val. "Drives me crazy to have to have all those idiots coming to me and asking if they can do things they should be able to figure out on their own."

"You have to stay on top of every detail, Dario. You don't, and someone's going to try to slip something past you the way Miceli did. The way Carmine Catani was doing."

Brielle bit down on her lower lip. She had identified

Carmine Catani as a traitor in Dario's organization. He was feeding Santoro information, and he'd provided the photograph of Elie to the traffickers.

"I'm on top of it. I brought in my boys just as you suggested, although that almost lost us Brielle. It didn't occur to me they wouldn't be welcome without being investigated first."

There was something in Dario's voice that captured Brielle's attention. She didn't make the mistake of turning her head toward him or tensing. She made certain to stay relaxed. Dario didn't like the idea of anyone investigating his two personal protectors. She'd been warned off and she'd done it anyway. Their bogus backgrounds were completely false, so good one had to be an expert to recognize they'd been given new identities.

She had wondered, for a brief moment, if they were in witness protection, but knew better when they were so blatantly guarding a known crime lord. "By now, Stefano's people must have done background checks on them. Why aren't they with you?" She couldn't keep the little edge of anxiety out of her voice.

Brielle still couldn't go to sleep without seeing Leone shot in the chest and falling backward, right in the doorway. She knew Elie had the same problem. Most nights, he still paced up and down restlessly, his eyes on her as she tried to reassure him that she was perfectly fine. They both knew she wasn't— not yet.

"You and Emme." Val sighed, shaking his head. "Does it never occur to you that we are capable of taking care of not only ourselves, but the two of you as well? Our regular security details are just outside your door. A few others are stationed close to the elevator. I've sent word to them to watch the windows. Now that I know the Winslow brothers could be involved in this, I asked for locations of their equipment on every floor. I don't want any surprises appearing at the window."

"I'm sorry Raimondo didn't let you into the house right away, Dario. I know you've been upset by that," Brielle murmured. Her belly felt so much better in this position. Maybe she would put some of her work off for a little while.

Valentino and Dario had made their pitch to her, explaining how they had only one investigator to cover both territories. He was extremely loyal to them, but they didn't have anyone to occasionally check up on him. That was needed. It was just the way they both were. They wanted her working for them. She was exactly what they needed. Fast, efficient, she would do a lot of the investigative work, which would free Bernado to do more of the bookkeeping work.

Elie had sat with her during the interview. She had made it clear that if anything involved the Ferraro family, she would have no choice but to inform them. Elie had remained silent throughout the interview, for which she was grateful. This was her business and she was very serious about it.

"There will be times we might have to ask you to work with Bernado during a sensitive meeting. We would include Elie." Valentino had leaned forward. "This is extremely important, Brielle. We are criminals. You have to know that going into this. We do illegal things. People sometimes try to take away our businesses and our lives. We retaliate in a very hostile manner. You might see and hear things that you can never repeat. The penalty would be death. I would signal to you, hopefully before things ever got out of hand, but I can't guarantee that I'd be able to see it developing in time to do that. At times, you'll be the one warning us that our lives are in danger. What I'm saying is, don't take this job if you would feel you would have to go to law enforcement. Or if law enforcement came to you if you would feel you had to tell them what you heard or saw."

Brielle had taken her time thinking things over. She had to admit she was an adrenaline junkie on the keyboard. It felt right to her to choose to work for Val and Dario. She hadn't looked at Elie, not wanting him to give her a clue as to

his thoughts. This had to be her decision alone. If she had harbored secret doubts that Elie was meant to be her partner, they were definitely put to rest during that meeting. He never once interfered or attempted to persuade her in any direction. He didn't ask questions of Valentino or Dario. When they named a salary and she negotiated up, he didn't bat an eye. She knew she was worth it and they'd pay it.

"I definitely understand confidentiality. I have no problem with that." She had been silent for a moment and then she held up her hand. "I would never, under any circumstances, go along with human trafficking. At the first sign, I would be texting my husband and handing in my resignation. The same with selling drugs to children. I have a real problem with that. I would do the same and quit."

"We are adamantly opposed to both," Val had stated, and Dario had nodded his head.

She had taken Dario's nod for his word. There had been a burst of elation when they finalized the agreement. She hadn't realized just how much she really wanted to work for the Saldis. Technically, Dario's last name was Bosco, but he was a Saldi through and through.

Elie had taken her out to dinner afterward, the restaurant amazing. They'd been surrounded by personal protectors, but she hadn't cared. They'd danced the night away, and when they'd gotten home, he'd made love to her, a sweet, hot fire that burned so bright, it brought tears to her eyes.

It was impossible not to fall more and more in love with Elie Archambault. She detested when he was away from her, like now, and she couldn't reach out to him to make certain he was all right. She knew the jet was in the air and on course to Barcelona. They were flying there straight from New York after wiping out the Santoro family.

The Archambaults would meet the Ferraros there. The investigators had done their jobs and uncovered every target. The local shadow riders, the Ignazio family, had to be seen leaving the city so no suspicion could possibly fall on them.

Stefano Ferraro had business at the bank with the manager there. He was meeting Jean-Claude Archambault as well. They would be seen along with their personal protectors. The others would be in the shadows, carrying out their assignments. Brielle tried not to feel anxious without Elie, but she did. Not for herself, but for him.

Emmanuelle came out of the shadows, appearing close to her husband. He didn't seem to startle easily. Val casually wrapped his arms around her to steady her. "You're cold, princess. Were you in the refrigerator?"

She nodded. "For a few minutes. There's a walk-in down there and Constantine was in and out of it. I can tell you, he doesn't intend to carry out his assignment."

Val rubbed her arms briskly. "How do you know?"

"I talked to him. He was very upset and writing a letter to Elie. I was able to look at the letter. It looked to me as if he planned to commit suicide. In the letter, he explained to Elie what happened to him and the others when he was twenty-three. He named Otto and Rupert. He said Rupert was the gentlest of all three of them and couldn't even kill spiders. No one could figure out how he would ever be violent with a woman. It didn't make sense. Rupert had wanted to stay in Spain and face what was coming to him, but the others insisted they bring him home. They were afraid of what would happen. None of them were willing to murder an innocent woman for the Tosellis. They all three planned to commit suicide rather than risk the Tosellis coming after Otto's and Rupert's families."

Brielle started to sit up, one hand covering her belly where the surgeon had done something to keep her from bleeding to death.

"Stay down," Val and Dario growled in stereo.

Emmanuelle burst out laughing and went over to the sofa to perch on the edge. "I have to say, I'm so glad I get to share them with you. They're so annoying. I just ignore them most of the time, but in your case, you really need to be careful. How are you feeling?"

Brielle rubbed her stomach over the ache. "It does hurt

a little. I think I moved around too much. I pace a lot when things don't add up. Movement helps me think. Usually, I can go outside in the fresh air, but those two and Elie are being very strict with me. You'd think someone was trying to murder me." She tried to make a joke out of it, but neither man cracked a smile. Only Emmanuelle.

"You'd think."

"What did you tell Constantine? Hopefully, you had him call his friends and let them know the Tosellis lied to them about what happened, that it was a scam and I have proof," Brielle said.

"You didn't, Emme." Val was horrified. "Princess, there's no way to know for certain if the Winslow brothers intended to follow through with what they've indicated to Babell. They could have been waiting for him to off himself and then they were going to try to kill Brielle. You are so fucking compassionate. That's always been your downfall."

"You're lucky she is," Dario said. "That's the only reason she took you back."

"Dario's so right," Emmanuelle agreed, blowing a kiss Dario's way. "I didn't check on the brothers yet, because I had Constantine call them and ask them to come to the hotel for a meeting before they did anything stupid. I can hear lies. When they talk to Babell, who is quite nice, I'll know their intentions. If either of them is here to carry out the instructions to kill Brielle, I'll bring justice to them."

Emmanuelle had sounded playful until she delivered her declaration, then she sounded wholly like a Ferraro. She was fierce, a shadow rider, experienced and in control. Brielle knew she was in charge of her husband's security. Few of his men realized it. Dario still, at times, gave the orders, mostly because in the world Emme now lived in, the women weren't treated quite the same as the men. Emmanuelle didn't seem to mind.

"Why doesn't it bother you?"

"Why doesn't what bother me?" Emmanuelle echoed.

She sounded serene. Confident in herself and who she was.

She didn't need others to see her as her husband's equal, or theirs for that matter.

"The men you're in charge of see you as less than they are. How can you stand that? Especially if you have to give them an order? Why would they obey you promptly if they don't really respect you?"

Brielle wasn't trying to stir up problems; she really wanted to know. She knew Elie wouldn't treat her as less when she was working, but when they played, he would always be in charge. She liked that. Needed it. Had someone other than Dario seen them, would that man have still treated her with respect? She doubted it.

"I know I can wipe up the floor with most men," Emmanuelle stated. "I've trained with my brothers, other riders and Elie. Have you trained with him? He's so fast, you don't see him move. Really, Brielle, his hands and feet blur when he comes at you with kicks or punches. He can stand in one place just watching you and then he's on you and you don't even know how he moved. I've seen him do it when he's working with my brothers and they're lightning fast. It's good to train with him because he brings up your speed."

"I hate to say this," Valentino said, "but it's the truth. I've had him spar with me for months now and can't believe how much faster I've gotten and the things I learned from him when I thought I knew so much already."

"He hits with the power of a fucking freight train," Dario added. "Sometimes he moves his fist a half an inch and it's like your entire insides turn to jelly."

Brielle knew everything they said about Elie was the truth. She had begun to train with him until she had gotten shot. They still meditated together every morning, but training was out until she was completely healed. She was getting anxious that wasn't going to happen for a while. She'd never had an injury that wasn't superficial. Not really, not like this.

"I trained with him before this happened to me," she

admitted. "I was getting faster." She was certain that was the reason she'd lasted longer in the shadows than normal.

Emmanuelle glanced at her watch and then stood up. "I think the Winslow brothers should be here by now. They were meeting Constantine in the lobby. I'll go on down and see what I can find out."

"I don't like you down there by yourself," Val objected. "Not with three of them."

"Send the boys down. They can wander around the lobby looking all badass. They live for those moments," Emmanuelle said, going up on her toes to brush a kiss on her husband's jaw.

She didn't wait, but stepped into a streaming shadow. It was a fast one. It yanked her inside and she was gone, disappearing right in front of them. Brielle had been trained from childhood never to allow someone outside the shadow-riding community to have knowledge of what went on in their world, but it was clear that both Dario and Valentino were aware of shadow riders.

"Emmanuelle didn't tell us," Val said, watching her closely. "We were watching the Ferraro family for years. The Saldi family and the Ferraro family have been entwined for centuries. Consequently, we have our version of the shadow mysteries. It wasn't a difficult leap to know the Ferraros were able to use the shadows in some way others couldn't. We also know the consequences if we don't stay quiet. I would never betray my wife, or her family. Neither would Dario."

"It honestly didn't occur to me that Emmanuelle would ever talk about what her family does. It's too ingrained in all of us not to. I just couldn't figure out where both of you came into the picture. Sometimes, I know that even in a marriage, one of the parties doesn't know everything. Usually, that's their preference, but over the years, some riders have married outsiders and they were never told."

"We're family, Brielle, not outsiders, as you're family to us."

"I don't know very much about being in a family," she admitted. "Mine was sort of dysfunctional."

Dario and Val exchanged a smirk and then both laughed, although neither sounded too humorous. "I believe our dysfunctional family might have yours beat," Valentino said. "Believe it or not, Emmanuelle's family would be considered dysfunctional if it wasn't for Stefano."

Emmanuelle returned a few minutes later. Again, she stepped out of a shadow quite close to Valentino. He immediately wrapped his arms around her. She leaned into him. "The two Winslow brothers were definitely preparing to end their lives rather than murder someone. They had letters on them and both had tried to write to their wives to explain things as well. When they spoke to Constantine, and he told them that Rupert hadn't actually committed a crime, that there was proof, Rupert nearly fainted. He wept. Both men comforted him."

She raised her gaze to her husband's. "That's why investigators don't want to name suspects until they actually have all the facts. And riders are very careful before they carry out sentences. Those men weren't going to kill Brielle. They would rather end their own lives than take hers."

"What did you tell them?" Brielle asked.

"I just told them that Constantine was a valued employee and Stefano had been concerned when someone mentioned he was acting out of character. I had done some investigative work and discovered the scam. I volunteered to ask Constantine what was worrying him and he told me. It was fairly emotional after that. Of course, they said they'd wait. Once it comes out that the Toselli family is no more, and the threat to them is gone, I don't think they'll worry anymore."

Her hand slid down her husband's arm. "If you'll excuse us for just a little while. I really need to talk to Valentino."

Brielle watched them leave, envious that when Emmanuelle had come out of the shadows feeling needy, her husband was right there for her. Brielle detested the fact that her husband would be riding shadows over and over again. She knew

that when he came out of them, his body would be utterly aroused and demanding. She wouldn't be there to take care of him. Worse, when he did return, and he needed the type of sex he enjoyed the most, she wouldn't be able to provide for him—or he wouldn't think she could.

"One more sigh and I'm going to gag you."

"You're so pleasant, Dario."

"I don't want to be pleasant right now."

"Why?"

"Because I'm still pissed at you."

"Why?"

"For fuck's sake, woman, why do you think? There was blood all over your house. *Your* blood. A lake of it. You died. Do you even get that? You fucking died. I saw your husband's face when he walked through the door and he didn't even see you die. He didn't have to give you compressions or breathe air into your lungs. I saw his face. His world stopped, all because you can't take a simple fucking order. So, yeah, I'm still pissed and I might be for a long time. You do something like that again, I'm locking your ass up when he's gone whether Elie likes it or not."

Brielle turned that over and over in her mind. Dario was still angry with her. Elie wasn't sleeping. They'd talked it over, but he was still pacing at night. Sitting on the edge of the bed watching her sleep. He was so careful with her. Always sweet, but so careful. Was he still angry? That was a possibility. Did he even know he was? She couldn't answer that question.

"I'm sorry, Dario. I really am."

"You just make me very glad I don't have a fucking woman I love. I never want to feel what Elie did. *Never.* I probably would have murdered your bodyguards and everyone else in that room. You're fortunate he's your man. You think about that, Brielle. Think about him."

She could hear the hint of anger in his voice, something rare for Dario. "I do, Dario. I didn't realize I meant anything to him. I knew what I felt for him, but he's lived a very different life

than I have. I thought . . . well, it doesn't matter what I thought. I realize I was wrong."

She had been. Apparently, everyone else knew Elie loved her. She was the only one to question it. She had to get over her issues of confidence and embrace the fact that she was very lucky to have the man she'd wanted her entire life.

CHAPTER NINETEEN

Although Barcelona during the day was gorgeous and full of things to do, at night, the city really came alive. The sun dropping signaled a change in energy, setting the streets on fire, so they bustled with raw vitality. Glittering lights illuminated the buildings in a riot of color, as if beckoning everyone to a dance party.

The door of the private jet opened, and a few moments later, Emilio Greco stood in the doorway, his wide shoulders nearly touching the doorframe. He surveyed the entire tarmac, parking lot and buildings before he turned to say something and then began his descent on the stairs leading to the ground below.

Shadows zigzagged across the asphalt and up the stairs to the very door of the jet, thrown by the giant overhead lights. Stefano Ferraro paused in the doorway of the aircraft, talking with his pilot, Franco Mancini, for a few minutes. He seemed relaxed, dressed in his immaculate suit, his body positioned sideways, as he spoke to the pilot, who was behind him, in the interior of the aircraft.

Elie chose his shadow and streaked past Stefano toward the meeting place the Archambaults had chosen. This was the first time in his entire history that Elie could remember being grateful he was related to the large, famous family. His uncle Marcellus was head of the International Council of Shadow Riders. They ruled over every rider family in the world. Jean-Claude, another uncle, was on the council ruling the French shadow riders. They were his father's brothers. Although he despised the fact that he'd been shuffled from home to home as a child, he recognized that his father, the youngest of the three brothers, had dominion over him during his younger years. His parents were at fault, not his uncles, as much as he wanted to blame them.

Elie knew both uncles kept a close watch on his training. He had exceeded every other rider in the history of their programs, not just when it came to times in the shadows, but in combat and language training as well. He had done so from the very beginning of his training, and that was part of the reason no one objected when he was sent away at such a young age. They were too excited and proud to have a protégé such as Elie in their already renowned family. They forgot all about treating him like a child and human being rather than a robot to train and shape to their will.

He stepped from shadow to shadow, going through the city, finding his way easily with the maps in his head. This was where Brielle had lived and studied. She loved Barcelona and the people here. She spoke often of her time there and how much she had bonded with her host family. They had treated her as a daughter. It was the first time she had ever been treated so well, and at first, she had been leery, afraid to believe they could be so good. She'd stayed away from them as much as possible, but she loved their children and eventually came to believe in the adults.

The city with its people had won her over as well. The culture and the beauty. The food. The passion and energy. Brielle's face lit up every time she talked about her stay there. Elie had made it a priority in his mind to take her back frequently

to visit her host family and the places she loved the most. He wanted to share those with her. Right now, he was going to make certain it was safe for her to do so. That meant taking down the Toselli family and removing their choke hold on Barcelona.

Riders had come from numerous families around the world to aid in the takedown of such a large empire. First, the freighters and ships used for human trafficking that had been traced back to the Toselli family had to be disposed of. At the same time, any paperwork that would allow them to profit from losses had to be erased as though it had never been.

They had so many investigators working on erasing the coffers of the Toselli family, emptying their bank accounts, both legitimate and illegal, ensuring the missing money couldn't be traced. Everything had to appear as if it had never been. In their homes and businesses, every safe was emptied. It was a huge undertaking and required a force of riders the likes of which had never been known before.

One of their precious shadow rider females had been targeted—nearly murdered—and that was unacceptable, never to be tolerated. The reason the shadow riders had scattered centuries earlier was for this very purpose—if someone threatened them, they could retaliate in force and no one could touch them. No one would ever see the shadow riders or know they were in Barcelona. They couldn't possibly be blamed for what was in store for the Toselli family.

Elie stepped into another shadow that took him fast, streaking through the streets toward the large party house the riders' support staff had rented. All cameras had been interrupted, making it safe for the shadow riders, once inside, to allow themselves to be out in the open. Heavy drapes were pulled so it would be impossible for anyone to see inside the windows.

Maps of the city were spread out on the tables. Marcellus Archambault waited for the riders to gather around in groups. He'd labeled each map clearly so each group of riders had their assignments and knew what parts of the city they would

be going to. The Tosellis had several estates the riders would be visiting. All other main leaders of the organization and anyone aiding them in the trafficking business were going to be eliminated as well.

Elie would be leading the strike team against the main cluster of homes belonging to Arnau Toselli and his two sons. Elie intended to visit Guillem and Angel Toselli, both of whom lived near their father. After speaking with Arnau, and making it clear what a very big mistake he'd made in targeting Brielle, he would seek out Izan Serrano. Serrano was the dominant who frequented the Toselli-owned nightclub Fantasía Más Oscura.

Marcellus had five sons and one daughter, all amazing riders and Elie's first cousins. He barely knew them, yet they had come immediately to free Barcelona from the grip the Tosellis had on the city. They greeted him warmly. He had met Maxence, the oldest, on more than one occasion, when they both frequented the clubs in Paris. Sacha and Gage, the next two in line, he'd competed against, although he rarely saw them. He just had his time posted against theirs. The last two of Marcellus's sons, Croix and Talon, he'd met briefly after one of the big tournaments. They'd acted happy to get to meet him. He'd been a little aloof when he spent time with them before and he regretted his behavior, wishing he hadn't been so standoffish.

Then there was Axelle, Marcellus's only daughter. Like Emmanuelle, she was one of the rare females born into the families of riders. She was a beautiful woman and very fast in the shadows, like her brothers.

Elie didn't understand why the rider families seemed to produce so few females. Their scientists were researching, considering the shadows might have something to do with it, influencing the bodies toward male genetics. After the revelation that Eloisa Ferraro had discovered—so many repeated trips into the shadows had given her brain bleeds—they were all much more cautious.

Jean-Claude had two sons, Roch and Arman, as well as

one daughter, Alize. They also greeted Elie warmly. They'd met Stefano Ferraro as well as Vittorio and Giovanni. Ricco had been introduced to Maxence and Sacha during the hunt for Mariko's brother. Looking around the spacious room that could barely contain the international contingent of riders, Elie was proud of belonging to something that important.

"The ships have been attacked by the riders from Portugal and Morocco," Marcellus said. "All freighters, both large and small, are gone along with the entire crews participating in human trafficking. If they were at sea, they went down with their ships. If they were at home, they died in their homes. The Italian riders and Greek riders took the ones in their homes along with the Toselli capos and all his advisors."

He tapped addresses to show the remaining riders the addresses of the estates and businesses. "All of the businesses must be taken down completely. These officials have been in the pockets of Toselli for far too long and made too much money." He gave the list of names to the next group of riders. The riders had to study the layouts of the homes and businesses as well as the various ways to get to each of them through the city.

"Elie, you have both sons, Arnau and their wives as well as Izan Serrano. You're used to working with Ricco and Mariko so they're with you. Let us know when to call in someone to come for the children if they're on the estate."

Elie nodded, studied the addresses, and then he, Mariko and Ricco together spent several minutes studying the layout of each of the homes they would be visiting. When they were done, they turned to catch a shadow that would take them to the home of Angel Toselli, Arnau's youngest son.

Angel's villa was located about a half hour's travel from downtown Barcelona and just down the street from the two houses belonging to his father and his brother, Guillem. He had a tremendous view of the Mediterranean Sea from his living room and upstairs master bedroom suite. Like his family's other two properties, his home had four floors and five bedrooms and seven and a half bathrooms. Each of the three

villas had been designed by the same architect under the scrutiny of Arnau Toselli. There were passageways and safe rooms built into each of the villas, and after their construction along the exclusive northern coast of Barcelona, the architect died tragically in a terrible accident. It seemed there was a mysterious curse that followed anyone who had worked on the villas as well. Those men died in accidents over time or just disappeared.

Angel kept his home very private. The villa was surrounded by a high, thick wall covered in green vines that kept out prying eyes. Heavily armed guards patrolled the grounds. They were extremely careful to stay on the paths that led through the beautiful gardens surrounding the modern, four-story villa.

Elie, Mariko and Ricco slid up and over the high wall and past the patrolling guards. Three had dogs. One immediately reacted, turning toward the shadows as they streaked by, warning the trainer with a short bark. The handler scanned the garden and then glanced toward the house warily, abruptly commanding the dog to be silent.

Elie stepped from one shadow to a smaller one that slid under a side entrance. He was nearly thrown out of the tube into the house, the shadow ended so abruptly. He was able to put the brakes on at the last moment and stood in the mouth of the shadow, allowing his body to come back to itself. His heart had accelerated and he deliberately slowed his breathing while he evaluated the situation.

Elie was just outside of the dining area. There was no sound coming from the living room, but he could hear music playing upstairs. He stepped silently out of the shadows and approached the stairs. Ricco stepped out of a shadow and signaled him that he was moving through all the rooms and would ensure the downstairs was free of guards. Mariko indicated she was taking a shadow to the second floor to do the same. Elie would clear the third floor and then go up to the master bedroom on the fourth floor, where the music was playing.

He stepped into a shadow and streaked up the stairs, going past the first and second landings, but stopping at the third. This floor boasted a spacious playroom containing a pool table and several old-style arcade games as well as a full bar. There was a full screen set up for virtual reality play. Another room had a state-of-the-art home theater. The entire floor was dedicated to entertainment. There were no signs of guards in the house. Apparently, Angel liked his privacy.

Elie took a shadow to the fourth floor, where the master bedroom and bath took up most of the entire floor. The windows in the villa were nearly ten feet high in the rooms facing the sea to give the occupants the best views. One entire wall of the master bedroom and part of the bath were nearly all glass.

The moment Elie entered Angel's bedroom, he knew why the man required privacy and wouldn't want any security guards in his home. He most likely required his father and brother to call him before they came to visit. He might act like his was the "party" villa, but that wasn't because he preferred all the hot women he entertained in his home occasionally. He invited couples over for a reason.

Angel had a partner. His partner had to know if he was indiscreet, it was a death sentence. The man obviously was careful never to be seen by anyone in what could be a compromising situation for Angel. Arnau Toselli would never, under any circumstances, accept a gay son. He wouldn't mind his son using men or boys occasionally for sex in rough bondage play, but he would never accept a permanent relationship. He would expect his son to marry and provide him with male grandchildren. Anything less than that would be considered unacceptable.

Angel and his partner were wound around each other on the bed, murmuring and occasionally laughing. Both were nude. In the corner of the bedroom was a large dog crate. Hanging on the wall was a spiked collar, a leash, a whip and what appeared to be dog brushes, combs and a scrub brush. Along the glass windows were a spanking bench and a Saint

Andrew's Cross. There were two luxury chairs facing the window and between the chairs was a table with a cage built under it. A dog bed sat beside one of the chairs and an open toy chest beside the other.

Elie's shadow took him right next to the chest and he could see the ball gag and various other sex toys. Beside the dog crate was a bowl of water and another bowl containing food. Inside the dog crate huddled a boy of about thirteen. He was curled up on his side, a black-and-tan furry tail hanging between his legs. He was very clean, the scratches on his skin showing signs of having been scrubbed too long and painfully.

Cursing under his breath, Elie took a few moments to gather himself to put aside his personal emotions. Under the circumstances, seeing the depravity of the people involved in the trafficking, and the way they used other human beings for their own pleasure, power and pocketbooks, sickened him. He had to compartmentalize. He brought justice. He couldn't look at the young boy, or think about what these people had done to his life. He had to do his job. At least the child was sleeping.

He made a note to have the Archambaults arrange to find the kid's parents. If he had none, then if the kid wanted a home, he would do his best to find someone who would be able to help him. It had to be someone who could relate to him. Elie had no problem paying for counselors and even the home, but he had no idea how to parent. He could barely manage his relationship with Brielle.

He crossed the room to the bed where Angel and his partner sat eating ice cream and drinking champagne. They faced the sea, looking out the window as they fed the ice cream to each other. The shadow spilled across the bed behind Angel's partner. Elie stood in the mouth of the shadow, a grim reaper going through the motions in his head.

He stepped out, kneeling behind Angel's partner and grasping his head, all in one motion, delivering the killing wrench. With blurring speed, he was on Angel, forcing his head forward and quickly breaking his neck. "Justice is served," he said quietly.

He found the key to the dog crate hanging beside the leash and spiked collar. There was a long scarf he could use as a blindfold. He couldn't allow the child to see him, but he wasn't leaving him there. He awakened him as gently as possible, extracting him from the crate while Ricco tied the blindfold around him.

It was Mariko who kept reassuring the boy that they were there to rescue him. They would have someone coming for him, but he had to stay very quiet, there were armed guards on the estate. Elie and Ricco had to clear a path for them to take the boy out. They were breaking protocol, and no doubt, Marcellus would be furious, but Elie wasn't leaving the kid. They pulled a dark T-shirt over his head after removing the offending tail.

Mariko took the boy down in the elevator and continued to reassure him. She used the phone in Angel's house and coded in the emergency number for their bodyguards. The phone the bodyguards used would be disposed of as soon as they hung up. She told them she needed a pickup and gave coordinates, but did so in code then hung up. The phone call lasted under fifteen seconds.

Elie and Ricco went first, ensuring the guards were out of the way as Ricco leapt to the top of the wall, Mariko handed the boy to Elie and he all but tossed him to Ricco. Mariko was already on the other side as was Elie. They brought him down fast and Ricco was with them. The three stayed in the shadows with their charge, avoiding cameras and light, keeping to foliage as much as possible. When a car glided up and a door opened, the boy was thrust inside with murmured reassurances and then the car was gone. In all, the rescue operation took under three minutes.

Elie turned his attention to Guillem Toselli's home next. Like Angel's, Guillem's and his father's villas were built overlooking the Mediterranean Sea and both commanded extraordinary views from what would be the living rooms, gardens and pools. Elie had been told Guillem and Claudia were home. They had returned from a night out to dinner

when news of the freighters exploding at sea had come in. Then the ones in the harbor had exploded. By now, Guillem had to have been told the crews of the ships were all dead.

Elie, Ricco and Mariko took the shadows into the living room, where the pair were alone. Security patrolled the gardens and around the villa. All were heavily armed and on alert. Guillem was armed and continually admonished Claudia to stay away from the windows.

"We're at war, Claudia," he hissed at her. "I'm aware you've never been through this before, but do what I say if you want to come out of this alive."

"Who would go to war with our families, Guillem?" Claudia wrung her hands together. "It doesn't make sense. None of this makes any sense. If you know why this is happening, I want you to tell me." There was suspicion in her voice.

He stalked across the hardwood floor straight to her, slapping her hard. "Don't talk to me in that tone of voice. If I knew what was happening, I'd tell you."

Claudia shrank back from him, turning one palm to cover her cheek. "I'm sorry, Guillem, I'm afraid for the children." She edged a little distance from him and fell silent.

He closed both hands into tight fists, staring at her for a couple of minutes as if he wanted her to say anything that could allow him to take out his frustration on her. "My father is coming over to talk to me about the situation. If you can keep your mouth shut, you can stay in the room. But I'm warning you, Claudia, one sound out of you and I'll take you up to the bedroom and beat you within an inch of your life. I'm tired of your constant whining about going home to see your daddy. I treat you like a damn princess and all you do is whine about New York and how great it is and how you want to go home."

"Because you promised me," she whispered. "You said we'd go there on our honeymoon if I married you. But we didn't. Then if I got pregnant. We didn't. Then again, and I had another child. We didn't go. I figured out all the shipments for us. How to lure the children in the parks away from their parents,

the ones you wanted. You told me if I did those things, we would go. You won't even let me plan a trip."

"There you go whining again. I told you I wanted sons. Girls are useless to me, Claudia."

"I gave you a son."

"One. Then that pathetic girl. What should I do with her?" There was contempt in his voice.

Claudia whirled around, her eyes suddenly bright. "Guillem, you said if I could find a way to come up with the money to go to New York, I could go. What if I sold her? She's really quite special and would bring in a lot of money in an auction. You don't want her. More than once, your father has talked about the idea of selling girls her age and what kind of cash they would bring in."

Guillem stared at her a moment then burst into laughter. "You're priceless. You'd do anything to go back to your daddy. He doesn't want you, Claudia. Don't you know that yet? He used you to make an agreement with my father to get in on the trafficking deal. That's all you were to him, a bargaining chip. When are you going to get it through your empty little head that you're better off here with me than there with him?"

He flung his glass of tequila sideways at the white marble fireplace, shattering the crystal and spilling the contents so the alcohol ran down the column in an amber trail. Before Claudia could answer, the door was flung open and Arnau strode in. He wasn't a big man, but he commanded the room instantly.

"Guillem, have you heard? It's being reported that Riccardo Santoro went insane and murdered his entire family. Everyone, parents, children, my daughter, everyone. His freighters are gone, his crews, his capos. All dead."

Claudia gasped and quickly covered her mouth with both hands when her husband gave her a sharp look. She backed up to a darker corner and peered over her fingers at the head of the Toselli family with shocked eyes. Behind her, in the shadows, Mariko stood waiting, a silent arbiter of justice, listening, just as Claudia was.

"The exact same thing happened to Alfredo Colombo. Everyone dead, his entire family wiped out. His entire organization. His ships, crew, everyone. Now, it seems, it is happening here, like a disease, a cancer spreading, and we have no idea who's doing it."

"I doubled security on the grounds and inside the house as you instructed," Guillem said. "Who would dare to come after us like this? Which family thinks they are big enough to take over our territories?"

"The only one with large enough balls would be the Rodrigo family, but I had them checked on and none of them or their soldiers are in Barcelona. I don't believe they are this clever. I think we're under attack by the Ferraro family and the Archambaults."

Guillem shook his head. "We did nothing to bring the attention of the Ferraro family to us. Nothing. We can easily wipe out the Archambaults with one phone call." He snapped his fingers.

"There have been rumors for years about the Archambault family, whispers that said they are very much like the Ferraros, but I paid them no attention," Arnau said. "Valeria listened to a conversation that took place in Riccardo's study just before he supposedly went insane. He had invited Valentino Saldi and Dario Bosco to meet with him in order to either offer them to come in, bringing the Ferraros with them, or compensate them in some way for putting them on a hit list."

"Bullshit."

"We were going to kill them eventually, but if we could get Ferraro under our thumb, we would have it made, so Riccardo tried to entice both Valentino and Dario by offering them a piece of our business. Valeria reported that Elie Archambault suddenly showed up in the office with them. She couldn't tell where he came from. Apparently, the guards didn't see him and he wasn't caught on camera. Not coming or going. Riccardo got angry with him and Elie told him he would regret his decision to murder his wife. That he would

take away everything from Riccardo before he killed him. Then he walked out and disappeared."

Guillem swore. "Have you found a connection between his wife and the Ferraros?"

"I received a photograph of that troublesome woman being escorted down the aisle by Stefano Ferraro at her wedding to Elie Archambault."

Arnau stepped forward to show his son the photograph of Brielle Couture in her wedding dress, on the arm of Stefano Ferraro.

"That bitch," Guillem snarled. "How many tries and no one has killed her yet?"

"This worries me," Arnau admitted. He dropped into a chair. "Why isn't she dead? She should be. We've tried so many times. A bomb that missed. Two full teams sent to her husband's house. That's ten men, *experienced* men, Guillem. Then one of our best information men, Asier Fredrick. How long has he worked for us? Years. No one has ever suspected." He pressed his fingers to his eyes. "He had a team with him. They've all disappeared. Some of our best men. We lost a couple of men we had planted in Saldi's organization."

"That was the nosy bitch. I'm sure of it," Guillem said.

"Probably. But how is she getting her information? Who's leaking it to her? She had rendezvous times with the freighters at sea. Did you know that?" Arnau peered across the room at Claudia. "There were only a couple of people who knew those times and coordinates."

Guillem followed his father's gaze. "Not Claudia," he denied. "She would never put her father or me in danger. It had to be someone in New York or LA. No one here would dare leak information. They know you'd kill every member of their family." Eyes on his wife, he snapped an order. "Claudia, get us drinks. You know what Padre and I prefer. Hurry up. I'm thirsty. And clean up the glass around the fireplace."

He turned back to his father. "Did Angel step up his security? Maybe you should have him come to the main house."

"I told him to come. He won't. He thinks I don't know about his lover, Guillem, but I know all about his pathetic friend, Rey Estay. That will get him killed if he isn't careful. You should talk to him. Better yet, go in and put a bullet in that worthless Estay's head and drag your brother out of there."

"I spend a lot of time putting bullets in my brother's lovers' heads," Guillem said. "When he's tired of them, he comes to me and cries like a baby. Says he can't do it himself because he still loves them but they're getting too clingy and he's worried they'll do something stupid and endanger the family." He sighed. "I guess I can go get him and bring him to your house."

His father looked past him to Claudia, who hadn't moved. "Your wife seems to have forgotten all the training you gave her, Guillem. You were so patient and took so much time making certain she understood that we don't allow our women to run our lives the way they do where she comes from."

Guillem swiveled his chair around and glared at his wife. Even with his sinister scowl, she remained defiant, unmoving from what she must have thought was the safety of her corner. Her husband leapt from his chair and stalked across the room, his hands curled into tight fists.

Arnau gave his daughter-in-law a cruel smile. "You really do need to remind your stubborn wife of her duty to you periodically, Guillem. Perhaps schedule her for training with the other women and girls we get from the States. Clearly, she would benefit."

Guillem swung his fist, his knuckles connecting with Claudia's jaw. She was flung like a rag doll out of the narrow chair she was in, her body flying from the corner toward the bank of windows where they spent so much time viewing the sparkling Mediterranean Sea.

Arnau threw his head back and laughed gleefully. "About time Riccardo's little princess realized she *serves* men, not the other way around."

Guillem followed the flight of the body, watching the way Claudia landed on the hardwood floor, her head hitting, almost

bouncing, arms and legs flopping, truly like a rag doll, with no attempt to cushion the fall. He slowed his approach and rather than pull back his foot to deliver a kick, he crouched beside his wife and touched her neck tentatively. His breath seemed to hitch.

"She's dead, Padre. Her neck is broken. I didn't hit her hard enough to break her neck." There was that hitch in his breath again. He gripped Claudia's shoulder and then stood up abruptly, his gaze scanning the room sharply. "Someone's here. In this room with us now. Someone else killed her."

"You hit her pretty hard," Arnau observed.

"No, she was already dead," Guillem reiterated. Still looking carefully around the room, he backed up to the chair he'd been sitting in and picked up his automatic. "We have to go, get you in the safe room and make sure Madre is alive. Right now. I know someone is here. Call Angel. Tell him we aren't playing games and they killed Claudia."

Arnau didn't waste time arguing with his son. He called Angel's cell. It rang and rang. He looked at Guillem, sudden fear creeping into his eyes. "He always answers me."

"I have to get my son. I'm not going without him," Guillem said. "Come with me. We shouldn't separate." He indicated the elevator.

Arnau pushed himself out of the chair just as his phone rang. A smile burst over his face. "This must be Angel." He answered without looking. The smile faded immediately and he began to swear. "Impossible. That's not possible." He looked at his son. "Find it, José, or you're a dead man." He stabbed at his phone with a shaky finger to end the call. "José says every account we have is wiped out. All our businesses are gone. Burned to the ground. The safes are empty. Every single one has been attacked."

"Where are the soldiers? The police we've paid all these years?" Guillem demanded.

"Dead. He says they're dead." Arnau's face turned a dark red beneath his skin.

"Padre, I have millions in the safe. You do. Angel does.

Between the three of us, we can leave here and go somewhere else and do whatever we want." His voice was soothing.

"Look in your safe, Guillem. Look and see if your money is there," Arnau encouraged. "I have to see it."

"Of course." Guillem went straight to the wall next to the fireplace. He had to step over his wife's dead body. He did so without looking at her. Pressing his palm to one small depression, he leaned in for a retinal scan once the panel slid back to reveal the safe. He opened it slowly and stared at the empty interior.

Arnau gasped and let out a loud cry of anger. "I'm going to tear them from limb to limb when I find them," he vowed.

"The bitch," Guillem declared. "We have to get to her. She's what this is all about. Once we have her, we're in the driver's seat. If Archambault is willing to go to these lengths for his bitch, imagine what he'll do for us to get her back."

Once again, he indicated the elevator. "We have to get to my son. Hurry. I want to get out of here. I feel like we're being watched."

Arnau hurried to the elevator and pressed the code to open the doors. They slid smoothly apart and he stepped in, turning and holding the door for his oldest son. Guillem sat on the floor, back against the wall, his automatic resting in his lap. His eyes were wide open, staring at Arnau, his head tipped to one side.

Arnau came slowly out of the elevator and looked around before crouching down beside his son. "Guillem," he said quietly, his voice quivering with sorrow. He reached for the gun and straightened, turning quickly, prepared to shoot anything that moved, but there was only silence in the house.

Not taking the time to check on his grandchildren, he raced outside, calling to his personal security guards, who instantly crowded around him. He took the path that led between the two villas and hurried into his home, insisting that several of his guards accompany him inside. Giving them orders to patrol downstairs, he took the elevator to the master bedroom and the little control room off of it. He had cameras

set up to record every perverted act in Angel's home. He would know if his son was alive or dead. He would know exactly who was behind this heinous crime.

He turned on the screens and watched Angel and Rey Estay hideously abusing the little teenage boy, pretending he was the pet dog and then raping him repeatedly. They beat him with the dog brush and the whip and then scrubbed him with the brush to clean him. They tried to force him to eat and drink before shoving the kid in the dog crate, locking it and going to bed with champagne and ice cream. Arnau fast-forwarded until the cameras began to glitch. He couldn't see anything but white snow. Then the men were dead on the bed and the boy was gone from his dog crate.

Arnau wanted to scream in frustration. Angel was dead. Guillem was dead. Even Claudia. The money was gone. His money was in the safe room with his wife, Adella. His marriage, like most, had been arranged, to better the family fortune. Adella had been a good wife, an asset to him. She understood what they needed to do to become powerful and she helped him in those early days no matter what it took. She was a good partner. He opened the door to the safe room and found his wife lying peacefully on the bed. He knew immediately she was dead.

He sank down beside her. The safe was open and empty. She must have opened it to retrieve their documents just in case they needed to leave quickly. She had their bags on the floor beside the bed. The cash was gone. He hadn't thought to check it before he left Adella alone with just the guards.

"It wasn't a very good idea to threaten my wife, Toselli," Elie said from the shadows. "Men like you think you're untouchable, but you aren't. I would have dismantled your human trafficking operation no matter what, but I most likely would have left you alone if you hadn't threatened her. Unfortunately for you, you were just too stupid to let it go."

"Damn you, show yourself."

"You think you're going to shoot me with your gun, but I can assure you, you're not. Every single member of your

family is dead except for your grandchildren. They've been spared, although they will be watched closely as they grow up. If they turn out anything like you or their parents, they'll be dealt with immediately. Your empire is gone."

Arnau did exactly what Riccardo had done, and what Alfredo Colombo had tried to do to Stefano's cousins. He lifted the gun and began spraying the house in the hopes that a bullet would find his elusive target. Suddenly the gun was turning toward him. Hard hands covered his, holding his finger to the trigger and preventing him from letting go. The bullets smashed into him, tearing through his body, up his chest and into his throat.

A man seemed to emerge right out of the shadows as the gun dropped into his lap, but he couldn't tell if he was real or part of hell. Elie looked at Ricco and Mariko. "One more stop and we can go home."

They found Izan Serrano at his home, an apartment in the middle of Barcelona. He had a small rooftop garden and that's where he was sprawled in a lounge chair listening to music and idly throwing knives at a wooden target several feet away from his chair. He had bundles of ropes, handcuffs and a ball gag beside his chair. His head bobbed up and down to the beat of the music as he threw his knives.

"You aren't very good," Elie observed. "You've missed the target more times than you've hit it."

Izan spun around, falling out of the lounge chair to his hands and knees, his head swiveling this way and that to try to see where the voice was coming from. Elie stepped out of the shadows right in front of him, causing him to sit back on his butt, eyes wide with shock.

Ricco stepped out of the shadows just in front of the target, crouching down to examine it. He sighed and shook his head. "Good thing the wall is here or you'd have complaints from the neighbors. What's your average? One hit for every three or four misses?"

"Who are you?" Izan sputtered, trying to recover, pushing up with his hands in an effort to get off the ground.

Elie scooped up the throwing knives, testing the weight and balance of them in his hands as he stepped into Izan, making it impossible for the man to rise. "You should know me, Izan." In rapid succession he threw all three knives he'd taken off the chair, picked up the last two from the small end table and threw them as well, all without a single pause. "Archambault. Elie Archambault. The man married to Brielle Couture. The Brielle Couture you put on a hit list that you sent to your good friend Riccardo Santoro. Sent her photograph to him, too. It was a beautiful picture of her. I decided to keep it for myself."

Izan shook his head and kept backpedaling, pushing with his heels in an effort to get away from Elie. He looked from Elie to the target board and then let out a squeak. Every knife had lodged in the smallest circle, dead center. Each blade sunk to the hilt, although Elie had merely appeared to flick his wrist when he'd thrown the knives so casually, not putting any real effort into it.

"She has scars from your little edge play with her. She said no. It was a very firm and clear no, but you had her tied down and you used your knife on her anyway, Izan. Is that your thing with women? You like to cut them up after they tell you no?" Elie kept his voice very mild.

Izan shook his head and looked behind him, shocked that Ricco now stood there. He had no idea how Ricco had gotten there. "I—she—she's different."

"Be very careful how you speak of my wife."

"They were going to traffic her, and I was going to buy her. *Save* her. I would have saved her." Izan puffed out his chest and managed to scramble back onto his lounge chair, sitting sideways, facing the two men.

"I see. You were going purchase a woman from an auction and keep her for your own. That was your version of saving her." Elie raised an eyebrow. "What about the other women? Weren't some of them really young?"

Izan shrugged. "I couldn't save them all. They weren't my concern."

Mariko slid out of the shadow directly behind Izan.

"That's too bad, Izan," Elie said. "I think all of those women should have been your concern. At the very least, you could have tried turning the Tosellis in to the cops in a different city. You knew enough to save at least one shipment of girls."

Mariko caught the man's head between her hands and wrenched. "Justice is served," she whispered and then gently guided the body down to the lounge chair.

"These gloves are not the best," Ricco complained. "We need to tell our cousin to go back to the originals. Either of you having a problem with them?"

Mariko inclined her head. "They make my hands itch."

"Mine, too," Elie said. "I was just thinking I couldn't wait to get back to the plane so I could take them off." He stepped into a shadow and streaked through the city toward the airport.

CHAPTER TWENTY

Brielle couldn't help staring at her husband, admiring the way he looked as he padded so silently around the room, muscles rippling smoothly beneath his thin gray shirt with the darker pinstripes barely seen. He'd removed his suit jacket and tie and left them neatly hanging on the end of the staircase. It took her breath away just looking at him—just knowing he belonged to her.

Never, in a million years, had she believed Elie Archambault would fall in love with her. She never thought he would look at her with his dark eyes filled with passion, with lust, with such complete and utter love. Sometimes, she woke up in the middle of the night and just stared at him in absolute wonder, afraid if she blinked, he would disappear.

Elie must have felt her eyes on him because he glanced up from where he was leaning over the bar. His gaze drifted over her very possessively. That look he got always made a thousand butterflies take flight in the pit of her stomach. She found herself swallowing the sudden lump in her throat.

ones. She didn't yet know which this was. The fact that he kept her off-balance only added to the excitement.

Elie came right to her, framed her face with both hands and kissed her. At once she found herself drowning in him. The moment she opened her mouth to his, her brain seemed to switch off and she floated in her wonderful Elie fog, giving herself to him. She wore a long gown and he slipped his hands to the back of the neck where it hooked and then slowly peeled down the zipper, all the while kissing her. She wasn't wearing a bra; the dress had one built in and her full breasts jutted toward him, her nipples already standing out.

"Step out, *bébé*," he whispered against her lips.

She obeyed him, the way she always did when he was kissing her. He kissed like a dream. His hands moved over her back, down the curve of her bottom. Rubbing. Kneading. He made her feel sexy when he pressed her tight against his front and she felt his hard cock, full, already in need of her.

"Did you wear your anniversary panties? The ones I laid out for you?" He kissed his way down her chin, then nipped at her.

Her heart seemed to contract. "Yes, of course." It was the only thing he'd asked her to wear. The panties were crotchless. Her stockings and garter made her feel sexy and she knew he loved them, so she'd chosen them along with her long dress and high heels.

He took her hand and led her across the room toward her favorite spot, the cozy circle of extremely comfortable chairs, four of them. The conversation area was in the corner between two banks of windows to catch sun or moonlight. The chairs, as a rule, were normally grouped around a single drum-shaped coffee table, but the coffee table was missing. The coffee table, like the chairs, was usually on the hardwood floor. Instead, there was a mat down and on the mat was a machine.

Brielle moistened her lips. She'd never seen one like it before and it looked dangerous and wicked at the same time.

"I bought you a six-month anniversary gift, *mon petit jouet très sale.*"

His dirty little sex toy. She loved when she could be his dirty little sex toy. She waited while he opened the jeweler's box and took out a very thick, extremely wide collar made of heavy-duty saddle leather. She could see it was padded, but it still looked wicked. There were two buckles in the back and several 3-D ring loops to enable restraint.

Elie wrapped the collar around her neck and buckled it at her nape. It forced her head up into a straight position. There was no way for her to put her chin down. "Remember, *bébé,* you can always say no and it's no. I am never disappointed and we go on to something else."

He reached for the second box and opened it to remove a wide leather restraint that veed into two thick leather cuffs. He held it up at eye level. "If you aren't there yet with me, you have only to say so and we'll use these another time."

Her heart beat overtime. She trusted Elie. She did. He would never hurt her. Not in a million years. He knew what she liked. She swallowed hard and nodded. He waited. She would have to have the courage to give verbal consent or they wouldn't go any further.

"Yes. You can use them on me."

Elie leaned forward and kissed her again, something he rarely did once they started in their roles, but she gathered even more courage from his mind-fogging kiss. Then he was all business, pulling her arms behind her back, clipping the leather into the rings in the collar and then fastening the cuffs to her wrists. The leather was the same heavy-duty saddle leather, but padded. Her hands were just above her buttocks and tight enough that she couldn't move them, although she could wiggle her fingers with no problem. The position forced her shoulders back and thrust her breasts forward.

"Very nice posture, Brielle. You will need to keep that posture. It's very important. You have been working on your core strength when I've been gone, haven't you?"

Already, she was slick and hot. So needy. He knew how to make her hungry for him. He sounded indifferent. As if she really was his plaything for the night or he was teaching her some extremely important lesson she had neglected.

"Yes," she managed to whisper.

"You do look beautiful in leather and arousal. I think something's missing though."

She couldn't turn her head or look anywhere but straight ahead with the thick leather collar keeping her neck stretched high. She waited in an agony of anticipation for what her husband had come up with for her anniversary surprise.

He clipped another leather strip to the ring in the front of the collar. Her breasts were fitted into leather demi-cups, so they rested on padded leather seats. He sucked on first her right nipple and then her left, elongating them, and sliding each nipple between two forks she couldn't see. The sensation wasn't one of pinching. She couldn't see what it was and had no idea what to think.

Hands at her waist, Elie guided her to the machine sitting in the middle of the mat where the coffee table had been. "You're going to put your leg over the saddle and lower yourself right down on the dildo."

Her heart jumped. She made the mistake of trying to look down and a jolt of fiery pain flashed through her nerve endings. A crop smacked the top of her breasts, the sting sending liquid flames racing through her body.

"You're forgetting your posture, *mon petit jouet très sale*, and we haven't even started. I have plans for my own pleasure, and if I have to stop every few minutes to correct you, I won't be pleased." While he spoke, his fingers slid between her legs to test her readiness. His lips pressed against her ear. "So slick, *ma chatte*."

The more he talked dirty to her, the more her body responded. Brielle's entire body was in goose bumps, endorphins already reacting as Elie lifted her carefully, guiding her leg over the saddle, and lowering her onto the thick length of the mechanical cock slowly. It felt almost an exact replica of

his. The girth and length filling and stretching her. Her high heels tucked into stirrups and her knees gripped the saddle.

"Only your core strength and posture will keep you where you belong." Elie came into view, naked now, his powerful body as aroused as hers. He placed a leather riding crop on the arm of his chair and a leather riding quirt beside it. Both were made of the same heavy-duty black leather as the cuffs and collar she was wearing. The sight of both sent hot blood rushing through her.

He sank into the chair and casually picked up a bottle of lotion, the one she knew was edible and tasted a little like cinnamon. In his other hand was a remote. The machine began to move, making her gasp. She had to get the rhythm of it, gripping it with her knees, as it went through the motions of a horse walking, then beginning to trot.

With her hands behind her back, she had to use her muscles to stay in the saddle and keep her perfect posture using only her core and knees. Her gaze never left the slide of Elie's fist as it glistened over his thick, long, mouthwatering shaft. She had the horse down now, and she could match the movements with her body, so she could give complete concentration to worshiping the shape and size of her man's cock.

Without warning, the dildo in her began to move, not slow, but using rapid, hard, deep strokes that took her breath and sent streaks of fiery electricity running along every nerve ending. She nearly toppled out of the saddle and only at the last minute was able to catch herself. The change in posture sent pain flashing through her. Instantly, the crop was smacking her breasts, the upper curves and sides, adding more flames racing through her until her body exploded and she cried out as the first orgasm rushed over her. It was powerful and seemed to move through every part of her so that she gasped for breath, desperate to find a moment to slow down what was happening.

Elie settled back in his chair and once more began fisting his cock as though nothing had happened. He didn't acknowledge that she had an orgasm, or that the machine was trotting

a little faster now so she had to adjust her rhythm to it. The dildo was relentless, slowing for a moment and then surging into her so there was no way to know what it was going to do next. Her body began to coil tighter and tighter all over again.

Brielle was in heaven and hell. If she moved wrong, pain flashed through her. Exquisite, perfect pain. She didn't dare lose her posture. She didn't want to topple out of the saddle. She couldn't get away from the pounding cock in her and she was already moving with the horse. Another orgasm was building and watching Elie's tight fist wrapped around his cock was so sexy. She wanted him in her mouth. She needed him there. She could already taste him.

Without warning, the small clips on her nipples began to vibrate. Really vibrate, stimulating them, sending waves of sensations through her body. She cried out and pulled back without thinking. There was nowhere to go and the thick collar didn't allow for moving that way. She received the collar's sharp correction of pain along her nerve endings and this time the riding quirt fell across her breasts, her belly and then the tops of her thighs.

The cock in her pounded hard and deep and the horse began to gallop. Her body exploded into another mind-numbing orgasm. This one went on and on, powerful and almost frightening in its intensity. Stars and colors burst behind her eyes. Her mouth opened into a silent scream, the only way to release the wild craziness in her that never seemed to be sated unless Elie gave her these surprises.

"I love you so much," she whispered when she could speak. Her voice was husky. The horse hadn't stopped moving, but it had slowed down to a fast walk so she could catch her breath. The cock in her had changed rhythms again as well, slowing to a much gentler thrust. The vibrations were still stimulating her nipples, sending little shock waves through her, so that her clit felt like it would light up as it pressed against the stimulator on the saddle. "So much, Elie." Her gaze went to his cock. "I need you."

"You have to ask. I'm not going to just give it to you when you made me punish you."

His stern voice made her shiver. Made the goose bumps start all over. Her body had already had a series of strong orgasms and she wasn't even being that stimulated, and yet the sound of his voice had every nerve ending coiling tighter in anticipation.

"Please, Elie, I want to suck your cock."

"It won't be easy with that collar on. Especially when you have to maintain your posture."

There was a wicked note in his voice. She was missing something, but it didn't matter. She was always the beneficiary of his games in the end. He stood up. He clearly had worked out the angles perfectly ahead of time because when he stepped right up to her, straddling the end of the saddle, crowding her body, his cock was the perfect height for her lips.

Elie smeared the delicious drops of precum over her lips, and when she opened her mouth, his fist in the back of her hair, he shoved his cock in. Her hands were behind her in the cuffs and for a moment her heart clenched and a ripple of fear went through her. Her body clamped around the dildo just as it began to thrust a little harder. The horse changed gaits, forcing her to adjust her body, knees gripping tighter. As the dildo retreated, his cock filled her mouth so the two worked in tandem. The vibrations increased on her nipples. Her body seemed to go up in flames with so much stimulation.

She concentrated on Elie's cock. She knew it so well. She loved it—and him. She wanted to give him the kind of pleasure he gave her. Using her body to ride the horse, she used every bit of the skills of her mind and mouth to give to him. She took him as deep as she could. She hollowed her cheeks, used her tongue, danced it, curled it, edged it. When he rose even higher above her so he could angle his cock down her throat, blocking her airway, she refused to panic, trusting him, looking up at him, as she rode the horse, swallowing him.

The expression on his face was worth it. She would gladly

have passed out. He pulled back to give her air and then he tightened his grip in her hair and the cock in her began to surge deeper. "Get there, *mon petit jouet très sale*, get there fast. I'm going to come down your throat and you're going to swallow every drop."

He thrust into her mouth and wasn't as gentle as before. She took him all the way down and her body once more impossibly went up in flames, the powerful orgasm rocking her, but his cock was jerking and pulsing, sending ropes of semen down her throat and she swallowed and swallowed to keep from choking. He pulled back to give her air but then stood there, waiting, expecting her to clean him as he slowed, then stopped the vibrations on her nipples.

Breathing heavily, she did the best she could, staying in position, until he stepped back and stopped the dildo. She didn't dare move position. She was so weak, she was really afraid she'd fall. The saddle stopped all motion and Elie's hands were there, unbuckling the collar around her neck and then the cuffs. He slid the nipple forks from her and then dropped the entire contraption on the mat. Lifting her, he cradled her against his chest.

"I love you, woman. So much."

"I love you, Elie. Thank you for this." Brielle slid her arms around his neck. "That was the best present ever. I don't know how you think of these things. I don't know why I need them."

"I love that you need them. I need them, too. That machine can simulate a bucking horse. Wait until you work up to keeping your posture on a horse trying to throw you off." There was laughter in his voice.

She buried her face against his shoulder. "You're very wicked."

"I am." He carried her into the master bath and began running hot water into the tub. "Your mouth should be insured."

The wild color slid up her entire body. "I'm so glad you enjoy my mouth."

"I enjoy everything about you, Brielle. I never believed I'd have a woman who loves me, or understands me. You're somewhat of a miracle."

Elie thought she was the miracle, but she knew he was. He was the one who understood her.

Keep reading for an excerpt from
Christine Feehan's thrilling new mystery

RED ON THE RIVER

Available Summer 2022

Vienna Mortenson pushed her shiny key into the private elevator to take her to the floor where her suite was located. She had never been impressed with money. Never. She preferred camping outdoors to hotels, no matter how luxurious they were, and casinos were *not* her thing. Being a nurse and seeing time and again what cigarettes could do to people, she despised the smell of them. Just walking through a casino floor made her want to tell all those people smoking what was inevitably going to happen to them. Yet here she was, being impressed with this particular hotel.

The Northern Lights Hotel and Casino was owned by billionaire Daniel J Wallin. Vienna was aware that he had partners, but Wallin had started the hotel; it was his concept and he owned the majority of shares. It was rare for a single hotel to do the kind of business that his did. It was popular, full to capacity at all times. The twice-a-year gambling tournaments drew the biggest names and had some of the biggest returns, which was one of the reasons she had decided to participate even though it required her to be there in person.

Normally, Vienna competed online. She'd built her reputation through her username *luckypersiancat*. She'd managed to pay for her mother's cancer treatments. She'd put herself through nursing school. Her mother still lived in Vegas with her partner, and Vienna paid her rent using her gambling money. Vienna owned a nice house in Knightly, where she resided with her Persian cat, Princess. She'd put quite a bit away for retirement and invested most of the rest of her winnings. She'd been careful to stay under the radar, living and working in Knightly at the local hospital. She was also head of Search and Rescue for the county.

"Honey, hold that elevator," a voice called out.

Vienna turned. She didn't particularly like to be addressed as *honey* by total strangers, but the gentleman calling out to her was older. He looked to be about seventy, with thick gray hair and faded blue eyes. He did look fit, even though he walked with a cane. She flicked a quick, assessing glance over him to see what his injury might be. He didn't appear to have one. He wasn't actually limping, or even leaning heavily on the cane. He wasn't even walking with it correctly. He did have a key to the elevator in his hand, so she held the door.

She looked past him to the man behind him and her breath caught in her lungs. Everything in her stilled. She nearly let go of the door. Zale Vizzini. The moment she saw him, she could taste him. The way he kissed. Feel him inside her. The way he moved. The way he filled her. No one was like him. No one ever would be again. Her eyes met his, and then caught the little shake of his head. It was almost imperceptible. His hand lifted to his chest and he waved her off—again, the smallest movement.

Vienna flashed a brilliant smile at the older gentleman who was nearly to the elevator. "You know, if security is watching, I'll probably receive a visit from them."

"And rightfully so," the man said cheerfully. He stepped inside the cedar-scented elevator, hooking the cane over his arm as he did so. "I'm Wayne Forsyne. You're actually more beautiful in person than in your photograph, and I thought

that was extraordinary." He completely ignored Zale slipping into the lift behind him and settling against a wall.

The doors slid shut silently and the elevator began to rise. Vienna kept her gaze steadfastly on the older man, although every nerve ending in her body was vividly aware of Zale. It was not only embarrassing and rather humiliating that she could feel his body heat when he was completely across the elevator from her, but that she could feel her entire body reacting to his presence. That *never* happened around other men.

Deliberately she sighed. "I suppose you're referring to that obnoxious wraparound photograph the hotel has of me along with the other tournament players going around and around the outside of the hotel and then in the lobby and again in the casino?"

"You look lovely, even more so in person."

"I think it's a little overdone to have us everywhere, not to mention it seems like it's miles high, but I suppose it's a good advertisement for the hotel and casino."

The elevator smoothly came to a stop and the doors glided open. Forsyne waved for her to precede him and she did so without hesitation. She didn't need to be in such close proximity to Zale. She would know his scent anywhere. The cedar in the elevator couldn't cover the way his skin hinted at first snow and fresh rain in the high Sierras.

She wanted to run to the door of her suite, but instead she turned calmly to smile at Forsyne. "It was lovely to meet you."

"If security takes you to task for helping an old man out, you call for me. I'm next door."

There were only four suites on the entire floor, and his suite was directly across from hers. She shared the elevator with Forsyne. The other two suites had their own elevator on the other side of the floor.

"I'll do that." She was very proud of herself for not looking at Zale as she inserted her gold key into the lock and the door opened for her. She stepped inside and closed the door, nearly going to the floor, her legs turning to rubber.

She had never thought she would see Zale Vizzini again.

Not ever—and she didn't want to see him. She wasn't a woman to make a fool of herself over a man. He'd walked away from her without a backward glance. That had hurt. Really hurt. She knew better than to have any faith in men, but she'd wanted to think she'd mattered to him. She hadn't. So, okay. She'd gotten her heart broken just like a million other women. She was tough. She could take it. She didn't want a repeat of the process, and seeing him and feeling her instant reaction to him told her she was susceptible to him.

Vienna slid down the door to sit on the floor. There was no one around to see her moment of weakness. She had learned to take those moments if they came. She was decisive as a rule. She'd been raised by a single mother and they had struggled financially. Not at first. They seemed to have money coming in and they lived in a nice neighborhood in a nice home. But when it came time to go to school, that hadn't lasted long.

She'd had to learn at an early age not to let other people's opinions bother her. Her clothes weren't good enough. The car her mother drove wasn't nice. They eventually lived in a run-down apartment so the money could go to the private school tuition. Soon, they didn't have the money for that. Vienna was grateful that they didn't have the money and she could leave that school. She got odd jobs to help out, contributing the money and feeling like it was the two of them—her mother and her—against the world. They were so close and she loved that.

Vienna took a deep breath and looked around the far-too-large-for-one-person suite. It was gorgeous, from the marble floors and the grand piano, the up-to-date high-tech gaming room, the deep soaking tub, the private hot tub on the balcony, the walk-in marble shower and enormous, far-too-comfortable bed with a fireplace and sweeping views. There wasn't anything she could possibly think of that had been left out. If she did need anything, she simply had to pick up the phone and her own personal concierge would immediately

provide it for her. Best of all, it was free. Why? Because she'd been invited to play in their tournament. The one with the enormous prize at the end. How could she possibly resist coming out from behind her anonymity for a chance at millions, especially since she was already going to be in Vegas?

Her phone buzzed and she glanced down. Stella Harrington. The bride. One of her best friends. "Right here, but I'm not sure I'm speaking to you at the moment," she greeted.

"Uh-oh. What's wrong? Are the other players being mean?"

"I can handle players in a tournament," Vienna said. She ran her finger back and forth along the beautiful table. There wasn't a speck of dust. Not one single speck. Now she was putting fingerprints on it. She felt a little guilt over that. "Do you remember when Sam had some of his friends take us to Shabina's house because he felt it was the safest place to be when the killer had threatened us?" She couldn't make herself say the killer's name. It still hurt, after all these months.

"He threatened you specifically, Vienna. And me," Stella said. "But yes, I remember."

"I wasn't so happy about being forced to leave work by some man I didn't know. He didn't give me much choice. And he didn't talk much, either. It wasn't like he explained the situation."

"As I recall, none of Sam's friends were big on talking, but then Sam isn't, either," Stella agreed. "We just got used to Sam over the years we've known him."

Vienna appreciated that Stella was allowing her to get around to what she had to say without hurrying her. Vienna wasn't certain how to explain the situation. "The man he sent to collect me was named Zale. I found him to be the most annoying and attractive man I'd ever met in my life. He was so damned intelligent and could actually talk when he wanted to, about a wide variety of subjects."

There was silence on the other end of the phone. Vienna could almost count the breaths Stella took. "When did you ever have a conversation with him? Certainly not at Shabina's

house. We were all together. And afterward, when we found out Denver was dead, we were all so shocked and devastated, we just kind of stayed together for a little while and talked things out."

"I know. But then I went backpacking up into the mountains alone. I didn't want to be afraid of a serial killer coming after me. I have to be able to go into all sorts of places without being afraid. I decided I needed to just go, to get it over with. I took a month's leave of absence, packed up and went hiking. Zale followed me."

Again, there was a long silence. Finally, there was the sound of a door closing. "Sorry, someone came in. I take it you didn't send him away."

"No, he stayed with me for the entire month. He was this amazing man. So intelligent, and you know how that matters to me. He could make me laugh. And he was great outdoors. On top of that, he was dynamite in bed. He could light up the night. I had no idea sex could be like that. We didn't talk about my home life or his because I thought we had all the time in the world. For some ridiculous reason, I believed he was as taken with me as I was with him. I mean, he didn't say so, and neither did I, but when he touched me, I felt it. So much for my intuition as a woman."

Vienna was very proud of herself for keeping any bitterness from her voice. She didn't even feel bitter. She'd been hurt, but she wasn't bitter. Zale hadn't given her false promises. If she had built a relationship between them, it had been all in her mind. He'd showed up, they'd talked. She couldn't even say he'd seduced her. The attraction had been mutual. He'd been respectful. Careful of her because they were alone out in the middle of Yosemite. He'd told her he'd pitch a tent away from her. She'd been the one to make the decision to allow him to stay with her.

"What happened?"

"He just packed up one day and disappeared without a word. I mean, I woke up, he was packing up, he leaned over

and kissed me goodbye and was gone. I never heard from him again."

"Are you kidding me?" Stella sounded outraged.

"No. He really is one of the Ghosts Denver was always going on about. In any case, he's clearly working some job here. He signaled to me that he didn't want me to acknowledge that I knew him. Or maybe he's married and his wife is here with him. Sheesh, I never even thought of that." Now that she did think of it, she was alarmed. Horrified.

"No, he's not married. Well, at least I don't think he is. Now I'm going to go grill Sam. Zale Vizzini is Sam's best man. I had no idea you even knew him other than for that brief moment at Shabina's or I would have told Sam he was banned from our wedding. I wonder if it's too late to kick him out. I'll turn into bridezilla for you."

Vienna laughed. "You can't do that. I can handle it. It was just such a shock to see him." She sobered up suddenly. "Although if he was married at the time, I'll have to retaliate even if it's in a childish way. That would be so disgusting. I do *not* mess around with married men. And that includes men in partnerships."

"I'll find out what I can and call you back."

"Please keep what I told you confidential."

"I'm very aware you're an extremely private person, Vienna. In any case, you kept everything about me confidential," Stella said. "I can't wait to see you in a few days."

"I'm looking forward to bouldering and some other outdoor adventures. After the tournament I'll need to be out of this building," Vienna assured. "Don't forget to text or call me back when you know something. I don't want to be up all night feeling guilty if I didn't do anything wrong."

"Will do," Stella promised.

Vienna paced around the suite several times. She'd meant to stay in and just relax but now she couldn't. She needed action. Something. Anything outdoors. She would have to work tomorrow, starting early afternoon, and play carefully

to stay in the game. She was playing against some of the top players in that world. She'd made it through to the semifinal table, a feat she was certain hadn't been expected of her.

When Vienna had first started, she'd had to borrow money to buy into her first online game. She'd won. She'd been able to borrow the money because those who knew her were aware of her uncanny ability to win at cards. It wasn't that Vienna counted cards or anything like that, she just "knew" things. She had a gift, and over the years, she'd come to believe in it and knew she could trust it. Because she saw her talent as a gift, she didn't overuse it, and she made it a point to give back in some way.

She knew that when she entered the room with the other players at the semifinal table, they would all be looking for anything they could about her to help them find an advantage over her. Vienna had been in charge of others as a surgical nurse and also as head of Search and Rescue for Inyo County. Sometimes that would spill over to Mono County as well.

She was experienced in all-weather rescues and could do avalanche control when needed. She'd climbed Mt. Whitney several times and rescued more than one person as well as retrieved bodies when weekend climbers thought they knew more than the experts warning them of the various hazards.

She had to make split-second decisions that could be life-or-death for others as well as for herself under extreme conditions. She didn't give much away unless she wanted to. She wasn't worried about the tournament. She had made it through to the semifinal table and had every confidence that she would make the final table.

Once, because she'd needed the money for her mother's cancer care, Vienna had made the mistake of playing in person at some of the tables in Vegas and someone had tried to rob her on her way home. As if she'd carry cash in her pockets. What idiot would think that? She'd arrived home shaken beyond belief, needing comfort from her mother, only to end up in a huge fight with her. Her mother had been her best friend all of her life. That night had changed her life

forever. Vienna had moved out and she'd never played poker at a table in Vegas again.

Vienna gambled online as *luckypersiancat*, a totally anonymous way to gamble. No one knew who she was or how much money she made. She no longer had to borrow money to get into the ten-thousand-dollar buy-ins with the five-hundred-thousand or million-dollar rewards at the end. She could manage that all on her own now.

She went running, one of the few things that could clear her mind completely. She drove out to Red Rock and parked, choosing one of the many trails that looped around. It was still fairly hot, although the sun would be setting soon enough. She made certain she was carrying enough water and had a filtration system with her just in case. She was a hiker, not a dedicated runner, and she knew any injury could suddenly change everything. If she was caught out in the blazing sun without the ability to call for help and with no water, she could easily lose her life. She'd seen that happen too many times.

Vienna had long legs, and within minutes she had hit her stride, covering ground with her steady rhythm. The sights were breathtaking. She wasn't going for speed so much as just wanting to be grounded by the beauty and peace of the outdoors. Red Rock had natural formations of rocks with various colors and unusual concretions. Red dots were scattered throughout some of the rocks, while brown rock balls were dense in others. Erosion caused many different shapes, from fins and spirals to caves and arches. It was difficult not to want to stop and explore them.

Shadows fell across the rocks towering above her at times, lending them different appearances, coloring them with darker varnishes, but she kept her pace even though, again, she wanted to go examine them closer. Her friends would be joining her in a week or so for Stella's bridal shower. Stella's event wasn't a traditional one. They were going to boulder first and then explore the various scenic trails Red Rock had to offer. They would also do some trad climbing there as well.

Next—and all of them were excited about this—they would

spend a day on the river, kayaking, starting at Hoover Dam. They planned to find out-of-the-way coffee shops, something they all loved. It definitely wasn't the traditional bridal shower, but for Stella, it was perfect. They planned to follow it up with hiking and camping the Tuolumne trail in Yosemite along the river for an additional adventure before the wedding.

Vienna felt lucky to have five such close friends as the ones she'd met in Knightly. They had been unexpected—and wonderful. Five powerful women, women who made each day count. They shared the same interests and loved the outdoors. They loved to dance and often met at the Grill, a bar where they danced, drank their favorite drinks and ate the owner's famous offerings surrounded by other locals. Had she not fought with her mother, she never would have moved and found a new life filled with friends and adventure. She detested that she'd never gotten back her friendship with her mother, but she truly loved her life.

Vienna was hot and sweaty, but felt so much better when she was once again back in her suite at the Northern Lights Hotel and Casino. After a shower, she soaked in the deep tub, enjoying the feel of the hot water on her sore muscles. It was nice to close her eyes and relax, to feel at peace again.

Wrapping herself in her robe, her long hair in a towel, she checked her phone. Stella had messaged her back. *No relationship ever.* Vienna breathed a sigh of relief. She wouldn't have been to blame, but it would have left a bad taste in her mouth had she been with a married man, even through no fault of her own. She hadn't asked Zale that question and she should have.

Refusing to allow Zale Vizzini to take up any more time in her brain, she checked out the menu to see what really great dinners she could order. Everything was first-class, including the food. She hadn't been disappointed yet.

The door buzzed and she swung around. No one knew where she was, with the exception of the hotel personnel, Zale and the gentleman he guarded, Wayne Forsyne. Maybe security was really going to lecture her. She hadn't even told her mother where she was staying. She planned to visit her,

but *after* the tournament. There were millions of dollars at stake. She didn't want anything distracting her. Well, maybe she'd visit sooner. She really wanted to see her.

Fortunately, her robe was the type that had buttons instead of a belt, so she was fairly decent. Vienna went to the door and peered through the peephole to see who her visitor was. The older man and Zale were outside the door. Zale was looking up and down the hall very alertly. Something in the way he did it sent chills down her spine.

She hit the intercom. "I'm not exactly dressed for company."

It was Zale who answered. He reached past Wayne to hit a button to respond. "Open the fucking door, Vienna. We need to get out of sight now."

He was *such* an ass. He was back to the man he'd been when he'd ordered her out of her place of work and into his car. When she hadn't cooperated, he'd simply abducted her. No second chances, just picked her up, tossed her over his shoulder as if she weighed no more than a child, and took her out. He had that same low voice with the commanding purr. Not a growl, a purr. It wasn't a nice purr.

She opened the door because Wayne's face was pale. If she could have, she would have allowed him entrance and barred Zale from coming into the suite. She must have stepped into the doorway, because Zale put a hand to her belly and pushed her inside, closing the door after him.

"I need you to check out Wayne for me, Vienna. I don't think he's hurt bad." As he spoke, Zale helped Wayne to the nearest couch. She trailed after them, watching the older man carefully. He carried the cane, rather than leaning on it, and even though Zale was helping him, he walked as a much younger man would.

She noted blood on Zale's shirt, a slash line on his belly and right arm. There was blood on Wayne's shirt, much more of it than on Zale's. Wayne's wound was on his left side, along his ribs. Zale unbuttoned Wayne's shirt as Vienna hurried to the bedroom to retrieve the small medical kit she always

carried with her. She also got warm water from the master bath.

"Tell me what happened and why you didn't take him to the hospital," she ordered, nudging Zale aside with her hip so she could take over.

"We were outside the casino, just taking a walk. It can be difficult staying indoors so much when you're not used to it."

She understood that. She also caught the "we." Wayne didn't have to go with Zale to take a walk. He could have stayed locked in the safety of his suite. She kept her mouth shut. The knife had sliced into the skin, under the ribs, missing all vital organs somehow. The wound was shallow.

"Zale blocked the attack," Wayne provided. "Otherwise, I would have taken the hit right in my heart. They came out of nowhere. I think they were in the flower beds."

"They were," Zale confirmed.

Her heart accelerated for a moment before she could get it under control. More than one attacker. Zale was obviously working under cover. This wasn't a random attack, and there had been more than one assailant. She washed the wound carefully.

"Knife wounds are tricky. This isn't deep. You don't need stitches. I can glue it, but if the blade had bacteria on it, you can get an infection that could eventually kill you. You need antibiotics. I don't have those, and I really mean you should have the wound flooded with them and you should take them orally. I've got a topical I can apply for now, but, Zale, if the two of you have access to help, get antibiotics for both of you. I can see the knife cut you as well."

She finished up with Wayne and turned her attention to Zale, indicating for him to take off his shirt, although that was the last thing she wanted him to do. She remembered his body all too well. She'd mapped every single inch of him with her tongue. He was there in her mind, never to be forgotten.

Refusing to meet his eyes, she kept her gaze fixed on the wounds. Maybe it was cowardly, but she told herself she was a nurse and she needed to make certain the laceration was

cleaned properly. "Very shallow. Same with your arm. But I'm very serious about the antibiotics. No doubt the blade of the knife contained bacteria." She hoped it didn't contain poison for their sakes.

She smiled at Wayne cheerfully as she sat back on her heels. "You're good to go." Meaning they could leave her suite.

"Do you want a drink, Rainier? Rainier clearly is a friend of Sam's as well, and you'll be meeting him soon enough at the wedding, Vienna," Zale informed her. "He's under cover as Wayne Forsyne."

She put her hands over her ears. "I don't want to know anything more. You two are obviously working on something important, and I don't need to know anything about it."

Zale ignored her and went to the bar, turning to raise an eyebrow at his friend.

Rainier sat up. "Nice to meet you as me, Vienna. Zale has assured me you know better than to break confidentiality." There was warning in his voice.

"I take it you're not seventy. I'd already guessed that. You don't walk with your cane correctly." She stood up and went to the master bedroom to change into actual clothes. Having no underwear around Zale made her feel vulnerable.

"You want a drink, Vienna?" Zale called out.

"No, thanks." She needed her wits about her. Dressing hastily in leggings and a favorite comfortable sweater, she unwrapped her hair and brushed it out, leaving it down to air dry. She wasn't going to try to make herself look good for Zale. If anything, she wanted him to ignore her, just as he'd done these last few months.

Zale and his colleague had made themselves right at home, sitting in the living room, Rainier going through the menu. He looked up when she entered. "You sure are a beautiful woman," he reiterated. He sounded like he was stating a fact rather than flirting with her. He just looked her over and then was back to looking at the menu. "You hungry?" he added. Even the voice was different, sounding much younger.

"Yes." Vienna went to stand beside his chair, looking

down at the menu. "I was about to order room service when you were announcing yourselves. Do you think you were followed?"

"No one can get up to this floor. In any case, Zale wounded all three assailants."

She didn't look at Zale but continued to peer at the menu as though she were really studying it. *Three* attackers. He'd managed to block the initial attack from Rainier, keeping him from getting killed, and then took on all three.

"Won't they go to a hospital and report that they were attacked by the two of you? There must be security cameras outside of the hotel." She took the menu right out of Rainier's hands.

"I jammed the cameras for a moment," Rainier admitted, "but the fight was over in under eight seconds. Zale wounded all three of them. They don't think the wounds are bad enough to seek help, but that's classic textbook. They'll bleed out slowly without even being aware they're going to die. They're heading to a safe place to lick their wounds, but it will be too late for them."

Rainier sounded very satisfied. Vienna couldn't blame him. If someone came out of the bushes and attacked her to kill her, she would want them just as dead. She wasn't a forgive-and-forget kind of girl. That was one of the reasons she wasn't going to look at Zale. No matter what, she wasn't falling into any traps—if he even thought about going there again.

"You've looked at that menu long enough to memorize it, Vienna," Zale said, using his purring, commanding voice after Rainier gave her his order. "Hand it over." He didn't come to her. He stayed across the room in one of the two-person cuddle chairs.

A red flag went up instantly. She thought about sailing the menu toward him, hoping to hit him right in his hard head. That wouldn't go along with the "calm, didn't give a damn that he'd left her and never contacted her again" façade.

"Sure. I do think I've memorized it." She shared a little laugh with Rainier and then walked slowly across the wide

expanse of the room to Zale. Before she reached him, she held out the menu. "I'll call it in for everyone. That way they'll only hear my voice."

Thankfully, Rainier responded, giving her the opportunity to turn back toward him.

"That's a good idea. We'll hide out in another room when room service gets here."

Unfortunately, with her back to him, Zale was able to lean forward and shackle her wrist, drawing her close to him, toppling her into the seat beside him.

"What are you doing? I was going to call in the order." She did her best to sound a little surprised at his outrageous behavior.

"I need time to look this over and you can sit here while I do it. You didn't seem to have a problem giving Rainier time. Or standing right over the top of him while you were deciding."

"You do need to eat. I think you have low blood sugar. I might have trail mix in the other room so you can snack on something while we're waiting for dinner," she suggested helpfully, starting to push up from the cuddle chair.

He didn't even look at her, but his arm swept across her like a bar, restraining her. "Just stay put. If my blood sugar starts to drop, you'll be the first person I'll tell."

She looked across the room at Rainier. "Is he always this grumpy before he eats?" She poured concern into her voice.

"I never noticed it before." Amusement colored Rainier's voice until Zale looked up, pinning his friend with a dark stare. Rainier sobered instantly.

"I'll have the steak, rare. Baked potato with everything. Salad. The roasted brussels sprouts."

"That sounds eerily like Rainier's order." Vienna took the menu out of his hands and once again made a move to go to the phone. Again, Zale blocked her.

"Are you going to look at me?"

"I have looked at you."

"You haven't."

She sighed. "I'm hungry and tired. *I* have low blood sugar. I just came back from a long run and I have a big day tomorrow. I can't afford any distractions, Zale. I appreciate that the two of you are in trouble. Maybe the fate of the world is in your hands, I don't know. But I have to keep myself under control. Whatever the two of you are into, I can't be a part of. I'm not in your world and you're not in mine."

There was a small silence. Rainier broke it. "I'm sorry, Vienna. We needed medical attention, and Zale mentioned you were a nurse. We couldn't go to the hospital, and you were on the same floor. You were going to meet me at the wedding anyway, so it wasn't like you weren't going to find out I was working under cover with Zale. We didn't mean to drag you into our problems."

She felt a little ashamed. It wasn't as if she didn't want to help them, especially when they were both hurt. She shrugged. "I don't really mind helping out. It's just that I know I'm not supposed to know what you do, and I respect that. Like I said, I'm just tired and hungry. I'll call in the order so we can get our food."

Zale had removed his arm, so she took that as permission to make a break for the phone. While she gave their orders for dinner, Zale made another drink for Rainier and himself. She took the sparkling water from him and sank into the single cuddle chair across from him, putting her head back to stare up at the ceiling.

"I guess whatever you're into is dangerous. If your cover is blown, shouldn't you pack up and go home?"

"Not necessarily," Rainier said. "No one saw the attack in the parking lot. We're betting the three die before they report to their boss. They aren't going to be too quick to tell whoever they report to they missed an old man and the lone personal protector wiped up the floor with them. At least, that's the hope."

Vienna studied the ceiling. "You're betting your lives."

"This is Vegas," Rainier said, humor once again tingeing his voice.

Vienna let the air move in and out of her lungs. Waiting. It was a bet. A wager. It didn't matter that lives were at stake. It came down to a bet. Three men were somewhere slowly bleeding internally. They were unaware they were dying. Would they call their boss and report to him or her that they had failed to kill their intended target? What were the odds? There were three of them. They wouldn't die at the same time. They each had a cell phone. The boss could call them. They'd grow cold. Weak. Would they try to call for help?

Vienna nodded her head slowly. "I do believe you have a good chance those men won't admit their screwup to their boss. By the time they realize what's happening, it's going to be too late." She knew things. How? She had no idea, only that she could bet on cards because she knew what each opponent had in his hand and what was going to be the card the dealer put down next. Bets were tricky things. "But there are a lot of variables. Their boss might just show up last minute."

Rainier laughed softly. "I was feeling good for a minute there. You just shot that down."

"That's the nature of the gambling beast," Vienna said, joining in his laughter.

"You seem to do fairly well. Did you expect to make it to the semifinals?"

"I expect to win," Vienna said. "I've been playing for quite a few years now. It isn't like I just walked in off the street. I was invited to the tournament, and it just so happened that Stella wanted to do a few fun things in Vegas, so I thought I'd come ahead of the rest of my friends and do a little work. I prefer to play online."

"Why is that?" Rainier asked.

"I'm not terribly fond of having my photograph plastered all over the casino. I like to sneak around under the radar. You should know something about that. You don't even use your real name."

Was Zale even his real name? Had she slept with someone and had no idea who he really was? Probably. She didn't look at him. She detested that she meant nothing to him at all

when, in her mind, he'd been *the one*. She had never been that kind of woman. She didn't build fantasies around men. She'd never grown up thinking she needed a man to rescue her or complete her. She worked hard and took care of her mother and herself. She was happy. Zale had been . . . unexpected.

There was a knock at the door. Zale snapped his fingers and indicated for Rainier to go to the other room. Both men were suddenly all business, expressions sober and weapons out. Zale concealed himself in the shadow of the bathroom off the living room. He left the door partially open in order to cover her.

The cart was rolled in and the dinner put on the dining room table. Plates and silverware were used, not Styrofoam takeout boxes. Linen napkins were set beside each dish along with wineglasses and water glasses. When the servers left, she made certain the door was properly locked while both men took out small devices to check the room for any listening bugs.

Vienna seated herself at the table. "Interesting way you have to live."

"We don't usually live around other people," Rainier said.

She nodded. "I'd forgotten that. Sam's been away from it for quite a long time. We're used to him. He doesn't talk much, but he participates. He goes to the bar with us. Most of the time he's our sober driver. He gets an earful. He works at the resort and fishing camp, but he normally works alone, unless he works with Stella."

She took a bite of her food. She'd forgotten how hungry she was. She decided less talking and more eating was in order.

"Sam just walked off the job one day," Rainier said. "He was like that. He'd make up his mind to do something and you couldn't talk him out of it. He wouldn't argue with you, he'd just do it." He indicated Zale with his fork. "He's like that. Decides and that's it."

"What's there to argue about?" Zale said.

"There's nothing wrong with discussions," Vienna said, savoring the roasted brussels sprouts. "Discussions are fun."

"That's not the same as arguing," Zale said. "Arguments lead nowhere and usually end up in hurt feelings."

"This is good steak," Rainier declared. "As in great. Notice, there's no arguing on the subject."